ASIA MONET

King of Ice

Dedication

For those who think they're undeserving of love

Content Warnings

This book contains mature content that may be disturbing to some such as:

- Graphic Violence/Death on Page
- Attempted Sexual Assault
- Discussions and descriptions of human trafficking
- Discussions and descriptions of assault and abuse
- Crude language towards women (from antagonists)
- References and discussions about self-harm and suicide
- Mentions of the deaths of familial members
- Perilous situations involving a minor

Readers who may be sensitive to these topics, please take care of your mental well-being before and while reading.

Playlist

Like This | NF
    When I See You | Fantasia
    Good Days | SZA
    How To Touch A Girl | JoJo
    Change Your Life | Kehlani featuring Jhene Aiko
    Agora Hills | Doja Cat
    Steal the Show | Lauv
    Un-thinkable (I'm Ready) | Alicia Keys
    It's Yours | J. Holiday
    1-800-273-8255 | Logic featuring Alessa Cara and Khalid
    Teachme | Musiq Soulchild
    Something Like You | *NSYNC
    Obvious | Ariana Grande
    Make it Alright | Jessica Mauboy
    Never Knew I Needed | Ne-Yo

Chapter 1

Javier

I hate when people beg for mercy.

The tears streaming down their cheeks. The helpless pleas. The list of useless reasons to leave them alive. It was all fucking pathetic.

Especially when it came from reputable crime bosses like the one laying before me.

The old man was strapped down to a hospital bed with a single handcuff. His free arm was restrained by the abundance of IV needles in the back of his hand and in the crook in front of his elbow. A mask connected to a nearby oxygen tank was strapped across his face. The transparent surface of the mask fogged and cleared with each quick, jagged breath.

His hazel eyes, wide with fear, stared up at me. Desperately, he shook his head back and forth in a silent plea for mercy.

He hadn't shown my family mercy when he organized and oversaw a violent hit on us. My siblings and I may have survived the massacre, but our father didn't.

I couldn't shake the image of my father's body drowning in a pool of his own blood. In my dreams, he reaches out for me in a silent plea for help. When I gave him my hand, a sinister smile spread across his face. Using all his strength, he pulled me down into the red pool and dragged me toward the bottom. The agonizing burn of liquid filled my lungs, clawing at my intestine like a cat caught in a ball of yarn. I kicked and punched and squirmed with all my might, but I couldn't break free from his iron

1

hold. As my chances of survival diminished, death crept closer and closer, wrapping it's arm around me like an old friend.

Just before I could lean into it's embrace, I'd shoot up in bed, sweaty and nauseous and out of breath. I wasn't a stranger to nightmares, but ones like these haunted my brain even when I was awake.

If I couldn't have peace, then neither would this asshole.

He'd already been dealt an unlucky hand. Lung cancer had crept up on him in his old age, and it wasn't kind to him. According to his medical records, the tumors were eating away quickly at his lungs, making breathing laborious and agonizing. But the pain didn't stop him from smoking cigars - or operating one of the largest sex trafficking schemes in the country.

It wasn't until the moment he couldn't take another breath without feeling like his body was on fire that he paused his daily activities and checked himself into a hospital.

His first mistake was waiting so long to let the doctors treat him. His second mistake was going to a hospital under my control.

He must have thought flying across the East Coast to Florida would have put some distance between himself and the war he'd started with my family. But little did he know that our cartel - hidden beneath the guise of a renowned pharmaceutical company - had ties all over this damn country. There wasn't a single corner he could hide in to save himself from our wrath.

I was patient over the past few months, perfecting my plan to take him, and the rest of his fucked up operation, down. Not only did I need the time to acclimate to the hierarchical changes the death of my father brought, but I also needed to prepare my men for the battles to come.

I hadn't expected the call from the chief of oncology, an old friend of my mother's, telling me that the man at the top of my hit list waltzed into his hospital. I don't think I ever hopped on a plane as fast as I did once I received the news.

I didn't bother telling my siblings about my trip. If our enemy was anywhere else, I would've let them tag along. But the twins were too loud and impulsive for a job like this. This man might deserve a torturous death, but in a civilized environment like a hospital, it needed to be a quiet one.

His eyes widened as he watched my gloved fingers remove the oxygen mask from his face.

"Please, please," he choked as his gaze went to the pillow in my free hand. "Please, don't."

As I leaned over him, I had half a mind to respond. To taunt him. To tell him every single detail of my plan before he died, knowing there was nothing he could do about it. But kicking a man while he was down wasn't my style. Alessandro Bianchi knew he was going to die. That was satisfying enough for me.

Without hesitation, I pressed the pillow down against his face.

Underneath me, his body instantly flew in a frenzy. He writhed and kicked underneath the weight. His free hand, still tangled in wires, raised enough to tap frantically on my forearm. Muffled pleas vibrated through the fabric. "No, no," he mumbled. "No!"

His chest's movements became sporadic as he began to run out of fresh air. He twitched from the agony as his empty lungs struggled to function. In seconds, his uneven breaths transformed into tight gasps. Beside him, the heart monitor raced with loud, rapid beeps.

It wasn't long before the annoying sound, and his body, came to a complete stop.

His lifeless body fell limp as the heart monitor chimed in the long, distinct sound of a flat line.

I kept the pillow there for a few moments longer. Unlike his sons, I was going to make sure my target was dead before going anywhere.

When I finally removed the pillow, his eyes, usually smug with greed, were wide with fear. His mouth gaped open from the struggle for air.

If it weren't for appearances, I wouldn't have closed his eyes or his mouth. He deserved to die with humiliation painted all over his face.

I reluctantly fixed his expression and tucked the pillow back underneath his head.

Quietly, I twirled the top of the tank, releasing the oxygen. The red indicator on the side dropped at rapid speed as the invisible air whisked

3

out of the tank. Once it hit zero, I reconnected the tube, snipped a tiny hole into the side, and carefully put his mask back over his face.

The nurses were going to come in and notice his dead body. Upon further investigation, the doctors will find his tube connected to the oxygen tank was damaged and let out essential amounts of oxygen. His autopsy would state he suffocated from the lack of air to his weak lungs. It was a natural cause of death due to the mix of his illness and the equipment error.

As far as anyone else is concerned, Alessandro Bianchi's death was an accident.

And that's exactly how I wanted it to look.

Turning on my heel, I exited the hospital room and slipped off the latex gloves I borrowed from the medical supplies in the room.

Easily, I slipped back into the small masses of people teeming in the hospital hallways. In my suit and medical mask, no one looked twice at me. For all they knew, I could be anyone. A family member or friend of a patient. A doctor consulting from another hospital. Or an attorney working with one of the medical chiefs on a malpractice case.

Knowing the amount of stress and anxiety being in a hospital brings, I might as well have been no one to any of the people I passed. And that was even better.

When his death is pronounced and his family is notified, my name won't be anywhere near it.

It's the one lesson I could never convince my siblings to learn: sometimes the best revenge is taken in silence.

Chapter 2

Brielle

"Good morning, Mrs. Morales! Good morning, Mrs. Worrell! Good morning, Mr. Andres!" I greeted the line of clerks at the front receptionist's desks as I jogged by.

A chorus of "Good morning, Brielle," followed behind me.

At this hour, the first floor was filling up with tiny crowds of people. Customers, vendors, delivery men, and employees milled around the spacious lobby. I weaved through the masses, balancing a cup carrier of four coffee cups in my hand.

One of the security guards on the first floor, Mr. Turner, chuckled at my sprinting figure. "Good morning, Brielle," he greeted. He stepped a few inches away from his post to click on the button for the elevator.

"Hi, Mr. Turner!" I plucked one of the steaming hot coffees out of the carrier tray and handed it to him. "This is for you! A fresh caramel macchiato from that new coffee shop down the street."

His brows rose in surprise. "Oh, Brielle, you didn't have to bring me coffee."

"It's your long day," I explained. "You're going to need as much caffeine as possible if you're going to make it to eleven o'clock."

His smile crinkled the ends of his brown eyes. "Thank you," he said as he accepted the hot cup.

The elevator beside us dinged as the car arrived.

Walking through the opening doors, I said, "Have a good day, Mr. Turner."

5

"You too, Brielle!" His figure disappeared as he stepped back towards his post.

I stepped to the side and pressed the number for the top floor of the building.

The doors quickly started closing just a moment after the button turned yellow.

I averted my eyes to the mirror-like wall to my right. With my free hand, I spruced up my kinky curls and checked the light coat of lip gloss I applied while I was waiting at the coffee shop.

With the tight time crunch between dropping my daughter, Chloe, off at school and arriving at work, I usually had little time to do anything else besides throw on some clothes and make sure my hair wasn't a mangled mess.

Today, Chloe was early. She was excited about her school's field trip to the aquarium, so she was up well before our alarm clock went off. I wasn't complaining about the extra half hour. It gave me more than enough time to swipe on some make-up and grab coffee. With the weather being a little kinder in anticipation of spring, I wanted to add some more feel-good moments into my busy mornings.

The elevator pinged when I finally reached my destination. I hopped off of the elevator and walked down the quiet hallway. Most of the rooms on this floor were for holding meetings, leaving it empty at the beginning and end of days.

I smiled at the tall, burly man standing outside the main door of our office. "Good morning, Mr. Torres," I greeted him. I grabbed one cup out of the carrier and held it out to him. "I bought you a Mocha Latte."

The line on his lips didn't waver, but his eyes softened the slightest bit. As he reached for the cup, the sleeve of his suit stretched past his wrist, threatening to expose the ink on his skin. "Thanks," he said. With his free hand, he grabbed the vertical silver handle of the glass door and opened it for me.

I thanked him as I entered the office. This space was bigger than our old one on the floor below us. On one side of the room, there was a waiting area with black cushioned chairs and a small bookshelf filled with magazines. On the other, two television screens, currently idle with the company logo, were placed above a long bookshelf. My collection of decorative plants and succulents covered the surface while pharmaceutical law and business books filled the shelves.

My work space was just beyond the waiting area. I'd graduated from a long, horizontal desk to a large U-Shaped desk with plenty of room for my computer monitors, calendars, stacks of files, and decorative Funk O' Pops. My daughter's photos and drawings hung on the walls above the curve of my desk.

I set down the carrier and my purse on top of my desk. After wiggling out one of the coffee cups, I walked down the narrow hallway next to my desk towards my boss's office. The glass walls covering his office were adjusted to the tinted feature, covering the interior of the space.

I gingerly cracked the door open and poked my head inside. The sunlight from the glass wall on the opposite side of the room poured through the room. From my spot in the door, I could see the shadow of my boss sitting at his desk. "Good morning," I sang.

"You're late," a deep, monotone voice shot back at me.

"I'm not late! I'm actually early today!" I said as I entered the room. A smile tugged at my lips as I walked closer to the long rectangular desk at the back end of the room. "And look: I bought you coffee! It's your favorite: dark roast with a shot of espresso!"

Butterflies stirred in my stomach as I caught a better view of him.

Bronze brown skin glistened underneath the golden sunlight. Dark, short curls covered his head. Well-kept stubble covered his sharp jawline and lips. Long eyelashes framed chocolate brown eyes, emphasizing their unique shape. Sharp, expensive suits always sheltered his tall, chiseled body. He was the type of man you could stare at for hours and never get bored.

He glanced at me as I set the coffee down on his desk. "*Gracias*," he mumbled.

I was used to the deep frown on his lips, but the dark bags underneath his eyes made me raise a brow. "Long night?" I asked as I tilted my head.

"Sure," he replied.

I refrained from rolling my eyes.

Javier was like snow: beautiful, but cold. I've never seen him smile or crack a joke. Getting over two words out of him was a challenge. To top it all off, he was a stickler with his work.

According to the grapevine, when I was hired, he'd run through more assistants than anyone could count. He required his personal office to run in a specific way, and none of them could satisfy his expectations or demands. Apparently, a few of them left the building with tears in their eyes and the fear of God in their hearts after being fired.

During my first week, it was clear everyone thought I wouldn't last. As I walked through the building each day, I was met with concerned brows and pitiful stares. "I hope he doesn't tear down that poor girl's spirit," one woman murmured, thinking I couldn't hear.

I didn't take their stares or rumors as cautionary tales. Instead, I made Mr. Ruiz my own personal challenge. This was the highest paying job I've ever had, and I'd be damned if I fucked it up. If my boss had a set of particular expectations, then I was going to do more than meet them. I was going to *exceed* them.

Truthfully, it was difficult in the beginning. Javier was extremely detailed about every inch of his office. He liked his files to be organized in a alphabetical order with distinct tabs. His calendar needed to be color-coded by the department or the type of clientele he was meeting with. His meeting notes, taken by me when he couldn't be in two places at once, needed to be outlined with the traditional Roman Numerals symbols, letters, and numbers.

At first, I was intimidated by the thick packet of rules and expectations he held for his assistants. I flipped through it with no idea of how the hell I was going to make this work.

Instead of winging it, like I guessed some others did, I went into his office and had an honest conversation with him. Staring into his eyes for the first time and fighting the sting of the icicles sticking out from them was unnerving, but the uneasiness was worth the wealth of knowledge I received.

Javier was more than willing to clarify and answer questions I had. I think he appreciated my eagerness to please and vulnerability. Not because of feelings of power, but because others had been so quick to dismiss his requests. Pretending to know everything was easier than asking for help. Especially when the person you're asking could invoke the fear of God into someone with a single look.

He might not have directly expressed his gratitude, but the five-hundred dollar gift-card left on my desk after my first month of working there sure did.

I quickly learned Javier's professional quirks and accomplished my initial goal of exceeding his expectations. Now, I was practicing new goals, like trying to establish a friendlier co-worker relationship.

He seemed like he was finally beginning to open up to me near the end of last year. We hung out at his sister's engagement party and her wedding reception. Each time, I thought I saw the faintest ghost of a smile grace his lips.

But, after his father died, he curled right back into his shell.

I couldn't blame him for it. Grief was an unpredictable storm. You never knew when the clouds were going to thunder and all the emotions you thought were gone poured down over you.

I've been through my own storms before, so I knew the feelings all too well. I just hoped Javier wasn't pushing through this alone.

"Well, I hope the coffee helps a little," I said. "Don't forget your meeting with the marketing department is at nine-thirty."

"Mhm."

Shaking my head, I finally left him alone. I walked out of his office and settled in for the day. I turned one television on to a hip hop lofi-beats radio on YouTube and flicked the other to a news station. As I waited for my computer monitors to reboot, I sipped on my coffee and looked through my to-do list.

With Javier at the head of the company now, my list of tasks was much longer than before. I had a few companies to call, an abundance of emails to send, a stack of files to organize, and two meetings I needed to take notes for. It was going to be another busy day, but I didn't mind. Having so much to do made the time go by.

Except for the occasional whoosh of the glass door opening from my boss's journeys to and from his meetings, the office was quiet for most of the morning.

Closer to eleven, the sound of harsh clicks against the ground accompanied the sound of the door opening. Looking up from my computer, I saw a beautiful woman with glowing bronze skin and a long mane of raven-black curls. Her red-frosted lips were pulled into a tight scowl as she stormed up to my desk in her thin stilettos.

"Good morning, Mrs. Ruiz," I greeted her as I stood up. "How are you?"

"Not great," she admitted, her voice tight. She pointed to the tiny hallway. "Is my brother in there?"

"Yes. He just came back from his-"

"Good. Do me a favor: If you hear anything concerning, pretend you didn't."

Both of my brows rose as I watched my boss's sister march down the hall. Alexandria Ruiz, our company's Chief Financial Officer, was absolutely gorgeous, but she was terrifying when she was angry. I was not getting in between whatever she was about to do in there.

I sat back down and attempted to resume my email. Again, I was only able for a few moments before I was interrupted. This time, it was the ring of the phone that broke my concentration. Checking the caller ID, I saw the call was coming from the public relations office in California.

"Hello, Javier Ruiz's office. How may I help you?" I answered.

"Good morning," a deep male voice replied on the other end. "Is Mr. Ruiz still available for our phone conference today? I've tried calling his direct line, but he's not answering."

Quickly, I pulled up my boss's calendar and noticed he had a scheduled call with the PR team. I glanced at the hall in which his sister disappeared down. "Um, he's not near his desk right now. I'll let him know you're on the line. Please hold."

I reluctantly stood up from my seat and headed down the narrow hallway.

Javier must've lifted the tinted feature on the glass covering his office. I could see clearly through the transparent walls.

Javier was leaning against the side of his desk. His arms were crossed, and he was staring at his younger sister with a hard expression.

Alexandria's hands were gesturing vigorously as she yelled harsh strings of words. "Just because you're the head of everything now does not mean you get to make decisions without consulting us first!" I heard as I walked closer to the office.

"And what would the two of you have done? Huh?" Javier challenged. "Blow the entire hospital up?"

"Well, it would've made a bigger statement!"

"It was best to keep this quiet."

"Why? What they did to my wedding wasn't quiet! They were going to make a spectacle out of us! It's only fair we make an example out of them!"

"And we will. I'm not done yet. Miles is still collecting the rest of the information we need for the rest of our plan. This was a complete surprise."

"Yeah, a surprise you kept secret. It's not fair that you took one of our chances to avenge our father away from us."

"There will be plenty more."

"Sure - assuming you don't think we're immature enough to take part in those, too."

"I never said I thought you guys were immature."

"You didn't have to," she spat, her voice filled with venom.

Javier opened his mouth to reply, but he wasn't able to get the words out before I knocked on the glass.

Both of their heads darted in my direction.

A shiver ran down my spine under the intensity of rage in both of their eyes. "Sorry to interrupt," I said as I poked my head in the door. "But the PR team is on line one. You have a phone conference scheduled."

His sister jabbed her index finger into his shoulder, pushing so hard he almost budged. "This conversation isn't over," she stated before turning on her heel.

I moved aside to let her pass me through the doorway. Frowning, I watched Javier run a hand through his short curls with a deep sigh. "Is everything alright?" I asked.

"Mhm." He straightened his composure and walked around the desk to his chair. "Line one, right?"

"Yes." I hesitated in the doorway. "Is there anything I can do...to help?"

His eyes almost softened as he looked up at me. "No. *Gracias*, Brielle."

Nodding, I closed the door and left him alone.

When I returned to my desk, I did my best to forget what I'd heard.

I wasn't ignorant of the type of man he was. I heard the rumors in the streets about his family's horrid deeds. I saw the gun in his hands when his sister's wedding was ambushed by supposed "robbers." I caught the flash of tattoos and scars on the security guards around the building.

Javier was a powerful man in more than just the corporate world, and it was best I kept my nose out of his business.

I continued on with my day, breezing through my tasks and some of the virtual meetings Javier asked me to take notes for.

As it neared five o'clock, I quickly tidied up my workstation, ready to pick up my daughter from her after-school program. As I was shrugging on my coat, I noticed Javier emerging from the narrow hallway with his laptop bag thrown over his shoulder. "Heading out early?" I asked. From my short gossiping sessions with the security guards, I learned Javier stayed late most nights - or at least later than I did. It was rare he ever left before me.

"I have a meeting," he explained.

"Ooh, a hot date with another pretty corporate heiress?"

Javier rolled his eyes, and I laughed. One of his father's missions before he'd passed away was trying to get Javier to settle down and marry. I watched women with drop-dead gorgeous looks and old money flounce in and out of here in search of Javier's attention. It was almost laughable watching them drape themselves over him and he swat them away as if they were pesky mosquitoes.

Yet, I couldn't help but wonder: if the city's finest bachelorettes weren't his type, then what was?

Buttoning up my coat, I noticed he didn't move from his spot. He still stood beside my desk, staring patiently at me with his hands in his pockets. Usually, when he stops talking, it's the end of our conversation. I was expecting him to walk away and continue with the rest of his day - not wait for me.

My fingers fumbled against the buttons as jitters twirled through my stomach. "Sorry," I said.

"Take your time."

Quickly, I finished with my coat and grabbed my purse.

Javier followed close behind me as we walked towards the office door. He briefly sped up in front of me to hold the door open.

I offered him a bashful smile in silent thanks.

He didn't return the smile. Instead, he averted his gaze and looked at the security guard standing beside the door. He spoke with his eyes and delivered a silent message to the burly man.

The other man responded with a curt nod, confirming his understanding.

"Have a good night, Mr. Torres," I said with a smile.

He lowered his eyes and gave me a nod as well. "Good night."

I took a step to my right to head to the main elevator on the floor. Suddenly, strong fingers wrapped around my bicep and gently tugged me in the opposite direction. My body instinctively stiffened as I followed the hand up to its owner.

"This way," my boss's voice commanded. He glanced at the crease between my brows and released my arm. Walking a few steps ahead of me, he led me to the private elevator on the other side of the floor. Only he, his sister, and a select few of the security guards had an access key to operate it.

Chills threatened to run down my spine as I thought of the rumors associated with this elevator. Some colleagues believed it was a special privilege for the acting CEO. A private elevator meant less foot traffic and less chances of bumping into someone who wanted to engage in unnecessary conversations. But most believed the elevator was used for more private matters like sneaking illegal products or associates into the building - or moving dead bodies out.

I could believe the former, since drug companies could dabble in a bit of experimental and unethical practices, but the latter was a bit extreme. The Ruizs may have a bone-chilling reputation in the city streets, but I doubted they'd bring any of their bad deeds in their professional place of business. Not unless they were asking for more trouble than they could handle.

I shook the thoughts out of my head. It was important to be aware of my surroundings, but I could only take the rumors with a grain of salt. At the end of the day, whether they were true or not, it was none of my business. All I needed to do was come to work, do my job, indulge in my schoolgirl fantasies for a few minutes at a time, and leave. It was in my, and my daughter's, best interest not to dive too deep into information that could hurt us later.

The elevator wasn't as intimidating as I thought it would be. Suspenseful talk aside, it looked like a normal elevator with mirror-like walls and automatic doors. As we stepped inside, I took a deep breath and released some of the tension in my shoulders.

Through the door's reflection, I saw Javier take his place beside me. A few inches lay between us within the large space of the elevator. He was too close for comfort, yet too far to brush fingers.

"Any plans tonight?" Javier asked, breaking the silence I thought he'd enjoy.

"My daughter has ballet class tonight," I replied. "They're going to start practicing for their recital in May."

He raised a brow. "What show are they doing this quarter?"

"Swan Lake. Chloe was chosen to be Odette in her class."

"That's the lead, right?"

"Yeah, she's super excited! She turned the playroom into her own personal ballet studio to practice in."

I was hesitant to allow her to start taking dance classes, but the energy and passion she had at such a young age needed to be placed somewhere. She started ballet and gymnastics when she was three, and she absolutely loved them.

I started talking about the progress Chloe has made and the signatures she's making for herself. Lately, she's been merging the skills from both of her classes and creating her own style. During gymnastics, I've seen her waving her limbs and coordinating her flips to a beat in her head. In ballet, she utilizes her flexibility to help her with high kicks and splits.

Her dance instructors often tell me she's a natural with the potential to have a phenomenal career when she gets older. I used to think they were just telling me that to keep her enrolled in their dance academy and continue collecting tuition checks, but after seeing Chloe blow everyone away in her first dance recital, I realized they were telling the truth. My baby girl had the potential to be a star one day. And I needed to make sure nothing took away her shine.

I hadn't realized Javier had walked me to my car until we stopped walking in front of my Chevrolet Equinox. I was too busy running my mouth to notice we'd walked a few blocks away from our corporate building and into the nearby parking garage.

"I'm so sorry," I cut off whatever sentence I was in the middle of. "I didn't mean to eat up your time. You didn't have to walk with me all the way to my car."

"I know," he said. "I like listening to you talk."

Heat rushed across my cheeks underneath his steady, serious gaze. "Oh," was all I managed to say as a volcano of butterflies erupted in my stomach. "I...I like talking. Talking to you. I mean..." I stumbled over my words as I struggled for the right ones to say without making things awkward or weird.

A deep, bouncing sound rumbled in his throat. It almost sounded like a laugh, but there was no happiness within it. His lips remained in a tight line, and the hardness in his eyes didn't waver.

Still, the sound made my belly do somersaults.

"I'll see you tomorrow, Brielle," he said.

I uttered a farewell as I watched him turn on his heel and head back the way we came.

I couldn't get rid of my smile during my drive to the learning center where Chloe's after-school program resided. As a twenty-nine-year-old woman, I probably looked ridiculous - kicking my feet and blushing over such a simple comment from a man I had no chance in hell with. But, I didn't care. I'd never experienced an innocent crush like this. I never knew how ticklish and giggly enjoying the short moments in someone's presence could be. And I wanted to bask in it for as long as I could. God only knows if I'll ever experience something so simple and sweet ever again.

Chapter 3

Javier

"Do you wanna fight or something?" I asked as I finally met my younger brother's livid gaze.

He was standing on the other side of the room with his inked arms crossed against his chest and a glare plastered on his face. He'd been staring at me with malice in his eyes since I walked into his best friend's technology-based headquarters.

After being appointed to official head of our cartel, I gave Miles, our hacker and inventor, a proper upgrade. I hired some men to knock down a few walls in the basement of our main warehouse and offer more work space for Miles's inventions and surveillance. In times like these, it was good there were more than a few feet between Adrian and me. Any closer and one of us would've been swinging sooner.

"Yeah," Adrian admitted. "Pussy."

"Oop," my best friend, Dante, instigated from beside me. "Don't let him talk to you like that, Jav. Beat his ass."

"Shut the fuck up," Adrian snapped at him.

"Make me," Dante challenged.

Adrian grabbed a metal wrench from off the table he was leaning against and chucked it in our direction.

Dante and I leaned in opposite directions to dodge the wrench. It whizzed past our heads and collided with the wall behind us with a loud thud.

"That's why you missed," Dante taunted.

Adrian straightened up, preparing to charge towards us.

"Aht, aht, y'all better take that outside of my new workshop," Miles said before his friend could move. He sat in front of a plethora of computer monitors, all plastered against the wall like tiles. His fingers clacked against the keyboard as he worked on an unidentifiable screen. "There's more than enough room for y'all to kill each other out in the hallway."

"Alright, say less," Adrian said as he stormed out of the room.

I rolled my eyes as I shrugged off my suit jacket. I really wasn't in the mood to put Adrian in a headlock right now, but I would if I needed to. He'd been giving me the stink eye since I arrived. Ignoring him worked sometimes in instances like this when he was holding a mini grudge against me, but if he really wanted to get physical, then we could.

"You want backup?" Dante asked.

"Nah," I said, rolling up the sleeves of my button up. "He's mad out of love, not vengeance. I'm not going to hurt him."

"Nobody said anything about hurting him. I was thinking I could hold him down and you could pop him in his head a few good times."

I almost smiled. "Maybe next time," I told him as I headed out of the room.

Adrian was pacing back and forth in the hallway, preparing for a fight. When he saw me emerge from the room, he stopped in his tracks.

"One last chance," I said. "You wanna talk about this or you wanna fight?"

He answered my question by swinging his fist at my face.

Easily, I stepped back and dodged his attack. I grabbed his outstretched arm and swung him towards the wall. As I pushed him against the wall, I twisted his arm behind his back and put some pressure on his wrist. I pinned him there, restraining him from any more harsh movements.

"Let me go!" He said as he wriggled in my grasp. "You promised me a fight!"

"I didn't promise you, shit," I said firmly. "You want me to hit you, and I'm not going to do that."

"And why the fuck not? You'd do it any other time."

"Because I'm not taking Dad's place in busting your face every other week.

Now, if I let you go, will you chill the fuck out?"

"No," he admitted.

Reluctantly, I released my hold on him. He wasn't going to be satisfied unless I popped him at least once. I swear there's a switch in there that turns his anger on and off, and sometimes it takes more than words to flip it.

Instantly, he turned around and swung at me again.

I blocked his arm halfway with one hand and used the other to punch him in the side of his temple. Not hard enough to leave a mark, but with enough strength to sting. "Cut it out," I scolded. "I understand you're mad I went on a mission alone, but I'm fine."

"What if you weren't?" He asked. The question, and each one that followed, was accompanied by quick swings. "Huh? What if you died out there? What the fuck did you expect me and Lexie to do about it?"

I weaved from side to side to dodge his fists. "Handle business as usual."

"How?" His punches were replaced with harsh shove, one that I let connect. "You're all we have left. How the hell are we supposed to operate without you?"

I sighed as some of the fire in his eyes diminished, giving me a peek into the real emotions lingering behind their flames. "You don't have to worry about that right now. I'm alive. I'm here. And I'm not going anywhere."

His brows twitched upwards, reminding me of the child he used to be. The one who'd climb into my bed during nights when he was anxious and doodle on my arm or listen to me tell elaborate stories to help him sleep. Despite the fearless, dangerous man he'd grown into, he'd always be my little brother, and whether I liked it or not, he needed me.

"You swear?" He asked.

"Yeah," I promised as I held out my hand.

Adrian didn't hesitate to clasp his hand around mine.

Tightening my grasp on his hand, I used my free one to pop him in the head. "Call me a pussy again, and I'll body slam you through this floor. *Comprendes?*"

Adrian chuckled. "I'm not scared of you, *pussy.*"

19

I had half a mind to hit him in his smart ass mouth, but the clicking sound of our sister's heels coming down the hall prevented me from doing so.

We both looked in her direction to see her strutting down the hall in her tall stilettos. With every step, her dark curls bounced and her red-frosted lips turned into a deeper frown. Her eyes fell on our intertwined hands, and she scoffed.

While both of the twins were reputable for holding nasty grudges, somehow Lexie's always stung worse. Whereas Adrian and I could duke out our issues, Lexie needed a softer approach. Don't get me wrong: she's dragged Adrian and I by our hair across the floor quite a few times in our youth. But in order to reach true reconciliation, she needed to talk to us. Discussing our feelings wasn't any of our strong suits - especially not mine.

Wordlessly, she brushed past us towards the door to Miles's office.

"Let her simmer," Adrian said. "I'll talk to her later and try to get her to come around."

Nodding, I followed him back into the technology-filled room.

My eyes fell on Lexie as she wrapped her arms around Dante's torso and rested her chin against his chest. She looked up at him, and the sharpness in her eyes softened.

Grinning, my best friend wrapped his arms around her and leaned down to give her a short kiss.

"Ew," Adrian commented as he reclaimed his spot near Miles's chair. "Get a room."

"Shut up, Adrian," Lexie and Dante said in unison.

Again, I almost smiled. Dante may get on my last fucking nerve sometimes, but he was good for my sister. Unlike other made men who sought to control their wives, Dante chose to empower his. He put Lexie on a throne and let her reign over him and his old territory on the West side. Through his respect for her wishes and her forms of self-expression, he was able to make her feel safe and loved. As her big brother, that's all I ever wanted for her.

The walkie on my hip crackled with static as a voice spoke on the other end. "Boss, your visitors are here."

I unhooked the walkie from my belt loop and brought it to my lips. "Send them down."

A few minutes later, a man and a woman appeared in the workshop doorway.

The man stood more than a head taller than the woman, with dark skin and jagged scars scaling over his face. The petite woman beside him carried a lion's mane of curly black hair that fell to her shoulders and umber brown skin that glistened underneath the fluorescent lights of the room. Both of them wore all black ensembles, cloaking them in the shadows where they often hid.

Mateo and Maria were the head members of a freelance assassination organization that serviced mainly cartels and other illegal operations. Sometimes legal ones too. If anyone wanted the best of the best to annihilate someone, Mateo and Maria were the ones to call.

"Hey, Mateo! What's up, Maria?" Dante greeted both of them happily.

While I was formally acquainted with Mateo and Maria through the business they've done with my father, Dante has actually worked with them. From the stories he's told me, they've utilized his charm and charisma to gain intel before a mission or as a diversion to keep attention away from their target. In exchange for his help, they offered their own to him free of charge. Becoming allies with them was one of his smartest ideas. With their wealth of skills, knowledge, and advanced technology, it'd be the worst mistake to make them an enemy.

"We bought a flash drive," Mateo said. "It should have all the information you need."

Maria left Mateo's side and walked towards Miles's chair. Ignoring his typing hands, she reached over him and put the small drive into a port on his hard drive.

"Hey," Miles started to protest. Swiveling in his chair, he looked up at Maria and choked on all the words he was going to say. His irises practically formed into hearts as they raked up and down her petite figure. Soaking in the view, he murmured, "Oh. Hi." He raised his hand and offered it to her. "I'm Miles."

Maria shoved him out of the way, sending his chair colliding into Adrian. "Yo," Adrian fussed from the impact. "Watch it!"

Miles held up his hand. "It's cool, it's cool," he told his friend. "She could push me around anytime."

Adrian snorted. "Yeah - push your dumb ass right into a grave."

She ignored them and focused on taking over Miles's monitors. With a few clicks of her fingers, she transformed all the screens to create one cohesive screen. On it was a large map of the country with red dots scattered across it. A few more clicks and blue dots accompanied the red ones, outnumbering and surrounding the red ones.

"All the red dots represent the clubs we've identified as Bianchi's territories," Mateo said. "Most are strip clubs, like the ones Dante and your sister infiltrated last year. But others are more high class and discreet. Gentleman's clubs or retail warehouses. We suspect the girls are held captive in the retail warehouses until they're worn down and trained. Then, they're moved to the clubs to bring in money."

"I bet some of the warehouses host their drug and weapons manufacturing sites, too," Dante chimed in. "It's not their primary focus, but they distribute other products, too. Those will be hard to hit, but not impossible to take down."

Mateo nodded in agreement. "I could spare some of my team to help with those locations if you need." He jutted his chin toward the screen. "The blue dots are the territories of the gangs you named. What do you plan to use them for?"

"Those are the gangs underneath our cartel; they distribute our drugs and weapons to their respective areas," I explained.

When my father married my mother and acquired access to my grandfather's pharmaceutical company, he only had one goal: to expand his cartel into an empire. He wasn't interested in running one city or one state. Having command over the city he resided in was simple, yet mandatory thinking. Thinking bigger, he sought to have control over every piece of land he could find. But, like any leader, he couldn't be everywhere at once. So, he came up with a solution: be the connect for as many gangs as possible.

Being the supplier gave us not only some control and surveillance of the gangs, but allies as well. Most of the gangs we worked with were reliable with their payments and shipments. After a few years of working with them, we've built mutual respect and trust. Enough for them to call on us when they need help with a gnarly situation - legal or otherwise. We always came when they called. Now it's their turn to repay the favor.

"Those are the crews that will be taking over the clubs," I continued.

Over the past few weeks, I've spoken to almost all the gang leaders the blue dots represented and delivered my plan. Their men would be on the front lines of infiltrating, destroying, and re-branding the clubs the Bianchis owned near their locations. In exchange for assisting the trafficked women, and killing the men responsible for their captivity, they earned more territory and an establishment to use as they saw fit. I even promised additional products to their next shipments free of charge for helping us out.

None of them turned down the opportunity. All of them were eager to expand and add more credit to their names.

Delegating was the approach my father had engraved into my head. "A king doesn't stand on the front lines," he once told me. "He dishes out commands and watches as his soldiers follow them through."

Instead of wasting all of my time and resources on the Bianchis, I was going to let the local gangs handle it. At the end of the day, we'd all benefit from their actions. They gained new territory, and I reveled in my revenge.

"It's a good plan," Mateo confirmed. "With all those bullets to dodge, they won't even realize who's behind the trigger."

"Good," I replied. The last thing I needed was a feeble attempt at retaliation. I didn't have time for distractions. I couldn't rest until I'd erased the Bianchi name from every single inch of this world.

My father may have been a shitty excuse for a parent, but he was the only one I had left. And since they took him from me, I was going to take *everything* from them.

Chapter 4

Brielle

Knock! Knock! Knock!

My fist rapped gently against the cracked door of Javier's office. I poked my head inside to see my boss typing away on his computer. His dark brows were pulled together in concentration, and his lips hung in their usual line.

He looked better than he did yesterday. No bags hung underneath his eyes and the whites of his eyes were clear of any red tints. I hoped he had a restful night. It looked like he needed it after the meeting-packed day he had yesterday.

I didn't see much of him today. He'd spent most of his time holed up in his office, catching up on personal tasks. I went inside and bugged him a few times, but he wouldn't let me last more than five minutes before he was sending me out the door.

I understood his silent need for space. Working so closely with Javier forced me to quickly learn that he was very introverted. He barely liked saying more than three words to me. I could only imagine how it felt having entire conversations and discussions with large groups of people. His social battery must've been empty after all the people he'd spoken to yesterday.

Still, that didn't stop me from poking my head in now and then to attempt to get a smile or a laugh out of him. I may have failed every single time, but I hoped this time may be different.

He glanced at me as I approached his desk. "What do you need, Brielle?"

He asked.

Smiling widely, I presented the paper in my hands. "I finished your itinerary for your business trip to L.A. next month! I booked you a nice room at the Ritz-Carlton, and I scheduled all of your meetings early in the day, so you'll have enough downtime to have some fun. I even marked down a few spots you could hit! There's Universal Studios, The Grove, some celebrity tours - and Disneyland!"

"It's a business trip, Brielle, not a vacation," he said, ignoring the papers in my hand.

"I know, I know, but you're leaving at an ungodly hour on a Friday morning and your scheduled meetings aren't long. You'll have at least one full night for yourself. If you sneak out of the Gala early enough, you might even have two." I swung the paper in front of his computer screen, blocking his view. "Say you'll think about it."

He snatched the paper out of my hand faster than lightning. Finally, he tore his eyes away from the screen and glared at me with a look that could scare even the most fearless of men.

Dark butterflies fluttered in my stomach. Rather than ticklish jitters, they threatened to send a chill down my spine.

Forcing my smile to grow wider, I fought against the need to shiver, to curl my shoulders inwards, to run in the opposite direction and never look back. If I wanted to chip away at him, then I needed to stand my ground. His intimidation tactics were no use without fear.

I didn't want to be afraid of Javier. When I first started working for him, the darkness in his eyes frightened me, but lately, fear was the last thing I felt around him. He could shoot me dirty looks all day and I wouldn't bat an eye. Maybe I've worked for him long enough to get used to him. Or maybe I've learned there was nothing to be afraid of.

The black butterflies transformed into golden ones as he let out a sigh of defeat. "Fine," he said. "I'll *think* about it."

"Say you swear."

"No."

"Why not? Come on. You act like you're allergic to a good time."

"I am. Whenever I'm having one, I tend to break out in hives. It's really bad."

I giggled at the way the joke sounded in his steady, monotone voice. "Well, pack an EpiPen because when you go to L.A. you are going to have a nice time. Doctor's orders."

"And what exactly does your prescription of fun include? Amusement parks and riding bikes on the boardwalk?"

"Sounds like a good time to me."

"I think you and I have different perceptions of what it means to have a good time."

I raised an eyebrow. "Oh yeah? Then tell me, what is your definition of fun?"

He opened his mouth to speak, but the vibration of his cellphone on the desk interrupted his statement before it could begin. As he looked at the unknown caller tag on the top of his phone, a deeper frown formed on his lips.

"We can continue this conversation later," I said.

"Hold on," he said. He grabbed a stack of folders from the opposite end of his desk. "I signed the documents you needed for the finance department."

"Thanks!" I grabbed the stack of signed papers to be faxed and filed out of his hands and headed out of the office.

Smiling, I walked down the narrow hallway towards the lobby of our office. My brows rose as I noticed a man in dark slacks and a black button up standing in front of my desk. From the side, I could make out a head full of dark, silky hair and a tall, muscular build.

"Hello," I greeted. "Sorry to keep you waiting! How can I help-" The stack of papers I was holding fell out of my hands as a pair of hazel eyes locked with mine.

The man, undeniably handsome with his short-cut stubble and almond-shaped hazel eyes, held my stare for a moment, staring at me in disbelief. "Diamond?" He asked.

A shudder ran down my spine at the name.

His eyes tracked the trembles as they ran through my body, and he smiled.

"Well, well, well, this is a pleasant surprise. I didn't expect to see you here."

I couldn't force any words out of my mouth. My entire body was paralyzed underneath his amused gaze. One wrong move and his smile would be replaced with a sneer or a glare. Another shiver trickled over my shoulders as I remembered what usually accompanied those sinister looks.

Tearing his eyes away from me, he fixed his gaze on a photo of Chloe on my desk. "Is that your daughter?" He asked. "She's cute."

"Leave," I commanded. "Now." The words clawed at my throat as they rose, but I needed to get them out. My daughter was the last thing he needed to be inquiring about.

"I can't," he replied. "I have a meeting with your boss. Eleven o'clock. Tim Randers. Check your calendar if you think I'm lying."

Shit, I thought. I remembered the name from a phone call a few days ago. But it wasn't his voice that I'd given it to. I guess I shouldn't be surprised. Tim wasn't his real name either.

A hand touched my back, and I jumped away from the touch. Looking over my shoulder, I saw Javier hovering over me.

His brows stitched together as he assessed the look on my face and the papers on the floor. He followed my gaze as it returned to the man standing near my desk. In a millisecond, his chestnut brown irises glazed over with ice, sharpening at the tip to create lethal icicles.

"This is Tim Randers," I shakily explained. "Your eleven o'clock appointment."

Our visitor smiled widely, exposing his rows of pearly white teeth. "Hello, Mr. Ruiz. It's a pleasure to *formally* meet you."

Underneath his black suit, Javier's broad shoulders rose and fell. "Same to you, Mr. Randers," he replied, his voice tight. "Follow me, please."

Our guest watched Javier turn on his heel and disappear back down the hall. Happily, he followed him.

I stepped aside to give him more room to pass. Still, a few feet wasn't enough. I needed an entire ocean between us before I felt comfortable.

"Don't worry, Diamond," he told me, pausing his journey to speak. "We'll have time to talk later. Clearly, we have *a lot* to discuss."

Chapter 5

Javier

It took every inch of willpower I had *not* to put a bullet in this man's skull.

Seeing Leonardo Bianchi's face in the comforts of my office was enough cause for me to whip out my gun. Then I saw the fear dripping off Brielle like sweat, and I wished I could pull the trigger. Petrified, she stared at him with wide eyes and trembling hands. Shooting the asshole in the face would've only made things worse. What the hell did he say to her, anyway?

"Ah, so this is where the newly risen king sits?" He said as he waltzed into my office. Nodding, his gaze wandered around my office. "Not as grandly decorated as I expected, but still spacious."

"What the fuck do you want?" I asked. Small talk was never my thing - especially with my enemies. Rarely did they ever want to talk. If Leo was here to fuck shit up, then I needed to be alert and ready.

"Pretty little receptionist you've got," he mused. "I didn't know you were interested in a full service gal. I could've gotten you a much nicer one for cheaper than what you're paying her."

"What the fuck do you want?" I repeated, adding venom to my voice.

Leonardo shoved his hands in his pockets as he walked towards the transparent wall overlooking the city. "How does it feel being on top of the world? Do you feel powerful? Unstoppable? Invincible?"

I remained silent. I wasn't entertaining the stupid remarks leading up to whatever point he was going to make. If he was going to say something important, I wish he'd spit it out already.

"You know, my father saw like this. He thought all the legitimate businesses hiding the dirty ones were going to give him all the bricks he needed to build a castle - just like this one. And he almost did it. We had all the money, all the resources, and the reputation we needed to make a legal brand for ourselves. We were inches away from the same greatness you hold now. Moments away from success. But then…well, then you killed him."

"And what evidence gave you that impression?"

He whipped around, his eyes now livid with a fire I recognized in my own younger brother. "My father did *not* die naturally. On his way to the hospital, he called me and promised he would hold on long enough to complete our plans - to make sure I could secure his legacy."

"The will to live doesn't always trump the body's need to die," I replied. "No one can defeat death. Especially not an old man with a fatal case of lung cancer. If he really cared about your legacy, he would've quit smoking sooner."

"I know you and your feral siblings had something to do with his death."

"My feral siblings would've sliced him open, ripped his weak lungs out of his body, and left his bloody body on your doorstep. Unless that's the case, then we didn't do shit."

"I know it was you," he snarled as he came closer. "D'Angelo Harris warned us about you. He said you were the smart one. The one who knew how to kill a man in all different ways and make it look like an accident - or like it was natural."

"D'Angelo Harris was a worthless piece of shit. His words have no meaning."

"But his son's words do?" He smiled as the glare on my face intensified. "Didn't he betray you not once, but *twice,* and yet he's still sleeping with your little sister?"

"Did D'Angelo tell you that before he died, too?" I tsked. "Your source really sucked. He gave you all the misinformation you need to get yourself killed."

His smile fell, and his eyes lit with rage. He stormed up to me with his hands balled into fists at his side.

I didn't flinch. I didn't cower. I didn't even blink. After all the hell my father put me through, I wasn't scared of anyone. Especially not a pussy like him.

Leonardo stopped inches away from my face. "I know *you* killed him," he whispered, his voice dripping with malice. "I don't need evidence or a source to tell me otherwise. And you're going to pay for your sins."

"And you're going to repent for yours," I retorted, holding his livid gaze. "By the time I'm through, you're going to be down on your knees *begging* for forgiveness. And when God rejects your apologies, He's going to throw you into the deepest pits of Hell."

He scoffed. "Are you God now?"

"No. Just another Angel of Death." Leaning closer, I added, "And I damn sure can't wait to deliver yours."

Leo saw something harsh in my eyes, causing him to take a step back. "You better watch your back, Ruiz," Leonardo said. "Even angels of death have weaknesses."

"Not this one." I jutted my chin toward the door. "Now, get the fuck out of my office."

Fuming in his inferiority, Leonardo finally turned on his heel and stormed out of the room.

Chapter 6

Brielle

I need to get the hell out of here, I thought as I scrambled to throw as many of my belongings into my purse as fast as possible. I don't know what Leo was doing here, but based on the anger radiating off his body when he stormed out of Javier's office, I could tell it wasn't anything good. This wouldn't be so bad if he hadn't recognized me. If he hadn't looked at me with rage in his eyes and a sadistic smirk on his lips before he exited the office.

I'll be thrown right back into hell if I stay here. When I clawed my way out, I swore I'd never allow myself to sink that low again. Especially not with Chloe by my side.

The poor girl was going to freak out when I told her the news. Living in Baltimore was the first time I'd let her lay some roots of her own with being in a dance academy and spending more time with friends she made from school. Her birthday was coming up soon, and I'd promised to give her a party at a local family entertainment center. She had a good life here - and I was about to tear it all away.

I blinked away the tears pricking at my eyes as I hurried out from behind my desk. I'll deal with Chloe's disappointment later. Right now, I need to construct the perfect lie to get me out of work early.

I collided head-on into my boss's hard chest after taking only a few steps down the hall. My body bounced back from the impact, and I stumbled backwards on my platforms.

Strong fingers wrapped around my arms. His hands were so large that his fingers enclosed around the entirety of my biceps as they wrapped around my arms.

Looking up, I met his dark eyes, frosted over with layers of ice. "Sorry," I uttered out quickly. "I need to leave early. My daughter's school called and-"

"You're shaking," he commented, ignoring my request. "Are you alright?"

"Yeah, yeah," I lied. I took a deep breath and tried to regain control of the jitters crawling over my body. "I just need to go pick up my daughter. Her school just called and said she's not feeling well. They said she threw up, and now she has a really bad fever. I'm sorry. I know I'm leaving a lot of unfinished tasks, but-"

"Don't worry about it," he said as he released me. "Go. Take care of your daughter."

"Thanks." I spun away from him, knowing I might break if I stared at the crease between his brows and the dissipating ice around his irises.

I sprinted out of the office and around the halls of the building. I didn't have any time to waste. If Leo knew where I was, then there was only a matter of time before his men would be on my tail.

When I reached the car, I debated picking Chloe up. It was barely eleven-thirty. She probably hasn't even eaten lunch yet at school. I'll pick her up later - after the car was already packed, and all we had to do was hit the open road.

I could already picture the look on her face when she saw the trunk packed with bags and our smaller items sitting beside her in the backseat. The initial confusion. The raising brows of realization. The moisture in her eyes as she accepted she was about to leave the life she knew behind.

I remembered it all too well from the last time we had to move. She was much younger then, but the city we'd fled had been the place where she created her first memories. There, she'd started preschool, made her first best friend, and discovered her love for dance at one of the weekend programs she attended while I worked. I'll never forget seeing the grief and pain in her eyes as she stared out the window, watching the only home she knew pass her by.

I wished I never had to do that to her again. But her safety was more important to me than anything else in the world. It was a shame it always came at the cost of her happiness.

Once I reached our small town home, nestled at the end of a row of houses on a quiet street, I began packing up our life. I threw all of Chloe's clothes and favorite toys from her room into suitcases. Realizing I wouldn't be able to fit all of her belongings in my SUV broke my heart. There were a few toys and knickknacks that Chloe was fond of, but wouldn't fit between all the other necessities we needed. I tried to be as mindful as possible when choosing which toys made the cut. I kept her favorite dolls out for the ride. She was going to need company for the long ride ahead of us.

I don't even know where we are going yet. In my head, I checked off all the states we've lived in so far: Maine, Connecticut, New York - and now Maryland. I guess we could continue moving south and head to Georgia or South Carolina. Although I longed for a small town, I knew we'd need to look into one of the larger cities, like Atlanta or Charleston. It'd be easier for us to blend in - and harder to spot.

After a few hours of thinking about my options while I packed, I decided on Atlanta. It was large and diverse and always moving. People moved there all the time looking for a fresh start or on a trail to follow their dreams. I'll be able to find Chloe another dance school, and she can continue building her passion. A new place always takes some time to get used to, but she's young and resilient and she is going to be fine. We were going to be fine.

I was just about finished gathering all our belongings by the time five o'clock rolled around. All our suitcases and storage containers were lined up in the hallway by the door, waiting to be taken into the car. It wouldn't take long to load everything into the car. I'd be a little late picking Chloe up, but maybe that was a good thing. She could spend a little extra time with the friends she'll never see again.

Bang! Bang! Bang!

Harsh knocks at the door broke my train of thought.

Raising an eyebrow, I pulled my phone out of my pocket and opened the home security app installed on it. On the camera above the door, I made out two burly, dark-haired men dressed in black standing in front of my door. One of them raised his enormous fist and rammed it against the door again, harder this time.

Uneasiness rolled through my stomach at the sight. Unfamiliar men showing up on anyone's doorstep was never a good sign. But, for them to show up on mine was like drawing a tarot card with a skull on it.

I backed away from the door as he knocked a third time. This time, his voice accompanied the loud banging. "Open up, Diamond! We know you're in there!"

"Shit," I murmured. I abandoned our luggage in the hall and jogged towards the back of the house. Reaching the laundry room, I peeked out the window beside the back door. Two more men stood on the small stoop there. A third kneeled in front of them, jostling the lock with a small, thin object.

My heartbeat thumped through my eardrums as I moved towards the stairwell and ascended the steps. All of my exits may be blocked, but my chances of survival weren't completely gone. I'd masked a ladder beside the window in Chloe's room with flower-filled vines. In an instance like this, my first thought was for her to have an easy way out. Now, it was going to be my saving grace.

As I hurried down the narrow hall, the creaking of the back door and the loud thud of the front door collided in a loud echo through the empty first floor. Heavy footsteps thumped on the floor, spreading through the rooms below me.

I crossed through the threshold of Chloe's room and shut the door behind me. I was prepared to climb out the window, hurry down the ladder, sneak to my car, and drive like a madman to get them off my tail. It'd mean a much later pickup time for Chloe, but she'll be alright. She wasn't attending dance class tonight, anyway.

My feet froze in their tracks as I noticed a figure standing beside the open window. A tall man shoved his large hands up and down his sleek suit, brushing away dirt and leaves from the fabric. At the sound of the door closing, he picked up his head, and hazel eyes clashed with mine.

34

I stumbled backwards as if I'd been shoved. My back collided with the closed door, the pain combating the shiver traveling down my spine.

"Hello, Diamond," he greeted as a sadistic smile spread across his lips. "Where did you think you were going?"

Swallowing the fear crawling up my throat, I turned around and opened the door.

A hand slammed against the surface and slammed it shut. "Aht, aht," he taunted. Leaning his head down to my ear, he pressed himself up against from behind, reminding me of every muscle I'd tried so hard to forget. He lay his other hand on the door, caging me between it and his body. "You got away from me once," he whispered, his warm breath tickling my skin. "But you're not getting away again."

Chapter 7

Javier

Brrring! Brrring! Brrring!

The loud chime of the landline on my desk tore me out of the daze I'd fallen into. I'd been staring at the door, silently hoping Brielle would waltz through it and help me with the email I was typing to my Public Relations team about the charity gala we were hosting next month. She was better at answering the decor and setup questions than I was.

Sometimes I swore she could see my face through the transparent wall that separated our spaces. She always managed to swoop in at the moment I needed her. Whether I was frustrated with my employees or annoyed by the stupid questions my PR team posed about events or worn down from the invisible weight laying over my shoulders. Each time, without fail, she strutted in here like she owned the place and brightened up all the empty spaces in the room with her lively energy and cheerful smile.

My office felt so strange without her. I've become so accustomed to hearing her music playing in the lobby, seeing glimpses of her pink outfits flitting around the file cabinets, and having my spurts of silence broken by the sound of her soft voice. With her gone, it's so quiet. Too quiet.

And that's usually the door the bad thoughts use to creep in and make themselves at home. I expected it when I was at my own house, but during work hours, I've been privileged to have Brielle's joy chase them away.

Blinking back into the present, I looked at my ringing phone. My brow rose at the sight of an unfamiliar number on the Caller ID. Usually, only company calls came through to my direct line. If my siblings or anyone else needed to reach me, they'd just call my cell. Who the hell was calling me at almost six-thirty at night?

I picked the phone up and held it up to my ear. "Hello," I answered.

"Hi," an innocent, high-pitched voice replied. "May I talk to Mr. Javier Ruiz?"

"Speaking."

"Oh. Hi, Mr. Ruiz. My name's Chloe. My mommy works for you."

I raised an eyebrow. Brielle's daughter? I thought she was leaving to pick her up because she was sick. Why the fuck was she calling me? "Okay," I said, confusion in my voice.

"My mommy put your number on my phone," she explained. "She said I should call you or 911 if there's an emergency."

"Why didn't you call 911?"

"Because my mommy said she had work today, and she hasn't picked me up yet. I tried calling, but she's not answering. Is she still with you?"

"No," I answered honestly.

"Oh," her small voice deflated. "Well, do you know where she went? My center is going to close soon, and I need to be picked up."

"I'm sorry, but your mom left a while ago. Let me call her on her cell and see-"

"I've already called twenty times," Chloe exclaimed, cracks forming in her voice. "She always answers her phone, and she's never late to pick me up, and I don't know who else to call."

"What about your dad? Do you know his number?" I asked. "Maybe he can pick you up."

The other end was silent for a moment. "I don't know my dad," she murmured.

Oh shit. Now, I feel like an asshole. I never made any assumptions about Brielle's personal life outside of what she's told me. All I knew was: she was single, she had a young daughter who she adored, and she was trying to make a good life for her small family. I never thought to ask about co-parenting or if she was still in contact with her daughter's father or any of that. Not because I didn't care, but because it wasn't a topic she seemed interested in talking about. And that girl could fucking *talk*. If she didn't bring it up of her own free will, then I figured she thought it wasn't worth speaking about.

"Alright. Um, how about I pick you up? Would that be okay?"

"I guess." She paused. "But, after you pick me up, you'll help me find my mommy?"

"Of course. What's the name of your center?" As she read off the name, I looked up the location on my cell. It was only ten minutes away. "I'll be there soon, Chloe," I promised before hanging up the phone.

I didn't waste any time gathering my things and bolting out of the office. A familiar twinge in my stomach let me know that something wasn't right. Brielle spoke about her daughter as if her entire world revolves around her. She'd never leave her behind or forget about her. So, where the fuck was she?

I tried calling her myself as I jogged to my car. Unsurprisingly, the trill rang for a few moments before sending me to her voicemail.

After hanging up, I called Miles. He was the only person I knew capable of tracking someone's location in under ten seconds.

"Her phone's pinging at her home address," Miles explained. In the background, I could hear the clicking of his fingers against the keys of his computer. "Her car's GPS is there, too."

"Does the address have a security system?"

"Yeah, but it has a thick firewall. It's going to take me a few minutes to break through it."

"That's fine. Just review it and call me back if you find anything interesting."

"Will do, boss!"

I raced down to the learning center where Chloe was waiting. Outside, the building was decorated with paintings of child-like cartoons and colorful signs. Kid-made crafts hung in the windows of the darkened rooms.

The front door was locked. I hit the small doorbell and waited for a response from the speaker above it.

"May I help you sir?" A woman's voice spoke through the circular speaker.

"My name is Javier Ruiz. I'm here to pick up Chloe Parker."

A soft buzz rang, and the door unlocked. Once inside, I walked down a long hallway, passing a long line of empty classrooms, towards a pair of double doors. Behind them lay a large carpeted gym filled with activity stations and round tables.

Only one of the abundance of tables around the room was occupied. A young girl I've only seen in photos sat with a solemn gaze, toying with a charm bracelet in her wrist.

The older woman sitting beside her widened her eyes as I approached them. Her gaze trailed over my sleek suit and the Rolex peeking out from under my sleeve. A noticeable crease appeared between her brows as she met my eyes. Her arm, thrown behind Chloe's chair, lifted and she cuffed the kid's shoulder. "*You're* the emergency pickup for Chloe?" She asked.

I nodded. "Her mom and I are friends." Turning my gaze to Chloe, I asked, "You ready, kid?"

"Yeah," she mumbled. Her eyes rose from the bracelet and traveled up my attire towards my face. Unlike her teacher, who damn near quivered when we made eye contact, Chloe held my gaze with a steady one of her own. Her eyes, bright amber rimmed with green, inspected me for a moment, determined to put a crack in the walls and peek to see what secrets lie behind them.

Hopping out of her seat, she said, "Goodnight, Mrs. Turner." Her eyes ran up and down my figure again. This time, she craned her neck back to meet my eyes. "You're really tall - like a giant."

"You're tiny - like an elf," I replied.

Her tiny lips tugged into a small smile. She raised her small hand and wrapped it around my larger one. Her entire hand only grasped three of my fingers. Still, she held on tight as we walked back down the hall.

"Do you live in a house in the sky like the other giants?"

"Do you live in a cottage like the other elves?"

She giggled. "I'm not an elf! I'm a dancer!"

I didn't care to feign the surprised expression she was expecting. "An elf who dances? I don't think I've ever seen that before. What book did you come out of?"

She giggled. "You're funny. No wonder my mommy likes you."

Ignoring her comment, I led her through the front door and towards the car.

"Are you hungry?" I asked as I opened the door and lifted her up into the backseat. The large leather seats swallowed her tiny body as she sank back against the cushions.

Looking around my clean, spacious car, her smile dimmed. "Yeah. My mommy said she was going to make my favorite meal tonight. She said I deserved it since I've been practicing so hard for my recital."

"Yeah, I heard you made the lead. Odette, right?"

Her eyes darted to me at the reference. "Mommy told you?"

"Of course she did. Your mommy talks about you all the time."

A crease formed between her brows. "Then how could she forget to pick me up?"

Fuck, I didn't know how to answer that question. I couldn't tell her about the panic her mother had left in earlier or the eeriness surrounding her unresponsive calls. Something was wrong, but I couldn't tell Chloe that. She was only six years old. She didn't need to know the fear that came with knowing your mother could be in trouble and there was nothing you could do about it.

"Your mother would never forget about you," I assured her. "She loves you very much, and she would never abandon you. Not like this."

"Well, then, where..." Tears welled in her eyes as she struggled to finish the question. "Where is she?"

"You let me worry about that. Okay?"

"Can you promise you'll find her?"

"I promise I'll do everything I can."

She nodded, content with my answer.

Sighing, I backed away from her. "Let's get you something to eat."

I climbed in the car and started driving to Adrian's fiancé's soul food restaurant. The cozy atmosphere and hearty food may not ease all of Chloe's worries, but it may comfort her for the next few hours. Hopefully, Kiara wouldn't mind watching her for a bit while I track her mother down.

The music humming through the radio paused as an incoming call came to my phone. Miles's name popped up across the dashboard screen.

I grabbed my cell from out of the center console and put it to my ear, so Chloe wouldn't hear the news he bought. "What did you find?" I asked.

"Footage of Brielle entering the home around twelve. Then, about two hours ago, there's two men slamming the door off the hinges and entering."

My fingers tightened around the phone. "Any visual of them taking her outside?"

"No. But, there's footage of a man leaving through the front door. I can't see his face, but he has dark hair, and he's wearing a suit. The first two men weren't with him."

"Shit," I muttered. God only knows what those men were doing to Brielle in that house. Two hours is a long time when you're being held against your will. The mental torture, even if your captors weren't doing anything to you at that moment, was excruciating. All you could do is stare and struggle in your bounds and pray that help comes sooner than later. I hope Brielle was doing more than praying. Life was one thing to fight for, but a child - a daughter - warranted a whole new level of strength.

"Call Adrian and Dante for me," I commanded. "Tell them to meet me at the address. Make sure they know not to make any moves until I get there. In the meantime, monitor her live security footage. Let me know if any more men come or go."

"Aye, aye, Captain!" Miles replied before ending the call.

As I stopped at a red light, I peeked at the rear view mirror for a glance at Chloe.

She was staring at me with her head tilted to the side. Obvious questions floated through her eyes, but her lips remained pressed shut. Her shoulders curled inward as she looked away and diverted her gaze out the window.

When we finally arrived at Kiara's restaurant, Sunflower Soul, I helped Chloe out of the car and led her inside.

Curiously, Chloe looked around at the gold-tinted lights, burnt orange booths, and decorative sunflower shaped lights on the tables. Her small hand squeezed mine as we approached the hostess stand.

Coincidentally, my brother's fiancé, Kiara, was behind the podium, standing beside a young woman with two big Afro-puffs on her head. Both of them looked up from the small tablet they were fiddling with atop the podium.

Kiara's eyes lit up with surprise as she met my gaze. "Hey, Javier," she said, offering a warm smile. "Pleasant surprise seeing you here. Dining in or taking out?"

"I need a favor," I replied.

Kiara followed my gaze as it lowered to Chloe's small head of curls. "Oh..." She moved from behind the podium, revealing her petite and curvy figure. Stooping to Chloe's height, she asked, "Who's this sweet little girl?"

"This is Chloe. Chloe, this is Kiara."

"Hi Kiara," Chloe said. Her eyes lingered on Kiara's micro braids, styled in loose curls around her head. "I like your hair."

"Thank you! I like your eyes. They're beautiful."

A bashful smile appeared on Chloe's lips. "Thank you," she said shyly.

"Bonnie, can you take Chloe to table fifteen?" Kiara asked the hostess. "I'll be there in a minute."

Nodding, the hostess picked up a paper kid's menu and a small pack of crayons. She held her hand out to Chloe as she moved from behind the stand.

Looking up at me, Chloe squeezed my fingers. "I want to stay with you," she murmured.

I stooped to her height again. "I'll be back. In the meantime, Ms. Kiara is going to make sure you eat dinner. Alright?"

Her eyes lowered as she nodded in reluctant agreement.

I put my finger underneath her chin and pushed it back up. "Don't do that. Keep your head up. Your mom is going to want to see your smiling face when she comes to pick you up."

She jolted forward and flung her tiny body against me. Her arms wrapped around my neck in a tight embrace.

Instinctively, I stiffened underneath her. I wasn't much of a hugger - never was and likely never will be. Chloe wasn't an exception to the uneasy sensation it summoned in my stomach. "Alright, kid," I said as I tried to wiggle myself out of her hug. It took a moment, but I escaped her grasp. "Be good for Ms. Kiara."

Chloe finally left my side and followed the hostess down the aisle towards a booth near the back of the restaurant.

I didn't take my eyes off of her as she hopped into the booth and started taking the crayons out of the box.

"Who knew you were good with kids?" Kiara commented. "Is she yours?"

"Hell no," I immediately replied. "But her mom is M.I.A. and it's not looking good. Can you watch her for a few hours until we have the situation under control?"

"Yeah, of course."

"*Gracias.* I'll have Adrian or Miles contact you about where to bring her and when, so keep your phone on you." I turned on my heel and started heading back towards the front door.

"Javier?" Kiara called from behind me.

I stopped and looked over my shoulder with a tinge of reluctance.

Tilting her head, she asked, "Is her mom going to be okay?"

"I don't know," I answered honestly. All I knew was that the men who had infiltrated her home were going to pay for trying to take advantage of the kindest woman I know.

Chapter 8

Brielle

The chain hooked around the post of my bed clinked against the metal rods as I tugged at my bounds. Digging my knees into the mattress, I pulled vigorously at the chain. My body, sore from all the straining, screamed in agony as I writhed, but I ignored it. The pain was minuscule compared to the ones I've faced before.

Thankfully, I didn't have to relive those memories - not yet, anyway.

Once Leo closed the door, I swung around and punched him square in the face. I didn't cause any damage but the sudden movement stunned him for a moment, giving me the opportunity to reopen the door and sprint into the hallway. I made it a few feet down the hall before his arms caged around my waist and he lifted me off of my feet.

I clawed at his arms as he dragged me, kicking and screaming, into my bedroom.

My heart fell into my stomach as he threw me onto the bed. The same fear that'd paralyzed me in situations like this years ago threatened to crawl up my spine. But I refused to let it consume me. I couldn't freeze up and remain idle - no matter how much I wanted to. I needed to get the hell away from him, pick up Chloe, and erase all traits of our existence from the face of the Earth *again*. My only job in this world now was to keep my daughter safe, and I was going to do so at all costs.

"You look good, Diamond," he taunted. His hazel eyes scoured over my body as he licked his lips. "Having a baby did wonders for those thin hips of yours. Boobs too. That baby weight filled you in real good."

I lifted my leg, intending to kick him in his groin. "Fuck you!" I spat.

He caught my ankle as it lunged towards him. Gripping it tight, he pulled me across the mattress towards the edge where he stood. "Made you feisty too. The little brat put some fire under your ass?" He pinned my legs down underneath him as he climbed on top of me. "Where is she, anyway? From the pictures at the office, she looks like a perfect doll to add to the collection."

I swung my hand at his face and dug my long nails into his flesh. I dragged them through his skin, creating a row of scratches across his face.

Almost immediately, his fist, closed tight and with full velocity, came down on my cheek. The crack of his knuckles against my bones rippled through my skull, blurring my vision. "All this freedom has made you forget your place." He grabbed a handful of my hair and pulled my head back so far that the arch of my neck strained my muscles. Staring down at me with livid eyes, he said, "Do I need to remind you of where you belong?"

I refused to cower underneath his glowering gaze. He wanted me to shake, to cry, to beg and plead for his forgiveness. And I would not do any of it. Chloe may not be with me right now, but I still needed to set an example for her. She needed to know to never back down from anyone - especially men like him.

I mustered up all the saliva around the inside of my mouth and spit it right in his face.

I was immediately met with another punch - this one colliding square with my mouth and nose. "That's it, you fucking bitch," he gritted. Tightening his grip on my hair, he moved from atop me and dragged my body up the mattress towards the headboard. He dug out a pair of leather handcuffs from his pocket. "I had a feeling I was going to need these," he mused.

Nausea rolled through my stomach at the sight. "No, no, no." I pushed at the fist in my hair, desperate to untangle his fingers from my curls. "Please, don't."

"It's too late for begging now, pretty girl." He substituted his grip on my hair for a tight hold on my wrist instead. He held it still and wrapped one cuff around it. He tightened the leather so tight around my wrist that it damn near stopped the circulation of my blood. "You remember the rules."

"No! No! No!" I swung my free hand frantically at his face and arms to escape his grasp.

Ignoring my flailing arm, he wrapped the rope connecting the cuffs around the poles of my headboard. Easily, he overpowered my other arm and confined it within a cuff. As he straightened up to hover over the edge of the bed, his hands undid the buckle on his leather belt.

I wiggled in my restraints. "No, no. Mr. Bianchi, please don't-"

"Get on your knees and face the headboard," he demanded.

I held his malicious glare, staring at him in silent defiance. I would've spat at him again, but the harsh lash of leather whipping against my face prevented me from doing so. My head swung to the side as my cheek burned from the impact.

"Don't make me repeat the instructions."

I took a deep breath, inhaling the tears pricking behind my eyes. I would *not* break. Not for him. Not again. I ignored my stinging cheek and turned to face him. "Fuck you," I repeated. My words earned me another slap with the belt. This time, the skin of my cheek split open, spreading a wildfire of pain across my face.

He grabbed a handful of my blouse and tore it clean off my body. My bra quickly followed. He forcefully pushed my body over onto my stomach. One hand pushed my head down against the pillow while the other lifted my hips to put me in position. "I can't wait to fuck you like this again," Leo said. "You look so pretty when you're praying for mercy."

I bit into the pillow to muffle my groans of discomfort. I couldn't risk letting him hear any sign of pain. It'd only fuel the sadism running through his sick mind. One whimper, one whine, one cry, and he'll be escalating to other methods to see what other sounds he can summon.

His phone rang before he could touch my pants. From my peripheral vision, I saw the belt in his hands lower.

"I'm in the middle of something," he said as he answered the phone. He was silent for a moment as the other end buzzed frantically. "What?" He exclaimed. "How?" He took a few steps away from me, his attention now taken from whatever news the caller had bought. "What's their affiliation? Who the fuck do they...?" He trailed off.

Turning my head, I saw an epiphany flash in his eyes. Fire that ignited the deepest pits of Hell followed it. "Those motherfuckers," he growled. "Keep surveilling the situation. I'll be right there." He hung up the phone and called for his men. Immediately, they filed into the room like obedient foot soldiers.

"I need to go to Philadelphia for a few hours, but I'll be back. In the meantime, I need you all to watch over my girl. Seems she's forgotten how we run things around here."

One man grinned maliciously. "Do you want us to remind her?"

My stomach rolled at the thought. Sometimes his henchmen were worse than them. They were more interested in fulfilling their own needs than giving a legitimate punishment.

Leo looked down at the belt in his hands as he debated the question. "No," he said after a moment. He threw the belt down on the ground. "I don't want any of you touching her. This little minx is mine, and if I find out one of you damaged my property, you're all getting a bullet in the head. Are we fucking clear?"

"Yes, boss," they all said in unison, all of their greedy hopes blowing out like candles.

"Guard the doors. Make sure no one gets in, and that this sneaky little one doesn't get out."

They nodded.

Leo turned his livid eyes back to me. He stalked over to me and leaned down to whisper in my ear. "Don't get too comfortable, Diamond. When I get back, I'm going to fuck that tight pussy of yours until it's black and blue. Then, when I'm done, I'm going to find that sweet daughter of yours and find out how much she'll sell for."

"You're a sick son of a bitch," I snapped.

Smiling, he backed away from me and exited the room. The men he commanded to guard the doors followed him.

Trembles traveled down my spine as the door closed behind them. I knew they'd be back. It was rare they ever listened when told the merchandise was off limits. I needed to get myself free before they thought Leo was far enough away to do what they wanted.

Once I heard their footsteps reach the bottom floor, I examined my restraints. The chain connecting the cuffs was metal, but the poles of my headboard were made of material just as strong. Writhing my body, I pulled the chain against the poles with all my might, hoping for either the chain to break or for the connecting loops to pop off of the cuffs.

As I worked, I kept an ear out for footsteps on the steps. If they caught me trying to escape, then I was definitely dead. I needed to survive. Not for myself, but for Chloe.

My eyes burned as I thought about my sweet girl and how worried she must be.

I've had plenty of talks with her before about whom to call and what to do in emergency situations like this. I stressed that if I didn't show up for any reason, then she should call one of the trusted adults I installed in her cell and wait with them until I could get to her. If they didn't answer, then the police were the next go-to. It wasn't an ideal solution, but at least she'd be safe.

I'd tried to engrave the instructions into her head, but she was still young. What if she freaked out? Or couldn't remember which names I mentioned? Or lost her phone? What would she do? Who was going to help her? What if Leo's henchmen got to her before one of our safety nets did?

I shook the last thought out of my head. Chloe might only be six, but she was smart. She'll make the right decisions that will keep her out of harm's way - for tonight, at least.

Keeping her sweet face and kind smile in my head helped me endure the burn of the leather around my wrists and the ache in my arms. Even when I could feel the chill of the air on my irritated flesh and the tickle of blood trickling over my fingers, I kept tugging. Giving up wasn't an option. I had a child who needed me. I had to return to her.

According to the clock on my nightstand, I'd been tugging at this damn thing for at least forty-five minutes, and I thought I was seeing some tears on the flap of my right cuff. Twenty more minutes of tugging, and I might be free.

Just as quickly as hope crossed my mind, it quickly vanished as the quiet chatter downstairs was interrupted by the loud crash of breaking glass.

The men's frantic, confused shouts echoed through the house. I could hear their footsteps as they scattered around.

Bang! Bang! Bang!

My eyes widened as gunshots followed.

Shit.

I needed to get out of here.

Now.

With no time to waste, I mustered up all my strength and pulled the chain against the poles with all my might.

The metal of the chain tore through the leather fabric and the hook slipped out from its closed loop. I nearly fell backwards from the force.

Two pairs of footsteps thumped against the steps, making their way upstairs.

Finally free, and topless, I scrambled off of the bed and went to the window. My heart rammed against my ribcage as I assessed the long distance between the window and the ground below. I could jump, but I'd be at risk of breaking my leg or my arm. Or god forbid, I bust my head open.

The steps, one pair looming closer to my door and the other moving farther down the hall, reminded me I didn't have time to decide. I could either jump or fight. In my condition, I wasn't sure the latter was going to do me much good.

I unlocked the latches of the window and started lifting it. To my dismay, the damn thing was stuck. It wouldn't budge farther than an inch.

Swearing under my breath, I gave up my first plan and opted for my second option. I grabbed the belt from off the floor and positioned myself next to the side of the door. From the angle, and the darkness, the intruder wouldn't be able to see me when I attacked.

Sweat trickled down my face as I struggled to steady my breathing. Every part of my brain screamed that this was a dumb idea. They had a gun and I had a fucking belt. There wasn't a chance in hell I was going to win this fight. But maybe winning didn't have to be my priority. I just needed to stun them long enough to get past them - or grab their weapon. Whichever came first.

Listening to the footsteps stalk closer to the door made my heartbeat pulse in my ears. Still, I took a deep breath and steadied my breathing. If I wanted to survive, then I needed to stay calm.

The doorknob clicked as it turned. Slowly, the door creaked open.

I saw the gun first, pointed straight ahead with firm hands wrapped around it. The mouth swayed back and forth as its owner scrutinized the room.

As they moved closer inside, I noticed their shadow hovered well over mine. It was going to be hard to get the belt around their neck without tipping them off. I'd have to use another part of it.

Once they crossed the threshold, I lunged from the darkness and slammed the belt buckle against the back of their head.

"Ow, what the fu-"

I didn't give them time to complete their sentence. I hit them again in the back of their head. The second hit sent them stumbling a few steps forward. I knew I couldn't make a giant fall, but this would buy me at least a few moments to make a run for the steps.

Turning on my heel, I darted out the door and sprinted down the hall. I almost reached the stairwell before a pair of arms wrapped around me. "No!" I screamed as I was lifted off of my feet. I pounded my fists against the arms that held me captive. "Let me go, you bastard!"

The hold tightened around me. "Relax, relax," a deep male voice replied.

I tried to wiggle myself out of his grasp. "No! Let me go!"

"Hey, hey," he said as he grabbed my arms and spun me around. "Stop. Look at me."

"No!" Lifting my arms as best I could, I pounded my fists against his chest. "Get off of me!"

A hand cupped the back of my neck and tilted my head up. "Brielle, look at me," he repeated firmly.

I hesitantly raised my eyes to meet his gaze. My shoulders sank in relief and confusion as my eyes collided with familiar chestnut brown ones. Raising my brows, I asked, "Mr. Ruiz?"

Chapter 9

Javier

Who the *fuck* blew the stars out of this woman's eyes?

The Brielle staring up at me wasn't the one I'd seen earlier today. Her brown eyes, usually filled with sparkles, were empty and despondent. Her shoulders, usually held high, were sunken and trembling. Her perpetual smile was nowhere in sight. Instead, a deep frown lay on her lips and wet tears covered her cheeks. Her lip was split, and a wide gash ran across her cheek. Blood trickled from the cut, staining her skin.

Whoever did this was going to regret ever being born once I got my hands on them. Killing slowly wasn't usually my style. My siblings got more pleasure out of causing physical pain than I did. But the person responsible for this didn't deserve a quick, painless death. They deserved to experience the sensation of having their body torn apart - piece by piece.

Brielle's trembles increased underneath the ill intentions forming in my eyes. Breaking out of my arms, she took a step back and asked, "Mr. Ruiz, what…what are you doing here?"

My eyes fell to her bare torso in search of other wounds. In the darkness, I couldn't see much, but I didn't doubt there were some blooming bruises.

Brielle's arms quickly lifted to cover herself, namely her breasts. The cuffs tied around her wrists looked too tight for comfort. Judging by the chain hanging from one of them, I assumed she added even more pressure to her wrists. I almost didn't even want to know what her skin was going to look like once they were taken off. "Mr. Ruiz?" She called again, her voice shakier than before.

I unbuttoned my shirt and shrugged it off my shoulders. "Put this on," I said as I wrapped it around Brielle. My shirt swallowed her slender body, covering her down to above her knees.

"Jav, you good?" Adrian called from behind me. I glanced over my shoulder to see him emerging from the other end of the hall, rubbing the back of his head.

"Yeah. Are you?"

"Mhm." He looked at Brielle as she hurriedly buttoned up my shirt. "She hit me in the back of the head."

Brielle's eyes widened. "Oh, I'm so sorry! I wouldn't have hit you if-"

"Don't apologize," Adrian insisted. "I just wanna know what the fuck you hit me with. That shit hurts."

"We're not having this conversation right now," I intervened. "I need to get her cleaned up, and you don't need any more ideas." I bent my knees and swooped Brielle up in my arms, bridal style.

Yelping in surprise, her arms flew around me, holding me tight as if I were a buoy sent to take her out of an aggressive wave.

Careful of the wounds I couldn't see, I turned towards the steps. "Close your eyes," I commanded.

Her brows creased. "Why? Are they...?"

"Close your goddamn eyes," I snapped. She'd already seen enough. The last thing she needed in her mind was the image of three men with bloody holes sliced through their body like Swiss cheese and a lone survivor being tied and gagged.

All four of the men were in the same room when we arrived, so the massacre was quick. But, it wasn't as clean as I preferred. Blood splatter covered the walls, and more seeped across the carpets from the bodies laying on the ground.

Brielle finally squeezed her eyes shut and shoved her face into my chest.

"Adrian, ride with Dante to transport our friend back to HQ. See what answers you can coerce out of him," I said as I glanced over my shoulder at my brother. "Try not to kill each other on the way there."

Adrian rolled his eyes. "If Dante keeps his mouth shut, maybe I'll think about it."

"And make sure the clean-up crew gets here *before* you two leave."

I heard his grumble of confirmation before I headed out the door. I carried Brielle to my waiting car near the curb. I opened the passenger door and gently set her in the seat.

Her fingers tightened around my neck, reluctant to let go. Against my chest, her eyes were still shut tight. As my hold released on her, she curled back into me.

"It's alright," I told her. "You can open your eyes now."

Slowly, she pulled her face away and cracked her moist eyes open. Tears escaped from her lids as she looked up at me with wide eyes. "Chloe," she whispered. "I…I need to go pick up Chloe. Can you take me to her? Please? Her after-school center is only down the street."

"I already picked her up," I assured her. "She's with my brother's fiancé now, and she's fine. I'll have Kiara bring her to the hospital after you're all cleaned up."

"The hospital? No, I can't go to a hospital. I need to grab Chloe and get the hell out of here *now*." She pushed at my chest as she tried to climb out of the car. "Mr. Ruiz, please get out of the way."

"No. You need medical attention. Relax and put your seat belt on."

"I am fine!" Her small hands curled into fists, and she started punching my torso. "Move out of my way!"

I firmly seized her wrists in one hand and used the other to strap the seat belt around her body.

Wiggling in my grasp, she yelled, "Mr. Ruiz, let me go! I'm fine!"

"You are not fine," I snapped back. "You're wounded and bleeding. You don't want your daughter to see you like this, do you?"

She ripped her wrists out of my grasp. Fire I didn't know she held flickered in her eyes as she glared at me. "Do *not* talk to me about my daughter! All I need is five minutes in the bathroom, and she'll never suspect a thing!"

"She will," I replied. "Kids always know when something's wrong - no matter how hard their parents try to mask it."

"How do you know?"

"Because I was the kid who saw through the masks."

Brielle's brows tilted up in something like pity. She didn't need to feel anything like that - not for me.

"I'm taking you to the hospital," I stated before she could reply. "After a doctor tends to your wounds, I will call Kiara, and she'll bring Chloe to you."

"Do you promise?"

"*Prometo,*" I replied without hesitation.

Sighing, she finally relaxed in her seat.

I left her side to head towards the driver's side of the car. As I walked, I fished my phone out of my pocket and shot Miles a text commanding that he dug up everything he could find on Brielle Parker. I wanted to know everywhere she's lived before. Her parents's occupations. Her schooling history. Any ex-boyfriends or casual flings she's had. I needed every piece of the puzzle of her life, so I could single out which piece of it led to this.

Miles promptly responded with a promise to compile all information.

On the ride to the hospital, Brielle was abnormally quiet. She sat in the passenger seat, watching the sights of the city passing through the window. I don't think there's ever been a moment where she's been completely silent. Usually, she was always chattering about something.

My fingers tightened around the steering wheel at the thought of the impacts this incident could have on her. She was already talking about booking it out of town. What if she stopped talking? Stopped smiling? Stopped being the bubbliest person in the room?

No, I wouldn't let that happen. Brielle was going to have the sparkles back in her eyes - no matter how long it took.

When we arrived at the hospital, Dr. Flores, one of the female doctors on our payroll, met us at the entrance of the emergency room. I'd made a quick phone call on the way to let her know we were coming.

She offered a kind smile to Brielle as she led us to an examination room. "How would you rate your pain?" She asked.

"A five, I guess," Brielle replied. "But I'm fine, really. It's just a few scratches."

"The cuffs on her wrists might have cut off her circulation and could've possibly damaged the joints," I explained. "She might need X-rays to make sure nothing is fractured."

Brielle shot me a sharp look. "Mr. Ruiz, I am-"

"You are not fine," I snapped. "Tell the doctor the truth and let them treat your wounds properly."

Looking away, Brielle crossed her arms. Her plump lips twitched, threatening to poke out into a pout.

I wish she would catch an attitude with me. She may be injured now, but her wounds will heal. I'll gladly take part in the "Who has a bigger attitude" contest once she feels better. I bet after I win, she won't do that shit again.

Dr. Flores shooed Brielle into an empty room. "There's a gown on the bed. Undress and put it on. I'll knock before I come in to make sure you're ready," she told her before closing the door. Turning to me, her brows creased with concern. "Welts to her face? Cuffs around her wrists? Javier, what am I looking at?"

"A group of men invaded her home. She'd freed herself by the time we found her, but it looks like they tied her up and knocked her around."

"Jesus Christ," Dr. Flores sighed. "Should I do a *full* exam?"

I nodded. "Let me know if you find anything else."

"Will do." She knocked softly on the door. After hearing Brielle's soft voice on the other end, she let herself in and shut it behind her.

I leaned against the wall across from the door and dug out my phone again. I dialed Kiara's number. It took her a few moments to pick up.

"Hey," she said when she finally answered. "Did you find Chloe's mom?"

"Yeah. She's banged up, but she's alive."

She let out a sigh of relief. "Oh, thank God."

"Did Chloe eat for you?"

"Well, she picked over most of it, but she ate enough to hold her over until morning. She's doing a good job hiding it, but she's really worried about her mom. I'm about to bring her some pie to get some more in her belly. Maybe that and the news her mom is safe will cheer her up."

"When she's finished eating, can you bring her down to Mercy Hospital? Her mom's wounds should be treated by the time you guys get here."

"Yeah, of course! I'll see you then."

Just as I hung up on Kiara, Miles's name flashed across the screen. "What did you find?" I asked, after accepting the call.

"Nothing," Miles admitted. Behind his voice, the constant clicking of keys was absent, leaving the background eerily silent.

I raised a brow. "What the fuck are you talking about? You always find something."

"I've checked every single database, but the only thing I can find for Brielle Parker - the one who works for you at least - are the basic identifications: I.D., address, place of employment, etc and some enrollment documents for her daughter's schooling. There's no birth certificate, no social security card, no known parents, no known associates, no legitimate educational history, no hospital records, no social media pages - *nothing*." He let out a sigh of defeat. "As far as records are concerned, Brielle Parker doesn't exist."

Chapter 10

Brielle

"Is this really necessary?" I asked. I was laying flat on my back with my legs propped up on metal prongs. Dr. Flores sat between my knees, inspecting the land between my inner thighs. After she finished bandaging my raw wrists and the cuts on my face, she insisted she needed to do a vaginal exam to make sure no other damage was done to my body.

"Yes," Dr. Flores replied.

"But I've already told you they didn't touch me there. My pants were still intact when Mr. Ruiz brought me in, remember?"

She laughed. "You're so formal. Why do you keep calling Javier 'Mr. Ruiz'?"

"Because he's my boss," I said with a shrug. And maybe old habits didn't die in addressing my superiors, but I wasn't telling her that. Especially not when she was doing a deep dive into my pussy.

"You work at the pharmaceutical company?" She asked.

"Yeah. I've been his personal assistant for almost a year now." I propped myself up on my elbows to look at her. Dr. Flores was pretty with her dark, curly hair, russet brown skin, and slender body. She radiated the type of sophisticated, intelligent women that often came by Javier's office with blush on their cheeks and ardor in their eyes. Raising an eyebrow, I asked, "How do you know Mr. Ruiz?"

"Mutual connections," Dr. Flores said, still focused on examining me. "Their company works closely with the hospital board, and by proxy, a lot of us physicians work with them for clinical trials and research and such. Being nice to some execs of the company made some of my research go fractionally smoother with access to more resources and treatments."

I leaned back against the cushioned bed. "Oh."

"Javier can be good company to keep once you get used to the emotionless void in his eyes," she continued. "Stay on his good side, and he can be very generous. He's helped me with grants, supplies, and abroad opportunities. I'm sure he'll be more than willing to help catch whoever did this to you."

After her gloved fingers left my skin, I closed my legs and pushed myself up into a sitting position. "Thank you for patching me up," I said, changing the course of the conversation.

"No problem. I'm going to give you some aloe vera gel to apply to the wounds daily. It'll help with pain and assist with the healing process. I'll also give you some ibuprofen to hold you over until you're able to get to the store - and clean clothes. We have some lying around that might fit you." She pulled off her gloves and headed for the door. "In the meantime, just try to relax. I'll send Javier back in to keep you company until you're set to go."

"Thank you," I repeated as I watched her disappear into the hall. Glancing around the room, I realized I didn't have any personal effects besides my pants and shoes. All of my stuff was still in the house, packed away in the piles of luggage by the door. The keys to my car were still on the table by the door. My car was still in the driveway. How the hell were we supposed to get out-of-town now? It wasn't safe to go back now. It didn't take a rocket scientist to figure out why Javier made me close my eyes. The men who held me captive were dead - and it wouldn't be long before their boss found out.

Going back for our stuff wasn't worth the risk of Leo catching us again. Once Chloe is back in my arms, I'll figure out our next steps. Maybe we can travel by train until we reach Atlanta. Then, we can settle our materialistic needs like clothing and convenient transportation.

Running away wasn't a great choice, but I didn't have any other options. I had no family or real friends to lie low with. And even if I did, I'd never risk their safety. Leo was a dangerous, sadistic man. He'll do everything in his power to eliminate any obstacle in his way. I was more than willing to bear the pain of his wrath for my daughter's sake, but I'll never ask anyone to bear it for me.

The door creaked open again. This time, Chloe burst through the doors. She rushed into the room, her curls bouncing with every step, and lunged into my arms. "Mommy, mommy!" She exclaimed as her tiny limbs wrapped around me. "Mommy, I was so worried."

I enveloped her in my arms and squeezed her tight. "I know, sweetpea. Mommy is so sorry."

She lifted her head to look up at me. Her brows stitched together as she noticed the bandage on my cheek. "What happened, mommy? Are you hurt?"

"I just had a little accident. But, I'm alright." I pulled her close again. My shoulders sank as I inhaled the familiar scent of the coconut oil in her hair. I thanked God my little girl was safe - and that she didn't have to witness any of what I've been through over the past few hours.

I looked up as two more women entered the room. I recognized Javier's sister right off the bat by her long, curly tresses. It took me a moment to remember the curvaceous woman with braids standing beside her. If I wasn't mistaken, she was Javier's brother's fiancé, Kiara. I remember chatting with her at Lexie's wedding. She seemed like an amiable lady, one I could have befriended in another life.

Kiara offered me a kind smile as we locked eyes. "Hey," she greeted. "How are you feeling?"

"Better now that Chloe's here," I replied. "Thank you for taking care of her for the past few hours."

"Of course. She's very sweet and well-behaved. I'm more than happy to take her anytime moving forward if you need a sitter." Walking closer, she held out a duffel bag. "Lexie packed some clothes for you."

I turned my gaze to the other woman, noticing she'd been oddly quiet. She remained by the door with her arms crossed and her head tilted. A mix of curiosity and suspicion twirled between her eyes as they looked me up and down.

"Thank you," I told her. Glancing around, I realized my knight in shining armor was nowhere to be found. Raising a brow, I asked, "Where's Mr. Ruiz?"

"He stepped out to handle some business," Lexie explained. "He'll meet us back at his house later."

"Wait, his house? No, no. Chloe and I aren't staying in town."

Chloe's head snapped upwards. "We're leaving?" She asked. "Why? I like it here!"

"I know you do, sweetpea," I murmured. "But it's not safe here for us anymore. We have to move on."

"But, mommy, I *like* it here," Chloe repeated. Moisture filled her eyes as her tiny heart broke into pieces. "I like my school, and I have friends, and I'm going to be Odette for our spring recital. I don't want to leave!"

"Chloe," I started.

"No!" She broke out of my embrace and hopped off the bed. "It's not fair! *You're* not fair!" Turning on her heel, she rushed towards the door.

I threw my legs over the edge of the bed to follow her and winced from the pain the movement caused.

"It's alright," Kiara assured me. "I've got her." She followed my daughter out the door and closed it behind her.

I let out a sigh as I ran a hand through my hair. I knew Chloe was going to have a hard time with this transition, but I didn't think she would throw this big of a tantrum. Hopefully Kiara could calm her down enough for me to help her understand this move was for the best. We were going to find her a new dancing school, new friends, and a new life. But, even then, we both knew she would eventually have to leave all of that behind too.

"What's the rush to get out of town?" Lexie asked. She took Kiara's spot by my bedside and unzipped the duffel bag laying beside me. "You won't have to worry about the men who broke into your house. They're being taken care of."

"It's not the men I'm worried about," I admitted. "It's their boss."

Lexie pulled out a tee shirt and a pair of sweats from the bag. "Who do they work for?"

"I...I can't say."

"Why?" she asked. "Are you afraid of him?"

I nodded. "He's...he's an evil man, Mrs. Ruiz."

"Why would an evil man send his goons to break into a good woman's home and torture her? What do you have that he wants?" Lexie raised a brow. "His child?"

My stomach churned at the reminder. "He doesn't know Chloe is his - not yet. And he can't find out. He'll ruin her." I grabbed her hands that were still pawing through the bag. "Please, promise me you'll keep that information between us."

She frowned. "I wish I could, but we need all the info we can get right now. The more we have, the better we'll be able to help you."

"Help me?" My brows stitched together. "Mrs. Ruiz, with all due respect, I don't need-"

"Don't say it," Lexie replied firmly. "Don't say you can do this on your own because you can't. I don't know what the fuck you're up against, but I know it will not end well if you continue fighting it alone. Those men could've killed you earlier if the boys hadn't stepped in. You don't want your daughter to grow up without a mother, do you?"

"No, of course not!"

"Then stop being stubborn and tell me the truth." Her eyes softened as she squeezed my hands. "What are you running from?"

I averted my gaze. Tears I hadn't cried in a long time pricked behind my eyes, desperate to be released from their prison. "Have you heard of the...the Bianchi family?"

Lexie's brows twitched. "Mhm. Why?"

"I...I um..." I trailed off as the words clogged in my throat. I never talked about this to anyone before. I wasn't sure where to start or how it would make me feel. The wave of nausea and shame caught me off guard, nearly knocking me back into the dark hole I once resided in. Taking a deep breath, I regained my footing and stood tall against the emotions as they came for me again.

"Mr. Leo Bianchi," I started over. "The eldest son… I was…I was his girl for a long time. I met him when I was a junior in high school. He saw me perform at an open-mic night at a restaurant, and he was very persistent in convincing me to let him take me on a date. At first, he was sweet and kind and he promised to make all my showgirl dreams come true. For a while, he did. He let me perform at his father's clubs and paid for studio time with producers he knew. But, after some time, I learned my so-called audience was never interested in my voice…and neither was Leo." My voice shrank as some of the bitter memories flashed through my mind. "Once he swooped me away from my hometown, he made me have private shows. Made me do things I didn't want to. Hurt me when I tried to refuse or didn't do them right."

"That bastard," Lexie cursed. "How long did you endure that?"

"Five years. Being claimed by the heir to the throne, all the other girls thought I was getting special treatment. Little did they know, I had it worst of all. He and his brother get off on pain, and Leo loved relishing in mine."

"How did you escape?"

"I never tried," I admitted. "One night, Leo saw me talking with one of their newer hires, and he swore we were flirting. In a blind fit of rage, he hurt me so badly that he thought he'd killed me. Hell, I thought I was dead too. I remember lying there, feeling the blood seep out of my skin and consciousness slip further and further away from me. When I blacked out, I thought death had taken me out of my misery.

"But then I woke up with a bright light in my face and a nurse at my bedside. Apparently, an older couple stumbled on my abandoned body and brought me to the emergency room. Once I was lucid, the doctors told me I was a few weeks pregnant, and by some miracle, the baby was unharmed. From there, I started all over. I used some funds from my previous life to restart my life.

"But that didn't last long before I started seeing telltale signs of their operation - the shady gentleman's clubs, the talent wanted fliers. Whenever I see them, or hear any sign that one of their operations is near, I move away as fast as I can. The problem is: now that Leo knows I'm alive…"

"He won't stop hunting until he captures you," Lexie finished.

"I'm scared," I admitted. Tears I'd been trying to restrain fell down my cheeks as the thought came to fruition. "I don't care what he does to me, but Chloe... I don't even want to imagine what he'll do to her if he gets his hands on her."

"He won't," Lexie promised. She pulled me into a tight hug. "My brothers and I will make sure of it."

Chapter 11

Javier

The man writhed in his chair as the hose poured bouts of water down over the towel covering his face. His legs, shuddering from the pain, lashed in every way. Sounds of his gurgles and gasps for air filled the room for more than a few moments. Before the man's body could cease their erratic movement, I turned off the hose.

Behind him, my brother ripped the towel off the man's face and kicked his chair back on its feet.

Our captive's eyes were wide and red as he inhaled air in quick, jagged breaths. His chest rose and fell in an uneven rhythm. Still, he fixed his face to glare at me.

"Are you ready to answer my questions now?" I asked.

"Fuck you," he spat.

Adrian didn't need to look at me to know the next move. He tilted the chair back and threw the towel right back on his face.

I adjusted the nozzle on the hose to increase the water pressure. I pointed the flowing stream of heavy, rushing water back over him.

He roared underneath the towel as his breaths eluded him again. His body shook helplessly in its bounds, desperate to escape from the wrath of the water pouring over him.

The asshole should consider himself lucky he didn't have more alone time with Adrian. I arrived not too long after my brother finished tying him up. He'd be dealing with much worse if it weren't for me. Shit, if he didn't talk soon, I was going to let Adrian do whatever the fuck he wanted with him.

I know I shouldn't have left Brielle - or whatever the fuck her name was - in the hospital by herself, but I couldn't be around her right now. Not until I had some answers about what the hell was going on.

I almost stormed into the exam room and questioned her myself, but I knew it wouldn't be right. She'd been through enough tonight. The last thing she needed was another terrifying man in her face, demanding something from her. Lexie could handle interrogating her once she and Kiara arrived with Chloe.

Hopefully she was having more luck than Adrian and I were having. Despite the nail-pulling, tooth-pulling, and now waterboarding, the henchman in our chair still refused to talk. Either he wasn't afraid of death or he was more afraid of what his boss would do to him if he snitched.

I waited just until his body was on the brink of losing consciousness from the lack of air before pulling the hose away.

When Adrian pulled the cloth off his face, the man's eyes were wide with shock. His breaths were jagged and short as he heaved new air into his lungs.

"Last chance to talk," I said. "If you don't, you're going to be butchered like the worthless pig you are."

He let out a weak chuckle. "What's so special about that washed up whore? Between you and the boss, I don't know who's more obsessed. Is her pussy that fucking tight?"

I grabbed my gun out of my waistband and shoved it into his mouth. I pushed the mouth of the gun all the way to the back of his throat, summoning uncomfortable groans from him. "Disrespect her again," I threatened.

Holding my gaze, he had the nerve to smile around the gun. Not even the first syllable of the word could rumble in his throat before I pulled the trigger and sent a bullet down his throat.

"Holy shit, Jav," Adrian muttered. "The hell is wrong with you?"

"I'm not letting some asshole call Brielle out of her goddamn name."

"Brielle isn't even her real name," Adrian reminded.

"Do you want a fucking bullet, too?"

"Whoa, whoa, whoa," Dante's voice echoed through the room. Footsteps accompanied his voice as he strolled into the room. "We're all brothers here. We're not shooting each other."

"Javier and I are brothers. You're just a charity case he adopted out of pity," Adrian spat.

"Shut the fuck up and go check in with Miles," I intervened before Dante could respond. *"Ahora."*

Adrian scoffed. He pushed his shoulder against mine as he passed. I inhaled a deep breath, resisting the urge to pop him right in his fucking head.

"What's his problem?" Dante asked, as he approached me. "He's been real mouthy since Alejandro died."

"He wants me to bust his face in. That's his goddamn problem."

"Why don't you? Oh, can I do it? One good knuckle sandwich ought to shut him up for a few days."

"No. You touch Adrian, and I'll fuck you up."

"And if he hits me first, then what? Do I have permission to punch him in his smart ass mouth?"

I rolled my eyes. I did not have the patience for their bullshit right now. "Sure. Whatever. What do you want? Did Lexie call you?"

The playful aura around Dante dampened as he nodded his head. "Turns out Brielle and her daughter have ties to Leonardo Bianchi."

"What? How?"

"How do you think, Jav?"

The memory of her wide eyes and stiff body from earlier rushed to mind. I'd been so focused on Brielle and her sudden behavior that I hadn't even thought about the way Leo had looked at her. Thinking back, I remembered the sly look in his eyes and the taunting smirk on his lips. No wonder Brielle sprinted out of the office like a bat out of hell after she saw him. She must've been scared out of her damn mind.

My hands curled into fists at the thought of the pain he undoubtedly put that girl through. I had a hard time imagining it when we first started pulling in girls from the club nearby. Their bloodshot eyes, bruised limbs, and broken spirits lived in my head for longer than I cared to admit. I understood this type of lifestyle called for a type of cruelty, but at some point, there needed to be a line drawn for the sake of saving some of your humanity. Looking at those women, I don't think the Bianchis ever had the decency to draw one.

God, I couldn't wait to burn that man to the fucking ground.

"Lex said Brielle was discharged, so she's taking them back to your house for the night. I know you're testy right now, but I have to ask: what's your plan? Leo is going to come back for them eventually. You can't keep them cooped up in your house forever."

"I wasn't planning on it."

Dante's brows stitched together. "Then what's your next move?"

A sinister smirk tugged at my lips. "The plan is to take everything from him, remember? It's only fair that I take his girl and his kid, too."

Chapter 12

Brielle

I've never been to Javier's house before. The thought made my stomach twist and turn as we filed through the front door behind Lexie. His house was smaller than I expected. Judging from his lavish suits and expensive cars, I thought he lived in one of those fancy mansions on the outskirts of town. I never imagined he'd be living in a two-story home with at least four or five bedrooms. Sure, a house like this was still more than I could afford, but nothing of the scale that most CEOs have.

The interior didn't take me as much by surprise. Just like his office, the walls were bare of any photos or paintings. The living room was adorned with dark carpets, a mahogany brown sofa, a cushioned armchair, and a small wooden coffee table. A large flat screen television was hooked onto the wall above the wooden entertainment center. Rows of video games and vinyl albums filled in the shelves, and a PlayStation 5 with two controllers hanging on a small rack lay atop it.

Tiny paws padded through the foyer, and yellow eyes glowed in the hall's darkness.

My heart almost dropped in my stomach at the sight.

Stepping forward, the tiny animal gave a short "meow."

I raised an eyebrow as the light reflected over shiny black fur and pointed ears. I hadn't taken Javier as a person who likes pets - especially cats.

The cat trotted over to Lexie and rubbed its body against her legs.

"Hey, Bagheera," she greeted as she ran her manicured hand over the cat's small head. She waved her free hand around the room. "Make yourselves at home."

Chloe approached Lexie's side and stooped to the cat's height. Eagerly, she petted the cat's head. "Hi, kitty," she said.

Bagheera leaned into her small hand, purring louder at the relaxing sensation. He followed her as she climbed into the large sofa chair. He hopped up beside her and lay his paws over her lap.

The cushions swallowed Chloe's small body as she lay back against the soft fabric. With fluttering eyes, she nuzzled into its embrace.

I didn't want to let Chloe out of my sight, but I didn't want her falling asleep in the chair either. Turning to Lexie, I asked. "Does Mr. Ruiz have any spare bedrooms? It's way past Chloe's bedtime. When she crashes, she'll be out for the entire night."

Lexie nodded. She started heading back into the hall from which we came. In the darkness, I could see a staircase looming on the other side.

I picked up Chloe and carried her in my arms.

Her little head settled against my chest. More weight fell from her body as she relaxed in my hold.

Bagheera and I followed Lexie up the steps into the wide hallway upstairs. On this floor, I could make out a bathroom through the open door all the way at the end of the hall and an empty bedroom cloaked in darkness. The other three doors were closed, cloaking whatever lay inside.

Lexie led us through the bedroom door closest to the steps. She lingered in the doorway, observing silently as I pulled back the covers and gently placed Chloe on the large king-size mattress.

"Mommy," Chloe cooed as she stared up at me through half-lidded eyes.

"Yes, sweetpea?"

"I'm sorry...for yelling at you earlier."

"It's alright. I know you were upset. You had every right to be." I caressed her round cheek. "We'll talk more tomorrow. For now, just get some rest."

She nodded. Her tiny arms reached out for me.

Smiling, I leaned into her embrace and pecked a kiss on her head. "I love you, sweetpea."

She squeezed me tight. "I love you too, mommy."

I kissed her cheek again before finally letting her go. I watched her snuggle against the fluffy pillows. Her eyes fluttered shut as she began to fall into a deep sleep.

"You're a good mom," Lexie commented as we tiptoed out the room. "Your daughter is lucky to have you."

I shrugged. Familiar guilt weighed down on my shoulders as I remembered the confusion and hurt in her eyes earlier. "I guess. I'd be better if I could provide her with the stability and consistency she needs. All of this constant moving isn't healthy for her."

She nudged my arm with her elbow. "Hey, don't beat yourself up. You're doing everything in your power to protect her. She may not realize it now, but when she gets older, she'll understand, and she'll be thankful to you for it."

We descended the steps and walked back into the living room.

"You need to eat something," Lexie said as she watched me sink into the cushions on the couch. "Javier never has food in here, so I'll have to order something."

"It's okay. I'm not hungry." The cushions underneath me, softer than the fluffiest cloud in the sky, pulled me into a comforting hug. The familiar smell of my boss's cologne wafted through my nose, and for a moment, it almost felt like I was wrapped in his essence. Enfolded in its grasp, the weight of my mind grew heavier and heavier. All I wanted to do was lay down, curl up in a blanket, and sleep the rest of the night away.

Lexie frowned. "Babe, I know you've had a rough day, but you need to eat."

Before I could answer, the click of turning locks sounded in the hall. Both of us turned our heads to the doorway as Javier, still dressed in his slacks and dress shirt, appeared within it. He held a takeout bag from Chick-Fil-A in one hand, and a drink carrier with three cups in the other. Immediately, his eyes darted to me.

Blood rushed up my cheeks under his intense gaze, and I averted my eyes elsewhere. I wrapped my arms around myself to shield the embarrassment rushing through my body.

"You came just in time," Lexie said. "I was trying to convince her to eat something."

"I've got it from here," he replied. "I bought you a milkshake for the road."

"*Gracias!*" She skipped to him and plucked her drink out of the carrier. "Be nice," she murmured sternly.

From my peripheral vision, I saw him roll his eyes. As the door closed behind his sister, he walked over to set the food on the coffee table. "I got your favorite," he said.

"Thanks, but I'm really not hungry."

"Don't make this difficult." He sat beside me on the couch. Inches too close, the fabric of his clothes brushed against mine. "I'll feed you myself if I have to."

More unwanted blush licked at my cheeks. "That won't be necessary."

He grabbed one drink out of the carrier, plopped a straw into it, and held it out to me. "Drink," he commanded.

Too tired to argue, I grabbed the cup and wrapped my lips around the straw. My brows threatened to rise as the taste of sweet Coca-Cola splashed on my taste-buds. In all the madness of the past few hours, I hadn't realized how dry my mouth and throat were. The soda served as a healing elixir, soothing every itchy scratch. Shamelessly, I gulped half of the large cup in a single sip.

As I drank, Javier retrieved the food from the bag and arranged it neatly on the table for me.

"Aren't you eating?" I asked, noticing there was only one meal in front of us.

"I'm not hungry," he replied.

"Don't be a hypocrite. If I have to eat, then you do too." I grabbed the paper bag of fries and held it out to him. "Here. You can have these."

Javier reluctantly took them out of my hand.

We ate in silence for a few moments, too busy devouring our food to make room for conversation. He held out the bag of fries to me in a quiet offer now and then, and I took one each time. I tried to extend the box of chicken nuggets in return, but he always declined with a shake of his head.

"Thank you," I said after my belly was full. "For saving me."

"Thank your daughter," he replied. "She's the one who called me."

"Yeah, I'm sorry about that. I gave her your work number in case of emergencies that happened during the workday. I told her that if she couldn't get in touch with me for whatever reason, then you'd be the next best person to relay the message. I didn't think she'd-"

"It's fine," Javier insisted. "She made the right decision."

"Still, you didn't have to pick her up or find me. So, thank you. You saved both of our lives tonight, and I'm very grateful." Reluctantly, I looked up at him. Knots twisted in my stomach as I met his gaze, already fixed on me. "If there's anything I can do to repay you-"

"There isn't."

I almost scoffed. I turned to face him better and tucked my ankle underneath my leg. "No offense, Mr. Ruiz, but I know men like you don't do good deeds for free."

He mimicked my stance, turning his body and throwing his arm over the top of the couch. Raising a brow, he asked, "What kind of man do you think I am?"

I almost shrank under his gaze, growing icier with every moment that passed without an answer. "Not an evil one," I admitted. "But, not good either."

"Hm." It wasn't an agreement nor a disagreement. Hell, it was barely even an answer.

Gathering the bit of courage still lingering in my chest, I asked, "So, what do you want in exchange for helping us?"

He stared at me for a long moment with an impassive expression. One that made me regret asking again. Finally, he said, "Protection is expensive."

"I know, but I can afford it."

"Not the type of protection you need."

"Mr. Ruiz, please. I need my daughter to be safe. She's all I have, and I can't...I *won't* let her be subjected to the same evil I experienced." I reached for his hand and squeezed as tightly as I could. "Please."

His eyes darted down to our intertwined hands. His fingers twitched beneath my touch, but he didn't pull away. "Fine. I'll guarantee protection for you and your daughter...on one condition."

My stomach twisted his last words. Still, interested in the offer and willing to do everything in my power to attain it, I asked, "Which is...?"

"Marry me."

"What?" I asked, recoiling back as if he'd hit me. "Marriage? Mr. Ruiz, that's insane!"

"It's the only way I can use my resources freely and without scrutiny to protect you and your daughter."

"But, if Mr. Bianchi finds out-"

"*When* he finds out," Javier corrected. "He'll be blind with rage and start making careless mistakes. It'll make him easier to kill." He tilted his head. "Because that's what you really want, right? His death?"

"No," I answered quickly. "I mean...I don't want to kill him, but I..."

"You don't have to be modest with me. Admit it: you wouldn't mind if he were dead. You'd feel much better if he was."

Shaking my head, I tried to reject the words I never said aloud. Leo made my life a living hell. He tainted every single piece of my innocence, staining it with blood and bombarding it with cracks until there was nothing left but ruins of shattered glass. And my life wasn't the only one he destroyed. I may have been his favorite, but there were countless other women whose bodies and minds were broken by the hands of Leo, his family, his men, and their long list of crude clientele. They all deserved to burn in the deepest, hottest pits of hell.

"I want my daughter to live a safe, happy life," I said, pushing away the flickers of shame and anger that arose when I thought of all the pain and suffering Leo caused me. I didn't want any of those emotions affecting the real reason I wished such malicious thoughts upon him.

"And she will," Javier promised. "If you agree to be my wife."

I averted my gaze in search of a moment to think. The thought of marrying Javier - my boss, the CEO of the most successful pharmaceutical companies in the country, and the head of God knows what type of organized crime ring - was crazy. Would it even be a *real* marriage?

I doubted it. Javier doesn't seem interested in me at all. So, what did he have to gain from this? Inheritance money? A trophy wife for his clean, CEO image? Or was he hoping to bear an heir to the throne he had freshly earned?

But now that Leo knows I'm alive - and Chloe exists - none of that mattered. Before, it was easy to duck and run before his men got too close because they weren't looking for me. If they ever caught me again, this time without adequate help, there would be no escaping his wrath. I could end up dead, and Chloe…

I shook the thoughts away before they could surface. I promised myself a long time ago that Chloe would never fall victim to the horrors I've witnessed at Leo's hands. If being Javier's wife - even if it is only for the public - meant keeping my promise, then I'd do it.

"Fine," I said. "I'll…I'll be your wife…"

Javier nodded. "Good. I'll make some calls tomorrow morning about drawing up the paperwork. Then we can head down there by tomorrow afternoon and sign everything."

"That fast?" I asked in disbelief.

"We don't have time to waste. He's going to be pissed when he realizes you're not chained up in the house anymore. It's best to have my men on guard before he throws a tantrum."

"Right," I murmured. I didn't want to think about the warpath Leo was going to be on when he found his dead men and my empty bedroom.

"We can talk more about it in the morning," he said. He rose to his feet and pulled me up off the sofa. "You need to get some sleep."

With our hands still intertwined, he led me up the stairwell and into another empty guest room. I couldn't help but raise an eyebrow as he pushed the covers back on the made bed.

He jutted his chin towards the bed. "Lay down. Your body needs to rest."

Once again, I followed his command without question. I almost moaned at the feeling of the fluffy mattress underneath my sore body. Wrapped in the snugness of the blankets, the fortress built to protect me throughout the events of the night crumbled into tiny pieces. The dam of tears I'd been holding back collapsed, and they slipped down my cheeks. I turned my head into the pillow, so Javier wouldn't see them.

Javier set his hand on my shoulder. "Brielle," he started.

"I'm fine," I said. My voice betrayed me, cracking as the lie left my lips.

The mattress sank lower under his weight as he sat beside me.

"Don't stay," I murmured into the pillow. "I swear I'm fine."

"You're not." He lay down on his side. Cautiously, he wrapped an arm around me. "And that's okay. You have every right not to be." He started rubbing his hand up and down my back.

Underneath his gentle touch, some of the tension in my body sprinkled away. I scooted closer to him, needing more of the comfort he was offering. Hesitantly, I curled my arms in front of me and pressed them against his warm, firm abdomen.

He stiffened from the contact, but he didn't shimmy away.

Without rejection, I moved closer, this time pressing my face into his chest. The familiar pine scent of his cologne wafted through my nose, transporting me into the foolish fantasies I indulged in at work. Only this time, it wasn't a daydream. Snuggling with him was now my reality. Maybe not forever, but at least for tonight.

Chapter 13

Javier

"Ah," a short, hasty gasp escaped my lips as my body jolted awake. My eyes flew open, and one of my hands darted to my throat. I dug my short nails into my skin, clawing at the liquid once invading my esophagus. Quick, uneven heartbeats pulsed in my ears, threatening to take my focus away from inhaling all the oxygen that'd been stolen from me in the sea of blood in my dream.

This time, it wasn't my father pulling my head underneath the water. It was my mother.

I've had this dream many times before. It always started with an image of my mother on the living room floor, bleeding profusely from a gunshot wound in the middle of her forehead. Her lifeless eyes stared directly at me, piercing through every inch of my soul with an unseeing gaze. When I walked closer to her, intending to close her eyes and lay a sheet over her body in respect, she inhaled a new breath of life. With a loud yell, she lunged at me and wrapped her arms around my neck in an iron grip. Then, she pulled me down into the red abyss surrounding her once still body.

I haven't had this dream since my father died. The novel image of his dying body triumphed over my mother's for the past few months. For a minute, I think I preferred it. After all, I was used to my father giving me hell. I was more familiar with his wrath and control than with his affection. But my mother was never cruel to us. Although she was the firecracker the twins's personalities took after, her sparks always provided light to our lives. She'd never burn us.

Being on the other end of her fury at her death, with no way to apologize or make amends, was unnerving. The last thing I wanted was for her to hate me. I could withstand the weight of disappointment, but I'd never survive in an exile of shame.

I've spent my whole life trying to make my parents proud. As the first-born son of a cartel king, it was my duty to be nothing less than perfect. I did a good job maintaining the image by excelling in school and rising above all the challenges in my father's intensive training. But all that hard work faded in the wind the moment I let my guard down and didn't keep an extra eye on the security system in our house.

The idea that one mistake could erase a wealth of love has been the bane of my existence since I was sixteen years old. From the longevity of the nightmare, I believed it was more than an intrusive thought - it was the truth.

Trying to shake the dream from my conscience, I raised my hands to my face. Confusion blurred my already foggy brain when I could only lift one of my arms. The other was pinned down under a soft weight.

As I looked down for the culprit of my paralysis, my nose was tickled by a mane of dark, curly hair. I almost raised an eyebrow, unsure of what sorcery a woman pulled to convince me to let her stay overnight. But the sight of my assistant's face, now free of tear stains and panic, stopped my muscle from rising.

Brielle's cheek was pressed against the corner of my chest. Her arm was wrapped around my abdomen, clutching a handful of my shirt. One of her legs was thrown over mine, and her calf was hooked around my knee.

"Shit," I muttered. I remembered laying beside her to give her some comfort while she cried, but I didn't remember falling asleep. In the moment, I didn't regret staying with her. I couldn't leave her all alone - not after all she'd been through yesterday.

Now, I was kicking myself in the ass for getting too comfortable. How the fuck was I supposed to get up without waking Brielle up?

Carefully, I used my free arm to fish my pockets for my phone. I squinted at the bright light as I read the time. Five o'clock. I slept longer than I usually do, but it was still too early for her to be awake.

Overcoming the stiffness that threatened to take over my body from her embrace, I slowly unhooked my leg from hers and started sliding my arm out from underneath her head. I almost achieved my goal without disrupting her sleep. But, as soon as her head hit the warm pillow, her brows creased. A quiet moan of discontent escaped her lips as she started stirring.

"Hm," she mumbled. Her fingers ran over the space I was making between us. Cracking her eyes open, she whispered, "Javier?"

"Shh," I replied, ignoring the soft, innocent way she breathed my name. "Go back to sleep."

She opened her eyes a little wider. Her lips fell into a frown as she watched me rise from the bed. "Wait, please don't... Don't leave."

"I'm just going downstairs."

"No." Her hand reached across the sheets and grasped mine. Looking at me with big brown eyes full of shattered stars, she pleaded, "Don't leave me."

Fuck.

I dreaded the thought of leaving her alone, but I knew if I stayed, she'd end up wrapped around my body like a snake again. Something strange whirred in my stomach from the brief memory of her warm body pressed against mine and her sweet jasmine scent wafting through my nose.

Ignoring the feeling, I withdrew my hand out from underneath Brielle's. "I have to make calls for our errands today."

As if she'd been burned, Brielle snatched back her hand and curled it against her chest. "Okay," she murmured in defeat.

I hurried out of the room, trying to avoid the frown forming on Brielle's lips. I headed into my room and slipped into the small half-bathroom attached to it. After a quick shower to wash off the lingering scent of Brielle's perfume, I sifted through my drawers to find a new pair of clothes. Rather than fabric, my fingers caressed crinkles of thin plastic and cold metal. I frowned as I remembered what I was hiding in my drawers.

79

Although I've lived alone for years, my siblings were always hanging around the house and they were experts at being in my business. The last thing I needed was them to dip into my weed stash or see the gun and start asking me questions I didn't feel like answering.

I shouldn't have this stuff out, unsecured, if Brielle and Chloe were going to be staying here. I dug the contents out and stuffed them in the small safe in the opposite corner of my room.

Once I finally changed my clothes, I moved back to the bathroom to dig through my organized cabinet of painkillers and supplements to find my antidepressants. I didn't want to go back on them, but our family's therapist didn't give me much of a choice after our father died.

Although I refused to speak during our group sessions, she was still observing me. She noticed the dark bags under my eyes, the gradual looseness of my clothing, and the stray marks I couldn't hide on my wrists.

She made me stay back one night after a session and asked, "Are you falling back into some unhealthy habits?"

I had half a mind to tell her to mind her fucking business. I only showed up to the stupid sessions to support Lexie. She was the one who wanted to go to a therapist, influenced by the classes she was taking for her psychology degree, but she didn't want to go alone. So, Adrian and I went with her. Although Adrian has been more active in those conversations lately, I still didn't want any part of it. And Dr. Quinn, our therapist, knew it.

I didn't want to disrespect her and potentially taint her relationship with my sister, so I gave her my cold stare. Usually it was enough to make her back off.

For the first time, she didn't cower underneath my gaze. "Javier, you don't have to talk to me. But, you can't let this continue." She pulled something out from her clipboard and offered it to me. It was a prescription for the antidepressant pills I used to take years ago. She pushed it into my hand when I didn't take it. "You need to take care of yourself. Not just for your siblings, but for your own sake too."

I found the orange pill bottle and popped one in my mouth. Exiting the bathroom, I swallowed the pill dry and headed downstairs. I made a beeline to the front door and opened it. As I requested from my men before I fell asleep, the piles of luggage that were once sitting in Brielle's hallways were all sitting on my porch.

I lugged everything inside and tucked them in the corner of the living room. Brielle could figure out where she wanted to put everything later.

Afterwards, I grabbed my laptop out of my work bag and parked myself in the kitchen. Rather than spending the next hour jogging like I would've on a normal day to chase the lingering nightmares away, I used it to clear my work schedule and reach out to my connections at city hall. Thankfully, the clerks on our payroll could pull some strings and get a certificate drawn up with the bits of information I could give. They promised the document would be ready by early this afternoon.

Around seven-thirty, I heard the soft pitter patter of two tiny pairs of feet coming down the steps. "Look, Bagheera," Chloe's voice echoed through the hallway. "It's our stuff!"

Her cheerful smile popped through the kitchen doorway. "Thank you, Mr. Ruiz!"

I gave her a curt nod.

She disappeared back into the hallway. The wheels of a suitcase clacked against the wooden steps as her steps retreated upstairs.

I listened to the trail of her footsteps in the other guest room and the hushed conversation between her and her mother.

"Please, please, please," Chloe's voice grew louder, carrying through the air upstairs. A moment later, she let out an exuberant cheer.

Her footsteps took off again and slower ones followed them. Within a few moments, Brielle waltzed through the kitchen doorway, rubbing her half-lidded eyes. "Good morning," she greeted wearily.

"Hi." I kept my gaze on my computer screen. "How'd you sleep?"

"Okay," she said with a shrug. "Thank you for getting our things for us."

"Sure."

In my peripheral vision, I saw her twist her hands as she walked closer to me. "Um, Chloe wants to go to school today. I know we still have a lot to talk about, but-"

"I'll drive her, and I'll have one of my men watch the building. She'll be monitored during her transport to her after-school program and until we pick her up."

"Thank you," she said, letting out a sigh of relief. "I really appreciate it."

"Mhm. Just let me know when the two of you are ready, and we'll go."

Nodding, she turned on her heel and hurried out of the room.

I waited for about twenty-five minutes before Brielle and Chloe were heading back down the steps. Both of them were wearing a fresh change of clothes, and Chloe's dark curls were pinned up in a high ponytail with a bow. Chloe offered me another wide smile as I rose from my seat and stalked towards them.

"Good morning, giant!"

"*Buenas días*, Chloe."

As I passed them to grab my coat and my keys, Chloe reached out and grabbed my hand. I looked down at her with a raised brow.

She wasn't looking up at me to see my confused expression. Her hazel eyes were fixed on the patchwork of roses on my forearms. "How do you get the pictures to stay on?" She asked with an innocent tone.

"They're tattoos," Brielle explained. "They use needles to push the ink into your skin."

"Oh." She looked up at her mother. "Can I get a tattoo?"

"Not until you're grown."

Chloe almost frowned at the answer. Huffing, she turned to me. "Mr. Ruiz, who drew your tattoos?"

"My brother," I replied.

"He draws pretty pictures," she mused, returning to examining the artwork on my arms. "Do you think he could draw me one someday?"

"When you meet him, you can ask him."

She momentarily released my hand, so I could shrug on my jacket. I couldn't even get my arm through the sleeve before her tiny fingers were curling around mine again.

The three of us exited the house and climbed into my car.

On the way to Brielle's school, we stopped at Dunkin' Donuts to pick up breakfast for Chloe. I've never seen the little girl happier than when she was skipping into school with a bag full of hash browns and a bacon egg and cheese sandwich.

After we dropped Chloe off, I took Brielle to one of the coffee shops nearby for our own breakfast. The place was small and quaint, offering freshly made goods and custom brews. Despite the appealing decor of cushioned mini egg chairs, low top tables, and soft jazz playing through the speakers, the place was rarely full. Most people used the spot as a quick grab and go.

I enjoyed sitting in the shop on days when I had free time in the city. I could work on my tasks, people-watch and not be bothered.

I sent Brielle to find us a table while I waited in the short line to order coffee and their signature breakfast sandwiches. From my spot, I watched like a hawk as she wandered around the small venue, searching for the perfect seat. The table in the corner beside the window facing the main street won her attention. She settled into the chair and stared curiously out the window at the pedestrians passing by.

Her eyes flicked to me when I approached her with our drinks and food in my hands. A smile spread across her lips, but it wasn't up to the same par as the ones she used to give. This one didn't make the sparkles in her eyes glimmer or show her pearly white teeth.

Soon enough, her genuine smile - full of joy and wonder - would return. I was going to do everything in my power to make sure of it.

"Thank you," Brielle said before taking a long sip of her iced coffee. Her shoulders perked up the slightest bit from the caffeine.

"How's your wrists?" I asked.

"They're fine," she replied with a shrug.

I raised a stern eyebrow.

She sighed. "They're a little sore, but I've endured worse. I'm fine, really."

I didn't want to imagine the "worse" she was mentioning. I didn't need to in order to add another nail into Leo's coffin.

"All I need is some ibuprofen, and I'll still be able to..." she trailed off. Her eyes widened as a light-bulb flicked above her head. "Oh my god, we have work today!" Frantically, she glanced around at her casual clothes and the cozy cafe. "I'm not wearing proper work attire! But, I don't think I have time to change before we have to be at the office. Is it okay if-"

"Relax," I told her. "I already cleared both of our schedules for the day and switched our voicemails to our out of office defaults. No one will look for us today."

"Are you sure?"

"Positive." I nodded to the plate in front of her. "Eat."

She complied, indulging in a few bites of the large sandwich and moaning in delight. She ate about half before taking a break to sip on her coffee. With food in her stomach, her shoulders were higher than they were before and soft hints of shine returned to her eyes. Noticing my stare, her gaze flicked to me. Her body curled the slightest bit as her sips slowed. Pulling the straw away from her lips, she said, "I guess we should start talking...about last night."

"We should." I leaned my forearms on the table and lowered my voice so only she could hear. "What's your name? Your *real* name?"

"It doesn't matter," she said. Her gaze lowered, and she picked at her fingernails. "She died *years* ago."

"How?"

"How all the other missing black girls die - in a cold case file in the basement of their local police department."

My frown deepened. "I'm sure there is someone still looking for you."

"No," she murmured. She blinked a few times, drying the moisture forming in her eyes. "Unfortunately, not."

"I am," I insisted. "Tell me your name."

"Gabrielle Anderson," she said.

"From?"

"A small town in Arizona. You wouldn't recognize it."

"Try me."

Sighing, she straightened her shoulders and looked back up at me. "None of this is relevant. Let's talk about the offer on the table. You asked me to marry you in exchange for protection. This marriage...what...what will it entail?"

"Exactly what it sounds like. You'll play my doting wife, and I'll make sure no harm comes to you or your daughter. We'll go to the courthouse later, sign the papers, snap a few pictures for documentation, and you'll wear my ring on your finger."

"Will I still be able to work for you if we're legally married? Doesn't the company have rules against bosses and their employees fraternizing?"

"You'll keep your job if you want it. Superiors have been in relationships with their subordinates in that building for as long as I can remember. We won't be the first, and we won't be the last."

"But aren't you worried about what other people in the building will think? I mean...we've been working together for a while now, and it'll seem absurd that we're married all of a sudden. The rumors that will spread around the office might be outlandish."

"I don't give a fuck what others beneath me think. As long as there's no disrespect, there won't be any problems."

"Okay, then what about in private? Are you expecting me to...?" Again, she trailed off as unwanted memories flashed behind her eyes.

"No," I answered quickly. "All I need is for you to play your part well enough for our colleagues, and my men, to believe you're my wife. It's the only way I'll be able to use my resources effectively."

"Why?"

"Why what?"

"Why do you want to help us?"

"Because I like you, Brielle." I almost didn't realize how it sounded until I saw her brows turn up in surprise. But, I couldn't tell her the alternative reasoning. Not unless I wanted her to dart out that door and not look back. Before she could get any bright ideas, I added, "You've been a good assistant for me for almost a year now. You're attentive to detail, patient, personable, and kind. You're a valuable asset and it's only right that you're treated as such."

Her lips pulled into a smile. Finally, a twinkle glimmered in her eyes. "Or, you actually *like* me. It's alright. You can admit it."

I rolled my eyes, and she laughed. It lacked its usual strength, but it was at least a promising sign. Her spirit didn't deserve to be broken by a waste of a man like Leo Bianchi.

We finished our breakfast and drove to the local car dealership associated with our organization. Ricardo, the dealership's owner, assisted with getting us new cars whenever needed. Most of the vehicles on his lot were basic black GMCs or Escalades. When I called him earlier this morning, I explained I needed a different vehicle this time around.

He eagerly guided Brielle and me behind his main lot. Behind the dealership building waited a silver Bentley Bentayga.

Brielle stared with wide, awestruck eyes at the SUV as Ricardo handed her a set of keys. "A wedding gift for Javier's beautiful bride," he explained.

Her eyes darted to me. "Mr. Ruiz, this is too much," she said.

"You needed a new car," I interrupted. "Driving the old one when Leo and his men could recognize it was too big of a risk."

"I understand, but I didn't need a *Bentley!* Do you know how much these things cost?"

"Price isn't a concern anymore. Don't waste your time trying to make it one." I dug into my pocket and fished out my wallet. "Speaking of money..." I took out one of my spare credit cards and handed it to her. "Here. Until I can add one with your name on my account, you can use this. There's no limit on it."

Her brows creased together. "Mr. Ruiz," she started.

Before she could finish her sentence, I grabbed her cheeks and gave a firm squeeze. "Stop calling me that. In less than a few hours, you are going to be my wife. You'll call me by my first name from now on, understand?"

She froze in my tight grip. The natural moisture in her eyes quivered as more water threatened to fill them.

Sighing, I released her face and ran my hand down her cheek. "There's no need for formalities anymore," I said, attempting to soften my tone. "I am not your superior in this relationship. I will be your equal - your partner. So, you need to view me as such. Alright?"

"Yes...Javier," she replied.

Unlike this morning, my name didn't sound natural on her tongue. It sounded like she was speaking a foreign language for the first time, and she was uncomfortable pronouncing every syllable. But that's alright. She'll get used to it.

Once we left the dealership, we made a quick stop at the bank so I could grab something out of my safety deposit box.

When we finally arrived at city hall, we were met at the entrance by my siblings and Dante. They were one of my calls earlier this morning. I asked them to meet us here and bring the proper wedding attire for photos.

With a dress bag and small makeup bag in one hand, my sister grabbed Brielle's arm with the other and whisked her away. Her voice echoed through the hall as she explained her plans for dolling Brielle up. "Don't worry about those marks," she told her. "They're easy cover-ups. And we'll just pull your hair up."

Brielle's gaze bounced between Lexie and over her shoulder at me as she was towed away.

I offered her a nod between one of her glances.

Her lips lifted into the subtlest hint of a smile just as they turned the corner towards one of the women's restrooms.

I turned to face my groomsmen and instantly caught Dante's sly grin. "Don't start," I told him. I grabbed the tuxedo bag out of his hands and started walking down the hall.

"What?" my best friend asked. "All I was going to say was 'congratulations'. It's about time you settled down."

"That's not what this is," I reminded him. "She needs protection, and I need more ammo against Bianchi."

"Are you sure marrying her is the only way to go about this?" Adrian asked.

"Unfortunately," I grumbled. "You know how strict dad was about when and for whom to use his men's services. Look at what he made you do with Kiara."

"That was different. I knew I was going to marry Kiara from the first moment I saw her. Dad just bumped up my timeline to pop the question."

"And yet almost a year later and not an altar in sight," Dante teased.

Adrian glared at him. "It may be my brother's wedding day, but I'll still fuck you up."

"Ignore him," I told Adrian. The last thing I needed was for him to spaz out in a place where the law was strictly enforced. The two of them could fight when we went back outside for all I cared. But right now, they both needed to act like they had some sense.

Adrian rolled his eyes. "Anyway, like I was saying, our circumstances are different. We were already in a relationship. Feelings were less likely to get hurt."

"We've already talked about it, and we both understand this marriage isn't real."

"I don't know, Jav," Dante said. "You might fuck around and start catching feelings."

"I'm not that type. I don't do feelings."

"Clearly," Dante agreed sarcastically. "But that doesn't mean she isn't. Shit, you might break that girl's heart if you're not careful."

"I'll *never* hurt Brielle," I replied, my voice firmer than I intended.

Dante chuckled. "Ain't that something? You haven't even put the ring on her yet and she's already got you wrapped around her finger."

I rolled my eyes. I didn't give a fuck what my brothers, or anybody else, said. Good deeds don't equate to attraction or attachment. I had no interest in falling for Brielle or getting close to her daughter.

I could piss off Leo and give Brielle and Chloe the peaceful life they deserve in one shot. When the bastard was six feet in the ground with the rest of his family, I was going to set them free from my gilded cage. And I'd be damned if I shed any tears when I watched them fly away.

Chapter 14

Brielle

"Are you okay?" Lexie's voice broke me out of my thoughtless trance.

Blinking, I refocused my gaze on the mirror in front of us. We were in a private office bathroom on one of the upper floors of city hall. A friend of Lexie's allowed us to use the space to get ready for our small wedding ceremony.

Lexie loaned me a simple, silk white dress she had in her closet and applied makeup over my healing cuts from last night. At the moment, she was working pulling my kinky curls up into a bun.

I don't know when I zoned out. One minute, I was admiring the beautiful work Lexie had done with me. The next, I was miles deep into a dark hole of unawareness.

"Yeah," I murmured.

Lexie's brow rose in the similar arch Javier's did when he knew I was lying. "You don't have to be modest with me," she said. "In the next few minutes, we'll be sisters-in-law. I know it doesn't sound like much, but we take family seriously around here. Your thoughts and feelings will be safe with me."

Warmth twinged in my chest from her kind words. "Honestly, this is all just a lot to process at one time. Last night I was a captive fearing her fate, and today I'm a bride bearing a similar weight. I may not be afraid, but I'm still nervous, still anxious. I just...I feel like I'm being ambushed by all these emotions, and I can't get my head above the water long enough to catch my breath. It's overwhelming and scary and I have no choice but to put on a brave face and endure it."

Lexie's arms wound around me from behind, and she gave me a soft hug. "You don't have to endure it alone," she assured me.

I almost started crying again in her embrace. Why were they all being so good to me? I've done absolutely nothing to deserve such kindness, but I was going to take advantage of it while I could.

"I'm not much of a therapist," Lexie continued. "But, I know a good one. I could connect you with her if you'd like. She's the best at navigating hard feelings like this."

"Yeah, I'd appreciate that." I grabbed her arms and returned the gentle squeeze. "Thank you."

"Of course." She held me for a moment longer before finally releasing me. Grabbing my hand, she said, "Come on. Let's go tie this knot."

We walked hand-in-hand out of the office suite and down the elevator to one of the small court rooms. Javier stood with his brother, friend, and an older brown-skinned man with a salt and pepper beard. He'd changed out of his comfortable clothes into a sharp black suit that hugged his lean muscles in all the right places. The butterflies rattling in my stomach banged harder on their cages at the sight.

At the sound of our heels clicking against the floor, all three of their gazes turned to us.

"My, my," the older man gasped in awe. "Such a beautiful bride you've chosen."

Javier's stony expression didn't crack as his eyes ran up and down the long dress falling over my body. "Yeah," was all he replied.

My cheeks burned underneath such an unreadable stare. Yet, I couldn't force myself to look away. As if compelled by a spell, I held his gaze throughout my walk towards him. I offered him a small smile to ease some of the jitters snaking down my spine.

His eyes fell to my lips, and the sensation intensified.

Once I was at his side, our officiant led us through signing paperwork and our brief vows. While we were getting ready, Lexie had given me a plain silver ring to present to Javier. Apparently, it was the quickest thing she could find in the jewelry store on the way to meet us. Slipping it on his finger didn't phase me. But, then I saw the ring he was offering me.

A cushion cut diamond sat atop a silver band infused with smaller diamonds. The rocks sparkled like tiny stars underneath the fluorescent lights of the courtroom. "Wow," I thought aloud. "It's gorgeous."

"It was my mother's."

I tore my eyes away from the glittering gems and looked up at him. "What? Oh, Javier, I can't accept-"

"You can, and you will," he cut me off. "She passed it down for me to give to my wife." He grabbed my hand and slipped the band onto my finger. To both of our surprise, it was a perfect fit. His hand lingered on mine as his fingers brushed over the band. "All I ask is that you take good care of it."

"Yes, of course! I mean…I promise I will." I could barely get the right words out with his hands on me. I never expected a man so cold to have such a gentle touch.

"By the power invested in me by the state of Maryland, I now pronounce you husband and wife," our officiant said with a proud smile. "You may now kiss your bride."

Oh, shit. I completely forgot about that part.

I opened my mouth to tell Javier he didn't have to. After all, this wasn't a true union that needed to be sealed.

But, before I could utter out a word, large hands were around my waist. My body propelled forward until it collided with a strong abdomen. Within the next second, soft, warm lips were crushed against mine.

The movement alone was enough to throw me off, but the kiss sent my head whirling in all different directions. He tasted like mint leaves, cool and sweet. Some of the scruff of his facial hair tickled my mouth and spurred more flutters in my belly. The scent of pine and sandalwood, fresh from a recent spritz of cologne, overwhelmed my nose and turned my knees into jelly. If it weren't for his hands holding me up, I might've melted into him. Held him closer and popped my leg up like the women in romance movies.

But the kiss ended as quickly as it began.

Javier pulled away and released my waist. He stared down at me with his usual indifference - as if kissing me was just another check on his to-do list.

The spike of embarrassment in my chest made me check myself. This wasn't the beginning of an epic love story. Our relationship wasn't real. And I'll be nothing more than a placeholder on his marital record.

It hurt, but it was reality.

After an afternoon full of taking romantic wedding photos and trying not to fall into the icy pool of his brown eyes, we picked up Chloe and headed back to Javier's house.

While I got Chloe settled for the night, Javier disappeared upstairs in his room. When he came back down, he had a duffel bag thrown over his shoulders. He walked past the living room without a glance or word in my direction.

"Where are you going?" I asked as I rose from my seat on the couch. I poked my head out the doorway to see him unlocking the front door.

"Work," he replied. "My men are posted outside. Don't wait up. I'll be back late."

Late must've been code-word for almost never. Javier didn't come around the house much after that night. The most I've seen of him was in brief passes when Chloe was already in bed and he was picking up another set of clothes to last him another couple of days.

At work, he busied himself with meetings or independent tasks. I rarely saw him unless he was entering or exiting the office suite. Usually, I had no shame in barging into his office whenever I pleased. But with his mother's ring on my finger and an indecipherable silence between us, I was uncomfortable bothering him. I didn't want to be too annoying and make him regret helping me. A part of me was also afraid his mind would change, and he'd ask for something I wasn't willing to give. If I pissed him off, I knew he'd throw me right back to the streets. Leo would have no problems getting his hands on us then.

For the moment, I needed to stay out of Javier's way and follow his cues. Eventually, I'll be able to follow the rhythm of our new dynamic.

The rumors quickly flew around our company building after a few people saw the enormous diamond on my hand. Although no one said anything to me, I could tell people were talking by the twisted lips and side eyes that followed me down the halls as I passed.

"What are they saying?" I asked Lexie one day when she came skipping into our office suite to deliver a large bottle of red wine as a wedding gift.

"That you're pregnant and he married you to be a proper gentleman," she admitted. "Have you guys found out the gender yet? The masses want to know!"

I rolled my eyes. "Your brother is a gentleman, but I am far from pregnant. He barely talks to me - let alone touches me."

"My brother is a psychopath. Let him fuck you and watch how fast that switch flips in his brain. You'll never get him to leave you alone."

I shook my head. "I don't think I have to worry about that. Javier doesn't seem interested."

"Girl, are you serious? Look at your hand. What the hell do you mean, he's not interested?"

"This," I waved my left hand, "is a shield to protect Chloe and me." Hearing it aloud almost made me frown. In hindsight, this was probably the easiest opportunity Javier had to take up a wife he didn't have to maintain. All the other women I've seen throwing themselves at him clearly aspired to be more than his arm candy. And from what I've seen, Javier was not the lovey-dovey husband material they were searching for.

"Don't lie to yourself," Lexie said. "Javier may be a closed book, but his actions speak louder than words. Focus on that rather than the silence."

I tried to take her advice, but it was hard when Javier was too busy to pay me any mind.

After a while, I became so accustomed to his silence that it didn't bother me much anymore. Rather than worrying about Javier, I focused my attention on what really mattered: Chloe.

Her birthday party was steadily approaching, and I needed to get all of my ducks in a row to make sure it was as perfect as she wanted it.

On a Saturday after her gymnastics class, we stopped at Party City to pick up decorations for her birthday party. I booked a reservation at the local trampoline park for the event and bought most of her birthday gifts. All I needed now was some light decor to decorate the private room the venue was providing.

Chloe had a blast throwing almost every item that fit her party's theme into the cart and picking out balloons.

As we drove down the street towards our new home, I noticed Javier's black Escalade sitting near the curb.

"Mommy, look! My giant is here!" Chloe exclaimed.

Once the car was parked, she hopped out of the car and darted toward the front door. I heard the echo of the security system alerting her entrance as I climbed out of the car. Quickly, I grabbed the Party City bags out of the backseat and hurried inside.

A smile spread across my lips at the sight of Javier and Chloe in the hall. Javier was staring down at Chloe in a mix of shock and confusion while her little arms were thrown around one of his legs. "I missed you, giant," my daughter said.

The crease between Javier's brows disappeared at her words. Gently, he patted her head. "Missed you too." His gaze rose to me as he heard the shuffling of the plastic bags. "Let me help your mom," he told Chloe. Upon release from Chloe's iron grip, he walked towards me and took the bags out of my hands.

"Where do you want this stuff?" He asked.

I led him into the living room. "You can just set it over here in the corner. Thanks."

"They're my birthday decorations!" Chloe exclaimed happily. "Everything is LOL! Surprise themed!"

Javier looked at me as he raised his brow in a silent question.

"They're dolls she likes," I explained.

"Oh," Javier said. "When's your birthday, Chloe?"

"Next Saturday! We're having my party at Sky Zone!" She trotted over to the coffee table where an envelope with Javier's name scribbled in her large handwriting. She grabbed it and presented it to him. "Here! I was going to have mommy give it to you, but I was hoping we'd see you soon, so I could give it to you myself."

"*Gracias*," he said as he accepted the small envelope.

"Go hop in the shower," I told Chloe, who was still sticky with sweat. "Lunch will be ready by the time you're finished."

"Okay, mommy!" She looked at Javier. "Do you want to stay for lunch? Mommy is making dino chicken nuggets!"

"Sweetpea, Mr. Ruiz is very busy," I told her. It'd be better if I was the one to break the news to her. "I don't know if-"

"I can stay," Javier interrupted. "I have a few hours before I need to be back at work."

"Yay!" Chloe cheered. "We can all watch Descendants while we eat!"

"Descendants?" Javier asked, glancing at me again.

"It's my favorite Disney Channel movie! It's about the Villain Kids: Mal, Jay, Evie, and Carlos and-"

"Don't spoil the movie," I told her. "Go wash up, so he can watch it for himself."

"Okay, okay." She grinned at Javier as she skipped backwards towards the steps. "Don't worry, giant. You are going to *love* it!"

I couldn't help but laugh at the crease of confusion between his brows. "It's actually a good movie," I admitted. "Personally, the second one is my favorite."

"There's two of them?"

"Three."

"Shit."

I giggled. "She'll only sit long enough for one, so you won't have to endure all three at once. But, just know she will not forget you've never seen them, and she will make you sit through the other two at some point." I started walking into the kitchen. "Oh, and fair warning: it's a musical, so be prepared for lots of singing."

"Great," he replied dryly. He followed me into the kitchen. Stopping in the doorway, he leaned his shoulder against the side of the wall. Quietly, he watched me flit around the kitchen, preparing my daughter's meal.

My nerves were teeming under his tense stare. "I can make you something else. I was planning on throwing some chicken tenders in the oven with her nuggets and making a wrap for myself. Do you want that or were you looking forward to the dino nuggets?"

"I like dino nuggets."

Smiling, I glanced over my shoulder at his tall figure. Without the armor of his sleek, expensive suits, I had a perfect view of his sculpted body, sheltered only by a long-sleeved tee and a pair of sweatpants. The fabric hugged his bulging biceps and stretched across his broad chest. In past conversations, Javier mentioned he enjoyed jogging daily, but he had to be doing more than that to sustain those muscles.

"You're a child," I told him.

"Says the one who likes Disney Channel movies."

"I am a mother. I have to find pleasure in the things she likes. What's your excuse?"

"Chicken is chicken. It doesn't matter what shape it's cut in."

I shook my head. "You could've said no to lunch. I know you have other places to be."

"I'm where I want to be right now."

Flutters twirled in my stomach from his blunt statement. I opened and closed my mouth, almost unsure how to answer. "Are you planning on coming to Chloe's birthday party?" I asked, deciding to change the subject completely.

"Yeah. She invited me," he said matter-of-factually.

"I know, but it's just going to be a bunch of kids running around a trampoline park. Are you sure you want to wrangle kids for three hours?"

"I don't mind helping." His voice was closer this time. "Chloe's a nice kid. She deserves to have her special day go as smoothly as possible."

I almost jumped as his figure appeared in my peripheral vision.

He idly leaned against the counter and crossed his arms against his chest. He stood so close I could smell hints of his cologne.

"Do you like kids?" I blurted out as I looked up at him. "Besides Chloe, I don't think I've ever seen you interact with little ones."

He shrugged. "I guess. I haven't interacted with many. I'm not exactly the type of person people ask to babysit."

"Why? Is it the monotone voice or the perpetually stoic, brooding expression?"

"Take your pick."

I giggled. I finished arranging the frozen nuggets and a few tenders on the cooking tray and popped them in the oven. Leaning my hip against the counter, I looked up at his eyes, thawing from the warmth of our conversation. "Well, for what it's worth, you've been great with Chloe. She likes you...a lot."

He raised a brow. "Really?"

"Oh, yeah. She hasn't stopped asking when she'll see her giant again."

"Maybe I'll try to stop by more often."

"You should," I blurted. "We'd - I mean, *she'd* really like that."

His gaze was steady as his eyes flicked down to my burning cheeks.

My stomach stirred at the thought of him noticing - or commenting. I averted my gaze, turning my body away from him, and scanned the counter for something else to occupy myself with. "Do you want something to drink?" I asked as my eyes caught an empty mug in the dish rack. I reached up to open the cabinet where the other clean cups resided. "We have juice, soda, water - and some alcohol."

"Soda is fine," he answered. He helped me around the kitchen, gathering drinks and paper ware for our lunch.

When Chloe came bouncing back downstairs, she dragged him into the living room and started showing him her wide collection of LOL dolls. From the kitchen, I heard her listing off all the different names and accessories and origins of each doll.

I couldn't help but smile as I walked into the room and saw them sitting together on the couch. Bagheera lay stretched on the headrest on the opposite side of the couch, watching them. Chloe was showing Javier a doll she received for Christmas, explaining with elation the surprise she experienced when she opened it and revealed a limited edition version.

Javier hung onto every word, nodding his head and asking questions to keep her talking.

Personally, I think he was trying to get out of watching the movie. But Chloe forgot nothing. As soon as she had her food, she grabbed the remote and turned on Disney+.

She sat next to Javier while the movie was playing. Happily, she sang all the words to the songs and imitated some of the choreography with her hands and arms. She answered questions before Javier could ask them, introducing each character that came on screen and explaining who their fairy tale parent was.

To my surprise, Javier was attentive to the movie, and Chloe's commentary, throughout the entire runtime. Not once did he touch his phone or try to make a break for the bathroom. His expression didn't give away much about his first impressions of the movie. Now and then, his brows would pinch together in a small crease, but it never lasted more than a moment.

Once the movie was over, Chloe ditched us to go play outside with some kids she recently met on the block. Usually, I'd park myself outside right along with her, but I knew one of Javier's men was outside watching her.

Whenever we stepped outside, there was a black car - sometimes a few - parked a few feet away from our house. Giving Chloe more freedom was easier with silent protectors hiding in the shadows.

Javier took charge of cleaning up the kitchen. He made me sit down at the small island in his kitchen and watch as he threw out all the trash and washed the few dishes in the sink.

"You don't have to do that," I told him.

"I know," he replied simply.

"What did you think of the movie? Be honest."

He shrugged. "I liked it."

I feigned a surprised gasp. "You liked something? A Disney Channel Original Movie at that? Hell must be freezing over."

"Leave me alone."

"Nah, you liked the music. I saw you bobbing your head to some of the bigger numbers. It's alright to admit it. This is a safe place."

He rolled his eyes. "You seem to be in better spirits."

"I'm trying to be. With Chloe watching, I don't really have much of a choice."

He finished washing the last dish in the sink and walked over to the island. Leaning his hip against the side, he asked, "How are you?"

"I'm fine," I answered, ignoring the tears pricking behind my eyes from the question.

His brow cocked into a perfect arch. Although he didn't speak, I could hear his voice, firm and demanding, ringing through the air. *Don't lie to me.*

"I'm serious, Mr. Ruiz," I insisted. "I'm fine."

"I told you to stop calling me that." Despite the steadiness of his voice, his words still carried a lash with them.

I wrapped my arms around myself to hide the flinch from the soft sting. "I know. I'm sorry. I-"

"Stop apologizing." He took one step closer, and I instinctively scooted myself backward in the chair. Confined in the small space, I couldn't go far. There was nowhere for me to run. The fact made my stomach ball into a knot. I just had to take it - whatever "it" was. No whining. No crying. No fear. Only endurance. It'd helped me survive before. Hopefully, it will save the day again.

Something soft flickered over Javier's face. His mouth fell into a frown, and his brows creased together. "Brielle," he said, the mask of monotone threatening to lift from his voice. "You don't have to be afraid of me."

"I know," I replied quickly, though it sounded more like an apology than an affirmation.

He cautiously took another step closer, caging me further into the chair as he hovered over me. "I'll never hurt you," he swore. "You may be my wife now, but before that, you were my friend. You can talk to me."

His kind words warmed my belly. Gazing into his eyes, kind and patient with some of the frost swept away from them, I couldn't form any sentiments of my own. "I know," I repeated. Finding some courage, I grabbed his hand and gave it a tight squeeze. "Thank you. I...I appreciate it...I appreciate *you*...so much."

His gaze shot down to our intertwined hands. The shadow of a crease flashed between his brows. He opened his mouth to speak, but the blaring of his phone broke the silence before he could.

The sound broke the bubble we were momentarily floating in, and Javier ripped his hand out of my grasp. The emotions once dripping over his face vanished, and the mask of indifference took their place. He fished his phone out of his pocket and looked at the Caller ID number. A frown replaced the content line on his lips. "I've gotta go," he said.

"Is everything okay?"

"Mhm." He headed out of the kitchen, keeping his eyes on his still buzzing phone. "I'll see you on Monday."

I shouted goodbye to him, but it was too late. He was already out the door.

Chapter 15

Javier

"What do we have here?" I asked, as I sauntered into my brother's torture room. I had to watch my step to avoid the puddles of blood on the floor.

In the middle of the room, a burly man was tied in chains to a wooden chair. Bruises and cuts littered around his face. His hands, strapped tight to the arms of the chair, were covered in blood. One of them was swollen, with fingers pointed in every direction. Fingertips, on his other hand, were engulfed in red. His shirtless torso mauled with wide cuts, fusing with small waterfalls of blood.

My brother stood in front of him, casually waving a machete in his black-gloved hands. He glanced back at the sound of my voice. "A sniper lurking around one of our clubs. Roman said one of his rookies found him setting up on a building across the street."

"Has he talked yet?"

"No. Claims he knows nothing."

"I *don't* know anything," the man spoke, his voice deep and even.

As soon as the words left his lips, the machete's blade flew across his cheek. He hissed in pain as his skin split into a long, wide gash.

"No talking unless you're telling me what I want to hear," my brother warned.

Raising a brow, I noticed the military tattoo on the man's breast. "One of America's finest," I commented. "Let me guess: dishonorable discharge?"

The man glared at me, but his focus remained on the machete in my brother's hand.

"And the bad guys pay a hell lot more money than the government does, don't they?"

He opened his mouth to speak, but stopped himself short when my brother raised the machete again. This one was smart. He knew he wasn't walking out of here alive, but he sure wasn't trying to speed up the process.

I looked down at his fingernail-less hand and immediately noticed the gold band around his finger. "Family?" I tilted my head. "They know you kill people for a living."

Something finally flickered in his empty eyes. He raised his palms up as best he could in his bounds.

"Don't worry. Hurting women and children is your boss's fetish, not mine."

Pinching his brows together, he adamantly shook his head.

"Playing stupid won't get you any leeway here. We both know who hired you. My question is: to do what?"

He looked between my brother and me, silently debating whether he should keep playing the long game or tell us the truth.

"I'll let him make it quick," I promised. "Patch your body up and send it back in a car wreck to your family for a proper funeral. Might even be able to make it an open casket. Answer my question, and your family won't spend the next few years wondering what happened to you."

"I was sent to scope out your territories for a woman and a child," he admitted, the offer too good to pass up. "Surveillance and communication were my only tasks. My trigger wouldn't be pulled so long as no one intervened."

"Because the well-being of my men is so much more important than that of an innocent woman and child?" I scoffed. "You're pathetic."

"What are you thinking?" Adrian asked. "Quick and painless, or can I take my time?"

I shrugged. "Do whatever you want." My gaze lowered to the ring on the man's hand. "Give the machete for a second."

Adrian's brow rose as he handed me the large blade.

I pushed the man's palms back down against the arm of the chair. Holding his hand still, I hovered the machete's sharp tip over his wrist.

"Wait, wait," the man yelled. "This wasn't part of the deal!"

"I don't make deals with scum like you." I slammed the blade down on his wrist with all my strength, slicing his hand clean off of his arm.

The man let out an inhuman scream as blood spurted out of the open gash that once held his limb. "You, motherfucker!" He yelled in agony. "Son of a bitch!"

Some of the blood stained my tee shirt, and I grimaced at the sight. I never cared for the gore that came with killing. It was too messy for my liking. Bathing in blood was more of my sibling's thing.

"Have fun with him," I told Adrian as I exited the room with the untethered hand in tow. "Come see me when you're done."

I carried the hand back out to the main hallway and headed back to my office. As I shuffled around my desk for a cardboard box, the bright colors of one of the wedding photos Lexie took outside the courthouse caught my eye. It was one of Brielle and I standing on the courthouse steps, pressed together in an embrace and Brielle smiling up at me. I'd set it there as a reminder to my men that Brielle was off-limits.

My lips twitched, threatening to pull into a smirk as I thought of another use for it.

I plucked the photo off of my desk and tossed it into the box. I set the untethered hand atop it. Quickly, I scribbled a curt note to accompany the items:

Don't worry. Your girls are in good hands.

I shoved it on the farther end of the box's interior, taped it up and scribbled one of Bianchi's club addresses on it. By the time I sent it off to one of my men to deliver, my brother was strolling through the door. He'd changed out of his bloody gloves and attire, now wearing clean, untainted clothes.

"Finished already?" I asked.

"You already did the fun part," he said. He flopped down into the chair in front of my desk. His leg bounced as he continued. "All I needed to do was shut him up and clean up the mess."

"My bad. Next time, I'll let you do the chopping."

"Please and thank you," he muttered. "So, what do you want?"

"To check on you. You're more irritable than usual. Are you alright?"

"I'm fine," he replied quickly.

The tightness in his voice let me know he was lying. This behavior wasn't unfamiliar. The heightened opposition to authority. The unpredictable aggression. The constant movement. He was feeling anxious about something, and I had a feeling I knew what it was.

"We never really talked about dad's death. If you want to-"

"I don't."

"That's too bad. I'm tired of dealing with your attitude."

With a roll of his eyes, he crossed his arms and averted his gaze. The bouncing of his leg sped up, and I almost felt bad for being too blunt.

Sighing, I said, "Talk to me. What's going on?"

"Nothing," he insisted, still avoiding my gaze.

"Just because you hated the bastard doesn't mean his death doesn't hurt. Trust me, I get it."

"I'm not upset about that. Fuck him. I hope he's in hell where he belongs."

"Okay." I said. "Then what's the problem?"

He was quiet for a moment. He glanced up at me a few times beneath his lashes, silently contemplating if he wanted to share. Hugging his arms closer, he finally murmured, "Mom would want us to be sad." He kept his gaze glued to the floor as he spoke. "She'd tell us he was still our dad and we should honor his legacy and blah blah blah. But, I don't give a fuck. Not even a little. Hell, I feel fucking relieved that he's gone. And I know she'd be disappointed in me for that. So, I'm trying to be angry - to give a fuck that he's dead, but it's just...it's not working. Just makes me feel worse."

"If mom was here, she would've thrown a goddamn party," I said. "She loved him, but she knew he was an awful father. After all the shit he put us through, she'd be happy we were finally free of his control - of his wrath. Don't beat yourself up thinking she'd feel any different. Okay?"

"Mhm."

I wish there was more I could say, but I was never good at things like this.

Talking through emotions was Lexie's area of expertise. Still, I tried to be here for Adrian when he needed me. He may not say it aloud, but I could tell he just needed his big brother right now. The way he sat a little longer in the chair, not eager to get up and go about his business, told me so.

"Do you want to run to the mall with me?" I asked. "I need to pick up a few things."

"Sure," he said with a shrug.

He waited a few minutes for me to change out of my blood-stained clothes before we headed out of my office. As we were walking down the hall, the sound of Dante's voice echoed through the halls. "Hey, hey, where are you two going?" He called.

I glanced over my shoulder to see him jogging up to us.

"Mind your business," Adrian told him.

"I can't. Not my specialty," Dante admitted as he wedged himself between us. "I needed to talk to both of you, anyway."

"About what?" I asked.

"So, my firm is having their annual Spring Carnival next month, and Javier, I wanted to convince you to bring Brielle and Chloe. Since Brielle's part of the family now, I thought it would be a marvelous opportunity for all of us to get to know her and her daughter. And there will be some good photo ops to rub in Bianchi's face. Could you imagine how big of a tantrum he'd throw if he saw the three of you together spending quality family time?"

I almost smiled at the thought. "Sure. We'll be there."

Grinning, he accepted his victory and moved on to Adrian. Throwing his arm over his shoulder, he said, "I was hoping you could do me a favor, and since we're bonded by law now, I thought you might be inclined to do it for me."

Adrian shoved Dante off of him and straight into me. "We aren't bonded by shit. What the fuck do you want?"

Dante grinned from the hit. "The face painters for our Spring Carnival Fundraiser unexpectedly dropped out, and I was hoping you and some of your tattoo artists could pull through."

"Do I look like I paint kids faces?"

"No, but for a fair wage, I thought you might think about it."

"How much money are we talking about?"

"I gotta ask my boss for the specifics, but it's decent money for a weekend's work. Plus, Kiara will already be there. I convinced her to sponsor one of the food booths. The two of you could turn it into a mini date on your breaks."

Adrian glared at him.

"Come on," Dante urged. "Do something nice for once in your life."

My brother rolled his eyes. "Fine. I'll do it. I'll talk to my crew and see if any of them want some extra cash."

Dante grinned in a sweet victory. "Back to my original question: where are you two off to? Can I come?"

"No," Adrian said.

Dante ignored him and looked at me.

"Sure," I told him. "Just do me a favor and leave Adrian alone."

"I can't. Also not my specialty." Proving his point, he pressed his hand against the side of my brother's face and returned the shove he'd given him earlier.

I rolled my eyes as I moved into the open space between the two before they could start tussling. If I didn't have something to do, I would've let them fight right here in the middle of the hall. It wouldn't be the first time they've gotten into it, nor would it be the last.

Adrian tried to push past me, but I held him back. "Relax," I told him. "The two of you can kill each other later."

We drove to the local mall, less crowded because of the evening hours. Adrian drifted off towards the art supply section to browse while Dante followed me through the near empty halls to the large Target on the opposite side of the building.

I ignored his raising brow as I grabbed a cart and made a beeline to the toy section. "Not a word," I told him. "Brielle's kid invited me to her birthday party, and I can't show up empty-handed."

A smirk tugged at his lips. "Let's back up a second: you're going to a *child's* birthday party?"

I peered through each of the aisles we passed, searching for the logo of the dolls Chloe showed me earlier. I spotted it in the aisles with the Barbies. "She invited me," I said. "It'd be rude not to go."

"How old is she? Five?"

"She'll be seven."

He chuckled. "Damn, her mama has you whipped like that *already?*"

"I'm not whipped," I replied, keeping my gaze on the abundance of small spheres and large dolls on the shelves. From what I gathered during Chloe's presentation of her dolls, she favored the larger dolls but appreciated the mystery of the smaller ones in the balls. I started grabbing a mix of both and throwing them in the cart. "This is temporary."

As if on cue, Adrian approached us with a few sketchbooks and painting tools in his hands. His brow rose as he looked at the growing amount of items in my cart. "Temporary, huh?" He mused.

"You just threw twenty different bug-eyed dolls into your cart," Dante chimed in. "I don't think it's as temporary as you think. You keep fucking around and that ice wall of yours might melt into a big old puddle."

"You keep talking and your body will be in a big old puddle of blood," I threatened.

Adrian and Dante shared a raised brow.

"What do you think?" Dante asked. "He's whipped, right?"

"Definitely whipped."

I rolled my eyes. After all these years of trying to keep the two of them from killing each other, the one thing they choose to come together about is my love life.

And that was bullshit. Absolute bullshit.

But, as much as I wanted to be irritated, I couldn't. Because it was in the small, annoying moments like this that scrubbed away some of the dark spots tainting the deepest corners of my mind and reminded me of the little things that bought some light to it.

Chapter 16

Brielle

The soles of my feet stung as I paced back and forth outside of the therapist's office. As promised, Lexie got me in contact with her therapist, Dr. Quinn. We had a quick conversation over the phone, and she fit me in for bi-weekly appointments on Saturday mornings while Chloe was at gymnastics.

I thought I'd be fine, but the harrowing beige walls and minimalist art were all too similar to a time in my life I'd much rather forget.

I hugged my arms close to my chest and tried to ease my racing heart. "It's fine, it's fine," I murmured to myself as I paced.

Thankfully, I didn't get here too early, so the door to the actual counseling room was swinging open within a few minutes.

I was taken aback when I met Dr. Quinn's kind eyes and warm smile. She was an older black woman with gray streaks in her hair and glasses that hung on her nose. "Hello," she greeted me. You must be Brielle. It's so nice to meet you in person!"

"You as well."

She shuffled me into the room and guided me to sit on the large couch against the right side of the wall. The scent of warm herbs and cocoa beans wafted through the air, reminding me of cozy winter nights spent wrapped in a blanket and hot chocolate. Portraits of nature landscapes decorated in soft blues and greens covered the walls. In the corner of the room lay a small coffee table with a Keurig, a carousel of different flavors, and colorful mugs. Dr. Quinn gestured to it as she spoke. "Would you like some coffee?

Tea?"

"No, thank you."

She sat across from me in a cushioned armchair. "Before we formally start, I wanted to say congratulations on your recent nuptials."

"Oh, thank you."

"How is that going?"

I shrugged. "Fine, I guess. Javier is…hard to figure out. Do you see him too?"

"Yes," she said. "But we're not here to talk about him today. We're here to talk about you." Leaning forward, she asked, "Where do you want to start?"

I hesitated at first, unsure of an answer. So, I started at the beginning: my picture-perfect childhood, the losses that shattered it, the horrible entrance into Bianchi's world that followed a few years later, and all the turmoil I experienced at Leo's hands.

I didn't expect to cry, but saying words I'd never let leave the confines of my mind summoned tears I'd been holding back for so long. When the first few tears fell, I started apologizing and wiping them away. Dr. Quinn moved from her seat across from me, handed me a box of tissues, and said, "You need to let it out. You'll drown in a sea of tears if you don't."

I thought the tears would never cease until I talked about Chloe. Sharing the story of the time I held my daughter for the first time reminded me of the reason I kept pushing through all the pain. From the first moment I looked at Chloe, I felt my heart burst out of my chest in adoration and love. She became the entirety of my world that day, and despite how she was conceived, I wouldn't have it any other way.

By the time I left Dr. Quinn's office, the weight of my shoulders, though a little lighter, was hard to ignore.

I dragged myself through the weekend and the better half of the work week, feigning my best smiles and pretending I wasn't suffocating underneath the pain of reopened wounds. Usually after some time, I found I wasn't faking anymore.

I was feeling better by Thursday afternoon. I happily bobbed my head and shoulders to the lofi beats playing through the speakers as I typed away on my computer. Time faded away as I buried myself in my monotonous tasks and relaxing beats. I was in a soothing groove when my bubble was abruptly popped by a deep, sharp voice.

"Clear your schedule for the rest of the day."

Startled, I almost jumped out of my seat at the sudden command. "What?" I asked as I looked up to meet my boss's - husband's - cold eyes. "Why?"

I cut myself off when his brow twitched, threatening to raise in frustration. My muscles tightened as an imaginary sting of a palm tingled on my cheek and a distant, "What the fuck did I say?" echoed through my ears.

Averting my eyes, I stilled the quiver in my hands and stood up. "Okay."

Javier took my coat off of the back of my chair and held it open for me.

My cheeks warmed as I slid my arms into the sleeves. "Where are we going?" I asked.

"The fundraising luncheon. It's on my schedule."

I remembered the red block I'd marked on his digital calendar. Their company held a fundraising luncheon every few months to raise money for cancer research and non-profits supporting the patients affected by the disease. I've cleared Javier's schedule for a couple since I started working for him, but I've never attended one. Nor had I been planning to.

"What?" I looked down at my simple pink dress. "But I'm not dressed for a formal outing."

"You always look beautiful," he replied without sparing a glance at my outfit.

Heat licked up my neck from his kind words. A clumsy smile tugged at my lips as I looked away to hide my blush. "Thank you," I murmured. "But...why are you taking me?"

"The public thinks we're married now." His fingers slithered from the corners of my jacket to the lapels. He firmly pulled it around me. "We need to act like it."

I tilted my head in silent question of what the acting entailed. We never discussed the specifics of the image we wanted to display of our relationship. Did he want me to fawn all over him or just look pretty on his arm? I know he definitely didn't want me to embarrass him.

"All you need to do is hold my hand, stay close, and smile," he explained as he untucked my curls from beneath the tips of my coat. "As long as you look happy, the masses won't pry."

"That's it? No hugging or kissing? I thought the press loved PDA."

His brow rose. "Were you looking forward to kissing me again?"

His comment summoned a tornado of butterflies through my stomach. The ticklish sensation temporarily paralyzed me. "No," I said quickly. "No, no I'm not. I mean, you're not a bad kisser. You're a *great* kisser. Shit, I mean -"

The rumble of his chuckle cut me off. Ghosts of amusement floated around the edges of his lips, making my cheeks hotter. God, I couldn't imagine how ridiculous I probably looked right now. I had to pull myself together - *fast.*

Shaking off the jitters, I grabbed a handful of the butterflies racking around in my stomach and straightened my shoulders. "I watch a lot of reality television and PDA, aside from drama, never fails to make audiences go nuts over a couple. I didn't know how much attention you wanted to draw to our new union."

"Enough to keep our PR department satisfied. I'm not a fan of being in the spotlight. But..." He grabbed my chin and tilted my head upwards to meet his gaze. "You're welcome to kiss me anytime you see fit."

The muscles in my knees quivered under the sincerity and amusement in his stare. "Oh...okay," I uttered.

Chuckling again, he finally released me and led me out of the office.

Together, we headed towards the private elevator. The idle elevator music filled the silence between us. While I wanted to talk more and ask questions about the event, I figured I embarrassed myself for one afternoon.

Through the mirror-like wall, I could see Javier's eyes on me. His dark irises bounced between my stiff shoulders and folded hands, but he didn't comment. Instead, he held out his hand in a silent offer.

Smiling, I accepted it and squeezed his palm tight.

Our hands remained intertwined as we walked out of the elevator and into the busy lobby.

The looks and murmurs that usually followed me through the halls increased with Javier by my side. But, with the security of my hand in his, I didn't mind.

We walked to the nearby parking lot and climbed into his car.

On the ride to one of the luxury banquet halls, we listened to the songs in Javier's music library. I recognized a few rap artists like J.Cole and Kendrick Lamar, but others like NF and Logic were new to me. I liked their style, though. All of their songs revolved around a personal message they were trying to send or an issue they were confronting.

Someone once told me music was another gateway into the soul. Certain lyrics, styles, and artists resonated with us for a reason, acting as a mouthpiece for all the things we felt but couldn't say. As I listened, I wondered how Javier connected to these songs. What issues was he facing? What messages was he hiding behind his cold and silent facade? What was keeping him from speaking out like the artists he listened to?

My questions were pushed to the side as Javier pulled into the nearly full parking lot of the event space. Almost every row was filled with Mercedes, Cadillacs, Porches, and Bentley's.

From what I could see of the building, large sun windows covered most of the lower level walls, allowing natural light to slip inside and sparkle against the crystal chandeliers hanging from the ceiling. Through them, I could see silhouettes of people lingering around, chatting and drinking.

"We won't be here long," Javier promised. "We'll just make a round or two, and then I'll take you to get real food."

"They don't serve a meal during these fancy luncheons?"

"No. Just a bunch of appetizers and champagne."

"Damn, what a scam."

We hopped out of the car and walked hand-in-hand toward the entrance. The security detail at the door nodded to Javier as we passed.

Inside the main ballroom, small clumps of people loitered around the room with glasses of champagne in their hands and smiles on their faces. A live band played on a tiny half-moon stage in the corner of the room, filling in the empty spaces between the chatter with covers of classic hits.

Pink banners with the company's logo and optimistic mottos for finding the cure for cancer hung from some of the walls. Waiters milled through the crowds, carrying an array of finger foods and drinks for the patrons.

In the doorway, Javier shrugged off his coat. I started to follow with my own, but his hands beat me to the lapels. Gently, he slid it off of my shoulders and handed both of our jackets to the closet attendee.

Before I could thank him, a pretty woman with rich brown skin and a high ponytail of kinky curls strutted towards us. I recognized her as the head of the Public Relations department, Naomi Grant. "There you are," she said with a sigh of relief. "For a second, I thought I'd have to drag you here by your tie." She glanced at me and shot Javier a tight, threatening smile. "And you've got company. How nice."

"This is Brielle," Javier started.

"Yes, yes, your assistant. I know." She aimed her slightly intimidating smile at me. "Nice to see you again. Thank you for kicking his ass into coming so I didn't have to."

"She's not here as my assistant." He held up my left hand and flaunted the large diamond ring on my finger. "She's my wife."

His words awakened an army of butterflies in my stomach, swooping and swirling every which way. I underestimated how it'd sound, hearing him introduce me as his wife. He said it with such conviction and honor, as if he was proud to have me by his side.

Naomi threw her head back and groaned. "Oh, I was really hoping those rumors weren't true. You were supposed to tell me when you got hitched. Give me time to plan an appropriate announcement for the public."

"Mentioning it in conversation with our donors sounded good enough to me," he replied with a shrug.

Naomi glared at him. "I swear between you and your brother, I don't know who I despise more. Both of you are walking PR disasters." She turned on her heel and motioned for us to follow. "Let's go. We'll do a test run with the Wargroves."

I stood on my toes to whisper in Javier's ear as we hurried behind her. "You, I understand, but what did your brother do to piss off the head of PR?

He barely associates with the company."

"Because she keeps track of more than just our corporate image. She cleans up our messes on the other side of our business too. And he makes a lot of those."

I couldn't help but laugh. Never did I think crime organizations needed a person to keep their image clean on the streets too. Then again, I guessed that made it easier to evade any scrutiny from law enforcement. I had to give them credit: the Ruizs were smart. Smarter than the Bianchis ever were.

Before I could respond to Javier's statement, Naomi had dropped us off in front of an older white couple who looked at us with beaming smiles. From the little I knew about fundraising events, I expected our time to be spent taking up the wealthy patrons into donating to the company's efforts to combat cancer. Knowing how much Javier hated talking to people, I was curious about how this was going to go.

To my surprise, Javier played his role in a way that suited him. He posed questions designed to keep his patrons talking for long periods of time. Nodding his head and silently agreeing with the sentiments, he built rapport and mutual respect without saying much. The only time he ever deterred from that route was when he was introducing me.

With every, "This is my wife," my stomach swirled with an army of ticklish butterflies. The term may be temporary, and far from an accurate description of our relationship, but it made me weak in the knees. There was something about the way the word dripped off of his tongue, tinted with gold and heavy with power.

In one word, he clarified I was more than arm candy. I was his partner, his equal, the center of his affection. And even though I was none of those things, hearing it sure made me wish I could be.

An hour into charming the patrons, Javier discreetly led me to a small corner, away from the crowds. I watched him lean against the wall and let out a weary sigh. The socialite mask he was wearing threatened to slip as his mouth fell into its usual line and frost peeked around the rims of his irises. His eyes grazed over the teeming crowds as he sipped on his glass of champagne. They fell on me, and my belly flipped under his steady gaze.

Offering him a smile, I asked, "Having fun?"

"Loads," he replied, his voice dripping with sarcasm. "Are you?"

"Yeah, I really like the band."

He followed my gaze over to the men on the small stage, now crooning an acoustic version of an old R&B hit. "You like music?"

"Oh, I *love* music. I grew up surrounded by it. My mom always played gospel music around the house, and my dad played the piano in his spare time. My parents used to let me sing in the choir at church when I was younger. The pastor thought I sang so well that he gave me solos and leads in the group numbers. He used to tell me God gave me an angel's voice to spread His word."

He raised an eyebrow. "You're religious?"

"My parents raised me in the church, but..." I lowered my eyes as a familiar ache throbbed in my chest. "They passed away in a car accident when I was twelve. We were on our way home from an evening mass, and a drunk driver in a truck hit us...practically shoved us off the road. He and I survived, but my parents didn't... Afterwards, I...I kind of lost touch with my faith after that."

"*Lo siento*," he murmured. "I didn't know."

"I don't talk about it much," I said with a shrug. "I still have a hard time wrapping my head around how good people leave this world earlier than the bad ones."

"*Lo siento*," Javier repeated.

My eyes flicked up in surprise as his hand curled around mine in an affirming hold.

I squeezed his hand to absorb the warm energy he was offering. "The Bianchis used my voice for their own pleasure and benefit. They stripped away all the good until there was nothing left. With my daughter, I've been trying to reclaim my voice - to remind myself it can be used for good. But, I...I'm not sure if I'll ever lay it out for a large crowd again."

"I understand. You should think about it though. I hear you singing at your desk sometimes, and you have a beautiful voice."

"Wait, you can hear me?" I exclaimed as a familiar blush crawled up my face.

His deep chuckle rumbled in his chest. "Yes. Our office isn't *that* big. Usually, I tune in just after lunchtime. When you turn on the showtunes." He tilted his head. "Do you like musicals?"

"*Love* them. Broadway artists' vocal ranges are absolutely insane! I wish I could belt like some of them."

"Have you ever performed in a theater show before?"

"Yeah!" I perked up as happier memories flashed through my brain. "Actually, I-" As quickly as the happiness came, it quickly blew out as my eyes darted to the side and connected with ones that sent an eerie chill down my spine.

Standing across the room from us was a familiar face - one I didn't care to reminisce on. Most would think behind his expensive suits, salt and pepper hair, and beautiful wife was nothing more than a rich businessman. But I knew better than that. My body still carried some scars from the sick fantasies running through his head. Even with his wife by his side, he still stared at me as if I was a piece of meat he couldn't wait to dig into. Seeing him again, with that smug smile and lustful eyes, made me freeze in my spot.

"What's wrong?" Javier asked.

"Nothing," I murmured. Lowering my eyes, I stepped closer to Javier and curled my shoulders inward to make myself smaller to hide from the other man's gaze.

"Stop lying to me." Javier grasped my chin and bought my head up. "What's wrong?"

I almost quivered underneath his tense gaze. "That man...over there..." I quickly glanced to the side again. "He...he um..."

Javier followed my gaze across the room.

"Don't look," I said as I grabbed his face and brought his gaze back to me. My breath got caught in my throat as I was hit by the sharp daggers forming in his eyes.

"An associate of your ex?" he asked.

I shook my head. "A client."

A muscle jumped in Javier's jaw as his eyes glazed over with an emotion that nearly sent more shivers down my spine.

"Maybe we should go," I offered.

"No," he said. "We have a few more people on our round. Let me handle this."

My brow rose as I watched him wave one of the security men over. He was a large, burly man with tiny scars on his face and tattoos peeking out from the cuffs of his sleeves. There was no doubt he was one of Javier's muscle men disguised in plain sight.

Javier leaned in close and whispered something in the man's ear.

The man nodded and hurried off without a word.

"Javier, what did you say to him?" I asked.

"Continue what you were saying," he told me.

"But, Javier, he's not-"

"Don't make me repeat myself," he warned.

I fought back shivers as I took a sip of my champagne and tried to catch my lost train of thought. "Um, I was saying I have performed in musicals before. When I was younger…" My eyes caught a waiter as he exited the kitchen with only two glasses on his tray. I watched him weave through the crowd, making a beeline for my old client and his wife. "And I also did a few in high school. I was the lead in my sophomore year for the spring musical. We did The Little Mermaid, and I was Ariel."

"Brielle," Javier called my gaze back. "Focus on me."

Nodding, I continued. "I liked it…acting and singing. It made me feel…" Against his orders, my eyes darted back to the man. A tremor cascaded through my body as I watched the man raise his new glass in my direction. "Javier, he toasted the drink at me," I whispered.

"Relax," he told me. He ran his thumb over my knuckles, soothing my tingling nerves. "Keep going."

From the corner of my eye, I glanced at the man, just in time to see him take a long sip of the champagne.

"How'd it make you feel?" Javier asked to get me talking again.

"Like I was floating on a cloud," I said, letting the memories take me back to a time when life was easier. "Performing has such infectious energy. When you're up on the big stage singing, with everyone entranced by your voice, you feel so powerful - like the entire world is yours to own." I paused as the darkness tainted the nostalgic sensation. "At least it used to...before it became another cage in my prison."

Clank! Clank! Clank!

Both our heads turned at the sudden clamor of body weight and champagne glasses. My old client was on the floor, one hand clutching his chest and another clawing at his throat.

"Charles?" His wife called as her face fell in horror. "Charles, what's wrong?"

"Oh my god," another couple nearby mused. "I think he's having a heart attack!"

"Someone call 911!" Another few occupants called.

"Don't worry everyone!" One of the security guards said as he approached Charles. He and another guard helped Charles up from his seat and guided him towards the back. "We're notifying the authorities! We'll take care of him from here!"

Like the innocent bystanders they were, the other occupants only stared as the twitching man was led out the back doors. They put their blind faith in the event staff, thinking they were going to help the poor man, and resumed their conversations as if nothing had happened. Little did they know they just witnessed a cold-blooded murder.

"Javier, what the fuck was that?" I hissed.

"What?" He feigned nonchalance. "Heart attacks happen unexpectedly all the time. It's a shame it snuck up on him in public. But at least there were people around to help."

I stared at him in disbelief. My mouth opened and closed in silent debate of an appropriate response. What kind of crazy was this man? He had to be some kind of sociopath in order to have another man poisoned in public.

"Why would you do that?" I asked as I tried to yank my hand out of his grasp.

He tightened his hold on me, keeping my hand still. "Because no one, past or present, disrespects my wife and lives to tell the tale. Now, fix your face. We need to rush through our last stops before Naomi catches wind of the situation and chews me out."

Reluctantly, I let him tow me back into the mingling crowds. Feigning a smile, I did my best to uphold my doting wife act and forget about the disturbing scene I just witnessed. After all, the sick bastard did deserve it. My sympathy lay more with his wife, unsuspecting of his infidelities and ignorant to his sick tastes. She didn't deserve to see him die in front of her. Even the money she'd make from his life insurance wouldn't make up for the emotional damage the image could cause. But, at least, in her own way, she was free of his control too.

After a few quick meet and greets, we were almost home-free. The front entrance was in sight, and we were making a beeline directly for it. But, before we could reach the threshold, we heard Javier's name called from a few feet away.

Irritation swished through Javier's eyes as he turned his head. But, it quickly vanished at the sight of the person seeking his attention. Instead, the faintest hint of a smile hovered over his lips.

I followed his gaze to see an older woman with long, silver-gray curls and a warm smile. She was dressed in a simple coral dress and a sash that read "Survivor." She held out her arms in silent invitation.

To my surprise, Javier eagerly entered them, enveloping the woman in a tight embrace.

"Oh, my Javi," she murmured as she squeezed him tight. "It's been too long again." Pulling away, she set her hands on his cheeks. "You need to come by the bakery more. I worry when I don't see you."

"I know, I know. I'll do better. Since dad's gone, things have been busier than usual."

"All the more reason to take a break, stop by and get a treat. You'll work yourself to death if you don't." Her gaze wandered to me as she noticed me standing nearby. "Who's this beautiful young lady?"

Javier hooked an arm around my waist and pulled me against him. "This is my wife, Brielle."

The woman's eyebrows shot up. *"Esposa?"* She exclaimed. "Ah, *dios mío! Salud!* I thought I'd never see the day!"

Javier chuckled at her excitement. "Brielle, this is Ms. Marisol. She's like our *abuela.* She and my mother were very close when we were younger."

"Mhm. Their mother, *bendice su alma,* saved my life - and filled it with *mis niños dulce.* Javi and his siblings used to be in my bakery all the time, grabbing treats after school. Little troublemakers, all three of them."

Javier rolled his eyes. "The twins are trouble. I'm not."

"Maybe, but you're not innocent either." Marisol's smile grew wider as she examined me. *"Es hermosa,"* she mused. "Maya would be proud. Alejandro too if he were still here."

"Gracias, Ms. Marisol."

"When are you two planning to have some babies? I'd like to have some honorary great-grandchildren."

My brows rose as I looked up at Javier in surprise. How the hell was he going to answer that one?

Ignoring my gaze, he started ushering me toward our original route to the door. "On that note, we are leaving," Javier said. "Bye, Ms. Marisol."

Her laugh followed us. "Bye, Javi! *Te amo!"*

Javier waved over his shoulder as we finally made it out the door.

Interesting, I thought. This man could order a hit on someone without blinking an eye, but was on the verge of blushing in the presence of an old maternal figure. I wondered how many other conflicting traits Javier was hiding behind his cold facade.

"Are we heading back to the building after this?" I asked as we reached the car.

"No," Javier replied as he opened the passenger door for me. "You need to eat, and then we have one more stop before I take you back."

We pulled through the drive-thru of Chick-Fil-A and parked in a nearby lot to eat our food. As we ate, I admired the sight of him in the driver's seat.

Now that the dreaded social hour was over, he seemed in better spirits. In the comfortable silence, he held less tension in his shoulders, and his eyes were almost soft. If he stripped off his suit jacket and unbuttoned the top of his shirt, I thought maybe I'd be an inch closer to the man he truly was inside. But, I wasn't going to push. Not after I've gotten a taste of the consequences of his temper. For now, I was going to relish in the small, candid moments he was able to offer.

After we finished our food, we drove towards the south side of the harbor and went down a long driveway towards an enormous building looming over the waterfront. The isolation from the rest of the city and the vast harbor before it sent a shiver down my spine.

It's fine. It's fine, I told myself. Javier made it clear I had nothing to worry about, and as he reminded me earlier: he wasn't a man who enjoyed repeating himself.

At the sight of the two men, stiff as boards with handguns strapped to their sides, I scooted closer to Javier and clasped my hand around his again.

The guards at the door gave Javier a curt nod as we walked through the doorway.

Inside, the halls were teeming with an abundance of men. Most of them carried large packages or duffel bags through the halls. We passed some men diligently counting the amount of small wads of money they carried. All the doors were closed in the hall, so I couldn't see the behind-the-scenes work they were completing. Though, I could hear the soft whir of machines and the soft chatter of conversation behind the walls.

I knew better than to ask questions about where we were and what the workingmen were doing here. I kept my mouth shut as I allowed Javier to lead me down into the basement of the building.

We walked down the wide corridors towards the far left side of the basement.

My brows rose when he opened a door to reveal a large makeshift shooting range. A long table held thick partitions for separate shooting panels. On the opposite side of the room, enormous posters held shooting targets with bodily outlines and circles. The smell of gunpowder and smoke lingered in the air, making my nose scrunch.

"What are we doing here?" I asked, as I turned to face Javier.

"Do you know how to use a gun?" He replied with a question of his own.

"No," I answered honestly.

"Then, I'll teach you." Gently, he towed me down towards one panel where a gift box, wrapped in pink paper and a bow on top, sat. "Open it," he said as he waved his hand toward it.

Obeying his command, I took the bow off and unwrapped the paper. Inside lay a pink gun, seemingly dainty, but deadly. "What do I need this for?" I asked. "I thought you guaranteed our safety."

"Just because there are others protecting you doesn't mean you don't need to know how to defend yourself." He took the gun out of the box and pushed it into my hands. "Tragic incidents happen quickly. You'll need to move fast if, God forbid, something ever happens to me or the men guarding you. Leo's men can be clever, so it's best for you to have protection from all angles."

The weapon was heavy in my hands, reminding me of all the damage it could cause.

"Here," Javier said, as his fingers sheathed over mine. "Hold it like this." He moved my hands up over the handle. "Put your right hand on the grip and have your left-hand cup underneath it. Good. Just like that."

Moving behind me, he pushed my arms up. "Now, hold your arms out straight and lock in your elbows." His hands caressed down my forearms to my elbows, testing their rigidity. "Alright. I'm going to turn the safety off, and then you're going to take a shot, okay?"

"Does it matter where I aim?"

"Not right now. We'll work on aim once you've gotten used to the kickback." He flicked off the switch on the side of the gun before his hands returned to my arms. "Put your index finger on the trigger. Whenever you're ready, you can pull it."

I hesitated for a moment, caught between the adrenaline of holding such a dangerous weapon and being held by an even more dangerous man. I took a deep breath to steady my rattling nerves. Focusing on the target in front of me, I braced myself for the impact and pulled the trigger.

Chapter 17

Javier

Brielle stumbled backwards as the kickback from the gun pushed against her arms. She collided into me with a force I hadn't been expecting.

I grabbed her hips and pushed my body against hers to stop her from falling. "Whoa. Are you good?"

"Yeah," she murmured quickly. She looked up over her shoulder at me. The gleam in her eye grew bashful as she felt the pressure of my body flushed against hers. "Sorry."

"Try again," I told her. I was getting sick of her apologizing all the time. Maybe if I started ignoring them, she'd stop saying them all together. "This time when you feel the gun kick you, push it back."

Nodding, she turned back to the targets. She held out the gun and identified her target. As she pulled the trigger, she tightened up her arms, bracing herself for the impending kickback. Only her shoulders jolted backwards this time, but progress was progress. She needed to learn how to tolerate the kicks and stand her ground before I could teach her anything else.

It took almost an hour before Brielle was immune to the harsh push of the bullets releasing from the barrel. Another hour and a half was spent on practicing her aim. Usually, I hated being in the teacher's chair, but Brielle made the time worthwhile. She might not have been a quick learner, but she was happy to listen and eager to please.

When she finally made a shot through the center torso of the target, she twirled around and gave me a big smile.

"Javier, I did it!" She exclaimed.

I almost smiled at the excitement beaming on her face. "I saw."

By the time we left, Brielle was a good enough shot on her own. She excelled with body shots, but she caught the head targets a few times.

I felt more comfortable knowing she was strapped and trained to use it. Although I didn't doubt my men's abilities to protect her, I wasn't underestimating our enemy's motivation to hurt her. I don't know how many tricks Leo has hiding up his sleeves, but I needed to make sure I wasn't the only one ready for them. In order to keep Brielle and her daughter safe, Brielle needed to know how to defend herself. She can't freeze in the face of danger. Not like earlier. This time may have been a harmless client, but God knows what other men from Leo's corner could emerge from the shadows. Brielle needed to be prepared to put the bastards down.

Now that she's somewhat comfortable using a gun, she needed to learn a few hand-to-hand moves. It wouldn't hurt for Brielle to know how to snap someone's neck. Just in case.

Brielle lingered outside of her driver's side door after I took her back to her car. "Thank you," she murmured. "For today."

"Did it help? I noticed you've been quiet the past few days."

Playfully, she crossed her arms and shifted her weight on her hip. "What are you trying to say? I really talk *that* much?"

"No," I admitted. "I just know how it looks when the bad thoughts grab a hold of your mind. Did the practice at the range help shoo them away?"

A smile played on her lips as she nodded. "I never thought I'd say this, but it felt great to shoot something."

"Wait until you're able to *hit* something."

"Oh, will a fighting lesson be a part of our next outing?"

"Maybe."

"Well, I'll need a few days notice beforehand. I can't fight wearing this!" She motioned to her dress and wedges.

"Why not? My sister does it all the time."

"That's because she is a superwoman in disguise. Me? Not so much."

124

"That's a lie. You're pretty amazing from where I'm standing."

Brielle averted her gaze as her shoulders curled inward and her smile grew wider.

Shit. How the fuck are these thoughts making it out my mouth? The constant jabbering of my best friend, and now my wife, must be rubbing off on me. I need to get a grip before I say something I didn't want her to hear. I opened my mouth to backtrack when she looked up at me again.

"Will you be around for dinner tonight?" She asked. "I'm not the best cook in the world, but I found a recipe for a pizza casserole that I'm trying tonight. You could come do a taste test."

I couldn't stop my brow from raising. "Pizza casserole?"

"Mhm. One of Chloe's friends had it for lunch one day, shared some with her, and now she won't stop talking about it. I told her mine probably wouldn't taste as good as her friend's mom's, but she has faith in me and that's honestly all that matters."

"I have some things I need to take care of back at the warehouse, but if I get done early, I'll stop by."

"Okay," she replied, satisfied with my answer.

We bid each other goodbye, and I headed back to the warehouse.

In correspondence with one of our street leaders higher on the east coast, I was made aware that one of Bianchi's men was seeking to befriend them and move their drugs through their club. Apparently, they weren't aware of their affiliation with our cartel and were looking for a genuine alliance. Our role in the shadows allowed us an advantage here. Rather than supplying them with our legitimate drugs, I was going to give them a package of laced ones. All I needed to do was make sure my men labeled the tainted batch correctly, so our recipient knew which one to deliver to his new friend.

I wished I could see the look of horror on their faces when their spot not only lost their customers, but their reputation as well. When that sector of my men were prepared, it was going to be almost effortless to tear down their club.

By the time the task was completed and the shipment was neatly prepared for its journey to New Jersey, it was almost seven o'clock at night. A little late for dinnertime, but early enough for me to pop by the house and try whatever concoction Brielle was talking about.

I was pulling on my coat in my office when one of my lead dock men, Wes, knocked on my open door. "Javier," he said, his voice strained with urgency. "We've got a problem."

Raising a brow, I followed him through the busy halls outside. He led me towards one of the nearby ports. On the dock, a few men stood around a box. Their noses were scrunched in disgust at whatever was inside.

"This package came through with one of our shipments. Captain on the boat claims he doesn't know how it got there," Wes said.

As we walked closer to the box, I caught a whiff of a nauseating stench. At this point in my life, I was almost too used to the wretched scent. It almost didn't surprise me when I peeked inside and met the dull eyes of the leader of one of the local, smaller gangs pushing our product through the city. A bullet hole was sunken in the middle of his forehead, and dried blood crusted over his dry skin. Instead of his body, the head sat atop a pile of others, all donning the same numerical tattoo behind their ears.

A small black card, wedged between the leader's head and the one underneath it, read "Congratulations On Your Wedding" in gold foil.

I almost chuckled at the sight. I've seen Adrian do worse, but this was a cute attempt on Leo's part.

"What do you want us to do with this?" Wes asked.

"Burn it and get rid of the ashes," I commanded. "Then, get in contact with our runners over in D.C. One of their cousins is in this pile. Let him know what's happened. I'm sure he'll take it from there."

Nodding, Wes started assigning individual tasks to the men standing on the dock with us.

As I started making my way back up to the soil, my phone buzzed in my pocket. A text from an unknown number flashed on my screen as I took it out.

Unknown number: Enjoy the gift, newlyweds! It will start your marriage off with a blast!

"Shit," I snapped. Turning on my heel, I yelled out to the men at the dock.

"Get the fuck away from that box!"

The wind carried my voice to them, and they all looked up at me with quizzical expressions. Yet, before they could take a single step towards me, the box exploded and licked up all of my men in one fiery blow.

Chapter 18

Brielle

"Throw your plates in the trash on your way out!" I called at the stampede of children rushing past me towards the doorway of the small private room of the Sky Zone complex.

Chloe's birthday party was today, and so far it was going better than expected. The trampoline park gave us our own private room in the back to decorate with balloons, tablecloths, and streamers. All the kids were given wristbands for access to all the park's attractions and game cards for the small arcade. We could use our private room for the full two and a half hours of time, so the kids could store their belongings in here and take breaks in between playing. I tried to structure the time to let them jump on the trampolines for a half hour before calling them back for pizza. Now, they were going to be out for another hour, and then I was going to call them back in for cake.

Two other moms accompanied me as impromptu chaperons. Lisa was the mother of Chloe's best friend at school, and Angela was the mother of Chloe's closest friend at her dance academy. The three of us have hung out a few times over the past year between play dates and the girls dance recitals. They reminded me of the friends I had in high school. Sweet, kind, and making light of their own situations. Lisa, who was married to her college sweetheart, had trouble conceiving and was in the process of adopting the child Chloe befriended. Angela was going through a divorce with her husband of ten years, but she didn't let the ugliness of their fight affect her smile or her children. I guess I should say it aloud more, but I admired both of them for their strength and resilience in the face of motherhood. Both of them have been helpful with supervising the kids as they roamed around the trampoline park and wrangling them in when it was time for pizza.

They lingered behind the kids, picking up stray plates and cups left on the tables.

"Thank you so much," I said once all the kids filed out.

"Oh, it's no problem," Angela said. "It's the least we could do after you've been such a great hostess."

"Yeah, you did a nice job booking this place," Lisa agreed. She peered through the long, rectangular window on the wall, watching as the kids raced back onto the trampolines. "The little ones are having so much fun!"

I followed her gaze out the window towards the group of kids bouncing on the trampoline. Chloe stood out in the group in her bright pink bows and sparkling skirt. Smiling, she jumped as high as she could on the trampolines, the truffles on her skirt flouncing with every bounce. My heart lifted at the sight of her happiness. "It was Chloe's idea. I just made it a reality."

"What other things are you bringing into existence?" Angela asked as she sauntered closer to me. "Some good things for yourself?"

I almost raised an eyebrow until I noticed her gaze on the diamond ring on my finger. "Oh, this?" I clasped two fingers around the band, admiring the diamond as it sparkled underneath the light. "This is, uh…this is new."

"Clearly," Lisa said. She joined Angela's side, smiling at me with curiosity. "Come on. Give us all the details. Who's the guy?"

"When did he propose?" Angela chimed.

"How long have you been keeping him in your corner? You've never talked about him before."

"Is the dick good?" Angela teased. "It must be because you are *radiating*."

Blood raced through my cheeks from the questions. Keeping my gaze on my task, I answered, "I met the guy at work. I kept things quiet because I wanted to make sure he was serious about me. I have Chloe, and I didn't want her to get attached if the relationship fizzled out."

"Has he met her yet? Since he's clearly very serious."

"Yeah. She likes him. She calls him her giant."

Lisa's brow rose as her gaze flicked back out towards the trampoline area. "Does this giant happen to be tall, handsome and dressed to the nines?"

"What? How did you..." I followed her eyes and immediately spotted Javier walking down the hall with a posse of children around him. Despite both of his hands being filled with gift bags, Chloe still found a spot on his wrist to hold on to while they walked. Happily, she babbled on and on as she escorted him into the room.

"Mommy, mommy, look who's here!" She exclaimed as they walked through the doorway.

I was surprised he could come. The night of our outing, he texted me saying something came up, and he wasn't able to stop by. I understood at first, but then he didn't show up for work for the rest of the week. Conveniently, I noticed his sister also had limited availability in her work schedule. I didn't want to stick my nose where it shouldn't be, but I was worried. I shot Javier texts here and there to update him on tasks at work. His one word replies weren't much, but they were enough to let me know he was alive.

A smile tugged at my lips at the juxtaposition of Javier's sleek black dress shirt and slacks against Chloe's sparkling pink ensemble. "Hey, Javier," I greeted.

"Hi," he replied, his voice tight.

Chloe towed him to the gift table, filled with other gift bags and wrapped boxes. "Set the gifts here, and then you can put the special socks on so you can play with us. Oh, we can play medieval times, and you can be the raging giant trying to capture us!"

Javier frowned. He lay the bags down on the table and stooped on his haunches to her height. "*Lo siento*, Chloe, but I can't stay. I just wanted to come by and wish you a happy birthday. But I'll tell you what: if it's okay with your mom, I'll take you out to Friendly's after ballet one night this week. How does that sound?"

Chloe's shoulders twitched from the bad news, but her smile didn't falter from the offer. "That sounds great, giant." She stepped closer and threw her tiny arms around his neck. "Thank you for coming by! And for all the gifts!"

Despite the tension gaining in his muscles, he lightly patted her back. "You're welcome." As she released him, he said, "Go have fun with your friends. I'll see you later."

"Okay!" She grabbed the hands of the friends closest to her and towed them back out towards the play area.

Rising to his full height, Javier looked to me. I almost frowned at the hardness around his brown irises. I hadn't seen it in a moment. A part of me was hoping maybe it was gone for good. Glancing at Lisa and Angela's curious gazes, I put my concerns on the back burner. We'd talk once we were alone. "Ladies, this is my husband, Javier," I said, motioning to him. "Javier, these are my friends Lisa and Angela."

He offered them a curt nod. "Nice to meet you."

"Oh, that explains the glow," Lisa whispered to Angela. "That's not her fiancé, that's her *husband*."

Angela eyed him up and down like a cat in heat. "Mhm. I'd be glowing like a nightlight too." Speaking a little louder, she asked, "Do you have any single brothers? Or cousins?"

"Angela!" I scolded.

"What? It's just a question. Women have needs too, and Lord knows mine have not been met lately."

I nearly face palmed. "May we have some privacy, please?"

Lisa grabbed Angela's arm and tugged her along. "Of course! Come on, Ang. Let the woman speak with her man."

"If I were her, we wouldn't be doing much talking."

I rolled my eyes as they finally exited the room. "Sorry about them. They were excited about the ring before-"

"It's fine," he said. "I'll be out of town until tomorrow night. I've assigned extra men to watch over you while I'm gone, so don't be alarmed if you see any dark Escalades a few miles behind you on the road or around the house."

I tilted my head. "Where are you going?"

131

He mimicked my action. His brow cocked in silent warning, reminding me of my place. I may be his wife now, but I was still on the outskirts of his icy fortress. I was naïve to think our alone time spent over the past few weeks meant anything. He would never let me in. No matter how hard I tried.

I averted my eyes. "Sorry, I know it's none of my business."

"Hey," he grabbed my face and pulled my gaze back up to his. "Stop saying sorry."

His hands had a rough touch to them. Not covered in calluses or clammy like most of the other men I've encountered, but still strong and demanding in the way they held me. Only this time, I didn't feel the urge to pull away or shiver in his grasp. Underneath his firm grip, there lay a smidge of gentleness, too.

No matter how I felt mentally, my body still reacted as it used to. Stiffening, quivering, bracing itself for what usually came after a face hold like this.

Javier must've noticed the change in my body language. The same moment I tensed was the same in which he released me. "There's some business in New Jersey that needs my attention. I'll be back by tomorrow night. I'll see you on Monday." With that, he turned on his heel and made a beeline for the door.

"Be safe," I called out to his back.

His steps slowed for a second, and I thought he might stop. His neck twitched as if he wanted to look back and promise me he would be.

But he said nothing. Instead, he let the words crumble upon a collision with the icy tips of the fortress he'd retreated into.

Chapter 19

Javier

I'm going to gouge someone's fucking eye out, I thought as I rubbed my fingers over my brow. I just returned from a meeting with some of my men, and their reports weren't anything I wanted to hear.

After Leo's present blew up a group of men, I stopped playing games with him. I didn't care about tearing down his clubs. I wanted to tear off his fucking head.

He must've known the repercussions of his actions were going to be fatal. None of my men have been able to find his bitch ass in any of the raids they've conducted on the East coast. The captives we've kept and tortured couldn't give us a straightforward answer on what hole he descended into. Even Miles couldn't find any activity in the accounts he hacked into under all of Leo's aliases.

For now, the bastard was in the wind. And I was fucking tired of being reminded of that.

The glass door sliding open caught my eye, and I slipped on a mask to hide my frustration. Training my eyes on my computer screen, I tried to ignore the flouncing pink skirts making their way towards me.

With the weather getting warmer, Brielle drifted away from flashy pantsuits to dainty dresses. Today, she was wearing a pastel pink dress that accented her slender curves and long legs. When she'd first pranced in her early this morning with a steaming hot coffee in hand, she'd nearly taken my breath away.

Like an angel skipping clouds, she flitted over to my desk with a beaming smile on her face and her black curls bouncing with every step. Humming a soft tune, she graced me with the subtlest hint of a voice that could bring the strongest of men to their knees.

I must've stared at her for a moment too long. A few seconds into our eye contact, her shoulders curled inward and her smile dimmed.

I tried not to make the same mistake again throughout the day, intentionally avoiding her path when I could. Making Brielle uncomfortable was the last thing I wanted. After all she's been through, she deserves to know what peace was.

"I made some adjustments to your itinerary for California," she explained, as she covered my view of the computer screen with a small stack of papers. "Naomi called, and she wants you to do an interview about our recent nuptials. She thinks it'll be good press after the tragedy you all experienced."

I grabbed the papers out of her hand and set them down on the opposite side of me. "Did you tell her I'm not doing a stupid interview?"

"I tried," she said, leaning backwards on the edge of my desk. "But you know Naomi doesn't take no for an answer."

"How long is this interview supposed to take?"

"She promised only an hour. It's an exclusive fluff piece for a fancy magazine, so she doesn't think it'll take long."

"Did it have a major impact on the schedule?"

"Not really. I mean, you won't have as much time to hang out at Universal Studios afterward, but that's alright. I'm sure there's some L.A. nightlife that might catch your attention."

I rolled my eyes. "Who gave you this party animal image? Because I sure didn't."

"It's always the quiet ones who come alive once they have a glass of something strong and a good song to dance to."

"Well, this quiet one turns into a pumpkin once the sun goes down."

She giggled. "Forgive me, but I don't believe that."

I finally tore my gaze away from my computer and looked up at her. "Then, tell me, what do you believe?"

"Hm…I think you have another side of you - not necessarily a wild side, but a fun, more carefree one."

"And what gives you that impression?"

"The hard evidence speaks for itself. Have you seen your best friend?"

"Dante is *not* a reflection of any part of my character."

"Aht, I never said he was a reflection! I'm saying that I could see his personality, and all the other stuff he probably gets into, bringing out that side of you. After all, you danced at his wedding."

"Dancing and having someone pulling on my arms, offbeat by the way, are two different things."

"I was not offbeat! You weren't cooperating!"

"It's alright to admit you can't dance. I do. It takes the load off."

She laughed again, the sound bouncing through the air like bubbles. "You still owe me a dance, you know - a *real* one."

"What we shared at the wedding wasn't real?"

She scoffed. "Boy, please. I mean a legitimate dance. You know, one with slow music and you twirl me around."

"Sounds like a scene out of a chick flick."

"Hey, I was robbed of my younger, dreamier years. At least humor your wife and entertain her silly daydreams."

My brow twitched at the term. She'd never called herself that before. I didn't realize how good it would sound rolling off her lips.

My wife.

Mine.

Fuck, now I was sounding like Adrian.

Getting a grip on whatever the fuck was trying to slip out of its cage, I turned my attention back towards my computer screen. "Humor your husband and head on back to work."

She groaned. "You always kick me out just as the conversation is getting good." Reluctantly, she straightened her composure and started heading towards the door.

My gaze wandered back over to her. As I watched the sway of her hips, an idea crossed my mind. "Brielle," I called her name before she was even five steps away.

Turning on her platform heels, she replied, "Yes, Javier?"

"Come with me. To California."

Her brows shot up. "What? *Why?* I mean, I can't! I have Chloe, and I've never left her alone - and never when I was in a whole different state! And with all that's happened with Leo, I couldn't possibly-" She cut her words short when I rose from my desk. Again, her shoulders curled inwards and her smile faded as I approached her.

"The PR department doesn't want a fluff piece on me - they want a fluff piece on *us*. It's only right that you're part of the interview. And the Gala on Saturday night would be the perfect time to debut our marriage to our company's donors on the west coast."

"But you're not hearing me about Chloe. I can't just leave her, and I completely understand that I can't bring her. We'll be in business meetings most of the weekday, and she'll be bored out of her mind sitting around a hotel room. Plus, she has gymnastics on Saturday mornings and-"

"Brie," I said, gently hooking my hand around her face. "Relax. Chloe will be in good hands. I'll text Lexie and Kiara and see if one of them can watch her for that weekend."

"I don't want to bother them. Kiara and Lexie are good with her, but what if they have plans? What if they don't want to watch her for *three* days? And, no offense, but isn't your sister a little...?" She pointed at her temple and swirled it around. "Isn't that what you tell me?"

"Both of my siblings are crazy as hell, but they'd let nothing happen to anyone under their protection - especially a child. There would be buckets of bloodshed before anyone could lay a hand on Chloe. She couldn't be safer."

Brielle looked down. "I...I don't know, Mr. Ruiz. We've never been apart for so long before..."

I traced my fingers along her jaw to grasp her chin. Tugging it upwards, I said, "I promised I'd protect you and your daughter. Don't you trust my word?"

She hesitated, her eyes welling with moisture. "I...I want to. But, I've been told a lot of empty promises, and I…I'm doing my best not to get my hopes up."

I frowned, but I understood. Trust was earned, not given. And after all she'd been through, her trust was going to be difficult to hold. But that wouldn't stop me from doing everything I could to pursue it. "None of my promises go unfulfilled," I assured her. "Even the ones made in malice."

Her eyes bounced between mine, searching for something I wasn't sure existed in them anymore. "You don't have to be so good to me," she whispered. "I've done nothing to deserve it."

"That's not true. Every morning, you skip in here and brighten everyone's day. Your smile makes *my* day. And for that, you deserve the entire world."

Brielle's eyes widened in surprise at my words. She opened her mouth to speak, but the blaring of my work phone interrupted her.

Reluctantly, I released my hold on her and backed away toward my desk. "Listen, I have an invitation to a benefit show next weekend for the Hippodrome Theater; it's raising money for their youth summer programs. We'll go, and I'll have the girls watch Chloe. It'll be a test run," I said. "How does that sound?"

She nodded. "Yeah. Sure." Still in a daze, she slowly turned on her heel and walked towards the door. She paused in the doorway, turning her head to look at me. "Wait, Javier?" She asked.

"Hm?"

A grin spread across her face. "You know dates are supposed to happen *before* marriage, right? We're moving backwards here."

I grabbed a post-it note off my desk, crumbled it in my palm, and threw it at her. "Get out."

Her bright smile finally returned and her laughter filled the air again. She graced me with her joy for a moment before she exited the room and happily skipped down the hall.

Chapter 20

Brielle

Knock! Knock! Knock!

The banging of the door broke me out of a sleep I hadn't realized I was falling into. I was lying on the couch, listening to the voices on the television and the quiet smacking of Chloe's mouth as she munched on her lunch. The morning had been long for Chloe and me. While she was practicing new skills on the balance beams at gymnastics class, I was discussing grief at my weekly therapy session.

Dr. Quinn warned me of the heavier conversations coming, but I thought I was better prepared for them. I've been in grief counseling before, so I recognized the directions of the conversation earlier. I thought I'd be fine. I was expecting questions about my parents and death and the nonlinear grieving process. What I didn't expect was Dr. Quinn asking me if I'd ever grieved for myself.

The question took me by complete surprise and opened wounds I didn't realize I had. When I got involved with Leo, I missed out on the milestones of my teenage years: prom, high school graduation, admission to college. He yanked me through the portal leading from childhood to adulthood. Even the few years of teenage hood I had before I met him were tainted with tears from losing my parents. The moment Dr. Quinn posed that question, I realized a part of me that had perished before it even could bloom.

Her question, too, made me think of Chloe and the childhood I was giving her. Although I was doing my best to maintain as much innocence and magic in her life as possible, I worried I wasn't giving her the childhood she needed. With the constant moving and uprooting of her life, I feared she may look back and mourn over the normalcy and stability she never had. We may stay in Baltimore for a while longer under Javier's protection, but I wasn't under the impression our situation was permanent.

My boss may be extending some kindness to me, but we both knew he wasn't *that* nice. Worrying over his true motives wouldn't help me, so I was content living in blissful ignorance. Whenever his good deed runs its course, I'll be ready. Whether I liked it or not.

Wearily, I pulled myself up from the couch and padded to the front door. My brow rose as I opened it and met the gazes of my new sisters-in-law. "Hey, Lexie. Hi, Kiara," I greeted them. I moved aside to let them in. "What's up? I wasn't expecting you until later."

"We wanted to help you get ready for your hot date tonight," Lexie said as she strutted inside.

"Is that alright?" Kiara asked.

"Yeah!" I replied. "That'd be great, actually. I don't have a vast selection of evening dresses, and I know I'm going to have trouble picking out what to wear."

"Don't worry about that because we are going to the mall," Lexie said. "We were thinking mani pedis and then we're going shopping. Kiara and I can handle your hair and makeup, but you're going to need a new dress."

My shoulders curled inwards. "I can't exactly afford a new dress right now. I'm still trying to sell my old place and-"

"You're not paying for it," Lexie insisted. "Javier said he gave you one of his credit cards."

"Yeah, but that's *his* money."

"And? He doesn't spend it, anyway." She took her phone out of the back pocket of her fitted jeans. "Besides, he gave me specific instructions." She pulled up a text thread on her phone and showed it to me.

Me: What's our budget?

JaviBear: Sky's the limit. Brielle has my credit card. Make sure she uses it.

I smiled at the nickname she had set for him on her phone. "JaviBear?" I asked.

"Yeah. I used to call him that when we were younger, since he's so warm and cuddly."

I shook my head at the sarcasm dripping from her voice. Despite the text confirming Javier's wishes, I still didn't feel comfortable using his credit card. I was already using his resources for free. I wasn't about to take advantage of his money, too. Not when I wasn't sure what he'll be expecting in return.

"Don't overthink it," Lexie told me. "It's fine."

Nodding, I led them into the living room. "Chloe," I called my daughter. "Look who's here!"

Chloe's head swiveled at the sound of my voice. A huge smile spread across her face at the sight of her new aunts. "Ms. Kiara! Ms. Lexie!" She shot up from her spot on the floor and darted across the room towards them. She grabbed both of their legs between her arms. Hugging them tight, she exclaimed, "I'm so happy you're here! I've missed you!"

Kiara giggled. "We've missed you too."

"Go throw out your trash and put your shoes on," I told Chloe. "We're going out with them."

Beaming, Chloe hurried around the room to complete the tasks.

When she was finished, she returned to Kiara's side and grabbed her hand.

Lexie and I followed behind them as we all walked out of the house. I made a beeline for my car, but Lexie snatched my hand and towed me towards the red Audi sitting on the curb in front of the house. "I'm driving," she said, her tone leaving no room for arguments.

We took the drive to the city and made our first stop at a nail salon.

The receptionist, a pretty woman with long, shiny black tresses, smiled as we all walked inside. "Good afternoon, Lexie!" She exclaimed as she hopped up from her seat. "We're all set for your party! Pick out your colors, and I'll lead you guys back."

The four of us milled over the wall of nail colors for a few minutes. Lexie and Kiara quickly identified the colors they wanted, while Chloe and I took more time browsing over our choices. "Which color do you think would look nice on me?" Chloe asked Lexie.

"Hmm," Lexie hummed as she skimmed over the rows again. She grabbed a vibrant fuchsia bottle. "How about this?"

"Yeah, that's pretty!"

For myself, I picked up a soft pink color for my toenails and decided I'd just do French tips for my hands. Since I didn't know what I was wearing tonight, I thought neutral colors were the best way to go.

The receptionist led us back to the massage chairs with the pedicure bowls underneath them. Once we were all seated, I asked, "So, how are you guys?"

"Good!" Lexie exclaimed with a grin. "Dante and I finally finished our honeymoon plans for the summer."

"Really?" Kiara asked. "Where did you both decide on?"

"Bora Bora. We're staying in an over-water bungalow, and we're going snorkeling! I already warned Dante that if he doesn't act right, I'm feeding him to a shark."

Kiara and I shared a giggle.

"Have you started making any wedding plans?" Lexie asked Kiara.

The question summoned a smile. "Yeah, actually. We narrowed the potential venue down to a few places in the city, and we think we're going to have it next spring."

"Aw, that's great! I can't wait! You're going to look so beautiful - and Adrian is going to cry."

Kiara scoffed. "No, he's not."

"Girl, that man worships the ground you walk on. He's going to break down watching you walk down that aisle - just watch."

Shaking her head, Kiara changed the subject. "How are things going with Javier?" she asked me.

I shrugged. "Fine. He's still very reserved and quiet, but he's been super good with Chloe. She really likes him."

"We heard the two of you might go to Cali together," Lexie said. "Is this a romantic getaway in disguise?"

I almost rolled my eyes. "No offense to your brother, but I don't think romantic is in his vocabulary."

"It's not," Lexie confirmed. "But that doesn't mean he can't learn. He asked you out on a date, and that's a start. What does he have planned for tonight?"

"He's taking me out to dinner and a benefit show at the Hippodrome Theater."

"What show are they performing?"

"I don't know. He won't tell me. I think he wants it to be a surprise."

Lexie and Kiara shared a smirk.

"What?" I asked. "What do you guys know?"

"Nothing," the women said in unison.

I raised a suspicious brow but dropped the subject. I didn't want to pry and spoil whatever Javier was planning. I wanted to continue relishing in the butterflies tickling my stomach whenever I thought about being alone with Javier tonight.

After our nails were finished, we headed off to the mall. Lexie dragged us through the large hallways towards a dress store with some of the most beautiful, and expensive, designer gowns I've ever seen. She and Chloe flicked through the racks in search of the perfect dress for the occasion. Kiara and I stood close behind them while they threw potential dresses into our arms.

I couldn't help but smile as Chloe followed Lexie around like a loyal puppy. Like most others, she was mesmerized by Lexie's beauty and powerful will. But it warmed my heart to see Lexie include Chloe in her contemplation over dresses and considering her comments. Usually, it was Chloe's yay or nay that determined whether the dress was getting thrown into our arms or back on the rack.

When the piles in our arms became too heavy to carry, they shooed us into the dressing room to test out the dresses while they shopped around for accessories.

"Do you think this is too much?" I asked Kiara as I smoothed out a dress

I was trying on. This one was a deep fuchsia color with off the shoulder sleeves and a sensual slit running through the skirt.

Kiara's lips pursed to the side as she examined the dress. "Hmm, not really. It's fitting for the occasion: elegant but simple. Do you like it?"

I shrugged. "I do, but it's a little dramatic. Did they pick up anything with less pizzazz? I want to impress Javier, but I don't want to be too obvious."

Kiara smiled as she wandered over the hanging dresses. "You really like him, don't you?"

I opened and closed my mouth, unsure how to answer. Having an innocent crush on Javier was one thing, but falling for him was a whole different ball game. There wasn't a chance in Hell he'd ever feel the same way. I'd be setting myself up for heartbreak and I knew it. Still, I couldn't fight the heat rushing to my cheeks whenever I reminisced about his gentle touch, his affirming words, and his sweet interactions with Chloe. He may not be a good man to the rest of the world, but he was the kindest one to us. I didn't want to mess that up.

"Hey, what about this one?" Kiara asked, distracted by the gowns on the rack. She held up a soft pink dress with a V-neck, butterfly short sleeves, and floor-length A-line skirt. "I think you'll look angelic."

I was amazed at the way the dress draped flawlessly around my body when I put it on. The bodice hugged my torso, and the skirt swirled around my ankles. With even the simplest of moves, the fabric swayed in gentle waves. The way it glided around my body reminded me of a princess gown. Smiling, I did a little spin and watched the skirt twirl around my feet. It was *perfect*.

When Kiara and I emerged from the fitting room with the dress in hand, Lexie and Chloe met us with some jewelry they'd found.

I paid for everything using Javier's card, and we went back to my house.

My brow rose at the unfamiliar Black Escalade sitting in our usual watch-guard's spot a few feet up the street. "Did Javier assign a new bodyguard?" I asked the girls.

"No, that's Adrian," Kiara explained. "He volunteered to keep watch tonight."

"Yeah, because he can't be away from Kiara for over twenty-four hours, or he'll have an aneurysm," Lexie commented.

I smiled. "I think it's sweet he cares so much about you," I told Kiara. "He doesn't have to stay in the car. He can come in if he wants."

"Are you sure?" Kiara asked.

I nodded.

As we piled out of the car, Kiara made a beeline down the sidewalk to the car. She stopped at the driver's window and conversed with the man inside. After a moment or so, the door opened and Javier's younger brother stepped out. He held his fiancé's hand as they hurried down the street to our house.

Chloe smiled at the tall man following us inside. "Who's this, Ms. Kiara?" She asked.

"This is Adrian," Kiara introduced him.

He nodded to my daughter. "What's up?"

She tilted her head. "You look a little like my giant." Her gaze lowered to the tattoos covering his arms. "You have pretty pictures on your skin like him, too. Are you his brother? The one who drew on his arms?"

Adrian's brows creased in confusion. "Your who?"

"She calls Javier her giant," I explained. "I don't know why."

"Probably because he's tall and awkward as shit," he muttered. Speaking louder, he said, "Yeah, I did those."

"Can you draw some on me? I have markers in the dining room!"

Adrian looked at me. "If it's okay with your mom."

"Yeah, it's fine. Chloe, just make sure you grab the *washable* markers."

Chloe beamed. "Okay!" She grabbed Adrian's hand and started towing him through the living room. "Come on, Mr. Adrian! I want a butterfly garden!"

I shared a giggle with Kiara and Lexie as we listened to Chloe ramble about all her artistic ideas.

The girls stayed downstairs with Chloe and Adrian while I headed upstairs to take a shower and wash my hair.

Kiara worked on my hair once I exited the bathroom. She massaged the leave-in conditioner in my thick curls and rubbed some curl activator cream onto my coils to enhance their shape. She used gel and a wet brush to slick down my hair as she pulled it up into a high, curly updo. A few curls near the front of my face were left out of the ponytail. She used her fingers to tighten the curls and style them to frame my face.

Lexie took over with my makeup once Kiara was finished with my hair. She gave me the full works: plucked brows, short false eyelashes, and subtle makeup that enhanced my natural features.

I could've cried when I looked in the mirror once the two of them were finished with me. Between the hair, the makeup, and the dress, I barely recognized myself. It's been so long since I've worn this much makeup. The last time I was this dolled up was when I was still performing as Bianchi's precious songbird.

Back then, my beauty didn't feel like my own. It didn't exist for my enjoyment, but for others. When I looked into the mirror after a long night, I didn't see the precious jewel my captor proclaimed me to be. Instead, I saw nothing but a mess of glittering ruins.

Tonight, though, I saw more than that. I saw a woman with, despite the pain in her eyes and the cracks on her skin, a joyful smile and a sweet demeanor. All of her pieces, though once shattered and broken, were glued back together. They may not glow as bright as they used to, but they still had a unique shine to them. She was resilient and breathtaking.

In awe of her beauty, I almost forgot she and I were the same.

And I wondered if the man whose ring she wore adored her as much as I did.

Flutters I was becoming all too familiar with brushed against my ribs as I remembered the look in his eye whenever we were alone. When he let the tips of frost melt away and exposed what was hiding on the inside. With all the emotions he never showed, I thought maybe one of them could be reserved for me.

Lexie was spritzing perfume on me when we heard the knock at the door. She met my eyes in the mirror as my fingers instinctively started picking at my nail beds. "Relax," she said with an assuring smile. "You look gorgeous."

I returned her smile. "Thanks."

"Mommy," Chloe called up the steps. "My giant's here! And he bought flowers!"

Lexie and I shared a laugh at my daughter's innocent enthusiasm. She fussed over me one last time before grabbing my hand and leading me out of the room.

As we padded down the steps, I glimpsed Javier's dark suit and the red roses in his hands. He was bent down to Chloe's height, listening as she showed off the detailed butterflies drawn on her arms. At the sound of our approaching footsteps, he looked up, and his eyes fell on me.

A flicker of emotion wafted through his usually empty eyes as he took me in.

I wanted to shrink underneath his gaze. To cover myself up. To hide from the intensity, trying to claw its way through the dark abyss of his pupils. My heart thumped in my chest as I watched him rise to his feet. Not once did his eyes waver away from me.

"Hi," I said.

"Hey," he muttered.

Chloe nudged his legs. "Give her the flowers now," she whispered. "And tell her she looks pretty."

"Pretty doesn't hold a flame to the way your mother looks right now," he told her. He held out the roses. "I don't think there are any words in the dictionary that can."

Hot blood rushed up my neck and face as I accepted the small bouquet.

"Ooh, okay Rico Suave," Lexie teased from her spot in the living room doorway. "Where did you learn that line from?"

"Probably googled pickup lines before he got in the car," Adrian added.

I giggled at the sharp look Javier gave his siblings. If looks could kill, they'd both be struck down. Yet they took the blow with amused smiles.

I stooped to Chloe to give her a kiss and hug. "Be good. I'll be back in a few hours, alright? I love you."

"I love you too, mommy!"

"Thank you," I told Lexie and Kiara. "For today."

"Oh, stop stalling," Lexie said. She started pushing Javier and me out the door. "Go have fun! We'll be here when you get back!"

Javier and I shared a glance as we heard the door slam behind us. I smiled at the roll of his eyes. "Excuse my siblings," he said. "They can be a lot sometimes."

"Nah, they're great. I like them."

He offered his hand. "Are you ready to go?"

My fingers intertwined with his without hesitation. "Yeah," I replied. "I'm ready."

Chapter 21

Javier

What did I do to deserve such a magnificent sight?

The epitome of grace and beauty sat across from me at the dinner table. Her eyes, wide with wonder and awe, examined the upscale restaurant I'd taken her to. It was one of the most expensive restaurants under my father's - *my* - reign.

The savory dishes and elegant ambiance attracted some of the most rich and successful citizens from all over the city. Growing up, I always thought it was a little snooty for my taste, but when compared to the other restaurants in the city, it was the best. And my wife only deserved the highest tiers of any dining experience.

Her gaze bounced from the other couples fancy attire to the glowing chandeliers hanging from the ceiling. More often than not, she stared at the live classical band playing their instruments on the small stage near the front of the restaurant and the couples waltzing on the small dance floor in front of them. Her shoulders melted with every soft harmonization between the airy harp and whimsical piano.

I paid extra to ensure the band played instrumentals of some of the music I've heard playing in the speakers of our lobby or in the car rides we've taken together. I hoped the familiarity would ease some of the tension constantly brewing in her shoulders.

Her brows creased in curiosity now and then, and I wondered if she recognized some notes. If she was impressed. If she suspects the lengths

I'll take to see her smile.

"Javier," she said, as her eyes locked with mine.

"Hm?"

Her shoulders threatened to curl inward. "You're staring."

"*Lo siento,*" I apologized. Still, I couldn't tear my eyes away. Not when there was so much to admire. The glow of the lights reflecting against the copper tones of her umber brown skin. The shine of the gloss on her plump lips. The halo of curls sitting perfectly atop her head. The way her dress swayed with even the smallest of movements.

Maybe it was the way I was raised or maybe I just wasn't a complete monster, but I'll never understand how anyone could mistreat such a beautiful human. Even if I envied her, I'd never think of breaking her spirit. If anything, I'd push myself to be on her level. To be a good enough person worthy of all the joyousness she effortlessly exerted.

Brielle looked away as a bashful smile tugged at her lips. "So," she started. "Are you going to tell me what show we're seeing tonight?"

"No."

"Oh, come on. I'm going to find out in an hour or two, anyway."

"Then you'll wait."

She rolled her eyes. "You're no fun, you know that?"

"So I've been told."

"Is it at least a musical? I know how much you love those."

"What's your favorite musical?" I asked to change the subject. I didn't want to spoil the surprise. Based on the music she'd played in the car the other week, I thought it was a nice coincidence. Still, I was curious about what other shows she favored.

"Hamilton," she said without hesitation. "The entire soundtrack is amazing: the lyrics, the vocals, the story! Seeing the show at least once is on my bucket list."

"I'll take you this summer."

Her brows rose. "Javier, do you know how much those tickets cost? Or how fast they sell?"

"Didn't I tell you money is no longer a concern?"

"But-"

"If that's what you want, I'll take you. We'll make a weekend out of it. How does that sound?"

A smile bloomed on her lips. "That sounds lovely, but…" As quickly as her smile arrived, it faded away. "It's *too* kind. You've given me enough, Javier."

"I've barely gotten started," I admitted. The goodness she possessed surpassed all the riches in the world, but I could still fulfill her desires for small joys. At least until I dropped Leo's dead body at her feet. Then, I was going to fill her bank account with more money than she'll know what to do with and make sure she uses it to build the life she deserves.

Brielle's eyes widened at my blunt statement. Only for a moment. Then a tender gaze replaced it.

One that stirred the most uncomfortable sensation in my stomach.

The opening strings of Lionel Richie's song "Endless Love" tore Brielle's eyes away. She looked at the musicians on stage and smiled. "My parents used to love this song," she mused. She glanced over at the other couples on the dance floor before looking back at me. "Dance with me," she commanded.

"How many times do I need to tell you I don't dance?"

"As many times as you want. I'm still not going to listen." She rose from her seat and held her hand out to me. "Come on," she said as she wiggled her fingers. "You owe me one."

Sighing in defeat, I grabbed her hand.

Brielle grinned as she towed me onto the dance floor. Her arms looped around my neck, and she stood so close I inhaled the scent of her sweet perfume with every breath.

I gently put my hands on her waist, keeping my touch light as a feather. I followed Brielle's slow steps, letting her guide us through the beat.

"Relax," she whispered. "You're still stiff as a board."

"I warned you I'm bad at this."

She stepped closer, positioning herself inches away from my body. "You're doing fine. You just need to loosen up. Hold me tighter."

Complying with her request, I moved my hands from her hips to the small of her waist. As I caged her in my arms, I pulled her closer, flushing her body against mine. "Like that?"

Her eyes held mine amidst the contact. "Yeah," she breathed. The chandelier lights glowed like tiny topazes in her eyes as she stared up at me.

With every step, the tension in her back eased. Her body melted in my arms, trusting me to uphold every inch of its weakening limbs. She scooted closer and laid her head against my chest. The scent of her perfume, warm and fruity, overwhelmed my nose as her curls tickled underneath my chin.

"I've never shared a slow dance before," she admitted. "Thank you for being my first."

I tightened my grip on her, determined to memorize the feeling of her body on mine. I didn't want to be the first person she danced with like this. I needed to be her *last*. Her *only*.

But I didn't know if she'd ever let me hold her like this again.

At the end of the day, she wasn't mine. Not mine to hold or to keep.

She belonged to the heavens. The devil himself may have dragged her down from her spot in the clouds, but she hadn't lost her angelic grace. Although her wings were broken and her purity stripped, her spot among the ethereal was still open, patiently waiting for her return. And she would - with another little cherub by her side. Together, they were going to live the rest of their lives in a peaceful utopia.

I was willing to cash in on my pile of sins to make sure of it.

Reluctant to break our dance when the song ended, Brielle made sure our hands were intertwined for the rest of the night. On the dinner table. On the center dash in the car. On the walk into the theater. On the armrest of the theater auditorium.

The only time she let go was to give me a tight hug when she saw the title "In the Heights" plastered on the playbill when we arrived at the theater. "Oh, my god! I love this play!" She exclaimed as she threw her arms around me. "Thank you so much for bringing me! It's going to be amazing!"

My body stiffened from the sudden contact. I thought she'd be content with the show, but I didn't think she'd be *this* excited over it. I guess I couldn't complain. Her burst of happiness was a big win in my eyes.

She was beaming in her seat as she happily watched the production. She swayed in her seat to the music and hummed some songs. During one of the slower love songs near the end of the second act, she laid her head on my shoulder and squeezed my hand tight. Swirls of sweet marshmallows and sensual jasmine invaded my nose and stirred that strange feeling in my stomach again. I tried to hold my breath and focus on the production occurring in front of me, but the scent was alluring. It demanded my full attention, brushing itself like a cat against my body. My shoulders tensed with the need to fidget - to get her off of me. But I couldn't bring myself to move, knowing it'd disrupt Brielle's peace.

I sat in an uncomfortable stew, fighting to ignore the emotions bubbling within me for the next fifteen minutes. Only at the curtain call did Brielle finally move her head.

She perked up to clap for the cast as they took their bows.

As soon as she moved, my shoulder felt too light without her weight and my nose missed her sweet smell. But seeing her wide smile illuminated by the reflection of the stage lights made up for any sense of loss I could've felt. Joy was the most beautiful thing this woman could ever wear.

On the ride home, Brielle chattered on and on about the show. She loved almost everything about it: the costumes, the vocals, and the choreography. "The actors were really cute too," she mused. "The one who played Usnavi was fine as hell."

I tore my eyes away from the road to shoot her a sharp look.

She giggled as her amused eyes met my stern one. "I'm just kidding," she said. She squeezed my hand tighter. "I'm already taken."

Ignoring her comment, I looked away and tried to suppress the tingling it summoned in my stomach.

When we arrived back at the house, I walked her up to the front door. Brielle stalled going inside by digging through her purse for her key. "Do you want to come in?" She asked, glancing up at me. "We still have that bottle of wine your sister gifted us. When our sitters leave, we could sit out back, have a few glasses, and share another dance or two."

152

The offer sounded nice, but I worried more alcohol and close proximity might blur the lines of our friendship. With the way Brielle looked in that dress, and the memory of how she felt in my arms, I don't know if I'd be able to control myself if she came so close again.

The ping of my phone saved me from answering the question. I didn't need to pull it out to know it was Dante, ready to bust my balls about our date. But when I did, the content was not what I'd been expecting. Rather than a cheeky text asking if I got laid, I was hit with an urgent invitation to the warehouse. What the fuck happened now? Between this silent war with the Bianchis and keeping our business in line, I couldn't get a fucking break even if I tried.

Brielle's smile dimmed. "Duty calls, huh?" She asked.

"Yeah," I murmured. *"Lo siento."*

"No, no. Don't apologize. I understand." She clasped her hands in front of her. "Thank you for tonight. It was wonderful."

"Yeah. Sure."

Brielle lingered in her spot. The stars sparkled like tiny topazes in her brown eyes, emphasizing the awe in her gaze as she stared up at me. Scooting closer, she said, "We should do this again sometime."

"We will."

"When we go to L.A.?"

"I'll take you to Disneyland."

She smiled. "And you'll wear Mickey Mouse ears?"

"Don't push your luck."

She giggled. "I look forward to it."

I raised my hand and caressed her cheek. My fingers traced down the line of moonlight trailing over her face. Gravity coerced me closer, tempted by the infatuation in her eyes and the subtle purse of her lips. But I couldn't kiss her. Not like this. Not when she was seeking something sweet and genuine. Not when I was the opposite of everything she deserved. Releasing her, I took a step back. "Goodnight, Brielle." I turned on my heel and made for my exit.

She grabbed my arm. "Hey, wait." Her shoulders bashfully curled in as I turned to face her.

Still holding on to my arm, she rose on her toes and pressed her lips against my cheek.

I froze underneath the soft, warm, gentle touch of her mouth. Light as a feather, it crashed against the wall I'd worked so hard to build and maintain. And while it didn't break, the impact sent cracks through its hard surface. The smile she gave me afterward was an additional hit, this time deepening the crevices by another inch.

"Goodnight, Javier," she said, my name slipping off her tongue as if she'd created it.

The sound, combined with the clatter of the ruins from the broken wall, stunned me for a moment. It took a second for me to form the simple words I'd spoken only a few seconds before.

"Goodnight, Brielle," I repeated, though I could barely hear my voice.

Brielle offered me one last smile before she finally stuck her key in the door and walked inside. I stared at the the closed door for a moment, my head still spinning from the touch of her lips. Struggling to steady my dizzy head, I stumbled down the steps to the car. As I climbed inside, I swore to myself.

This woman was doing more than chipping away at my walls. She was demolishing them.

Chapter 22

Brielle

I nearly jumped out of my skin from the sudden touch of strong fingers on my bouncing thigh. Instinctively, I turned my eyes away from the beautiful view of clear skies and tall palm trees. My shoulders couldn't resist curling inward as I met steady chestnut eyes.

He instantly lifted his hand off of my thigh. Raising it in surrender, he asked, "Are you alright?"

I almost lied and told him I was fine. But, I was *far* from that.

Early this morning, I dropped Chloe off at Kiara and Adrian's house, knowing I wouldn't see her for another few days. Although my daughter was ecstatic to spend time with Kiara again, the separation anxiety was tearing me apart. Before we left, I kept babbling and babbling to Kiara about everything I could think of relating to my daughter. I told her about Chloe's bedtime routine, the directions to her gymnastics studio, her comfort foods, some of her favorite movies and shows, and activities she enjoyed.

Kiara intently listened to me, nodding her head to my every word. "Don't worry," she said once I ran out of breath from talking too much. "We've got the entire weekend planned out. Tonight, Lexie is going to come over for a little girl's night-in. Saturday night, after gymnastics and some errands, Adrian and I are taking her out to Chuck E. Cheese, and Sunday morning, we're going to cook breakfast together. By the time we've eaten, cleaned up, and rested a little, you'll be picking her back up."

The game plan sounded like a good time, yet my nerves still shook from the panic of "what if" questions bumbling around in my brain.

On the plane ride, I had to bury myself in mundane tasks on my work laptop so I wouldn't get on Javier's last nerve. I continued on as if we were in the building to pass the few hours on the plane. But even answering emails and filing digital reports became boring after a while. I almost envied Javier's ability to hop on a few virtual meetings and engage in something other than mindless typing. Admittedly, I skipped out on work for a little while and caught up on some reality TV to keep my mind occupied.

When we touched down in Los Angeles, the distance, and the jet lag, became too real for my liking. I've spent the entire car ride fidgeting and checking my phone. Seeing the time a few hours behind what it should've been almost threw me for a loop. Although it was easy to search up the time in Baltimore, acknowledging I was in a whole different time zone from my daughter made my stomach uneasy.

"I'm just a little worried," I answered Javier's initial question. "I know she's in good hands, but it's still an adjustment."

"I understand." Cautiously, he set his hand back on my thigh, ceasing its bouncing again. "Just try to relax."

I lay my hand on top of his, hooking my fingers underneath his palms in a soft squeeze. I turned my gaze back to the novel city sights passing through the window. L.A. was gorgeous. While the busy streets and bustling sidewalks reminded me of cities I've lived in before, there was an invisible aura of serenity and happiness pulsing through the air. Pedestrians, sun-kissed and dressed in comfortable clothes, casually strolled down the streets. Tall palm trees with thick brown trunks and full, green leaves were scattered between the city corners. Beyond some of the highway roads, I could see miles of tan sand and sapphire seas. Sunlight reflected against the swooshing waves as they splashed, colliding into a million tiny diamonds.

I rolled down the window and let the cool breeze brush across my face. Closing my eyes, I inhaled the fresh air and relaxed underneath Javier's comforting hand. As much as I missed my daughter, I needed to cherish this time. I've never had a weekend to myself like this before. The least I could do was make the best out of it.

Our company building here was almost identical to the one in Baltimore - on the outside and the inside. Walking through the spacious lobby was like walking through the one at home. The only thing that was different was all the unfamiliar faces.

I've been in places where I haven't known a single soul before, but I could never let the uneasiness show - not with my daughter watching me. But now, without a reason to uphold the shield, I inched close to Javier.

He ignored our arms, bumping against each other. His eyes were trained forward, just as conscious of our new surroundings.

My fingers wrapped around his palm in search of some security. I squeezed his hand to fight the tingling nausea rolling through my stomach.

He offered a soft squeeze in return.

We continued through the busy lobby and made a sharp turn down a quieter hall.

Javier led me to yet another private elevator at the end of the hall and used his ID card to access it.

We rode up to one of the higher levels of the building and took a short walk down to the designated CEO office suite.

Naomi was pacing back and forth in the suite's lobby when we waltzed inside. As her eyes fell on us, relief washed over her face. "Ah, it's about time!" she said. Her dark curls bounced as she hurried towards us. "The reporter from the Los Angeles Business Journal will be here any minute!"

She snatched our bags out of our hands and swatted us towards the bathroom. "Go wash the plane ride off your faces! You need to look refreshed, rejuvenated, and radiant! We're going for the newlywed glow, so Javier slap a smile on or I'll stitch one on for you."

I giggled at Javier's blatant eye roll.

In the bathroom, we splashed some water on our faces and tried to rub away the weariness from traveling. From the corner of my eye, I couldn't help but watch Javier as he straightened himself up. His large hands raked over his freshly shaved face, unintentionally tracing over every tiny scar. He re-did the top buttons he'd opened on the plane to give his neck some breathing room and tugged at the ends of his suit jacket until he deemed it

157

pin straight.

You look fine; I wanted to say. But fine wasn't the word to describe the perfection Javier embodied. His dark suit hugged his muscles in all the right places. The sharp line of his jaw was emphasized by the glow of his smooth, bronze skin. His curly hair, freshly cut and no longer curling around his ears, was still neatly brushed despite the long morning. If the reporter came with a camera, he'd be well prepared for perfect candid shots.

His eyes flicked down at me, catching me staring up at him.

I quickly averted my eyes and pretended to spruce up the tendrils of curls.

Through the mirror, I saw his lips twitch in the slightest hint of a smile.

When we emerged from the bathroom, another woman wearing a sleek gray pants suit and short black finger waves was talking with Becky. At the sound of our footsteps, both of them turned to us.

"Javier," the unfamiliar woman said, a flirtatious smile appearing on her face. "It's so nice to see you again!" She strutted towards him, opening her arms for a hug.

He offered his hand before she could invade his personal bubble. "Same to you, Sharon."

Her smile tightened around the edges as she shook his hand. "Never thought I'd see the day you settled down." Her eyes flicked to me, and something green flickered through them. "Especially to one of your employees."

I opened my mouth, ready to defend myself, but Javier's touch distracted me from any words that were going to come out of it.

His arm snaked around my waist, and he pulled me against his chest. Giving my hip a soft squeeze, he said, "She's my right hand. There's nobody else I'd rather have by my side."

Blood rushed to my cheeks as I looked up at him, shocked by his words. The half smile I was given almost knocked me over.

Sharon didn't contain her scoff. "Well, let's talk about it, shall we?"

With his arm still wrapped around my waist, Javier guided us down the hall into his office. While Naomi and Sharon took a seat in the chairs across from his desk, Javier sat in the large, cushioned rolling chair behind it.

I glanced around for a second, wondering where I was going to sit. The thought barely crossed my mind before Javier's hands were on my hips again, this time pulling me backwards onto his lap. Heat rushed through my pelvis as my ass pressed against his dick.

It hardened underneath my novel weight.

I tried to move - to shimmy myself further away from him - but his arm was locked tight around my waist, silently forbidding me from going anywhere.

"So," Sharon said after she was set up with her small notebook and recorder. "I guess we know how you two met. But the real question is: how did you fall in love?"

I looked at Javier, unsure how to answer the question. We never decided on a joint cover story about our romance. At the luncheon fundraiser, the patrons cared more about admiring the rock on my finger than a fairy tale story, so we never even thought about creating one. In hindsight, this could've been one thing to work on during our long plane ride. I'd been so worried about Chloe that I forgot the intimate questions that this interview required.

Thankfully, Javier didn't skip a beat. Immediately, he said, "Brielle lights up every room she walks into. She always has a smile on her face, and she's kind to everyone she meets. Naturally, the entire staff was drawn to her light like moths to a flame, myself included. For months, I secretly admired the way she gifts coffee to people, decorates our office with plants and music, and excels at every task she's given. Then one day, she wrote a note on the margin of the agenda notes she was taking for me asking if I wanted to go out to lunch. She must've known I was having a bad day because she refused to take no for an answer. She practically dragged me out of my office and then talked my ear off through the entire lunch hour about a new show she started watching. For a while, she wiped away the dark clouds in my head and shined some of her light onto me. It was that day I knew I wanted to be more than her colleague. I wanted to be the person who held the umbrella on her rainy days too. So, we started hanging out more outside of work, and our relationship bloomed. Now, here we are: happily married and a bright future ahead of us."

I couldn't stop my brow from raising up my forehead. First, I've never heard so many words leave his mouth in such a small span of time. Second, I was taken aback by his loving description of me. And third: I wasn't expecting him to pull a story from an actual event between us.

There was, in fact, a day where I noticed he was having a rough day. It was when his sister first got engaged, and he was clearly not happy about the news. He hid in his office all day, sulking and burying himself in paperwork. I didn't like seeing him in such a bad mood, so I tried to take his mind off of whatever was bothering him and entertain him with long-winded summaries of a new dramedy I was watching. In the moment, he didn't look at all interested or appreciative of whatever I was talking about. But I noticed the subtle shift in our relationship afterwards. He started being more open to my presence in his office, babbling about nothing or joking with him, and he stayed by my side through some work events and his sister's wedding festivities. I thought we were becoming less like colleagues and more like friends, but I was never sure he felt the same budding connection.

"Oh, isn't that sweet," Sharon said dryly. "If the two of you were so close, emotionally, and in proximity, why did you keep your relationship a secret?"

"I wouldn't call it a secret," Javier retorted. "I keep my affairs private. You know that."

Sharon's lips twitched, threatening to purse into a pout. She took a deep breath to maintain her composure. "And the wedding - was that private as well?"

"We didn't have a traditional wedding. We went to the courthouse and had an intimate ceremony."

"Really?" she asked, her voice full of feigned curiosity. "Why? Were you afraid of another fiasco like your sister's wedding?"

"We wanted to continue keeping our business private," I jumped in, noticing the muscle jumping in his jaw from the last question. "And we didn't see a need for a huge wedding."

Her eyes begrudgingly flicked to me. Raking over my pink dress, she said, "Well, that's a surprise. Sunshine-y women like you love a flamboyant wedding."

Oh, she was desperate to piss one of us off. I almost couldn't tell what she was more upset about: another woman sitting on her old flame's lap or seeing the ring she likely wanted on a finger that wasn't hers. Either way, this awkward exchange definitely was not what we signed up for.

"Now that the knot is tied, what's next?" She continued. "Beach houses? Shared investments? Children?"

"We have a child," Javier took back over. "Her name's Chloe. She's Brielle's daughter from a previous relationship. She's our little dancer."

"Wow, just married and already a family unit. Any plans to give your little one a sibling?"

"Not now, but eventually maybe."

"Yeah, I guess you'll have to, right? The company will need a proper heir to the throne."

"Just because Chloe doesn't have my last name doesn't make her any less of my daughter. If she wants to run the company when she's older, she can. If not, that's fine too. As long as she's happy, that's all that matters to me."

I smiled at his words. Hearing him call Chloe his daughter made my stomach warm. I never thought I'd be able to give her a true father figure - not when I was constantly looking over my shoulder and didn't have the emotional capacity to date someone. Seeing Javier interact with Chloe let me know his words weren't reserved for this interview. He may be exaggerating for the sake of perception, but he really cared about my daughter, and he only wanted the best for her.

"What about your wife?" Sharon asked. "Will she continue working as your assistant, or will she be taking a higher stake in your company?"

"Only she can answer that question." He looked at me. "What do you want to do, Brie?"

"Oh, I...I don't know," I replied. I honestly wouldn't mind continuing working for Javier, but with our new relationship status, I worried it wouldn't be tangible for much longer. Not with eyes like Sharon's on us. But, I wasn't sure what other job or career I might want. I've spent the past eight years prioritizing jobs that would bring in enough money to support my daughter. It's been so long since I had an actual choice in what - or *who* I wanted to be.

"Looks like I have to wait until another interview for an answer," Sharon said. "Perhaps then, maybe it'll have a vastly different headline."

I almost narrowed my eyes at the duality of her statement. This woman was out of her mind if she thought I was going to let her hurt my feelings. Despite the extenuating circumstances, Javier chose me to be his wife. She wasn't going to take that satisfaction away from me.

Thankfully, our time with Sharon only lasted a little longer. She asked Javier a few business related questions before she finally strutted her salty ass out of Javier's office.

The moment she and Naomi were out the door, I tried to slide off of Javier's lap. Again, his hand tightened on my hip.

"Are you alright?" He asked.

"Yeah. I was just moving because..." I glanced down at our position and my stomach whirled with butterflies.

He followed my gaze and his brow rose. "Am I not comfortable enough for you?"

"No, no, you're *very* comfortable. It's just I'm sitting on your - you know - and I can feel - you know - and -" I stopped myself short when I heard the deep rumble of his chuckle. "Stop laughing at me," I scolded as I lightly shoved his shoulder.

Splashing imaginary water on the sparks crackling in my chest, I wiggled out of his grasp and stood up. I shook off the butterflies tickling my spine and regained my professional composure. "You need to head off to your meetings, anyway. The next one is in ten minutes. Is there anything you need me to do while you're gone?"

"Yeah, actually." He grabbed a pen and a pad of sticky notes from off of the desk and scribbled down a number. "This is the number for the head director at the Hippodrome Theater. Last time I saw him, I told him how much you loved the theater's production and about your background in theater. He told me he has some positions open if you were interested. Call him and let him tell you the rest."

My brows came together as he pushed the sticky note into my hand. "Why?"

He rose from his seat. Closing the distance between us, he said, "Because you deserve to do something that makes you happy."

"But, I like my job."

"Yeah, but you could do something you *love*. Your face lights up whenever you talk about theater. You deserve to pursue your passion."

I offered him a soft smile. "Thank you, Javier. Truly. I don't think there will be a way to repay you after this is all over."

"Your happiness will be more than enough."

My stomach swirled as the ghost of a smile hovered over his lips, daring to spark something in his usually cold, empty eyes.

As I turned on my heel to leave, I thought maybe my form of repayment didn't have to be my happiness alone - perhaps I could bring him some joy as well.

Chapter 23

Javier

I can't wait to lie down, I thought as we finally pulled into the parking lot of the Ritz-Carlton Hotel. Between the plane ride, the obnoxious interview, and all the meetings I attended throughout the afternoon, I was fucking exhausted. My social battery was close to zero, and I was desperately craving a recharge.

During the ride, Brielle mentioned she was going to call Chloe once we were settled in our rooms. That would keep her occupied long enough for me to take a quick nap before we went to Disneyland. Despite the exhaustion weighing on my mind and body, I didn't regret making the commitment. I was looking forward to spending more time with her.

I lugged most of our bags through the parking lot and into the main lobby of the hotel. Beside me, Brielle curiously glanced around the spacious lobby, tinted in hints of brown and beige wallpaper and furniture. Her hand wrapped around my biceps, gently squeezing.

"Good evening," the receptionist at the front desk greeted us. "Checking in?"

"Yeah," I replied. "There should be a reservation for Javier Ruiz."

The receptionist tapped the keys on his small computer. "Yup, I've got you right here. One deluxe guest room with city view, club lounge access, and a king sized bed."

"Oh, shit," Brielle muttered as she slapped her palm against her head. "I forgot to update the reservation for two rooms."

"It's alright," I said. "You seem to like sleeping close to me, anyway."

Brielle's shoulders curled inward, but bashfulness opposed to fear flushed through her face. It was an expression I was becoming all too familiar with. Maybe even starting to look forward to seeing. The innocence in her gaze and the adoration that flickered through her eyes enhanced her angelic features, reminding me of all the purity she still possessed.

After verifying my credit card and ID, the receptionist gave us our room keys and sent us on our way.

We rode the elevator up to our room on the twentieth floor and trekked down the long halls.

The inside of our room was modestly plain, but spacious enough to give both of us breathing room when occupying it. A king-sized bed lay out against the left wall of the room. A flat screen television atop a dresser sat a few feet opposite of it. Underneath the large window sat a small couch with small decorative pillows. Next to the couch was a marble bathroom with a walk-in shower and a small bathtub. A small round table with a cushioned chair sat a few feet away from the dresser near another large window. The wall sharing the doorway held a closet filled with hangers.

"Wow," Brielle murmured as she wandered towards the windows. At the five o' clock hour, the sun was high in the sky, reflecting off of the other buildings in the city. "Los Angeles is so beautiful."

While her eyes were on the city, mine were on her. Sunlight beamed through the windows, cascading over her umber brown skin. The golden glow illuminated the shine of the gloss surrounding her wide smile and emphasized the amber hues in her eyes. The pink of her dress twinkled under the light, creating a subtle glow around her body.

Fuck the city. Her beauty outshone any picturesque scene this town offered.

I shook the thought away as I tore my eyes away from her. What the fuck was coming over me lately? This fuzzy, ticklish sensation in my stomach wasn't normal.

I don't do this. I don't get attached. I don't catch feelings. Especially not for good women like Brielle.

Our so-called marriage was only for protection and a subtle taste of revenge. I hated that I needed to keep reminding myself of that.

"I'm gonna take a shower," I told Brielle as she dug her phone out of her purse. Quickly, I brushed past her and headed into the bathroom with my suitcase still in hand.

I took my time in the shower, wearily washing and rinsing my body. After I dried myself off, I changed into a black polo shirt and a pair of jeans.

When I emerged from the bathroom, Brielle was curled on the couch with her phone against her ear. "Oh, really?" she asked as she glanced up at me. "What else did you do in school today?"

I plopped myself down on the bed. Settling on my back, I threw my hands behind my head and closed my eyes. As I relaxed on the soft mattress, I listened to Brielle's melodic voice. She talked little, leaving as much room as possible for her daughter to speak, but when she did, it was a lullaby for my brain, so soft and soothing. Each time I heard her voice, it sounded farther and farther away.

My mind drifted off into another world, leaving my physical surroundings behind it. Before I could surrender to the bliss of unconsciousness, a soft weight smacked across my face.

"Hey," Brielle's voice cut through my ears. "You can't fall asleep! We have-" She wasn't able to finish her senses before my instincts kicked in.

I grabbed her arm and flipped her over me onto the bed. With my free hand, I grabbed another pillow off the top of the bed. Climbing on top of her and straddling her waist, I held up the pillow, ready to strike. "Dammit, Brielle," I muttered as I met her wide-eyed gaze. "You can't catch me off guard like that."

A smile tugged at her lips. "Why? Are you gonna maul me with a pillow?"

"Damn right. Next time you see Adrian or Dante, ask them about it. I used to fuck them up."

She giggled. "I think I could take you."

I took her words as a challenge. Without hesitation, I brought the pillow down on her, hitting her gently.

Her giggles grew in volume as she wiggled under me. She tried to block her face with one hand and grab a pillow with the other. She used it against me, smacking the soft cushion against my chest.

Easily, I snatched it out of her hand and threw it over my shoulder. My free hand darted to her stomach. Tickling her, I almost smiled as her laughter grew in volume.

She twisted and turned underneath me, trying to find a way out despite being pinned beneath me. Her hands tried to grab mine, but I moved it away whenever she got too close.

"Okay, okay!" She said between her laughs. "You win! You win!"

I ceased my attack. From above her, I watched her chest rise and fall as she caught her breath.

Her smile was wider than it's ever been before, bright with a child-like glee. Her eyes were cheerful, but watery from laughing too hard. Her kinky black curls lie around her head like a halo.

Giggling, she said, "You're staring again."

Reluctantly, I tore my gaze away and climbed off of her. "Are you ready to go?"

"Almost!" she replied as she sat up. "Let me freshen up in the bathroom real quick." She pointed a stern finger at me. "No resting your eyes!"

I shook my head at her as she grabbed her toiletries bag and skipped into the bathroom.

After a few minutes, she emerged with her curls pulled up in a high ponytail, a fresh coat of gloss on her lips, and a pink tennis dress hugging her body. As she came closer, I could smell soft hints of sweet perfume.

Smiling at me, she offered her hand.

I grabbed it without hesitation and let her tug me out the door.

We took the half-hour drive to Disneyland. At the later hour, the park wasn't as packed with other pedestrians walking down Main Street. It was easy to keep track of Brielle's ponytail of bouncing kinky curls as she skipped down the walkway towards the Sleeping Beauty Castle. My eyes fell from her head to the skirt of her dress, twirling around her long legs with every step. The sun cascaded down her calves, shining against her smooth skin, and the thought of running my hands over them crossed my mind. She turned around, and I raised my gaze to her smiling face.

Grinning, she ceased her steps and held out her hand to me. "We need to buy some ears before we do anything else! This place is too beautiful not to take photos!"

I let her tow me through the air-conditioned stores to find the perfect Minnie Mouse ears for her and Chloe. For herself, she found a pair of pink sequined ears that matched her dress. For Chloe, she found a Little Mermaid Inspired pair with ombre blue and purple ears and a shell-shaped bow in the center.

At the sight of a pair of regular black mouse ears without the bows, she grabbed it and tried to plop it on my head.

I dodged her hands and walked away.

"Oh, come on, Javi," she whined as she followed me. "Entertain your wife for five seconds!"

The sound of my old nickname, dripping in the soft satin of her voice, hit me like a ton of bricks, paralyzing my body mid-step.

Brielle collided in my back, letting out a soft "oomph."

I looked down over my shoulder at her. "What did you just call me?"

Her brows came together as she tried to remember. Noticing the tension stemming from my body, she cut her recall short. "Nothing. Sorry. I won't do it again."

"No, it's okay. It's just…only my sister really calls me that now. My mom used to before…" I trailed off, not wanting to summon unwanted memories on a night like this. "I'd like it if you called me that more," I told her.

Beaming, she scooted closer. "Okay, Javi." Taking my moment of distraction, she set the ears on top of my head. "But, you're still wearing these."

"The hell I am." I swiped the ears right back off and threw them in the nearest bin.

Brielle laughed as I walked away from her again.

With her and Chloe's ears secured and paid for, we started our journey around the park. Brielle was much more interested in all the photo ops opposed to the rides at first. Handing me her phone, she posed in front of all the famous decorations and buildings around the parks. I became her own personal paparazzi. Following her around, I flicked an abundance of candid and planned shots. I even took a few videos of her twirling in front of some of the main attractions, like the castle and the Haunted Mansion.

Now and then, she wanted to share the camera with me. She'd pull me from my spot in front of her and snatch her phone out of my hand. "Smile," she'd demand as she flipped the camera and positioned it in front of our faces.

I couldn't fake full smiles that matched hers, but I could soften my expression enough not to look bad on camera.

Once Brielle was satisfied with her album of photos, we grabbed dinner and started making our way through some rides. Brielle whooped and hollered on the Space Mountain and Big Thunder Railroad Mountain coasters. On Buzz Lightyear Astro Blasters, we competed for the highest score. Brielle hit me in the arm and accused me of cheating when I hit nearly every target. On the slow-moving rides, Pirates of the Caribbean and It's a Small World, Brielle looked around at all the animatronics like a kid in the candy store.

The song on the latter one gave me a fucking headache. Only the sight of Brielle's beautiful face helped me survive the torture. The colorful lights splashed on her face, highlighting the curves of smile and the glee in her smile. I don't think I've ever seen her so happy. Filled with nostalgia and surrounded by child-like magic, she glowed like a lantern, lighting up all the darkness in our lives. Such an amazing view was hard to look away from.

Brielle glanced in my direction, and I quickly looked away. I've been staring at her a little too much lately. I didn't want to make her uncomfortable. Especially not when she was having such a good time.

Her gaze lingered on me for a moment. In my peripheral vision, I caught a glimpse of the same tender look she'd given me at dinner the other night. She scooted closer and wiggled her arm around mine.

As she leaned her head onto my shoulder, I caught a whiff of the coconut oil in her hair. The scent pulled me towards her. Accepting the call, I set my cheek on top of her head.

Against my shoulder, I felt her cheeks rise from a bigger smile.

When we exited the ride, it was almost time for the fireworks. Brielle and I grabbed a cup of soft serve ice cream to share and found a less-crowded spot in Adventureland to watch the fireworks.

"Wow," Brielle murmured as she watched the colorful rockets paint pictures in the dark sky. "I definitely need to take Chloe here someday."

"Take her to Disney World. It's bigger, and you can make a longer trip out of it. I'll even book a Disney Resort for you two to stay in."

She turned to me. "Would you go with us?"

I tore my eyes away from the sky and looked at Brielle. The colors of the fireworks illuminated her eyes. "If you want me to."

"It's not about what I want," she said. Lowering her eyes, she stuck her spoon back into the cup. "I can't ask you for more than you're willing to give. The two of us are one thing, but the *three* of us..." She glanced up at me. "Do you even want kids?"

Honestly, I'd never thought about it. As the eldest son, it was assumed eventually I'd have children - heirs to take over the throne after my death. There wasn't a question of *if* I wanted them. Now that I was thinking about it, I wasn't sure of the answer.

Brielle took my silence as a cue to continue. "Look, I understand the basis of our marriage, but Chloe won't understand if...*when* we don't need protection anymore. Because this - *us* - isn't permanent...is it?"

The right answer felt like poison on my tongue. I opened and closed my mouth, trying to endure the burn enough to get it out. "No," I confirmed. "But that doesn't mean we can't be friends afterwards." Slipping my arm over her shoulders, I pulled her close and added, "Maybe more than that."

Accepting my embrace, she leaned into me and lay her head on my shoulder. Her nose nuzzled against my neck. Her lips brushed against my skin, pulling into a small smile. She pressed herself deeper against me, soaking in all the warmth my body offered.

The possibility lingered between us as we watched the fireworks and wondered what life would look like if our relationship was more than the deal we sealed it with.

Chapter 24

Brielle

"No, no," a voice broke through my ears, breaking the blissful dream I was having. "Let me go."

Wearily, I cracked my eyes open. In the darkness, I glimpsed Javier's body laid out on the other side of the bed, rustling back and forth. My brows came together as he spoke again, louder this time.

"No! *Soltarme!*"

I popped my head up at the urgency in his voice. "Javi," I murmured as I scooted across the bed towards him. "Javi, are you okay?"

He didn't hear me. He continued tossing and turning, muttering defenses in his sleep.

"Javier," I said, as I lay a gentle hand on his shoulder. "Javier, wake -"

Javier's body instinctively reacted to my touch. One of his hands gripped my wrist while the other grabbed something from beneath his pillow. In one swift movement, he threw my body down against the mattress and climbed atop of me, straddling me with his long legs. The hand holding my wrist pinned it down on the bed above my head. The other pressed something cold and hard against my forehead.

Unlike earlier, I froze underneath him, paralyzed by the fear of unpredictability. Before, I knew he wouldn't hurt me - not with a pillow in his hand. But, with the familiar mouth of a gun pressed against my forehead, I wasn't so sure.

Above me, Javier's eyes were wild with emotions I've never seen before.

Misery. Rage. Panic. *Fear.*

For a moment, I glimpsed everything hiding behind his walls. His pain. His sadness. His hopelessness.

Staring at the eye of the silent storm he was terrifying and heartbreaking. All I wanted was to push all of the clouds and rain away.

His walls rose back up as he assessed the situation. In the darkness, his squinted eyes scanned over my face. "Dammit, Brielle," he said with a sigh. He moved the mouth of the gun off of my forehead. Leaning down, he replaced the cold metal with his soft lips. *"Lo siento. Lo siento mucho."*

I took advantage of his closeness and wrapped my arms around him. "It's alright," I whispered. "Are you okay?"

"Mhm." He tried to move off of me, but I tightened my grasp. "Brielle," he started.

"You had a bad dream," I said, more of a statement than a question.

"Yeah."

"Do you have them often?"

"Every night."

I frowned. No wonder he looked so tired all the time. I always chalked it up to the natural exhaustion of running a company. But now, I realized there was so much more.

His legitimate company wasn't the only thing he needed to protect. He had his illegal affairs, his siblings, his pet - me and Chloe. He spent so much time shouldering burdens to protect others. Who was helping him carry his own?

"Do you want to talk about them?" I asked.

"No." He fidgeted in my grasp, subtly trying to break out of my hold. "I'm alright, Brielle. You can let me go."

"But, it might help if-"

"Soltarme," he repeated, his voice prickling with sharp icicles.

My chest stung from the distinct change in his tone. Reluctantly, I released him.

Javier rolled off of me and scooted close to the edge of the bed. Sighing, he ran his hand over his face.

"What can I do?" I asked as I closed the distance between us. "How can I help?"

"I'm fine," he gritted.

I gently lay a hand on his cheek and turned his face toward me. "All of your thoughts will be safe with me."

He stared at me for a long moment. The moonlight beaming through the windows poured over his eyes, slipping through his chestnut irises like silver linings. Eventually, he raised his hand and cupped my cheek. His thumb raked back and forth across my skin as he spoke. "You're kind," he whispered. "But I won't make my sins yours to bear."

"You say that as if I don't have my own."

"There's a difference between mine and yours. You were stolen from heaven and made to endure pain that wasn't meant for you. I was born in Hell. My suffering is a prerequisite for all the havoc I was raised to wreak, and a consequence of all the mistakes I dared to make. I'll never subject you to that."

"But you can't carry all of this weight alone. It'll destroy you."

"It already has," he admitted. He pulled me close and kissed my head again. "Go back to sleep, Brielle."

"Wait," I called as I watched him slip out of bed. "Where are you going?"

He slid off his pajama pants and traded them for a pair of joggers. "I'll be back later."

I glanced at the digital clock on the nightstand. "Javier, its four o' clock in the morning. Just come back to bed."

Ignoring me, he stepped into his sneakers and grabbed his keys off the dresser.

Before I could say another word, he was already out the door.

I had trouble sleeping after he left. Although Javier hadn't slept close to me, his absence was apparent in the gigantic bed. I had way too much room, and the sheets were cold without his body warmth.

I also couldn't stop thinking about where he could've gone. There weren't many places in L.A. open at this time of night. *Legal* facilities, at least. Knowing Javier, he could've been taking care of things that I'd rather not concern myself with.

Still, I worried about his safety and the state of his mental health. He clearly was not fine after his nightmare, and I didn't want him doing anything reckless.

I wished he'd just let me comfort him. He didn't have to talk if he didn't want to. We could've just lay here in silence. Maybe I could've rubbed his back and eased him back to sleep. Or held him while he wrestled with his demons.

I wanted to offer the same protection and safety that he generously gives everyone else.

The sound of the door opening woke me not too long after I finally fell asleep. Groggily, I opened my eyes, expecting to see Javier's tall figure strolling through the door.

Instead, I was met with Naomi's tight smile. "Good morning," she sang as she strutted closer. She held out an iHop takeout bag. "I brought breakfast."

"Thanks." I kept my eyes on the door, still waiting for Javier to walk through it.

Naomi followed my gaze. "Javier said he has some errands to run today. He asked me to drop off breakfast before I took you down to the spa. You have appointments for massages, facials, and mani pedis. By the time you're finished, the hairstylist and makeup artist should be here to get you ready for the gala. Your dress should arrive before they're finished with you."

I raised an eyebrow. "A dress? But I already packed one."

"Javier bought you a new one from Versace's latest evening gown collection. Don't worry. I've seen the picture, and it's gorgeous. You'll steal the show at the Gala tonight wearing it."

I almost frowned at her. I knew this dance all too well. Boyfriend makes the girlfriend upset, and instead of having a civil conversation about it, he throws money at the problem and prays it distracts her long enough to forgive him.

Leo and I used to do it all the time. But in that case, his gifts disguised the bruises decorating my skin. And he wasn't seeking my forgiveness - he was just trying to offset his wrongs with a good deed that appeared genuine.

He didn't care if I was mad at him. At the end of the day, no matter what I felt, I still belonged to him.

I thought Javier was more mature than that.

Naomi cleared her throat, breaking me out of my thoughts. "Javier really loves you," she mused. "He's never done anything like this before."

I almost scoffed. Love was a strong word. One that I doubted was in Javier's vocabulary. I may like him, but I wasn't naïve. I knew my chances of his feelings matching mine were slim to none.

Still, I guessed the gesture could've been made with well intentions. I knew his schedule was blocked off most of the day anyway with errands he wouldn't disclose, so maybe he'd planned this ahead of time to keep me occupied. For the sake of my sanity, and the enjoyment of this trip, I'd like to think of it that way.

"Eat your food," Naomi demanded. "You have a busy day ahead of you."

Chapter 25

Javier

The pungent smell of weed and liquor greeted me as I walked into my uncle's large office. The room sat above an old MMA gym, now restructured into an underground fighting arena. Below me was a large octagon, with chains around the perimeter and blood staining the off-white padding. Judging from the wet blood on the mat, I assumed there was an event not too long before I arrived.

I was planning to come here later in the day to monitor the shipment of products that accompanied Brielle and me on the trip, but I came by earlier than expected.

I wanted to punch myself in the face for shoving my gun in Brielle's face. Still, amid my nightmare, I thought I was being attacked and reacted accordingly. I was not expecting to be met with Brielle's brown eyes, wide with fear and confusion, when I finally broke through the realms of the dream and confronted my mind's intruder.

I couldn't erase the image of her frozen body and terrified expression from my mind. That she thought for even a second that I would harm her stung like hell. My father raised me to respect all women, but he put special emphasis on never hurting the women you care about.

Protect and provide is the motto he'd engraved into my head.

I always thought the former was meant for enemies. I never dreamed I'd have to protect my wife from myself.

It didn't help that she was so kind - too kind - afterwards. I didn't deserve her concern or affection - not when I'd dangled her life in front of her face. She was supposed to be angry with me. I needed her to yell or curse or hit me for making such a horrible mistake. Her forgiveness and soft touch weren't warranted after my actions. Yet, like the angel she was, she extended her grace anyway.

Perhaps my plan of taking her as my wife wasn't the best idea. I liked Brielle, and I wanted to keep her safe, but not at the expense of her righteousness. She's had enough stolen from her. I didn't need to take any more.

"What's up, Jav?" my uncle, Rafael, greeted me as we locked eyes. He was sitting behind his large desk. Grinning, he rose from his seat and crossed the side of the desk to approach me.

He passed his son, Max, who sat in the seat at the side of the desk with a first aid kit open beside him and a strip of gauze half-wrapped around his hand.

Rafael and Max weren't my family by blood, but by loyalty. Rafael grew up in Mexico with my father. Together, they busted their asses in their local cartel and climbed their way up the ranks until it became their own. When my father married my mother and inherited access to her father's pharmaceutical company, he expanded their empire and created two thrones at the head. While he operated behind the cloak of a legitimate business and became a quiet supplier, my uncle wore his power like a crown and boldly tore through cities as a well-known kingpin. Though both of their roles were the same, and both benefited from the money flowing through the venues, each served their own personal goals. Whereas my father wanted power, my uncle wanted respect.

I haven't seen him since my father's funeral, too busy with running operations as normally as possible. Hell, I haven't seen Max since he was in elementary school.

From the stories my uncle tells, Max wanted nothing to do with him after he and his mother separated. He assumed Max was taking his mother's side in the divorce, potentially brainwashed from the bad things she might've said about him. But, I didn't buy the lie. Growing up, it seemed like Max was close to his dad. He followed him around like a loyal puppy. It was odd he'd suddenly drop such idolization. But, I didn't ask too many questions. Their family issues were none of my business.

Reaching out my hand, I accepted his handshake and accompanying one-arm hug. "What's up?" My eyes went to my cousin. "Hey, Max."

He glanced up from his task to nod at me. Time took the innocence out of his dark brown eyes and covered it with hard walls instead.

I noticed blood seeped in scattered spots through the gauze on his hand. In the dim lighting, I could see swelling around his left eye and bruises on his cheeks. "You were in one of the matches tonight?" I asked him.

"Yeah," he said, his voice deeper than the last time I spoke to him. "The other guy looks worse."

"Hm."

"We weren't expecting you until later," my uncle said. "What brings you here this time of night?"

"I took a drive and happened to be in the neighborhood."

My uncle smirked. "Now, that's a load of bullshit. Why are you really here so early?"

A soft ping went off, stealing his attention and saving me from answering the question. My uncle pulled out his cell and frowned at the screen. "Excuse me, boys. I have to go handle something." He waved his hand. "You two catch up. I know it's been a while."

Max glanced up from his task to shoot a dirty look at his father's back.

I almost chuckled at the sight. "Still don't like the man, huh?"

"He's a bastard," Max grumbled.

"Aren't they all?" As I walked up to him, I watched him finish wrapping the bandage around his hand and secure it with a clip. "How long have you been working for him?"

"A few years now," he admitted.

I leaned my hip against the desk. "Voluntarily?"

Some of his walls fell as he looked up at me again. "Is anything voluntary when it comes to them?"

I shrugged. "It's been a long time, Max. I thought you found a loophole -

a way out."

"Almost," he murmured. "Are you sticking around long enough for a smoke?"

"Sure."

My cousin plucked a blunt off of his father's desk. "Freshly rolled," he explained as he stood up and led me to the couch on the other side of the room. "Best painkiller in the world, I say."

I sank down onto the soft couch cushions. I didn't need the weed, but nothing else was going to push away the gnawing sensation in my chest.

Max handed the blunt to me, and I held it between my teeth as he flicked a flame at the end. Relaxing against the cushions, I took a long inhale of the smoke, needing every ounce of serotonin I could get from it.

"So," I said after he'd taken his own puff. "What's been up with you? Besides the work with your dad?"

"I've been doing some legitimate work in mixed martial arts: competing in tournaments, exhibition matches, and teaching some classes down at the local gym."

"Nice. I remember you loved MMA when we were younger. You used to have Adrian putting you on your ass trying to show off."

A smile finally appeared on his lips. "That's only because he was older and bigger than me. I could probably take him now."

"Nah, he'll still body slam the shit out of you. Try him if you want to."

He chuckled. "I miss him," he mused. When we were younger, Max used to take a break from following his father around and be on Adrian's heels instead. Despite both of their hot-heads and tastes for trouble, they always got along well. If we would've lived in L.A. longer, or if Max hadn't taken a hiatus from this side of the family, they would've been the perfect duo to raise hell when our fathers needed.

"I can give you his number," I offered. "I'm sure he'd love to hear from you."

"I don't know. It's been so long. He's probably pissed I ghosted all of you."

"If he is, you can test your theory of beating him in a fight. After he kicks your ass, he'll be cool."

My cousin smiled wider, remnants of the youth I knew shining in his eyes. He pulled out his phone and let me plug my brother's number into it. "So, what's been going on with you?" He asked once I was finished. "Rumors have been flying around like moths."

"What are people saying?"

"First, that you're behind a coup against some powerful Italians. Second, you've settled down and found yourself a wife. Third, said wife has a little one on the way."

I coughed on the smoke at the last comment.

Max chuckled. "Guess the last one isn't true, huh?"

"Attention is a hell of a drug," I muttered.

"But the others are true." He tilted his head. "These Italians. Are they the ones who killed Tío Alejandro?"

"Yeah."

"Oh, so that's why our packages have been having some extra goodies in them? We're gonna tear some of their shit down?"

"Mhm. The only condition I have is none of the females they're trafficking are harmed. The Bianchis have been reckless lately, and some of them have gotten hurt or worse. I told your dad to try to ease them out first before you all shoot up the place."

"Still such a gentleman," he mused with a sly grin. "Though, I didn't take you for the type to settle down. Who's this woman you've married?"

"She was one of the Italian's prized possessions. Now, she's mine."

His brows rose. "You married one of their girlfriends?" He burst out in laughter. "Javier, what? I may have expected something like this from Adrian, but you..." He couldn't stop laughing. "You are a menace!"

"She's a good woman," I insisted. "She deserves better than what the Bianchis put her through."

His amusement simmered down at the solemnity of my words. "I understand. So, it's not just about taking a dig at them?"

"She's a friend," I explained. "I didn't know until recently about her affiliation with them. Marriage was my best option to keep her and her daughter safe."

"A daughter?" He let out a few more laughs. "You're just taking this whole man's family, huh? And here I thought the twins were petty."

I rolled my eyes and took another puff of the blunt.

"What's she like?" He continued. "I'm curious."

I fished my phone out of my pocket. Quickly, I scrolled through the photos I took earlier. I stopped at a selfie she made us take in front of the Sleeping Beauty Castle.

In the photo, I held the camera up high over our heads to capture both of our faces and the castle behind us. Brielle was pressed up against me, smiling as if she'd won the lottery. I refused to smile in the photo, but she didn't mind. Her happiness radiated bright enough for both of us.

"Wow," Max said as he examined the picture. "*Ella es muy hermosa.*" Looking at me, he asked, "Do you love her?"

"Love is a strong word," I said. "But, I do care about her."

He nodded. "*Ten cuidado,*" he warned. "Families are nice to keep you warm at night, but they're weaknesses - liabilities. The last thing anyone would want is for yours to get hurt."

He didn't have to tell me about that. I knew all too well how easily one's enemies could use their families against them. Our family was used as a pawn in that game once, and we lost our mother because of it.

As much as I wished I could say I'd never let Brielle or Chloe be subjected to that, I couldn't make any guarantees in this life. All I could do was cover all of my bases at all times for their safety.

We talked for a while longer before I started falling asleep on the couch. He left me alone for a few hours to catch up on the sleep I missed.

When I awoke, I helped my uncle review the contents of his shipment and brainstormed strategies for his men when they hit the Bianchi's territories. My uncle wanted a massacre, but he needed to be smart about it. The last thing we needed was for him to draw unnecessary attention to the conflict at hand.

I left the gym close to four-thirty. On the ride back to the hotel, I called Adrian to see how things were going with Chloe.

"She's a little scam artist," he told me. "I'm out fifty bucks."

I chuckled. "How'd she do that?"

"Swear jar."

"Then, learn to watch your mouth."

"I'm trying, but even when she's not in the room, she's eavesdropping on my conversation. Right, Chloe?" His voice raised on the last sentence, and I heard Chloe's giggle in the background. "She's over here hiding near the door."

"I was coming to tell you something," her tiny voice said.

"I'm about to make you a lie jar. Earn my money back."

She giggled again. "No! I like being rich!"

"Here." Static cackled on the other end. "Say hi to Javier."

"Hi, giant!" Chloe exclaimed. "I miss you!"

Hearing her voice, full of joy and excitement, bought a tiny smile to my lips. "I miss you too. I heard you're wearing out my brother's pockets. Is that true?"

"No. Ms. Kiara said I'm holding him accountable."

"Accountable my ass," Adrian mumbled.

"Aht, swear word! You owe me another dollar!"

"You tell him, Chloe."

I could perfectly imagine Adrian's eye roll. "Man, both of y'all can get off my phone."

Chloe giggled again. "Don't let Mr. Adrian fool you. He loves me!"

"Oh, does he?"

"Mhm. After gymnastics class, he gave me a drawing lesson and he taught me how to draw butterflies. I made you and mommy some for when you get home!"

"Nice. I can't wait to see them." Another voice, probably Kiara, echoed from afar. "Oh, I've gotta go help Ms. Kiara finish cleaning up. We're about to go to Chuck E. Cheese! Bye, giant!"

The phone crackled again as she handed the phone back to my brother. She told him to start putting his shoes on before her small footsteps padded away.

"Sounds like she likes you," I told Adrian.

"Yeah. I guess I like her too." The smile in his voice when he spoke about her was nice to hear. Adrian may act mean and tough, but he had a soft spot for kids. I was glad he and Chloe were getting along.

Brielle was still locked away in one of the private rooms in the spa when I arrived back at the hotel. Having the room to myself gave me the privacy to take a shower and compose a proper apology for my actions last night.

Reacting from my nightmare aside, I shouldn't have left her in bed by herself. Not after every tough conversation we've had. Every time she reaches me, I walk away. I needed to break the pattern before it became a habit. At least once, I needed to stay and accept the comfort she was trying to give me - no matter how much it hurt to receive it.

My nerves shook with anxiety from the words bouncing around my head as I waited for her in the main lobby of the hotel. I didn't apologize often. I rarely made mistakes that required one. But, usually I didn't care if others accepted my apology. With Brielle, I cared about every little thing that crossed her mind.

I ambled back and forth in the lobby, avoiding the eyes of the people admiring my suit as they passed by.

As I turned around to do another short lap, my eyes fell on the most magnificent sight.

Walking down the stairwell from the upper main floor was an angel descending straight from the steps of heaven. Her skin glistened underneath the golden lights of the hotel lobby like rich hot chocolate. A pink silk gown was snug around her slender body, hugging the curves of her breasts and hour-glass hips. Her black hair fell in graceful waterfalls of loose curls over her shoulders to the small of her back. Natural-looking browns and bronzes sparkled on her eyelids, and long, full lashes batted as she blinked. Her lips, pulling into a shy smile, were painted with pink-tinted gloss.

One look at her and all the words I had diligently prepared in my head were blown away.

I slowly moved towards her, entranced by the sight. I'd never seen beauty so mesmerizing, so exquisite, so heavenly. I couldn't tear my eyes away from her, worried that if I did, she might disappear and become another portrait of the wall of unforgettable memories in my brain.

I stretched out my hand as I reached the bottom of the steps.

Her own hand, freshly manicured with long, acrylic French tips, extended towards me. The touch of her soft skin against mine reminded me she wasn't a figment of my imagination.

Looking at the sparkling ring on her finger as my fingers curled around hers, I was reminded that this angel was not only real - she was *mine*.

Chapter 26

Brielle

"Wow," I murmured as we entered the large venue space of Candela La Brea.

String lights hung through the rounded wooden planks on the ceiling, illuminating the faintly lit space. Round wooden high-top tables lay in neat columns between wide open spaces, occupied by other patrons dressed in elegant gowns and expensive suits. The company logo was projected on the walls sandwiching the large stage where a live band stood, playing their own renditions of popular hits. Animated portraits of bouncing ball-like cells, waterfalls of bright colors, and swirling beams of light decorated the walls between the windows, immersing the room in a whirlwind of movements occurring in the inner body. The room itself was teeming with a plethora of people, all dressed in the finest of threads.

"This event is so much fancier than the luncheon," I commented.

"The luncheon was a celebration of the survivors in our trial programs; it was meant to highlight success stories and persuade existing donors to keep throwing money our way," Javier explained. "This is a horse-and-pony show to bring potential donors on board and convince them our research is worth contributing to."

Nodding, I watched Naomi scurry up to us. Her simple black gown accentuated her slender curves and highlighted the perpetual sharpness in her eyes. "You remember the game plan?" She asked Javier.

"Like the back of my hand," he replied.

"Good." She pointed a stern finger at him. "Don't embarrass me."

"No promises," he muttered under his breath as we started following after her.

Like the last fundraising event, we made our way through the clusters of guests around the room. Most of the donors took over the chatting, talking about whatever was on their mind.

I learned about children, grand-children, vacation homes, hospital funding issues, and even some gossip. A lot of the women must've seen a potential friend in me and wasted no time airing out the business of some of the others in the room they didn't care for. I quickly found out who was sleeping with whose husband and the blow-outs that occurred at some events. From the way two of the women were glaring at each other from across the room, one lady I was talking to thought there might be another one tonight. With every piece of information, I raised my eyebrows and sipped my champagne. I wouldn't say it aloud, but these rich women were entertaining as hell. Listening to their catty drama made the first few hours fly by.

Around nine o' clock, Javier was practically dragging me into an empty corner, desperate for a break from the empty conversations..

I watched as he leaned back against the wall and sipped on his glass of champagne. His eyes roamed over the crowd, watching contently as others mingled around the room. As they flicked down to me, something stronger than content flickered in his irises, and he quickly looked away.

"Why cancer?" I asked to break the silence between us.

"What do you mean?"

"Your company's work, and charity brand, is mostly attached to the cure for cancer. I was just curious why that is."

"My grandmother passed away from breast cancer," Javier explained. "My mother said she died with a smile, as if she was mocking cancer's face. She used to say that the disease may have destroyed her body, but it never destroyed her spirit. She spent her life dedicated to making sure it didn't break the spirits of others. Most of her medical career was spent conducting cancer research and searching for a cure. No matter how many trials that failed or people she lost, she always kept her head high and never gave up on her cause. Just before she died, she had a trial that was going extremely well. She had a high success rate, and was planning to open her study up to more candidates. After she passed, my father made sure her research was passed on to her apprentices, and now they're doing all the work she wasn't able to finish."

"But, with an increasing success rate, right?"

"I don't know," he admitted. "I haven't really kept up with the research. I just know when to wire money into the account and attend events as their sponsor."

I frowned. "Have you ever thought about checking in on it?"

"Sometimes."

"Why don't you?"

"Because it'll only remind me of everything I'll never be able to do."

My brows creased together. "You wanted to be a doctor?"

"Mhm," he sipped on his champagne. "A long time ago."

"Why didn't you?"

"You're not new to this world, Brielle. You know that in this life, the first-born son of cartels like mine don't have a choice. Whatever their father says, that's what they have to be. It looks different for everyone, and it has a lot of layers, but for me, in the public eye at least, it's the CEO of this stupid company."

"Your father isn't here anymore," I reminded him. "You can be whoever, or whatever, you want."

"Physically, he's not here," Javier said, his voice tight. "But that hasn't unlocked the chains he's put on me."

I stepped closer and grabbed his hand. "I'm sorry, Javier," I said. "For what it's worth, I think you would've made a great doctor."

His gaze flicked down to our intertwined hands before coming back up to my face. He stared at me for a long moment, his expression indecipherable.

I blushed under the intensity burning in his eyes. I couldn't tell if it was anger, fear, or desire. For all I knew, it could've been all three, battling against each other in a war that didn't need to be fought.

Before either of us could speak again, Naomi's voice pierced through the air between us. "Why are you two hiding in a corner?" She exclaimed as she hurried towards her. "I've been looking all over for you! Javier, some donors from John Hopkins would like to speak with you about the new clinical trials your team is conducting!"

Javier's chest rose and fell in silent irritation. Still, he took a step towards her, prepared to follow her through the crowd.

His grip tightened on my hand as I tried to wiggle it out of his grasp. His brow rose as he looked down at me.

"You go ahead," I told him. "I have to use the restroom."

I almost regretted my words as our hands fell away and my skin was nipped by the air conditioning in the room. But I'd drunk a considerable amount of champagne and needed to relieve the pressure on my bladder.

I would've gone sooner if it weren't for the constant conversation with the donors, and my selfish desire to savor the brief spurts of one-on-one time we had.

I shuffled out of the bustling room down one of the quieter halls towards the restroom. There, I took care of my business and washed my hands.

Eager to return to my husband's side, I exited the bathroom and suddenly crashed into a hard surface in front of me.

"Oh, I'm so sorry," I said, stunned by the sudden impact. Blinking back into consciousness, my gaze traveled up a dark suit towards a pair of sly, dark eyes.

"That's alright, Diamond," he replied, his voice filled with feigned joy. "You were just the person I was looking for."

Chapter 27

Javier

What is taking Brielle so long? I thought as I nodded along to the mundane ramblings of one of the event donors. I couldn't stop glancing at the entrance way, waiting to see her float through the doorway in her pink gown. She'd only been gone five minutes, but an uneasy feeling was waving through my stomach. I tried to attribute it to the usual anxiety I fought with during social events like these. I barely liked talking to the people close to me - let alone strangers. It'd subsided somewhat with her by my side. Her soft hand around mine and the sweet smile served as a pillar of support throughout these boring conversations, reminding me of all the good things I had to look forward to once we finally left.

I remember all the little fun activities she'd added to my itinerary. Although we wouldn't get through all of them, there were one or two I thought she might enjoy at the late hour. After all, it was our last night alone. The least I could do was try to make it special.

Glancing at the doorway again, the uneasiness transformed into a harsh nipping at my body. I felt harsh pinches, like little bees stabbing their stingers into me, all around my shoulders, pushing me to escape this stupid conversation and find my wife.

I didn't hesitate to listen to their calls. Quickly, I excused myself from the wealthy couple I was speaking with and stormed out the room.

The hallways were empty since all the patrons were occupying the main room. Only the music from the DJ and the distant chatter occupied the space.

I turned the corner to the hall where the bathrooms and I almost stopped in my tracks.

Brielle stood just outside of the women's bathroom door, staring up at the person in front of her with wide, fearful eyes and trembling hands.

Although only his expensive suit and dark hair were visible from behind, I knew only a certain criterion of men could summon such a reaction from her.

There weren't any cameras in this area. Whatever he was planning to do to Brielle, he must've been hoping to keep it quiet.

My hands itched for my gun as I stormed towards them. With every step, another layer of red was added to the tint around my gaze.

The asshole sealed his fate when he wrapped his filthy hands around Brielle's arms and greedily caressed her arm.

Gritting my teeth, I restrained the urge to shoot him straight in the back of his head. We were in a public place, and I had to attempt to act like I had some sense.

"There you are, Brielle," I interrupted whatever the man was saying. Taking my place beside her, I slipped my arm around her waist and pulled her out of the man's grasp. "I was looking all over for you." Reluctantly, I turned my gaze to the man she was conversing with. "Who's your friend?"

"This is Carlo," Brielle murmured, her voice barely high enough to hear. "Carlo Ricci."

The stranger chuckled. His eyes bounced between my hand on Brielle's hip and the glare on my face. "I'm an old friend," he explained. "I heard she'd gotten married, and I wanted to offer my congratulations. I didn't think anyone would put a ring on this one. You know she's been around."

"Mr. Ricci," Brielle hissed. "Please, don't-"

"Don't what?" Carlo asked sharply. "The man deserves to know the pussy he married is loose. And you know what they say: you can't turn a whore into a house-" His words were barely out of his mouth before my hand was around his throat.

I pushed him through the doors of the men's bathroom and slammed his head against the hard, marble corner of one of the sinks. I made sure his head was angled so the sharp edge collided into his temple, the weakest part of the body. In the first few hits, his eyes crossed from the sudden pain. After three or four slams, the side of his skull cracked under the pressure and sent his neurons into distress. Blood splattered onto the sink and nearby walls as the skin gave way underneath the pressure. The sharp corner of the sink dug further into his body, chipping away at the bone and exposing the raw flesh inside. The tenth one finally killed him, making him go still in my grasp.

I dropped his lifeless body on the tiled floor beside the sink.

No one - and I mean no fucking one - was going to disrespect my wife. It wasn't in my plans to kill this asshole so quickly, but clearly he was asking to be made an example for others stupid enough to cross me.

"Oh my God," Brielle gasped from behind me. She'd followed us into the bathroom and watched the entire attack. She stood a few feet away with her hands clasped over her mouth. "Javi, what the-"

"Who the fuck was that?" I snapped at her. "One of Leo's associates?"

She averted her eyes as she sadly nodded.

Of course, Leo sent one of his men to spy on our event. His association alone shouldn't have guaranteed him an entrance into our event. My men have been keeping tabs on all of his associates and allies. They should've sent him away the moment they saw him. Unless they were bribed or dead.

Knowing Leo's tactics, I assumed the latter to be true. With his snipers, he probably took out the guards before waltzing in here. I'll have to enhance our security measures in order to keep up with his eyes in the sky.

Sighing, I dug my phone out of my pocket. "Naomi," I said after she picked up. "There's been an accident in the bathroom. I need you here, *now*."

I moved to one of the other sinks and rinsed the blood off of my hand. I glanced up at Brielle who was still frozen in place, staring at Carlo's body as if he was going to rise from the dead. "Are you okay?"

She nodded, but I could see the moisture forming in her eyes.

Although I don't regret killing him, I shouldn't have done it in front of her. I didn't want her to view me as yet another monster hiding in the shadows.

The click of Naomi's heels greeted us as she came hurrying into the bathroom. She frowned at the sight of Carlo's deceased, bleeding body. "Goddammit, Javier. He just donated ten thousand dollars to our research. How the hell am I supposed to cover this up?"

"Claim the asshole tripped on the wet floor and hit his head. As for his money: refund the money back into his account and erase all history of the transactions."

Any other enemy's money I would've kept, but I didn't want any of his money, made off of the torture and pain of innocent women, touching the good work my mother created. And the body was going to serve as another warning for Leo to stop fucking testing me.

"Alright," Naomi replied with a sigh. "I'll make it work."

"Come on, Brielle," I told my wife as I gently grabbed her arm. "We're leaving."

Brielle didn't protest. Obediently, she followed me down the long hall, out to the car.

I didn't bother checking on my men. That was a tragedy waiting to happen. The best decision I could make at the moment was getting Brielle the hell out of here before Leo's men pulled another stunt.

"Lay down on the backseats," I told Brielle as I opened the backdoor of the rental car. I shrugged off my suit jacket and shoved it into her arms. "Put this over you and don't sit up until I tell you to."

Her brows came together in silent question, but she didn't voice it aloud. Sensing the urgency in my tone, she did as she was told.

I shut the door and climbed into the front seat. As I pulled out of the parking lot, I noticed two cars on the street turn on their lights and leave their parking spots.

"Fuck," I whispered. I couldn't take Brielle back to the hotel now. If Leo's men killed mine, then the hotel staff would be easy pickings. I needed to get Brielle somewhere safe.

Pressing my foot harder on the gas, I swerved through the lines of cars on the busy road. I knew all of them like the back of my hand. When we came up here for vacations in the summers, Dante and I used to drive around the city all the time. Usually, it'd be late at night when there were no other cars on the road. We'd ride around for hours and hours, talking and getting into shit we weren't supposed to be in. The latter built good experience for times like this. This wasn't the first time I'd been chased by an enemy around L.A. - and it certainly wouldn't be the last.

The unmarked cars swerved in and out of traffic, desperate to keep up with us.

I hit a few sharp turns positioned near traffic lights. Timing it right, I swept the car around the edges just as the lights were about to turn red.

The tactic shook off the cars for a few moments at a time, but failed to get them off my tail completely.

As we sped down a quieter street, I saw a long shadow poke out from the passenger side of one car behind us. Not even a moment later, loud bangs erupted through the air.

Bullets collided with the back of the car, sounding off like a chorus of fireworks. Most hit the trunk and bumper of the car, but a few crashed straight through the window, sending glass throughout the backseat.

Brielle whimpered in the backseat. Through the rear view mirror, I saw her fidgeting underneath my jacket.

"Don't move!" I barked at her. I unhooked my gun from my waistband again and slowed the car down. The hand on the wheel whipped and jerked it, guiding the wheels in jagged movements.

One car moved into the next lane and sped up to ride beside us.

As soon as our cars lined up, I rolled down the window and fired into the car.

The first bullet struck the passenger's head. The rifle in his hands clattered against the dash as his body fell limp.

The driver, too busy focusing on the road, caught the following ones. The bullets split through his face and head like holes in a bowling ball.

Without proper guidance, the car swerved off the road. Through the side-view mirror, I watched it collide into a pole.

With their comrades lost, the remaining car picked up speed and started shooting at us. This time, both the passenger and the driver had their weapons stuck out of the windows. More bullets clattered against the metal exterior of the car like raindrops on a stormy day.

Learning from their team's mistake, this pair stayed behind us. Their aim was sporadic, aiming at any inch of the car they could see.

I pressed my foot on the gas as we approached yet another traffic light. The green light flashed to yellow. I slammed the gas pedal all the way to the floor to zoom through the light before it turned red.

Our attackers followed us through the small intersection just as the opposite light turned green. A loud beep echoed through the air as an approaching truck crashed into the car, violently pushing it a few feet down the street.

I glanced in the backseat at Brielle. Bits of glass covered the fabric covering her body, but on first impression, she didn't have any major scrapes or scratches.

Leo better thank whatever devil he worships she wasn't hurt. It spared a few more moments for his pathetic waste of a life.

With our tail gone, I made a beeline towards my family's old beach house in Malibu.

The large, three-story house sat by itself near the sands of the ocean, miles away from other neighborhoods and the nearby town. Very few men on my payroll knew the location.

When we were younger, my father used the house as both a safe haven and a vacation home. If he ever felt we were in danger and needed to stick us somewhere no one would find us, this was the spot. We had others around the world, specifically in Mexico and the nearby islands, but this one was always my go-to. Likely because this was the one that carried the most memories from when my mother was still alive.

I waited until I drove all the way down the long driveway to look back at Brielle again. "You can sit up now," I told her.

Sighing, she lifted herself up. Her chest heaved as her eyes darted between the glass on her lap and the broken windows. Looking at me, her eyes widened. "Are you alright?" She asked. She pointed at my arm. "You're bleeding."

I followed her gaze to my biceps. Amid all the chase, I hadn't realized one bullet whizzing through the window grazed the side of my arm. The jagged rip in my shirt exposed the long, wide gash spreading across my skin. Blood seeped from the wound, staining the white fabric with red. The pain was like a bee sting compared to the other wounds I've faced.

"I'll clean it when we get in the house," I said with a shrug.

Holding my suit jacket tight around her shoulders, Brielle followed me out of the car and into the house. Curiously, she examined the furniture, lightly worn out over the years, and the photos decorating the walls. A smile threatened to bloom on her lips as we passed a decorative table filled with photos of the twins and me in our youth.

I shed my blood-stained dress shirt and inspected the wound more. The bullet scratched tore through the surface of my flesh, slicing through some of the meat of my muscle. The wound will heal in a few days with stitches, but it will leave a nasty scar. Another addition to the collection, I guess.

I grabbed the medical kit from the hallway closet and plucked out the materials I needed for my sutures.

Parking myself on the floor, so as not to get blood on my mother's favorite furniture, I started twisting the cap off of the alcohol bottle.

Brielle snatched the alcohol and gauze out of my hands before I could begin. "Let me do it," she said. "You shouldn't have to stitch and dress your own wound."

"Why not? I've done it plenty of times before."

Brielle frowned. Ignoring my comment, she poured some alcohol on a gauze pad and started dabbing it along the bullet wound. "Did you patch the rest of these up yourself, too?" She asked as her free hand traced over some of the other scars on my arm.

"Most of them."

Her fingers descended lower towards the longer scars on my inner forearms.

I snatched my arm away before her fingertips could reach them.

"Sorry," Brielle murmured. Cautiously, her hand wrapped around my bicep and pulled it back to her. The sting of the alcohol on the cut returned as she continued her task. "May I ask what happened there?"

"What does it look like?"

Her gaze drifted towards my forearms again, traveling up and down the perfect lines running across the middle of my skin. Her frown deepened as she noticed the smaller, horizontal ones closer to my wrists. "How old were you? When you…" she trailed off, the words too heavy for her delicate tongue.

"Eighteen."

"You were young," she murmured. "May I ask why?"

"The weight of my family's burdens and expectations are heavy, and there isn't anywhere to put it down. After a while, there's only so much will to keep carrying it. At that time, I didn't have the strength to hold it anymore, and I let it crush me."

Brielle picked up the needle. As gently as she could, she pierced the sharp end through my skin and tugged the skin up to cover the gash. "What knocked you down?"

"The night my mother was murdered was the last straw. My father trained me to tolerate a lot of ugly shit, but watching my mother bleed out on the living room floor wasn't one of them. The experience alone damn near tore all of us apart. Then, my father dragged my brother through hell and back as punishment for letting it happen."

"But, weren't you guys young when she-"

"We were old enough to protect her," I cut her off. "We were just too busy being kids for once that we forgot we were supposed to be soldiers."

"I'm sorry," she murmured. "You don't deserve all the pain you carry."

"Neither do you."

Her eyes darted up at me. She may hide it with her pink dresses and bright smile, but the beast gnawing at her conscience reared its ugly face with every flinch and quiver. If I, alone, could slay it for her, I would. But, once beasts like these wrapped themselves around their host, it was going to take an entire army to destroy them.

She finished stitching up my wound and wrapped gauze around my arm to protect it.

"You should wash off and change," I said once she was done. My blood stained her skin, and I hated that I'd tainted it. "We'll stay here tonight and leave tomorrow morning. My men will get our things from the hotel and bring them to the jet for us."

I grabbed Brielle's hand and towed her upstairs into my old room.

As I rustled through my drawers to find a change of clothes, Brielle floated over to the window. She stared out at the beach, her eyes glowing with awe. "Is it safe to go out there?" She asked.

Nodding, I handed her an old button-up of mine. "Clean yourself up, and I'll meet you downstairs. Bathroom is the door at the end of the hall."

While Brielle was gone, I changed into a pair of sweats and a tank top. I rustled back through my drawers in search of some pre-rolled blunts I'd hidden the last time I was here.

I stuffed the joint and a lighter in my pocket before heading downstairs to wait for Brielle.

While I waited, I called my uncle to let him know about the situation. Los Angeles, and most of California, was his territory. As expected, he was pissed that an enemy was stomping all over it. Over the phone, he promised me he'd take care of the rest of the men Bianchi had lying around the city. "You just relax and focus on that pretty wife of yours," he said shortly before hanging up.

As I heard the click of the dial tone, Brielle's footsteps padded down the carpeted steps. The trade between her extravagant pink gown and my old button-up didn't change the scale of her beauty. The white shirt may have been its own version of a gown with the way the open collar drew the eye to her neck and the ends flounced around her slender legs. She'd rolled the sleeves up to her forearms in cuffs to resemble quarter-length sleeves. Her dark tresses still fell over her shoulders, bouncing with every step.

Gracing me with her smile, she skipped across the living room towards the glass doors leading to the back patio.

I followed close behind her as we walked across the smooth wood of the patio and descended the porch steps onto the beach.

The sand was warm underneath the soles of my feet. The crashing of the waves and soft whistling of the wind blew through my ears. In front of me, Brielle skipped ahead, her dark curls bouncing behind her.

She pranced all the way to the spot where the water kissed the land. Pausing for a moment on the wet sand, she allowed the water to stretch up and caress her toes.

I stopped on the dry sand and sat down. I took my blunt from out of my pocket, lit the end, and took a long puff. In times like this, weed was a better painkiller than pills. After a night like tonight, it was what I needed to put my body, and my mind, at ease. As the cannabis clouds fogged my thoughts, I watched Brielle journey further into the water.

She swayed from side to side with the music in her head, embracing the waves in a playful waltz. Stretching her arms out, she twirled in the waves. The ends of my shirt lifted and swirled around her thighs. Above her, the moonlight shone on her umber brown skin. Long silver linings cascaded down her arms and a halo hovered over the crown of her head.

The only thing she was missing was the wings protruding from her back. Between her twirls, the light traced over the curve of her back where they once laid, wide and radiant.

When she smiled at me, I could imagine her in all of her grace, beaming with happiness and radiating with kindness.

Remembering Leo tried to rip all of that goodness away from her made me want to break his fucking skull.

"What are you doing back here?" She asked innocently as she strutted towards me. Her brows rose at the sight of the blunt between my lips. Feigning a gasp, she asked, "And you weren't going to share?"

"Don't tell me you smoke this shit," I replied.

Grinning, she fell down on her knees between my parted legs. "I used to once upon a time." She held out her hand. "Give me some."

I handed her the blunt. My dick twitched in my pants as her glossed lips wrapped around it. I couldn't help but stare as she took a long puff.

She held the smoke in her cheeks for a moment, rocking back and forth in a little happy dance. Tilting her head up towards the sky, she blew out the excess smoke. In her position, the moonlight dripped over the curve of her neck and trickled down over the tops of her breasts. As her head came back down, the silver light trickled over her face, illuminated the twinkling stars in her brown eyes.

I don't think I'll ever understand how the all-powerful creator could allow his most precious angel to fall from the sky. But, at this moment, I was glad He let her past the pearly gates. Grateful He allowed me to spend even a moment in her divine presence.

Noticing my stare, a bashful smile bloomed on her lips. "What are you staring at?" She asked.

"*Un angel*," I replied, letting my hazy mind speak for me.

Her shoulders tilted inward, but stopped midway. Taking a deep breath, her shoulders fell instead. "You shouldn't say things like that," she warned. "I'll start thinking this marriage might be the real deal."

"A man and his crew are dead tonight because he dared to call you out of your name. Does this marriage feel fake to you?"

She averted her gaze as she took another hit of the blunt. "I guess not," she murmured between exhaling the smoke.

My eyes darted to her lips, tracking the clouds of smoke floating around them.

Brielle held the blunt back out to me, and I accepted it.

I inhaled another puff and held it in my cheeks. With my free hand, I curled my index finger and motioned her closer.

A smile tugged at her lips as she scooted closer and draped her arms over my shoulders. Her plump lips opened, ready to accept the smoke.

Holding her gaze, I closed some of the distance between our lips and blew the smoke into her mouth. My dick throbbed as her lips puckered, sucking every single cloud in. Usually, weed gave me a case of the munchies, but every now and again, it gave me an appetite for something better than food.

Watching Brielle tilt her head back once more and blow the smoke above our heads, my body yearned to devour every inch of her silver-dripped skin. I sucked in another hit to battle the fearful thought she'd never let me.

As if she read my mind, Brielle leaned in again, closer this time. The scent of her perfume, a mix of light florals and sensual herbs, wafted through my nose in silent assurance. Her gaze flicked up and down from my eyes to my mouth as she continued to close the distance between us. Soft as a feather, her lips brushed against mine as I blew the intoxicating smoke towards her.

She inhaled again, this time taking the smoke amid a soft kiss.

Chapter 28

Brielle

Oh, I fucked up; I thought as my hazy brain registered the sensation of my lips on Javier's. His mouth was soft, smooth and warm - the latter likely from the cannabis we've been smoking. On his breath, I could still smell the mint of his mouthwash. The scent of his cologne meshed with the freshness, sending hints of pine and sandalwood through my nose. Flutters tickled my stomach as I inhaled the familiar yet foreign smell. The sensation jolted me further out of the trance I'd fallen into.

Ripping my lips away, I exclaimed, "Sorry! Sorry! I'm so-"

As I spoke, I saw a crease furrowing in his brow, bouncing between emotions with every word. Confusion. Irritation. Determination. Amid the last one, he cupped his hand underneath the side of my face and pulled me back to him.

Javier's lips crashed back onto mine, cutting off my words.

His lips molded mine, slowly, attentively, as if he was trying to engrave their shape into the back of his mind. Cautiously, his tongue flicked against the curve of my lips in a subtle lap. It traced around the outline of my lips before moving closer inward, making a beeline for the crease between my mouth. As if knocking on a door, it lapped against the entrance of my mouth, politely asking for permission to enter.

Fighting the chill threatening to run down my spine, I opened my mouth and allowed him in.

His tongue darted for mine, grabbing it into a sensual waltz. One my body felt safe taking part in.

As our kisses deepened, his hand fell from my neck and slid down my arm. He cupped my hips and tugged me upright. Craning his head back to keep the contact between our lips, he lowered his hands to my thighs. Firmly grasping my muscles, he dragged my legs through the sand.

My knees collided with his thighs, and I almost pulled away.

At the subtlest threat of movement, Javier's hand raced to cup the back of my neck, keeping our lips locked together.

With his free hand, he lifted one of my legs and set it over his hip.

Following his silent command, I moved my other leg to straddle him. Our abdomens meshed with each other, fitting together like perfect puzzle pieces. As I settled myself on his lap, I was met with the novel feeling of his dick, hardening with every passing moment, pressing against my pussy.

A chill ran down my spine as my muscles stiffened.

"Hey," Javier whispered against my lips. His arms wrapped around me, embracing me in a sight, secure hold. "It's alright."

"Yeah?" I asked, my voice smaller than I'd prefer.

"Yeah," he replied. He solidified his answer with a kiss, wiping away the doubts and fears budding in my head.

Javier had proven he can be a safe haven. Maybe he can be one for my body, and my heart, too.

Reclaiming control over my body, I relaxed my muscles and lowered myself down on Javier's lap. My pussy pulsed as it came in contact with his dick again. This time, it pressed through the fabric of my panties, desperate to push through and make contact.

Warmth trickled through my pelvis from the touch. Rather than the impulse to jump away, I felt the desire to be closer to him. To feel him.

Desire was once something I only experienced once in a blue moon when times with Leo were good. When he'd perfected his lies to make me believe for a millisecond that he cared about me. When I let myself relish in my own outlandish dreams that maybe his kind words were true.

But, even then, it'd felt nothing like this. Butterflies fluttered in my stomach and my heart pounded a mile a minute in my chest. My hips grew a mind of their own, scooting closer and closer to him until there was no space left between us. I draped the hand still holding the lit blunt over his shoulder. My free hand curled around the back of his neck. I raked my nails through his shortcut curls.

His hands slipped down my body, over my arms and back, to my thighs. Gently, yet firmly, he rubbed his hands back and forth over my legs.

The motion mimicked the waves crashing behind us, pushing and pulling the flow of the desire moving through my body.

My hips moved in sync with his hands, rocking in slow, sensual grinds.

Between my legs, I could feel the friction it created between his dick and my pussy. As I thrust myself back and forth across his rock-hard member, the ache to feel him completely intensified.

My body yearned for more than to be filled. It needed to be kissed, touched, held - loved. Emotions I didn't realize I'd been neglecting poured over me. I've spent a lot of time redefining intimacy for myself. Discovered alternatives for what it could be. Snuggling with my daughter. Curling up in a blanket in a book by myself. Having deep conversations with friends. Yet, I did little exploring of the romantic side. After all of those years of seeing it in such a negative way, I thought I'd be afraid when life gave me the opportunity to do it the right way.

Sitting here, entangled in Javier's lips and limbs, fear was the last thing I felt. Maybe it was time. Maybe it was the emotional work I've been putting in. Or maybe it was the security Javier had so selflessly given to me. But, I sincerely felt safe. And I wanted to feel all the good things this man offered.

Breaking our kiss, he started peppering kisses across my cheek and jaw in a trail towards my ear. His hand slipped from my neck to the collar of the button-down shirt I was wearing. "I want to touch you," he whispered, his deep voice sending pleasant shivers down my spine. Tugging at the hem of my shirt, he asked, "Is that alright?"

"Yes," I murmured, entranced by his intimate spell.

His mouth traveled down my neck in another trail of soft kisses. With every peck, he popped a button open on my shirt.

The soft breeze blew through the novel opening and chilled my bare skin. Shivering, I pressed myself closer to Javier, desperate for more of his warmth.

As if reading my mind, his hands slid from my waist up to my chest. His palms cupped my breasts in a soft hold. Massaging the muscles with his hands, his thumb flicked over my nipple.

The jolt of pleasure shooting through my pelvis intensified from the sensitive touch. My hips bucked more desperately against his, needing more friction to satisfy the ache pulsing in my pussy.

As he rolled circles into my nipple, he sucked and nipped at my neck. His teeth lightly grazed the surface of my skin, barely leaving a mark. Still, his tongue flicked at every tiny dent, soothing the hints of pain.

"Javier," I murmured, as the sensation between my legs became too strong to ignore.

He jerked his head away from my neck and looked up at me. Even his hand ceased its massage as we made eye contact. "Are you alright?" He asked. "Do you want me to stop?"

"No," I replied. My cheeks warmed as I admired the moonlight pouring over his hooded brown irises. Underneath the silver light, his irises were like pools of hot chocolate, dark and rich. Staring into such a beautiful sight made me feel even more absurd for the question lingering on my lips. "I…I want…"

Words were going to sound stupid coming out of my mouth, so I showed him instead.

I grabbed the hand on my breasts and pushed it down my stomach towards my throbbing pussy. My hips bucked to the touch of his fingertips, brushing against the lining of my panties.

Javier licked his lips as he comprehended my silent message. Bringing his gaze back up at me, he asked, "Are you sure?"

"Yes," I said without hesitation. I pushed his hand down further. His fingers brushed against my clit and my hips bucked again at the touch.

His brow raised as he felt the moisture leaking through my panties. Taking the lead, he pressed his fingers against my pussy. Slowly, he moved his fingers in circles, rubbing my sensitive nerves in all the right ways.

Closing my eyes, I tilted my head back and allowed the bliss to pour over my body. A moan climbed up my throat as one of his fingers hovered over my clit to give it the same attention. I locked my jaw closed to keep it from escaping. Still, it slithered out between the tiny gap between my lips.

The sound encouraged him to take it a step further. He ripped his wrist out of my grasp and shoved his hand into my panties.

A gasp left me from the novel sensation of his hands on my bare pussy. His fingers caressed my pussy in slow, meticulous waves. My juices coated his fingertips, and he used it to twirl smoother circles around my clit. Another one accompanied it when he plunged a finger into me.

"Are you good?" He asked.

I nodded.

His free hand grabbed my face and jerked my head upright. "Look at me," he demanded.

I complied and opened my eyes.

"Are you good?" He repeated in a firmer tone.

"Yes," I answered. I bucked against his fingers as an additional confirmation. He didn't need to keep asking me. I wasn't fragile. I wasn't broken. I wanted to be filled with his essence - his bliss. But even if I told him that, I knew he wouldn't listen. Somehow, that made me want him all the more.

Adjusting myself on my knees, I moved myself up and down on his hand.

He matched my slow, steady speed, pushing his finger in and out of me. He leaned in to capture my lips again. His kisses almost distracted me from the pressure of him adding a second finger inside of me.

"Shit, Brie," he muttered against my lips. "You're wet as fuck." Shoving his fingers deeper into me, he asked, "Is all this for me?"

I couldn't find my voice to speak. Between the euphoric sensations of his fingers wedged into my pussy and his tongue twirling around mine, my brain couldn't form proper words. All I could do was offer moans of confirmation into his mouth.

He abruptly yanked his fingers out of me. His hands cupped my legs again and wrapped them around his waist.

"Wait," I whined as I reluctantly pulled out of the kiss. "Why are you stopping? That felt nice."

Lifting me up with him, he rose to his feet. "Because I want to eat your pussy," he replied. "And I don't want a mouthful of sand when I do it."

"Oh," I said, surprised, and aroused, by his bluntness. I tried to hide the blood rushing to my face by burying my face in the crook of his neck.

I felt the rumble of his chuckle as he carried me back to the beach house.

He took me all the way upstairs into his bedroom and laid me down on his mattress.

He eagerly snatched my panties and pulled them down my legs. He licked his lips again as he examined my body, bare and spread wide for him on the bed. A mix of hunger and adoration floated through his eyes. "You're angelic," he said. "Do you know that?"

My legs came together as my body curled inward to dodge the compliment.

"Aht, aht, Brie," he said. He snatched the blunt out with one hand and grabbed my ankle with the other.

I yelped as he pulled me down the bed towards the edge where he stood.

He threw my ankle to the opposite side of the bed, spreading my legs again. "Don't hide from me," he said. He snuffed out the end of the blunt on the nightstand. "Keep those beautiful legs spread and let me show you what a real orgasm is supposed to feel like."

Without another word, he threw one of my thighs over his shoulders and stuck his face between my legs.

I gasped as the flat of his tongue dragged over my wet pussy, licking up every inch of moisture in its journey.

He stopped when he reached my clit and twirled the tip of his tongue over the sensitive bud. His lips came down around it as he sucked it into his mouth.

My back rose into an arch as he lapped at my pussy as if he were drinking from the fountain of youth itself. I lifted my other leg over his shoulders, wrapping them around his head to bring him closer.

Javier obeyed my silent command. Grasping my thighs again, he dove his tongue deep into the depths of my pussy. He explored as far as he could go, licking and sucking and devouring me whole.

I rocked in sync with his tongue. With every flick, my body was overwhelmed with blissful tension and indescribable pleasure. The sensation was so addictive, and I couldn't resist wanting more.

My wish was granted as Javier added a finger onto my clit, giving more attention to the already throbbing bud. His rubbing combined with his tongue inside of me caused my legs to tremble and an overwhelming wave of euphoria to crash over my body. I didn't bother containing the loud moan of content as I lost control of my body. Succumbing to the orgasm, it twitched and shook in Javier's grasp.

Ignoring my jerking movements, Javier continued to suck the soul out of my pussy.

I moved my hand on top of his head, about to push him away. "Javi...Javi, I...I already..."

He snatched my wrist and pinned it down on the bed. "I'm not finished," he said. He continued lapping at my pussy until he licked up every single drop of my cum.

I fell limp in exhaustion when he finally pulled away. My tummy tingled as I watched him emerge from between my legs. His mouth glistened with my juices, and he greedily licked it away.

As he rose to his feet, my eyes fell to the giant bulge in his pants. His dick was so hard that it damn near was about to rip through the fabric of his slacks.

Heat rushed to my cheeks. All of this time had gone towards making me feel good. I hadn't given him any affection. I was embarrassed by my selfishness.

Javier followed my gaze. "Don't worry," he assured me. "We can stop if you want."

"Why? Done with me already?"

Scoffing, he climbed on top of me. He pressed a soft kiss on my lips. "I've barely gotten started. If I could, I'd fuck you all night. Well into the morning. Until you can't take anymore." Tilting his head, he asked, "Can I do that, Brie? Make you cum over and over until your pussy can't produce another drop?"

My pussy throbbed at the proposition. Still, my brain shivered from the memories of how sex used to feel. The humiliation. The pain. The shame.

But Javier wasn't like the men I've encountered in the past. His intentions weren't built on masochistic fantasies or prideful egos. I might not have the full picture of what he wanted from me, but I knew I didn't need to be afraid. Rather, I could trust him.

Finding my voice amidst the anxiety bubbling in my stomach, I said, "Yes."

The ghost of a smile floated over his lips. I only glimpsed it before he was leaning over to grab a condom out of his nightstand drawer.

He pushed his pants down and slipped the condom on. He captured me in a sweet kiss as his fingers returned to my pussy, gently petting in preparation. After a few moments, his fingertips were replaced with the tip of his dick. Slowly, he rubbed it up and down my entrance.

From the brushing alone, I could tell he was wider and thicker than the sizes I was used to. Although my pussy still ached to be filled, my stomach tingled with nerves from how it might feel.

Once his dick was coated in my slickness, he started pushing himself into me. He stopped after every inch, allowing me to react and adjust to the novel sensation.

My fingernails dug deeper and deeper into his shoulders with every move. His colossal size was going to be uncomfortable for a minute, but I was determined to get used to it.

"Relax, Brie," Javier whispered in my ear as he pushed himself all the way inside. "I've got you."

Nodding, I took a deep breath and loosened the tight muscles in my legs. I held onto him tight as he eased himself back and forth in slow, gentle thrusts.

"Shit, Brie," he groaned. "You're tight as fuck."

I opened my mouth, ready to apologize, but was interrupted by a quicker thrust. The movement, though, took me by surprise, eased some of the pressure from his unfamiliar size. In its place, I felt hints of the bliss I was feeling moments before.

Javier pulled his hips back again and rolled them against mine, gradually plunging himself deeper into me.

I wrapped one of my legs around his waist and hooked the other around his. Lifting my hips, I met his thrusts halfway.

Together, we established a rhythm of our own in no time. First, we moved slow and steady, like the beat of an old school R&B song. Javier took his time indulging being between my legs, lazily rocking as if he had nowhere else to be. Now and then, his muscles tensed and his dick throbbed inside of me. He had to grip the sheets underneath us to keep his rhythm, fighting the urge to go faster.

"Don't hold back," I whispered. "I want to feel you - all of you."

My words opened floodgates I was nowhere near prepared for. In a split second, he unhooked my legs from his waist and turned me over onto my stomach.

Gripping my hips, he pulled me up onto my knees. Mercilessly, he slammed his dick into me, pushing himself far enough to collide with the end of my walls.

I shoved my face into the pillow to hide my surprised gasp. Instinctively, my body tried to jolt away from him. But his grip on my hips prevented me from going anywhere.

"Is this still what you want?" He asked. "Because I'm not usually gentle."

"I'm not fragile," I insisted. "I can take it."

"Then pick your head up and hold on to the headboard."

I did as I was told and wrapped my fingers around the rails of his headboard.

"If you want me to stop, you tell me." He grabbed a handful of my hair and yanked my neck back as he gave me another harsh thrust. *"Comprendes?"*

"Yes, Javier," I replied, moaning more than actually speaking.

His hand drifted from my hair back to my waist as his strokes picked back up again. What was once nice and slow quickly became quick and ruthless. His dick hammered into me as if we were in a boxing match, relentlessly assaulting the inside of my pussy with enough intensity to potentially leave a bruise on its walls.

The force of his hips colliding with my ass sent me a few inches forward, and his own hands, still holding my waist hostage, pulled me back into him. With every move, I felt the tip of his dick probing past my pelvis into my stomach.

I held on to the headboard for dear life, struggling to balance myself amidst the pain and intense pleasure. If I wasn't holding myself up, my head was going to go straight into the headboard.

Javier was aggressively beating the shit out of my pussy, but I didn't think he was trying to knock me out.

One of his hands released my waist as I adjusted to the quick, harsh rhythm. One hand slithered down my back and over my shoulder to my neck. His fingers wrapped around my neck and gave it a firm, yet delicate squeeze.

My pussy throbbed from the novel pressure, and I pushed myself harder against his dick to soothe it.

Sensing my need, he slipped his other hand underneath me and feathered his fingers over my clit. Pushing the pads of his fingertips down against my sensitive bud, he twirled quick circles in sync with his thrusts. The sensation sent my eyes rolling the back of my head.

"Shit, Javi," I groaned as stars brimmed the corners of my vision. My body hungrily ground against him, seeking more stimulation. The familiar wave of exhilaration crept up my body in a tiny tremble.

"It's alright, angel," he whispered through gritted teeth. "Go on and cum for me."

His words, firm and reassuring, pushed me over the edge. As I let out a high-pitched scream from the depths of my throat, my entire body exploded into a sea of tremors.

Javier's grip on my neck tightened to keep me steady. He adjusted his thrusts to match the speed of my climax. Not even a moment later, I felt Javier's hot cum pulsing through the layer of the condom, desperate to collide with mine but contained in its cage.

His thrusts, once quick and passionate, slowed into lazy, soft motions.

My body collapsed against the mattress when he finally stopped. Closing my eyes, I tried to steady my uneven breaths.

Javier leaned down to bury his face in my neck. He pecked a trail of kisses to my ear. "How'd that feel, Brie?"

"Good," I sighed. "Really good."

His chuckle rumbled through my ears. It sent another shiver down my spine and straight to my pussy. God, what the hell was this man made of? Almost everything he did made me trip head over heels.

He slipped his hand between my legs and caressed my wet pussy. "Do you have one more in there for me, Brie?" He asked.

I nodded. "Maybe two if you take your time."

He chuckled again. This time, it didn't sound so empty. He flipped me onto my back and captured my lips in a soft kiss. Our lips and tongues tangled again as Javier slipped back inside of me and started fucking me back into a sweet abyss.

Chapter 29

Javier

Buzz! Buzz! Buzz!

For the first time in God knows how long, something other than a nightmare woke me up.

I groaned as the sound pulled me out of the peaceful sleep I'd fallen into. After spending the better half of the night between Brielle's legs, I was exhausted. I'm pretty sure we both fell asleep still intertwined with each other. Too tired to move and too comfortable to care.

I hadn't been expecting Brielle to take me so well last night. Hell, I hadn't been expecting to fuck her at all.

I shouldn't have taken advantage of her - especially since we were both high as a kite. She may have kissed me, but it was my responsibility to squash that shit. I wasn't the type of man Brielle needed in her life. I was only a shield to protect her until the dragons threatening her life were slain. Not her knight in shining armor.

She deserved someone who'll make love to her every night and hold her when she cries. Someone with the emotional capacity to carry her baggage and walk with her through the rough roads towards healing. Someone who could truly love her.

That's not me.

I can't even deal with my own fucking trauma - let alone help someone else with theirs.

I liked Brielle, but I couldn't help her in all the ways she deserved.

The thought pushed me out of the peace I thought I'd found. Coming out of unconsciousness, I felt Brielle's warm body pressed against mine. Her head lay on my chest, and her arms were wrapped tight around my abdomen. Underneath my chin, her hair tickled my neck. In the silence, I could hear the soft sighs of her breathing.

Between narrow and heavy eyes, I looked at the nightstand towards my buzzing phone. I cursed at the sight of my brother's name across the top. As the call ended and the lock screen appeared, I saw a glimpse at the abundance of notifications in a long tower.

I picked up my phone and scrolled through the pile of messages with narrowed eyes. Still half asleep, I skimmed through the messages, only focusing on any repeating words or phrases. There were quite a few questions asking what happened and if Brielle and I were safe. I was almost confused by the urgency of the texts until I cleared some of the smog in my brain to remember the other events of last night.

Leo's spies. The car chase. The bullet wound on my arm.

Now, why the fuck would my dumb ass uncle tell the chaos twins about that shit? He must've been hoping for them to come up here and help him raise hell in the city. It wouldn't be the first time he'd masked his own ill intentions under the guise of a loved one in danger. Probably won't be the last either.

Gritting my teeth, I reluctantly started shimmying out from underneath Brielle's body.

She quietly groaned in disapproval. Her eyes fluttered as she stirred. "Javier," she murmured. Her eyes cracked open at the touch of the space beside her. "Where are you going?"

"I've got to make a call," I told her as I pulled on some sweatpants. "I'll be back."

Heading downstairs, I dialed Adrian's number.

"What the fuck happened?" He snapped not even a moment after the dial tone.

"Nothing Tío Raf isn't handling. I'm fine, so I don't need you worrying."

"Is that Javi?" Lexie's voice echoed in the background. I heard the

214

whooshing static of the phone as she snatched it out of her twin's hands. "Javi, what the fuck is wrong with you? How could you call Tío Rafael, but not us?"

"Because there wasn't anything either of you could do. This is Tío Rafael's turf, and he's going to handle the situation from here."

"Are you hurt?" Adrian asked, his voice clear. I guessed they put me on speaker.

I wanted to lie so fucking bad. The last thing I needed was to set off Adrian's short fuse and have him raise hell up here. "I'm fine," I repeated firmly. "The men are dead, and Tío Rafael will take care of the rest lingering around."

"Tío Raf said you were shot," Lexie said.

Fuck. Why did he tell them that? Hell, maybe he was banking on Adrian coming up here. I bet he'd love to have an actual partner-in-crime.

"Where?" Adrian barked.

"A bullet grazed my arm. It's not a big deal."

"A few inches over and it could've been. I'm going to rip those mother-fuckers apart."

"You are going to stay right there and babysit like I fucking asked you to."

"Is that an order?"

"Yes, and if you break it, I'm going to break your fucking face."

He scoffed. "Man, fuck you!"

I could hear the thumps of his stomping through the phone. "Shit," I murmured as I realized what I said. "Adrian."

"He's already gone," Lexie said. Her voice was closer now that she was alone. "He was just worried. You weren't answering your phone, and you know how he gets when we do that."

"Yeah," I sighed. "I'll apologize to him later."

"Are you sure you're okay?" Lexie asked, her voice softer this time.

"Yes," I assured her as I plopped down on the living room couch. "Listen, I need you guys to tighten up the security measures around our establishments and tell our men on the streets to keep their heads on a swivel. Bianchi likes hiding his men in plain sight. We need to be ready for a fight at all times. Understand?"

"Yes," she replied.

"Good. I'll be home in a few hours, so just hold down the fort and keep cool heads until I get there."

"We will," Lexie said. "Do us a favor and get home safely."

"I will."

I heard footsteps behind me as I hung up the phone. Turning around, I saw Brielle walking into the living room.

My shirt from last night was still draped over her body, and her dark curls were tousled around her head. She wearily rubbed her eyes. "Good morning," she greeted with a sleepy smile.

"Hey."

She sat down on my lap and buried her face in the crook of my neck. "Who'd you call?"

The compulsion to stiffen underneath her warmth spiked through me. But so did the urge to wrap my arms around her and hold her close. I was never good at intimacy. Never thought I would be. For Brielle, I thought maybe I could try. Wrapping my arms around her, I replied, "My siblings. They were freaking out after they heard the news about last night."

"I understand. I'd be worried too." She nuzzled her nose against my skin. "I'm just happy we're both safe."

I shifted underneath her soft touch. "I need to apologize about last night."

"Why? What happened on the ride from the gala wasn't your fault."

"I know, but you could've gotten hurt. Chloe needs her mother."

She picked her face up to look at me. "She has her mother." Smiling, she placed her hand on my face and rubbed my cheek. "Her gentle giant has been doing a great job protecting her."

I lay my hand over hers to cease the movement. "It's not just the shootout I need to apologize for."

Her brows came together. "What do you mean?"

"I mean, we shouldn't have had sex last night. We were high, and while I don't regret it, I don't think I should've taken advantage of your feelings in that state. *Lo siento.*"

"Don't apologize. I kissed you, remember?"

"Doesn't mean we needed to take it as far as we did. I mean, with all you've been through -"

"Don't," she said, her soft voice firm for once. "Don't use my trauma as an excuse to run away from me." Straightening her composure, she adjusted herself to straddle on my lap and meet my eyes directly. "I have had no sense of security in *years*. Then you come along and you treat me better than any man has ever thought to. Around you, I feel like I'm on top of the world and nothing can knock me down. You make me feel protected, cared for, and cherished. Even before all of this, you're the one person I sincerely enjoyed talking to. The only person I felt like I could tell anything to. You're my safe place, Javier, and I want to share this part of myself with you." Her eyes drifted downward. "If you want it..."

I cupped my fingers around her chin and pulled her in. I was never good at words. I probably never would be. So, I offered my reassurance to her with a kiss instead.

In a clearer state of mind, I appreciated the tenderness of her lips and the lingering scent of her perfume from the night before. My tongue flicked against the entrance of her lips, desperate for another taste of her sweet mouth.

Brielle eagerly parted her lips. Welcoming my tongue with hers, she flushed her body against mine. Slowly, her hips began the same slow rocking motion that tempted me last night on the beach. She moved as if moving in the waves, pushing and pulling against my dick. Today, panties didn't stand in the way of her wetness.

Through the fabric of my pants, I could feel her pussy moistening for me. I wrapped an arm around her waist and tilted us to the side. Gently, I lay her down on the couch.

Brielle's legs wrapped around my waist, keeping me close as we adjusted to our new position. She lowered one of her hands to the waistband of my pants and shoved it down to release my dick. Holding it in her hand, she glided it up and down the slit of her pussy, coating it in all of her juices.

Feeling it again, and without a condom, was fucking glorious. So warm and slick and *mine*.

Fuck giving her back to an ungrateful God. This angel belonged to me. And I was going to indulge in her every chance I had.

"We need a-" I cut myself off as I noticed Brielle wave a condom wrapper in her free hand. "When did you grab that?"

"While I was upstairs," she admitted. A bashful smile played on her lips. "I may or may not have come down here with a motive."

I almost smiled. "Addicted to me already?"

Pecking a kiss on my lips, she asked, "Can you blame me?"

Our conversation ceased as Brielle's peck turned into another sensual kiss. Between our entangled tongues and lips, I slipped the condom onto my hard dick and pushed myself into her.

Brielle's pussy fit around my dick like a glove, snug and hot. It took every inch of willpower in my last night not to ravish her like a goddamn caveman. But now, I wasn't holding back. Not when she's already given me the green light to take her as I pleased.

After a few slow strokes to let her get readjusted to my size, I picked up the pace and slammed into her with all the strength I had.

She gasped at the sudden change, but she didn't back down. Locking her ankles around my waist, she used me to pull herself up and down, pushing me deeper and deeper inside of her with every thrust.

I broke our kiss to lower my lips to her neck. I licked my way down to her jugular and sank my teeth deep into her soft skin.

"Oh, Javier," she moaned from the pressure.

Hearing my name encouraged me to bite down harder. Her skin was sweeter than berries and aromatic of all the best smelling flowers. I licked and nipped and devoured every inch of skin I could find. When I ran out of room on her neck, I unbuttoned the shirt she was wearing and turned my attention to her breasts.

I hungrily lapped her nipples into my mouth and rolled my tongue around the hardening buds.

Brielle's hands curled into my short hair, damn near digging the tips of her acrylics into my skin. Her head flew back as another moan eluded her lips. Trembles dripped down her body, and her legs tightened around my waist.

"Uh-uh, Brie, not yet," I said as I pulled my lips off her breast. I grabbed her arms and pinned them down on the armrest above her head. "I want to look at your pretty face while you cum."

"But, Javier," she whined. "You're so deep. I...I'm gonna..." Her words trailed off as I pounded harder into her, determined to push her past the brink she was toddling on.

I watched her eyes roll in the back of her head. Her back followed the movement, arching way off the cushion of the couch into my chest. Her plump lips gaped open as a long note of a beautiful symphony traveled from them.

With her arms above her head and the white shirt flapping around her torso, I saw her celestial form in all its glory. She'd fallen from a sacred place, but found her own slice of heaven on Earth.

Seeing her in all of her glory and beauty sent me over the edge right with her.

Together, we rode out the high ends of our orgasms, bucking and grinding against each other as if our lives depended on it. As we came down, our thrusts gradually slowed to a stop.

Releasing Brielle's wrists, I pecked a kiss on her cheek. I lay my head down on her chest and listened to the rapid beating of her heart.

Her arms looped around me. One hand rubbed my back while the other fiddled with the short curls in my hair.

My eyes fluttered shut in the warmth of her embrace. Some of the perpetual tension in my body eased underneath her fingertips. For a moment, I didn't feel the weight of the demons haunting my mind. The thudding of her heart shooed them all away.

As I lay there, in this masterpiece of a woman's arms, I realized I might've found a safe place of my own.

Chapter 30

Brielle

My leg bounced up and down as I glanced around at the event posters plastered around the lobby of the Hippodrome Theater. When I called the theater director while we were in Los Angeles, he eagerly arranged a time for us to meet. The only convenient time we could find was during my lunch break during work.

Javier offered to come with me, but I didn't want to take more time out of his day. Ever since our night together in Los Angeles, things have been different between us.

He's been coming home at night - and staying until morning. Some days, he'll drive Chloe and me and buy her breakfast on the way to school. We hold hands in the hallways. He kisses me on the cheek or the head whenever he passes by. If I was lucky, sometimes he'd shoot me the faintest hint of a smile. The edges of his lips quirked up the slightest bit, and some of the frost was wiped away from his eyes. The gesture was so quick that I'd miss it if I blinked. Yet, it never failed to stir the army of butterflies in my stomach.

With every instance, the swarm traveled further up my body and started making nests in my chest. Rather than going wild with every glance and kiss, they nestled deeper into their homes and draped themselves over my heart.

I only experienced that feeling once before in my life - when I naively viewed the world through rose-colored glasses and mistook manipulation for affection. The emotions lasted for a moment in time. One so short I'd almost forgotten it.

Feeling it again, and all consuming, was terrifying.

Javier may be sweet, but his emotional capacity clearly had limits. He could have sex with me, but I doubted he could ever *make love* to me. And accepting that was much easier said than done.

I shook the thoughts away as they threatened to bring tears to my eyes. I needed to bring my best attitude if I wanted to impress the director. Over the phone, he didn't give me many details about the positions he was hoping to fill, but a tiny part of me hoped for one in particular.

The theater director, Gabriel Toro, came out from one of the side theater doors wearing slacks and a charismatic smile. He opened his arms wide with excitement as he approached me. "Mrs. Ruiz! It's so good to see you!"

My brows twitched at the surname. Very few people called me by that name - most of them being at the Gala in Los Angeles. It was strange hearing my boss's name on mine. But, I think I liked the ring of it.

Shooting him my best smile, I rose from my seat and extended my hand. "Hello, Mr. Toro. How are you?"

He shook my hand with a soft grip. "I'm well! How are you? You look nervous."

"I am," I admitted with a shrug. "It's been so long since I've been involved in the theater."

He started leading me through the double doors of the main theater and down the velvet steps. "Ah, yes, I remember you telling me over the phone about your past productions. You last performed in high school, right? Female lead in the spring musical two years in a row."

I nodded. "I know that's not a lot of experience compared to the actors you work with now, but I'm well versed in other aspects of the theater, too. I can help with stage management, set design, costume design - I used to do similar tasks at some of my old gigs."

"Well, I'm looking for someone who could fill a few different shoes." We reached the stage, and he tapped the glossy wood. "Hop on up there."

"Wait, you want me to perform? Right now? I - I have nothing prepared!"

"Talent is natural - not rehearsed." He tapped the wood again. "Come on. Show me what you've got."

I timidly walked up the side steps onto the lit stage. The lights warmed my skin and blinded my eyes. My stomach swished and swirled with nerves underneath the director's expectant gaze.

Memories of being up on a stage like this and being watched with greedy eyes rushed to the surface. The familiar feeling of bugs crawling up my spine summoned tremors down my arms. I had to clasp my hands together to cease the shaking.

Closing my eyes, I mouthed the words Dr. Quinn taught me to say in situations like this.

You are strong.

You are secure.

You are *safe*.

At the last one, I took a deep breath and sang my daughter's favorite tune. The silence was filled with my voice, floating through the air like clouds on a sunny day. I felt the vibrations of the sound waves as my tone rose and fell to hit the notes needed for the song. Behind my closed lids, I pictured Chloe laying on my lap, staring up at me in innocent awe as I stroked her hair. Her presence wrapped around my shoulders and pushed me to sing more confidently.

By the time I reached the second verse, I was belting more comfortably and feeling the rhythm in my body. I swayed from side to side, letting the music take over for me. A genuine smile bloomed on my face in its warm embrace. In my brain, we waltzed and twirled to the romantic melody. And before long, it wasn't my daughter's image in my head, it was my lover's.

In his arms, my voice gained more passion and strength, soaring loud enough to reach the galleries.

Sensations I thought were lost flooded back to me. The bliss of flying. The superiority of being on top of the world. The peace that came with the beautiful view.

God, I forgot how much I missed this.

Suddenly, loud claps broke through my ears, snapping me out of the small world I momentarily returned to.

I opened my eyes and looked down to see Gabriel's wide smile.

"Wow," he said as he continued his round of applause. "Javier wasn't kidding: you have the voice of an angel."

"He said that?"

"Yeah. I know Javier isn't one to bluff, but I didn't expect such an eloquent powerhouse! You are amazing!"

My cheeks warmed and my shoulders curled inward from his compliment. "Oh. Thank you."

"And you wanted to stay behind the scenes? No, no, your talent is one that we put front and center." He held out his hand and helped me down from the stage. "I'd love to have you as the leading lady in some of our shows next season."

"I would love to, but I have a young daughter in a dancing academy, so my schedule is a little tight."

"Oh, that's alright. A good chunk of our cast members have children with busy schedules, so we try to accommodate them when we're working on the rehearsal schedule." He started guiding me up the steps again. "You know, Javier also told me you do good clerical work. I've been looking for an assistant theater director for a few months now, preferably someone with a background in theater and business. It's often forgotten that it takes knowledge of both to run a theater. How would you feel about coming to work for me full time as well?"

My brows crinkled together in disbelief. This was all happening too quickly and too easily. There had to be some kind of catch. How much did Javier pay him to give me a job offer? Rather, how much did he donate to the theater?

Gabriel chuckled at my expression. "Don't look at me like that. I'm giving an honest offer."

"Why?" I asked.

He sighed as we reached the top of the theater steps. He leaned against one row of chairs and looked down at the empty stage. "People don't appreciate the smaller theaters like they used to. Most are here because they're passionate about it, but enough of them are here for the cash and the recognition. They see this place as a stepping stone to get them into bigger spaces. And while I don't blame them, I just…I need someone committed. Someone who does this because they want to, not because they're searching for something else out of it." His gaze traveled to me. "Being a director for the past fifteen years, I've learned how to read people. Learned to tell the difference. When I watched you on that stage, your passion shined in more than just your voice."

I smiled.

"Listen," he continued. "I think we could do a lot of great things here together. Now, I don't know how much Javier is paying you, but I can try to match it. I can also offer paid time off when you need it, and we'll work on a schedule that works for you. Whatever I have to do to make sure you're on my team."

"That sounds like more than enough to me."

Grinning, Gabriel offered his hand to me. "Well, welcome aboard, partner."

I eagerly shook it, solidifying our new professional relationship.

I stayed for a little while longer to go over the logistics of my new job. True to his word, he was more than accommodating of my schedule and matched the salary I made at the pharmaceutical company. He went over his tentative schedule for shows and suggested a few he thought I would be perfect to lead in.

My smile couldn't have been bigger by the time I left the theater. The butterflies in my stomach were alive with excitement as I skipped back to the corporate building.

Too excited to hold in the news, I bypassed my desk and went straight into Javier's office.

He was sitting behind his desk and typing on his computer when I entered. Catching the movement of the door, his eyes darted in my direction. "How'd it go?" He asked.

"Good," I replied. "So good that I'm putting in my one-month notice."

"One month?" He asked.

I strolled over to his desk. Standing beside his chair, I leaned my hips against the surface. "Why'd you say it like that? Itching to get rid of me?"

"No." He pushed his chair away from his desk and rose to his full height. He took a few steps to stand in front of me. Gently, he brushed his hand across my cheek towards the back of my neck. Gripping it, he said, "I've been itching to lay you out across this desk."

Blood rushed up my neck to my cheeks as he leaned down and kissed me.

Our lips moved together in a slow, sensual waltz. His tongue traced the perimeter of my lips before flicking between them. Granting his silent request, I opened my mouth and let his tongue collide with mine.

As our tongues tangled, I felt his hand on my leg. Light as a feather, his fingers trailed up my thigh, lifting the skirt of my dress on its journey. "Isn't this a human resources violation?" I teased.

"You're my wife; not my employee," he replied. His fingers traced the hem of my panties, inching closer to my moistening pussy. "And even if you were, what was HR going to do about it?"

A moan crept up my throat as his fingers went beneath the fabric of my underwear and brushed against my pussy. "Javi," I murmured. Reluctantly, I broke our kiss. "You have a meeting in fifteen minutes."

"Fuck that meeting," he grumbled as he peppered kisses along my jaw. "It isn't every day your wife scores her dream job."

I raised a brow. "How did you know Mr. Toro was going to give me an offer?"

"Because you're amazing," he said, pecking another kiss on my lips. "Anyone in their right mind could see that."

Smiling, I grabbed the collar of his shirt and pulled him back in for another kiss. Our kisses grew heated again, and this time, I didn't dare stop them. Desire stirred between my legs, aching to be fulfilled.

Reaching behind me, Javier swiped off the papers lying around his desk. He grabbed my thighs and lifted me up onto the now empty space. Moving closer between my open legs, he pressed his firm torso and hardening dick against my body. He pushed the skirts of my dress up to reveal my panties. As he shoved the fabric to the side, his fingers returned to my pussy. He pressed two digits against my clit and swirled quick circles around it.

My hips bucked into his touch. Moaning into his mouth, I hooked an arm around his neck and my legs around his waist to keep him close. My free hand slithered down to the waistband of his pants and undid the buttons there. Returning the favor, I stuck my hand between the fabric of his boxers and gripped his dick.

He groaned as I pumped my hand up and down. "I need to be inside you, Brie," he murmured against my lips.

I pulled his dick out from his boxers and scooted closer to the edge of the desk to brush myself against the tip. "I need you there, too."

Another gasp escaped my lips as he pushed me down onto my back. One hand went around my neck and the other spread my legs wider for the taking. He took a moment to grab a condom from out of a drawer and slip it on. His fingers grip tightened around my windpipe as he pushed himself deep into me.

My eyes rolled to the back of my head from the combination of pain and pleasure. "God, Javi," I whined.

My words summoned a chorus of harsh thrusts and a tighter grip on my throat. "Don't call out that bastard," Javier demanded. "He had his chance. You, and all your divinity, belong to me now."

His free hand gripped my hips, pushing and pulling me in sync with his as he plunged into me over and over and over again.

With only my lower half getting all the attention, the sensitive spots on my torso ached from the neglect. To ease the sensation, I lay my hands on my breasts. I rubbed my palms over my covered nipples. But, there was too much fabric in the way to stimulate them. And it wasn't my touch they were craving.

I placed my hand atop of Javier's wrist on my neck and gently tugged.

Reluctantly, he released my throat and followed my guide from my neck down to my chest. Understanding my silent message, he grabbed a handful of the neckline of my dress and pulled it down to reveal my bra. Quickly, he shoved his hand underneath the padded fabric and cupped my breast with his large hands. Gently massaging them, he pressed his thumb over my nipple and rubbed circles into the bud.

The sensations from his dick filling my pussy and his hands on my chest collided together in my pelvis, adding more heat to the fire already burning there.

I opened my legs wider for him, granting him more access. Keeping up with his pace, I shifted my hips back and forth across the desk, meeting his strokes head on.

"Shit, Brie," he groaned. His fingers dug into my thighs, pinning them down as he stared down at me. The frost usually covering his eyes was almost gone, giving me another glimpse into all he hid behind it. Lust. Hunger. Passion. Adoration.

If he wasn't fucking me silly, I might've blushed under such a gaze. Right now, though, it fueled motivation for me to keep up with his fast pace. Hell, if I could move better, I might've tried to move faster. Anything to keep him looking at me like this. Like I was the brightest star in the sky.

My legs trembled as the sensations became too much to bear. My head flew back again, and my back curled up into a high arch. Shamelessly, I let a scream escape my lips as euphoria enveloped the entirety of my body and I was sent on a first class trip to cloud nine.

On the other end of the condom, I could feel the warmth and pressure of Javier's release. My pussy throbbed at the thought that one day I might feel it completely. Feel *him* completely. No barriers. No walls. Just him and all the goodness he had to offer.

He stared at me as we came down from the high. His head tilted slightly to the side, and I wondered what he was thinking about. What did I look like in his eyes draped over his desk like this with my dress half undone and my skirt a mess around my waist? Like the loose woman my ex tried to make me out to be? Or something more? Something beautiful? Something pure?

He extended his hand to me and helped me up into a sitting position. Cupping my cheek again, he leaned down to capture me into another kiss.

As much as I wanted to indulge in him again, I needed to remind myself we were still at work and his office door was unlocked. Anyone could walk in on us. And he had a meeting in less than five minutes.

"Javi," I murmured as I reluctantly broke our kiss. "The logistics department will be very upset if you miss that meeting."

"I don't give a fuck how they feel."

"Maybe not. But it'll be me who faces the bitch fest, not you." I pecked a kiss at his lips. "Go. Clean yourself up and head down. A few minutes late is better than nothing."

He tucked himself back into his pants as he moved away from me and headed towards the adjoining bathroom. He stopped midway across the room. "Wait," he said, turning around as if he forgot something. He strolled back over to me and pressed another kiss on my lips. "Congratulations, angel." His lips looped up into a one-sided smile. "I'm proud of you."

My heart exploded into a million tiny fireworks as I admired the expression. It didn't last more than a moment, but I saw it, memorized it, and locked it away in the most sacred depths of my memory. Even after he cloaked it with his usual mask of apathy and walked away from me, I still stared after him in astonishment.

Dimples.

This man had fucking dimples.

Chapter 31

Javier

> **Brie:** I think your sister killed us.
>
> **Brie:** Okay, not Chloe, but me.
>
> **Brie:** Chloe lived her best life. I am dead.
>
> **Me:** I thought you were excited for self-defense boot camp.
>
> **Brie:** I was excited to hit something.
>
> **Brie:** Not to be choked out and bruised.
>
> **Me:** You don't seem to mind when I choke you in bed.
>
> **Brie:** NO ONE ASKED YOU THAT!
>
> **Brie:** ANYWAYS
>
> **Brie:** When will you be home?
>
> **Me:** I'll be there in about an hour.
>
> **Brie:** Okay!

Three little dots appeared under her last message. They bobbed up and down for a moment before disappearing. I stared at my phone for a moment, waiting to see if Brielle had anything else to say.

Today, she and Chloe spent most of the day with Lexie learning some beginner mixed martial arts moves while I hung around the warehouse to oversee some incoming shipments. It's been quiet since I sent Leo's man back, chopped up into pieces on his doorstep, but I wasn't taking any chances. After the past few stunts he's pulled, I needed to keep a closer eye on my product and my men.

Thankfully, this delivery wasn't interrupted by any explosives or unwanted guests. Good thing too. Most of the cargo included new, upgraded guns and weapons I had ordered solely for Leo and his shitty ass men. I would've been pissed if they fucked up the shit I just bought.

My phone buzzed again, and I looked down at the message Brielle sent.

Brie: Drive safe!

I stared at the simple message for a moment, relishing in the jittery feeling it sparked in my stomach.

"Ooo, who's got you smiling like that?" Dante asked from beside me. We were sitting up on the rooftop of an abandoned building we found when we were kids. It had an amazing view of the city. Up here we could see the brightly lit skyscrapers reflecting their lights onto the harbor, filling the water surface with an abundance of stars and comets. We used to come up here often for a break from the wretched deeds our role in crime gave us. Sometimes I came up here alone, just for a slice of peace and quiet. In the mayhem of my life, it was pretty scarce.

Today, we came up here together to decompress after the busy day we had at the warehouse. We split a weed-infused gummy to avoid going home with the stench of cannabis on us. This one was lightweight so we could still drive, but it was enough to put us in the clouds for a little while.

I glanced at Dante to see his stupid smirk plastered on his face. "None of your business," I told him. I locked my phone and shoved it into my pocket.

"Uh-uh, don't hide shit now." He held out his hand. "Let me see. I have twenty bucks that says it was Brielle."

I rolled my eyes. "Fuck you and your twenty bucks."

"Ah, so it was Brielle?" He threw his head back and laughed. "What happened to 'I'm not the type to fall in love'?"

"Shut the fuck up."

He nudged me with his elbow. "Seriously, though: how has married life been? Must be good since you haven't seemed as grumpy lately."

"It is," I confirmed. "Too good."

His eyes fell to the line forming on my lips, and he frowned. "What's wrong?"

"Nothing."

"Don't lie to me," he said. For once, the air of mischief left his voice.

"What's bothering you? You think the relationship is too good to be true?"

I sighed. I could mask my stress and emotions from many people, but not Dante. For as long as we've known each other, he's learned to read between the words I didn't say. No matter how hard I tried, he always saw through my bluff. I used to hate that shit when we were younger, the way he could take one look at me and instantly know what I was thinking. As we grew older, I became grateful for it. Dealing with emotions was hard enough. I didn't want to explain them too.

"Life never stays good like this for long," I said. "I'm worried about Brielle and Chloe when everything goes to shit."

"Ah, don't be so pessimistic. Brielle and Chloe have twenty-four-hour surveillance on them, and they've got you. No one could penetrate that steel fortress even if they tried." He tilted his head. "But that's not what you're really worried about, are you?"

"No," I admitted. I averted my gaze to one if the lights sparkling off the water like a tiny star. "Brielle and Chloe are good people. They're sweet and kind and innocent. They...they make me feel good when I see them. And I don't know... I...I think I'm afraid."

"Of the way they make you feel?"

"Yeah. You know, nothing good ever happens to the people I care about."

"Don't let that fear cause you to miss out on a chance at happiness. You deserve that shit - whether you believe it or not."

I tried to hold on to Dante's words as I drove home. As much as I hated to admit it, he had a good point. Usually, it was easy to lock people out. Most of them only wanted to use me for the things I could offer them, anyway. It was rare any of them were actually interested in the person underneath the money and power.

But Brielle barely asked for anything. All she wanted was for her daughter to be safe, and she would sacrifice her own wants and dreams to get it. I respected her for that. Her selflessness made me want to shower her in all the things she truly deserved.

I just hoped her dreams weren't crushed before she ever had time to live them.

"Giant!" Chloe's voice echoed through the hall as I walked through the front door of the house. The little girl appeared in the doorway from the living room. Her damp curls bounced with every step as she darted down the hall towards me.

I leaned down to her height and caught her in my arms. "Hi. How was your day?"

She gave me a tight squeeze before pulling away. "It was awesome! Ms. Lexie is so cool. She taught me how to do a jump kick! Look!"

She raced down the hall and lunged into the air, thrusting her foot forward in a smooth motion. She stumbled a bit when she landed, but caught herself before she could fall. "I know, I know," she said before I could comment. "I'm working on my landing."

"That was good for having just learned it today."

She zoomed back over to me and wrapped her arms around my legs. "Really? You think so?"

"Yeah." I ran my hand over her head. "With some more practice, you'll have it nailed in no time."

"Mommy said I can start taking mixed martial arts classes once a week. She signed me up and everything already!"

"Yeah, she wouldn't leave until her name was on that list," Brielle chimed in. She appeared in the living room doorway. "Tell Mr. Javier your new goal."

"I wanna be a warrior ballerina! Graceful *and* dangerous."

I chuckled. "If there's anyone who could become a warrior ballerina, it's you, Chloe."

Chloe beamed at the assurance. She grabbed my hand and started towing me into the living room. "Come on, giant! Mommy and I were about to eat dinner and watch a movie! Now that you're here, we can watch Descendants 2!"

I shot a look at Brielle, and she giggled.

"I told you she wouldn't forget," she told me.

We all sat around the living room and ate Chinese food takeout as we watched the movie. Bagheera nestled himself beside Brielle, resting his tiny head close so she could pet it.

Halfway through the film, Chloe lay her head down on my lap. She wrapped a blanket around herself and used my leg as a pillow. The weight of her head grew heavier and heavier as she fell asleep. Before long, I could hear the soft snores rumbling through her nose.

Beside me, Brielle sat curled against my side with my arm over her shoulder and her head on my chest. Her own eyelashes were fluttering, struggling to stay open.

"Are you ready to head upstairs?" I asked her.

"Yeah," she murmured as she reluctantly moved off of me.

I gathered Chloe in my arms and picked her up. The young girl stirred in my arms, but she didn't wake up.

Brielle followed me as I carried Chloe into her room. She moved the sheets back so I could lay Chloe down on the bed.

I took a few steps back to let Brielle tuck her in and give her a kiss on the forehead.

Brielle offered me a weary smile as we walked out of the room and shut the door behind us. She shimmied closer to me and looped her arms around my neck. "Are you trying to stay up for a little while?" She asked. She stood on her tiptoes and pecked a kiss on my lips. "I missed you today."

My arms slithered around her waist. Pulling her close, I said, "How are you feeling about a bath, hm? Ease those sore muscles?"

She smiled. "I'd like that."

"I'll go run the water. How about you go in my room and grab us a little something to keep us awake? There's blunts and gummies in the safe in my tall dresser. The code is 5866. Take your pick and meet me in the bathroom. Okay?"

Nodding, she leaned up to give me one last quick kiss.

We released each other to go our separate directions down the hall. I headed into the bathroom while Brielle disappeared into my room.

I kneeled down on the floor and turned the faucet to run the hot water. As I felt the steam rise from the water, all the ways I wanted to run my hands over Brielle's body crossed my mind.

I may not have said it aloud earlier, but I missed her, too. Lately, my days have become consumed by her and Chloe. Their sweet smiles. Their joyful laughter. Their frilly pink wardrobes. Their bright auras.

Every day, I woke up looking forward to pressing my face into the satin of her bonnet and inhaling the coconut scent of the conditioner she'd put into her hair the night before. I was eager to get out of bed before her to meet Chloe halfway in the hall and get her ready for school. The moments spent alone with Chloe made me feel warm. In her, I saw all the innocence my sister used to have. All the hope she used to hold on to. All the love she used to crave from our own father. And it made me want to pour all the affection we never received into her.

It wasn't my place to do so. I wasn't Chloe's father, nor was I trying to be. But, it was something about seeing how wide she smiled when I dropped her off at school after our short time together that made me think maybe I could be.

The thought, a tremendous and heavy wave, crashed over and damn near sent me scrambling back towards the sands of the sea I found myself in. This shit was getting too deep. My head was well underneath the water, and the liquid was invading my lungs. But, for the first time in my life: I wasn't afraid to drown in the emotions overwhelming me. Instead, I thought maybe it was time to embrace them.

"Javi," Brielle's soft voice cut through my thoughts.

I turned around at the sound. "The tub's almost-" I started. I cut my statement short as I noticed the crease between her brows and the tears welling in her eyes. Before I could ask what was wrong, she held up a small black pistol.

"What's this?" She asked.

Fuck. I forgot I hid the gun in that safe when Brielle and Chloe moved in. The sight of it in her delicate hands made my skin crawl.

Rising to my feet, I stormed over to her and snatched it out of her hand. "Nothing," I told her.

She followed me as I walked back down the hall. "It doesn't seem like nothing," she said. "Why is there only one bullet in the chamber?"

I stopped in my tracks and whipped around. "You checked it?"

Brielle collided into my chest. Looking up into my eyes, growing more livid by the second, she cowered away from me. "I was just curious. Usually, you carry Glocks, not-"

"Don't touch my guns, Brielle. Any of them. The only one you need to be worried about is the one I bought you, understand?"

A shiver started down her shoulders. Gritting her teeth, she stopped it midway and squared them. "Why is there only one bullet?" She repeated her question.

I turned on my heel and continued the journey back to my room.

Again, she continued after me. "Javi, we have to talk about this."

"We don't have to talk about shit."

She scooted around me and stood in front of my bedroom doorway. "Javier, please."

"Move, Brielle."

"No. I won't let you ice me out." She put her hands on my face. "I want to be here for you, but you have to let me."

I pushed her hands off and moved past her into the room. I made a beeline for the open safe. Quickly, I shoved the gun back in its place near the back and changed the code on the safe. The last thing I needed was for this motherfucker to go missing.

As I turned around, I was met with the frown forming on Brielle's lips. I couldn't scrub the image of the gun in her hands. No one was supposed to know about that shit. Not her. Not Dante. Not my siblings. No fucking one.

I was pissed at myself for not being more careful. I've always done such a good job at hiding my razors. My scars. My pills. Even living alone, I still hid all of that shit, afraid a visitor might stumble upon it and start asking questions I wasn't prepared to answer.

Sighing, I slowly approached her. *Lo siento,* I mumbled. I lay my hands on her shoulders and ran them up and down her arms. "I shouldn't have snapped at you."

"No, I'm sorry for pushing. I didn't intend to make you upset. I just..."

Tears welled in her eyes. "I saw it, and I got scared. I care about you…so much, and I don't…I *can't* lose you."

My chest twisted as a tear fell down her face. This is why I kept the gun a secret. I didn't want to hurt the people I cared about any more than I did the first time. It was better they didn't know. Whether the bullet ended up in my skull or not.

I softly brushed the tear away with my thumb. "I'm not going anywhere, Brie." I assured her. "*Prometo.*"

I started towing her out of the room. "Come on. The water will get cold if we wait too long."

We headed back into the bathroom and undressed. In the tub, Brielle sat between my spread legs with her back to me. The silence hung over us like a cloud for a few moments as I massaged the tense muscles in her back. I waited patiently for her to speak, knowing good and well her questions were far from over.

"When were you going to use it?" Brielle finally murmured.

I wished I could tell her it was none of her fucking business, and that I didn't owe her or anyone else an explanation. But she wasn't just a random girl I was fucking. She was my wife. And if she was going to be a widow eventually, I guessed she had a right to know when to expect the blow.

"Supposed to be this year," I admitted. "May or June."

My words felt heavier knowing the months I mentioned were upon us.

"What changed your plans?"

"My father's death." The bastard wasn't supposed to die last winter. His responsibilities weren't supposed to fall on me. His world wasn't supposed to land on my shoulders.

My plan was always to empty the gun when the twins were in a good place. Ideally married and with someone who'd take good care of them. Their partners now were more than capable of handling the twins with patience and care. They'd be alright without me.

Then, my bastard father died, and all of his responsibilities fell on my shoulders. Now, it wasn't just the twins, I needed to be in a good spot. I had our empire - and now a wife and kid - to fucking worry about. I didn't see any of those standing on their own feet without me - not anytime soon.

"Why?" Brielle asked.

"Taking a knife to my wrists didn't work. Thought a bullet would get the job done." The pain I didn't mind. All of my nerves had become numb to the sensation already. It was the damn time it took for the blood to seep out. Had it been any quicker, maybe Adrian wouldn't have walked in on me. Maybe he wouldn't have called for Dante. Maybe they wouldn't have dragged me to the hospital. Maybe I wouldn't have had to see Lexie cry or hear my father's disappointed scoldings. Maybe I wouldn't be alive right now.

She turned in my arms to face me. "Do you still think about using it?"

"Sometimes," I admitted. "It's hard to get rid of thoughts like that, but seeing how much I have to live for helps chase them away."

"What can I do? To help with the load you're carrying."

I looped my arms around her waist and pulled her close. I buried my face in her neck and inhaled her sweet scent. "This," I murmured into her skin, letting her essence chase all the dark thoughts away. "This is enough."

Chapter 32

Brielle

Walking into a carnival was like stepping through the threshold of a time machine. The last time I attended a carnival was when I was in middle school. I remember my parents dropped me off at the entrance and I met up with my friends. One boy in our group, Wesley, spent most of the night trying to convince me this wasn't a normal hangout - not for us, anyway. He bought me a funnel cake, sat close to me on the rides, and even won me a few prizes to take home. Somewhere in the chest of my sacred memories, I still held the sight of his wide smile, filled with braces and dimples, when I kissed him on the cheek at the end of the night.

Staring at the bright lights of the rides and games illuminating the enormous field and hearing the whimsical music blasting through the speakers surrounding the area reminded me all too much of my first date.

Walking with my hand intertwined with my husband's warmed my belly with a sense of déjà vu as we followed Chloe towards the ticket booth.

Javier walked beside me, pacing his long strides to match my speed. His eyes darted around the busy carnival in silent inspection.

When we parked in the parking lot a few feet away, I noticed a few cars lingering on the perimeter. On the premises, I saw a few cops dressed in their uniforms and their gun holsters visible to the naked eye. Clearly, there would be no trouble of any kind taking place here.

My shoulders carried less tension, knowing there were so many people readily available to step in just in case Leo or any of his men were hiding in plain sight again.

Tonight, all I wanted was for the three of us to have some fun. After our tough conversation last weekend, I was trying to spend more intentional quality time with Javier. It wasn't much in comparison to all the help he's given us, but it was all I could give. My hope was that he could begin to see me as a confidant, someone he could talk to if his intrusive thoughts became too heavy to bear or if the compulsion to use the gun struck again. It hasn't been long, but with each little check-in conversation, he seemed more comfortable sharing how he was feeling - even if the answer was always a simple "I'm fine." Maybe I'd be able to get a "I'm good" out of him eventually.

At the ticket counter, I barely had time to reach for my purse before Javier was holding out cash to the clerk. He paid for wristbands for the three of us and led us to a quieter area away from the crowds.

Javier bent down and wrapped Chloe's wristband around her small wrist.

Returning the favor, Chloe took one out of his hand and tied it around his. The bright orange band covered some of the horizontal scars on his wrist.

When he rose to his feet, he gently grabbed my arm and tugged it up.

My skin tingled underneath his familiar touch as he put my wristband on.

Chloe didn't give me time to relish in the sensation before she was pulling Javier off towards the Tilt-A-Whirl.

We spent the next hour and a half letting Chloe drag us into her favorite rides. On the Tilt-A-Whirl and Buccaneer, she whooped and laughed with an infectious joy even Javier couldn't fight. By the end of each ride, I saw his lips tugging up into a small smile, threatening to expose his dimples. In the teacups, we all worked together to meet Chloe's goal of being the fastest spinning teacup in our group. She even towed us on a few rides that lifted us high in the air. I noticed Javier's arm going around her on an airplane ride that dipped up and down as it spun, weary of the ride's durability and ready to protect her at any moment.

Next, we headed towards the carousel. I hopped into one of the cushioned carriages while Javier helped Chloe onto the horse in front of it and strapped her in. Then he came and sat beside me. Throwing his arm over the backrest, he stretched his legs out.

"She's busy, isn't she?" I asked as I watched the mechanical horse rock her up and down.

"Yeah, but she's having fun. That's what we want, right?"

I nodded.

"Are *you* having a good time?"

The question made me look up at him. Flutters ticked my belly as my eyes collided with his. "Yeah, of course. I like hanging out like this - the three of us."

Spending time with both of them made me feel warm and fuzzy. Watching my daughter's joy and seeing someone else contribute to it was an indescribable feeling. Since she was born, I carried the guilt of not being enough for her.

Children needed a village, and besides the ones she created at school and her dance academy, Chloe didn't have one. And while she didn't say it aloud, she desperately sought one. I noticed the frowns she tried to hide whenever we were around larger families, and she saw all the things she didn't have. I found the father's day cards she made at school out of compliance, but threw out the moment she came home. I saw the extra figure in some drawings she made, standing on the other side of her with shorter hair and a mustache.

I wasn't sure how long Javier was planning to stay around now that our relationship has shifted, but it wasn't the time to worry about the logistics of potential heartbreak. I just had to take the moment to relish seeing Chloe indulging in the thing she's always wanted.

After the carousel ride, we paused the rides to get a much-needed snack. We roamed around the food booths until we came across one for Kiara's Sunflower Cafe. Kiara was manning the counter with a younger woman with dark hair pulled into an Afro-puff atop her head. Both of them smiled at Chloe as she skipped up to the counter.

"Oh my gosh, hi Chloe," Kiara greeted. She stepped around the counter to envelop Chloe in a hug. "How are you?"

"I'm good! May we have some of your beignets? I told mommy all about them!"

Kiara smiled. "Of course!" Rising to her feet, she greeted Javier with a wave. As she moved closer, I was surprised when she held her arms out and pulled me into a hug. "Hey," she murmured as she gave me a tight squeeze. "How are you?"

"I'm good," I replied. For the first time in a while, it didn't feel like a lie.

"Hi Bonnie," Chloe greeted the other young woman. She sparked up a conversation with her while Kiara returned behind the counter to pile the powdered beignets into a large paper cup.

"Dante is looking for you," she told Javier. "He's sprinted by here like ten times, asking if I've seen you yet."

"What does he want?"

She shrugged. "Each time there is a different reason. First, one of his sponsors wanted to chat with you. Then, he wanted me to tell you to get your brother. Then, he said he wanted to do a shoot-off at one of the basketball games. After that, I kind of lost track. Is that bad?"

"Nah, that's about right." He pulled out his phone and texted his friend. "What did Adrian do?"

"I don't know - something involving a paintbrush and paint landing on his shirt. I think he was actually mad and blows might've been thrown if Lexie was not there."

I giggled. "Do Adrian and Dante fight a lot?" I asked.

Javier and Kiara shared a scoff. "A lot is an understatement," Javier said. "As much as they bicker, they might as well be thicker blood than Adrian and I are."

"Have they always been like that?" Kiara asked.

"Mhm. They've been picking at each other since Adrian saw him in my room, playing video games when we were younger."

"Aw, maybe he's just jealous," Kiara said. "You know how territorial he is over the people he loves."

"Maybe," Javier agreed with a shrug. "But Dante's not innocent either. He

241

does shit intentionally to set Adrian off. Dumb ass thinks it's funny."

"Dante thinks everything is funny." Kiara finished piling the beignets and held the cup out to us. "Here. On the house."

"*Gracias*, Kiara."

"For sure!" She smiled wider at me. "Maybe I'll see you guys around later!"

I could barely bid her goodbye before Chloe was towing Javier and me off again.

We wandered towards the cluster of small tables to sit and eat our snack.

"Mmm," Chloe hummed in delight from the first bite. "Ms. Kiara makes the best food. Mommy, you should ask for her recipes."

"I would, but I'll probably butcher them." Tasting the beignets myself, I don't think I could recreate the melt-in-your mouth magic Kiara concocted with the fluffy dough and sweet sugar. I knew when to try new things and when to leave it up to the experts. In this case, the latter was clearly best.

I jumped as I felt slender arms fly around my shoulders from behind.

"*Hola!*" Lexie's voice sung in my ears.

I turned around to see my husband's sister hovering over me. Her mane of curls were contained in a high ponytail, with a few tendrils artfully left out to frame her face. A detailed painting of a rose lay on her cheek, matching her red frosted lips.

Beside her, Dante stood dressed in a collared polo shirt, stained with a big blob of paint and jeans. "Hey Brielle!" He said before turning his gaze to Javier. "You better get your brother before I fuck him up."

Javier's deep chuckle rumbled in his throat. "What did you do to piss him off now?"

"Hi Ms. Lexie!" Chloe exclaimed. Her voice stole my attention away from the conversation happening beside us. "You look so pretty! I love your rose!"

Lexie smiled. "Thank you! My brother did it earlier!"

"Mommy, can I get my face painted?" Chloe asked.

"Yes, after you've finished your food."

Nodding, Chloe turned her full attention to her snack. She gobbled up the beignets whole. She hardly chewed any of the bites she consumed. As soon as she was finished, she hopped up from her seat and glued herself to Lexie's side. "What face painting do you think I should get?" she asked.

"Hm." Lexie tapped her chin in fictitious thought. "I think you'd make a beautiful butterfly." She extended her hand to Chloe, and my daughter eagerly grabbed it. In her free hand, she grasped mine. "We'll catch up with you guys later," she told the men before towing us along.

We walked through the crowds towards the face painting station. The space was set up with an array of chairs filled with young kids. Sitting across from them were artists with tattoos and paint on their skin, diligently painting intricate designs on their faces. A young woman with voluminous black curls and a pretty face manned the front of the station, chewing idly on a piece of gum. Adrian stood beside her, sipping on a bottle of water.

"Where's your bitch ass husband?" He asked as he saw us approaching.

"Behave," Lexie warned. "There are child ears present."

"Yeah, that's one dollar in the swear jar," Chloe said. She held her hand out. "Pay up."

Rolling his eyes, Adrian dug in his pocket for his wallet.

"Aw, who's the cutie pie robbing you blind?" The woman asked as she looked down at Chloe.

"My name's Chloe," my daughter replied. "What's your name?"

"Sophia."

"You're really pretty, Ms. Sophia."

Sophia held a hand to her heart. "Oh, why thank you!"

"Don't lie to her, Chloe," Adrian said. "We all know she looks raggedy."

"Shut the fuck up!" Sophia exclaimed as she slapped Adrian in the chest. "Before Dante and I jump you."

"Nobody is scared of y'all."

Lexie shook her head. "Ignore him, Sophia. He's just jealous that your looks bring in more clients than his artwork."

Adrian opened his mouth to tell his sister off, but caught Chloe's eye and thought better of it.

Sophia laughed. "Well, I'll be damned. You *can* control yourself. What a surprise."

Adrian shot her a glare.

Smiling, Chloe wandered closer to him. "Mr. Adrian, can you paint more butterflies for me?!" She pointed around the side of her face. "A butterfly wing around here?"

"Of course." He walked around the counter and held out his hand.

Chloe didn't hesitate in dropping Lexie's hand to grab Adrian's. She skipped along to his long strides as he led her to a pair of empty chairs a few feet away.

I remained with Sophia and Lexie at the front of the stand. I didn't feel the tense need to hover over Chloe. The energy I'd felt over the past few minutes was welcoming and secure. Embracing it eased the tension in my shoulders and the anxious flutters in my stomach.

From my short distance, I saw her chatter away. I couldn't hear what she was saying, but I saw a small smile tugging at Adrian's lips from it.

"Your brothers are so good with kids," I told Lexie.

She followed my gaze. Her eyes softened as she watched Adrian display an array of colors for Chloe to choose from. "Yeah," she murmured. "Who would've thought?"

"I sure wouldn't," Sophia admitted. "But it's cute to see they're nothing but a bunch of teddy bears underneath those hard facades." Turning her gaze to me, she asked, "Do you want to get a little something painted?"

"Might as well while we're waiting," Lexie encouraged.

"Okay. Sure."

Sophia gathered a small paintbrush and a mini easel from around the counter. Grabbing some tubes of paint, she asked, "What would you like?"

I shrugged. "Surprise me."

Grinning, Sophia poured a few drops of white and light blue into empty sections of the easel. She dipped the brush into the white paint and smoothly ran the soft bristles over the side of my face.

Chapter 33

Javier

"Five for five!" The smiling man working the basketball shooting game shouted. "You've earned one of the extra large prizes."

I looked down at Chloe. The little girl stood beside me, cheering me on while I shot the balls into the hoops on the opposite side of the booth. Her arms were filled with stuffed animals I'd won from the other carnival games she'd convinced me to play. Blends of pink and purple filled in the wings of a beautifully painted butterfly around the sides of her face.

"Which one do you like?"

"Hm." Chloe pursed her lips as her eyes raked over the line of over-sized stuffed animals hanging above the basketball hoops. "I think mommy should choose this one, since it's the biggest."

I raised my gaze to Brielle. She was standing on the other side of Chloe with glittery white wings curling around the sides of her eyes. She looked down at her daughter with a raised brow. "Are you sure?"

"Yeah!" She held up her full arms. "I think I have enough! Now, you need one!"

Brielle took a moment to examine the selection. She pointed at a pink and white panda. "Can I have that one?"

The game clerk unhooked the toy and held it out to Brielle.

The panda was damn near twice her size. Still, her slender arms held it up with ease. Her eyes fell down to her daughter as Chloe let out a loud yawn. "Are you ready to head out?" She asked.

Chloe nodded.

We ambled back through the carnival, illuminated by dazzling lights, towards the parking lot.

Only the music of the radio filled the car ride back to the house. Both of the girls were too exhausted to make conversation, and my social battery was too low to break the silence. I had fun with them tonight, but being surrounded by so many people and having to speak so much was draining. In the time I wasn't with the girls, I was dealing with Dante's annoying ass and entertaining some of his company's sponsors. After so much talking, I just wanted a few hours of peace and quiet. I couldn't wait to go back to my apartment, pop in my headphones, and take my ass to sleep.

Brielle's soft giggle yanked me out of the zone I had unintentionally slipped into.

Our gazes clashed as I glanced at her, and she turned hers away from the backseat.

"Chloe's knocked out," she explained.

I peeked into the rear view mirror. My lips twitched at the sweet sight of Chloe with her head propped against the window and her tiny arms around an army of stuffed animals.

"It was a busy day for her," I said. "Didn't she have gymnastics class this morning?"

"Yeah." Weariness dripped from Brielle's own voice. It wasn't long before she was yawning herself.

When we finally arrived at the house, Brielle carefully plucked out all of Chloe's new toys from her grasp. She juggled the stuffed animals in her arms while I unstrapped Chloe and picked her up out of the car.

Still asleep, she rested her head on my shoulder.

I carried her into the house and upstairs into her room.

She stirred as Brielle wiped the paint off her face with a makeup remover cloth. "Mommy," she whined.

"I know, I know, but you can't sleep with it on." Brielle moved as quickly as she could to remove all traces of the paint. Once she was done, she leaned down to peck a kiss at her daughter's head. "Goodnight, sweet pea," she whispered. "I love you."

Her arms looped around Brielle's neck in a soft hug. "I love you too. Goodnight, mommy." Releasing her mother, she looked across the room at me through narrowed eyes. A sleepy smile bloomed across her lips. "Goodnight, giant!"

"Goodnight, Chloe."

Brielle and I exited the room, and she shut the door behind her.

"Are you up for hanging out a while longer?" Brielle asked as we headed towards the steps. Stopping in her tracks, she stepped in front of me and looped her arms around my neck. "We could crack open a bottle of wine and watch TV."

I raised a brow. "I think you and I have very different tastes in television shows."

"Hey, you leave me and my reality television alone! It's entertaining!"

"Well, I guess it's a good thing we won't be doing much watching."

Brielle's smile grew as I set my hands on her hips and leaned down to capture her lips. I kissed her slowly, savoring the sweet taste of her lip gloss. My tongue provocatively flicked at her lips, easing them open. Hers met mine halfway as it entered her mouth. As our tongues collided and tangled, my hands slithered from her hips to her ass. I cupped the bottom of her soft ass cheeks and pulled her closer against me.

Giggling, she reluctantly pulled out of our kiss. "Let me go grab the wine."

"No," I said. "I'll do that. You go into the bedroom and take your clothes off. I want your pretty legs spread wide across the bed by the time I get there."

Her cheeks darkened. "Okay," she said, her voice threatening to tremble.

To ease the tension I saw building in her shoulders, I pulled her close and pecked a soft kiss on her forehead.

We parted ways for a moment while I headed downstairs. I scoured through my wine cabinet, searching for one of the best brands I had on hand. Wine wasn't my first choice of drink, but it was a popular gift from the companies and charities our company sponsored. I decided on an aged bottle of Chateau before grabbing two wine glasses and heading back upstairs. I made a pit stop into my old room to grab my box of condoms in my beeline towards Brielle's bedroom.

When I entered, I damn near dropped everything in my hand.

Just as I'd ordered, Brielle lay naked in the center of the bed. The moonlight splashed across her body. Her skin glistened underneath it, resembling constellations of sparkling stars. The silver light trickled on the surrounding sheets. Large, white streaks flowed underneath the arm draped over her head and curled around her slightly arched back. One of her hands was lodged between her open legs. Her fingers twirled around her moistening pussy in small circles. Quiet hums rumbled in her throat, and her hips rolled in sync with her fingers. Her closed eyelids fluttered as she indulged in the sensation.

This woman truly was an angel.

My angel.

And I couldn't wait to make her feel like she was prancing on the clouds she came from.

Admiring the view, I set the wine and condoms on the dresser.

Brielle's eyes flew open at the soft thud of the items hitting the wood. She snatched her hand away from her pussy as if she were caught trying to steal from a cookie jar. "Sorry," she stuttered. "I - I - I was just-"

"Continue," I demanded. I leaned against the dresser and crossed my arms against my chest. "Show me how you like to be touched."

She pushed herself up onto her elbows. "I'd rather use your hands."

A smirk tugged at my lips as I climbed on the bed. I crawled between her legs and lay my hands down on either side of her hips. I leaned in close enough for our lips to brush as I spoke. "My hands?" I asked. My gaze lowered to her wet pussy, and I licked my lips. "Or my tongue?"

Brielle's eyes fell to my mouth from the movement. "Your...your um..."

"Don't be shy now," I told her. "Tell me what you want."

She leaned forward and closed the bit of distance between our lips. As our mouths locked, her tongue darted into my mouth and made a beeline for my own. A sweet moan rumbled in her throat as our tongues collided and wrestled for dominance.

Her arms looped around my neck, and she scooted closer to flush her hips with mine. Pushing herself forward, she used her body weight to roll us over. Brielle adjusted herself on top of me, settling her wet pussy atop my dick. She rocked her hips against mine, slipping herself back and forth.

I palmed both of her ass cheeks and encouraged the movement with soft pushes.

Brielle moaned into my mouth as I lifted my hips to meet her grinds. With every thrust, my covered dick pushed deeper into her pussy, desperate to enter.

She slipped her hands between us and unbuttoned my pants. Her soft fingers wiggled between the waistband of my boxers to grasp my dick.

It was my turn to groan as she started moving her hand up and down my length.

Brielle giggled at the sound. She pulled out of our kiss and trailed her lips down my neck. I like your moans," she whispered against my skin. Her head dipped lower, cascading towards my abdomen. She tugged my pants down and freed my dick. "I want to hear more."

"Aht, aht," I said before she could put her pretty lips on my dick. "If you're going to suck my dick, then you're going to do it while you're sitting on my face. Get up here."

Brielle's eyes widened at the command, but she didn't protest. She swung herself around and scooted upward to position her pussy over my face. Her hands started pumping my dick, preparing it for her mouth.

I pulled her hips down and latched my lips around her throbbing clit. I sucked it into my mouth and flicked my tongue over it.

Above me, Brielle gasped in surprise. Her hips rocked forward to break my hold on her.

I wrapped one arm around her waist and hooked the other around her leg to keep her still. Pushing her body further down against me, I moved from her clit to the slickness coating her skin. I lapped up every bit, savoring the taste as if it were sweet ice cream on a hot day.

Tightening her grasp around the base of my dick, she lowered her mouth down and swallowed my dick.

The feeling of her warm mouth and slick tongue took me by surprise. I groaned into her pussy.

Bobbing her head up and down, she twirled her tongue around my dick and sucked at my skin. She pushed herself as far as she could go, damn near taking all of me into her throat with every motion. Her hips moved in sync with my lapping tongue.

I picked up the pace as I returned to her neglected clit. I nipped and swirled my tongue over the bud, needing to hear more of the moans rumbling around my dick.

"Javi," she whined as she eased off. "I can't concentrate when you're-"

I dove my tongue deep inside of her to shut her up. She was failing to realize my goal for our intimacy. I didn't give a fuck about whether or not I got off. All I cared about was making her tight pussy explode with euphoria until there weren't any sparks left.

"Shit," she gasped. Her head flew back as she rode the waves of my tongue. She pushed herself harder against my face, suffocating me with her wetness. "Don't stop," she whimpered. Her nails dug into the skin of my thighs as her hips sped up. "Please don't stop."

Obeying her command, I kept up with her rocking hips and whisked my tongue around deeper inside of her. The juices of her orgasm poured all over my mouth as she succumbed to it. I licked up every single drop.

Brielle groaned as she shifted off of me. She turned herself around to straddle me. "Your mouth is dangerous," she said with a weary smile.

"Your pussy is delicious."

She looked away as her smile became bashful. "And let me guess: you're not done with it?"

"Aren't you a quick learner?" I slithered my hand between us and grabbed my dick. Slowly, I traced the tip back and forth between her slit. "Do you like being on top of me?"

She nodded. Her teeth caught her bottom lip as she followed my motion with her hips. "I like being under you too, but..." She took my hand off of my dick and pinned it down above my head. "Tonight, I want to ride you."

"I'm all yours, angel. Do whatever you want with me."

A grin bloomed on her face. She moved off of me for a moment to grab a condom. She slipped it on as she leaned in to kiss me. She licked the remnants of her essence off of my lips before sucking the rest off of my tongue. Her hand slithered between us again, and she positioned my dick against her entrance.

Without hesitance, she pushed herself down onto my lap, taking every inch of my dick in a single thrust.

"Fuck," I muttered against her mouth.

Giggling, she pulled out of our kiss. She lay her hands on my chest and started bouncing up and down on my dick. Her wetness helped her move with ease.

She looked divine. Her dark brown skin sparkled in the silver light. Every curve and line was laced with threads of stars.

Staring at her alone was going to push me over the edge.

I grabbed hold of her hips and met her thrusts halfway, pushing myself deeper into her. "Damn, angel," I murmured. "You ride my dick so fucking well."

My praise encouraged her to pick up the pace. Her hands slid up to my shoulders, and she dug her fingers into my muscles to hold herself steady. She threw her hips back with more force, shoving herself as far down onto me as she could go before coming up. "Javi," she whined.

"You've got it. Keep going just like that." I slipped one of my hands over her hips to her clit. I pressed two fingers against it and rubbed circles in sync to our rhythm.

Brielle's head flew back from the novel sensation. "Oh, Javi!" she exclaimed. Her muscles tightened around my dick, and her legs shook.

"That's right, Brie. Show me how beautiful you look when you cum all over me."

Her body shook as she became undone on top of me. As she tilted her head towards the sky, an angelic cry escaped her lips and she gripped my muscles so tightly that it almost hurt. Despite the waterfall running between her legs, she didn't stop moving. She rode her way through her orgasm, exhausting every single second of it.

Feeling her explode around my dick and watching her pleasure wash over her face was all I needed to reach the same peak.

Brielle collapsed on top of me when we both ran dry. She buried her face in my neck and lay a hand on my face. Her fingers gently traced up and down my jaw.

I wrapped my arms around her and softly traced my fingertips up and down the curve of her spine.

As I lay there, rubbing her back and absorbing the warmth of her body, only one thought raced through my mind: I loved this woman.

I loved her. I loved her daughter. I loved this little family - *our* family.

And fuck did that scare the hell out of me. Not because of the false foundations of our relationship or fear Brielle didn't feel the same way. But because bad things happen to the people I love, and I didn't know if this was something I could afford to lose.

Chapter 34

Brielle

The bright rays of the sun beaming through the windowsill seeped through my eyelids, waking me out of a deep sleep. I groaned as I clutched the pillow I was lying on. My body ached from the walking and riding I'd done the night before. I reached out my hand across the bed in search of Javier's warm body. To my surprise, my hand only caressed the soft sheets.

I reluctantly cracked my eyes open and noticed Javier's side was vacant. Judging from the coolness of the sheets, he hadn't been in bed for a while. Where did he sneak off to?

I pushed myself up and climbed out of bed. Wearily, I padded to the half bathroom connected to the room to wash myself up and throw on a pair of pajamas. As I walked into the hallway, I wasn't met by the sounds of clanking pans or the smell of hot food on the stove. I didn't even hear the television playing in the living room.

Knots threatened to form in my stomach as I instinctively went to my daughter's room. "Chloe?" I asked as I pushed the door open.

Inside, the bed was unmade and her stuffed animals from last night still lay across her mattress. My eyes darted around the room in a desperate search for my daughter's curly hair. Yet, no matter where I looked, I didn't see her.

"Chloe? Javi?" I called as I backed out of the room.

Only silence responded.

Was I dreaming? I had to be dreaming. There's no way in hell they would just disappear like this.

Right?

Maybe they were just outside and couldn't hear me.

I held onto that thought as I jogged downstairs. But they weren't in the backyard or on the front porch. The usual guard dogs were outside in the black vehicles, and so was Javier's car. So, where the hell were they?

Did Javier take her somewhere? Did one of Leo's men break in and take them? Had I woken up into a nightmare? What the fuck was going on?

My surroundings spun around me as the questions whirled around in my head. I needed to know where my daughter was - *now*.

I headed back upstairs to grab my phone and check my messages. My chest tightened as I didn't see any new notifications from my husband or my daughter. Running a hand through my hair, I dialed Javier's number and listened to the dial tone.

On the other side of the room, his cell phone sang the tunes of his ringtone.

"Shit," I muttered. How'd he forget his phone? He never left the house without it.

He must not have been planning to leave. Which made my question so much more urgent. Where did they go? Were they okay? What could I do to find them? Was there anything I could do?

The questions hammered against my brain as I paced back and forth. Chloe doesn't have her phone when we're home on the weekends, so I couldn't call her. I guessed I could go out and ask our guards, but that also meant risking stumbling upon dead bodies if something happened to them. But if Leo took them, then why would he leave me alive? Javier may have killed Carlo in L.A., but it was me he wanted. Unless he was planning to use them as some kind of sick bait.

My worries paused for a moment as I heard the chime of the security system. I hurried back downstairs and let out the biggest sigh of relief as my eyes fell on Chloe.

She smiled at me as I approached her. "Hi, mommy! Giant took me to-" Her sentence was cut off as I enveloped her into a tight hug.

"Oh, sweetpea," I murmured. "I was so worried." I pulled away to look at her. "Are you okay? Are you hurt?"

She shook her head. "No, I'm fine! We walked down to this breakfast cafe a few blocks from here, and they had the best cinnamon rolls I've ever tasted! We bought you back one!"

I smiled. "Thank you, sweetpea."

"You're welcome, mommy!" She turned her head to look at Javier. "I'm going to get my supplies ready! The salon will be open soon!" She wiggled out of my grasp and ran upstairs.

Sighing, I looked up at Javier.

He was staring down at me with a crease between his brows. *"Lo siento,"* he said. "I didn't mean to upset you. She was awake and hungry. And you were sleeping so peacefully that I didn't want to wake you."

"Well, could you leave me a note next time? Or take your phone? I almost had a heart attack." I lunged towards him and wrapped my arms around his torso. "I thought something happened, and I got so scared."

"Hey, hey," he said as he cupped the back of my neck and tilted my head back. "I would *never* let anything happen to Chloe. You know that, don't you?"

I nodded. "I trust you. It's just...sharing her is still new for me."

"I understand. This is new for me too, and I'll be better at communicating when I take her next time. Okay?"

Nodding again, I snuggled myself into his chest. In his embrace, all of my anxiety melted away. If it weren't for his arms around me, I would've sank into a giant puddle. The stones of sleep still lingered on my shoulders, and the panic from a few moments before left me with a small headache.

"Come on," Javier said, as he started ushering me towards the living room. "Let's get you settled down."

He made me lay down on the couch and threw a blanket over my body. He gave me the cup of iced coffee he was holding before going into the kitchen to heat the giant cinnamon roll they'd bought back for me. He was handing the steaming hot plate to me when Chloe came skipping back into the room with her nail polish kit and hair supplies in hand.

I raised an eyebrow as she started unpacking her things. "Do you have an appointment at the salon today?" I asked Javier.

"Mhm," he said. "During breakfast, Chloe told me I needed to add some color."

She grabbed his hand and made him sit down on the floor. "You do!" She held up a royal blue nail polish and held it up to his face. "I think this would go great with your complexion. Right, mommy?"

"Yeah, blue is definitely your color."

Javier rolled his eyes at us.

"Oh, and you can watch Descendants 3 while you're getting worked on! Mommy, can you turn it on for us?"

I grabbed the remote off the coffee table and turned on the movie. Between bites of my food, I watched Chloe pretend to be a nail technician. She attentively prepped Javier's nails with a file and a buffer block. Then, she reached for the bright blue nail polish.

I didn't think he was going to let the paint touch his hand, but to my pleasant surprise, Javier sat perfectly still throughout his entire "appointment."

Once his nails were finished, Chloe moved on to his hair. She wet his short curls and put some conditioning milk in them. She massaged and brushed his curls. Rather than adding butterfly clips in his hair like she does to me, she slicked back his curls into a sleek, suave look.

"Can I do your face?" She asked him. "Mommy bought me some face stickers last time we went to the store, and I haven't tried them out yet."

"You're the stylist here," he told her. "Whatever you need to do, I trust you."

Chloe beamed at the assurance. She ran upstairs to grab some facial moisturizers, her stickers, and the mini makeup kit I bought her for Christmas.

I couldn't help but giggle as I watched her work her magic. She moisturized his face, brushed some blush on his cheeks, applied some silver sparkles on his eyelids, and dabbed some clear lip gloss on his lips. To top off her look, she added some sapphire-gem like stickers in lines on the corners of his eyes.

"There!" she exclaimed when she was finally finished. She handed him her small handheld mirror. "What do you think?"

Javier examined himself. "You did good," he replied. "Really good."

"Now, you need more tattoos! Mr. Adrian has been teaching me how to draw butterflies, and I wanna give you one! Is that okay?"

"Sure. I'm your canvas today."

"Okay! Stay right there! I'll be right back!"

Javier and I shared a smile as Chloe raced back out of the room to grab her markers.

"You do look handsome," I complimented. "The gemstones and the sparkles accentuate your eyes."

Javier shook his head. "Just promise me you won't take a picture. Dante would never let me live this down if he saw this."

"Who said I was going to show the picture to him? What if I wanted it for my own personal collection?"

"Don't tell me you already snapped a few."

"I couldn't help it! You and Chloe just looked so cute! I had to capture the moment!"

"Guard those pictures with your life."

I giggled. "I will. Don't worry. Evidence of your makeover session is safe with me!"

The ends of his lips tugged up the slightest bit, and I remembered how he looked when smiled. His straight white teeth. The crinkle of the corner of his eyes. His dimples. He looked even more beautiful than he normally does.

How rare is it that he lets himself embrace such joy? Besides the time in our office, when was the last thing that summoned such an expression? What was the final straw that almost erased it from his muscle memory?

My heart grew heavy at the last questions. I remembered our conversation in L.A. about his scars and the reasons behind them. I wished I could take off some burdens weighing down on his shoulders. Even if it was just for a moment. Just long enough to see him smile. To see him *happy*.

My thoughts were broken by the sound of someone knocking on the front door.

Javier rose from his spot on the floor, but I waved my hands. "You stay," I told him. "I got it."

I hopped off of the couch and passed Chloe on my way to the front door. I peeked through the peephole to see a man with a suit standing on the front porch. Since there wasn't a bullet in his head, I assumed our guards didn't deem him as a threat. He was likely just a salesman or something.

"Hello," I greeted him as I opened the door. "How may I help you?"

"Brielle Parker?" He asked.

I glanced around behind him. From what I could see, there weren't any other men lingering around the sidewalk behind him. "Yes?"

He held out a packet of papers to me. "You've been served."

"Wait, what?"

The man didn't give me time to blink before the papers were in my hands and he was making his way back down the walkway.

Confused, I looked down at the papers and flicked through the content.

"Brielle?" Javier asked, as he walked up behind me. He set his hands on my waist and leaned in close to look over my shoulder at the papers. "What's that?"

"It's a petition for a paternity test and full custody," I said, my voice shaking at the confirmation. "Leo wants to take Chloe away from me."

Chapter 35

Javier

That *fucking* bastard.

Why the hell was he bringing Chloe into this mess? She was an innocent child. She didn't know about her mother's trauma, let alone the battle between Leo and I. Why the fuck couldn't he just leave her alone? Why couldn't he just leave both of my girls alone? He's already done more than enough damage to last a lifetime. How much chaos and suffering did he want?

Seeing Brielle breakdown as she processed the true meaning behind the petition damn near broke my heart. She'd worked so hard to get to a place where she was smiling every day again. It hurt to see her be knocked right back down to the position I'd found her in not too long ago.

I didn't want Chloe to see her mother's tears, so I called my siblings and asked if one of them could come over and keep her occupied for a few hours. To my surprise, both of them and their significant others showed up on the front door prepared to help.

They all stayed downstairs playing salon with Chloe while I consoled Brielle upstairs in her room. I sat beside Brielle on the bed, holding her while her body shook from her sobs.

"He can't take her," she croaked. "We don't know what he'll do to her."

"He won't," I assured her. "He won't lay a hand on Chloe. I'll take care of this. *Prometo.*"

True to my word, I spent the better half of the night in Miles's workshop.

He tracked down the petition back to the lawyer's office from which it was filed and gave me all the information I needed to take my ass down there.

I took Dante with me. The lawyer was probably dirty, but he thought it'd be good to at least try to approach him civilly. I was too pissed off to be friendly, so Dante planned to do most of the talking.

We strolled into the small, storefront office closer to the South Side of the city late in the early evening - right before closing time. Inside, the office was pristine and stylishly furnished. The receptionist's desk was empty, but the door leading to the main office was open. A man with brown hair and silver specks sat behind the desk in a suave black suit. He stood up and greeted us with a smile.

"Hello! Hello! How may I help you, gentlemen?" He asked, his voice full of charisma.

"Hi, Martin Geisman, right?" Dante asked as he extended his hand. "My name's Dante, and this is my partner, Javier."

The man eagerly shook it. He offered his hand to me, but stopped short when he noticed my icy stare. "Nice to meet you both." He motioned to the cushioned chairs across from his desk. "Sit. Please."

I followed Dante's lead and sat down.

"We wanted to look into a custody suit," Dante explained.

"Custody or adoption?" Martin asked. "I've had a few couples come by here, confusing the two. Do one of you have a child from a woman, and the other would like parental rights? Or are we looking to start a new family altogether?"

Dante chuckled. "Nah, nah, we aren't looking to file. We were hoping you could answer some questions about a suit you recently filed."

Martin's air of charm diminished as his bright smile fell. "Questions? Are the two of you police officers?"

"Not necessarily." Dante opened the jacket of his suit to flash his gun. "But we have some authority in this case."

Martin's Adam's apple bobbed at the sight. "Right." Clearing his throat, he folded his hands on his desk and tried to cease the tremble traveling down his spine. "Ask away."

"There was a custody petition you filed about two weeks ago for Leonardo Bianchi. Is that right?"

"Yes. He filed for a paternity hearing, following a petition for full custody of his daughter. Pretty cut and dry on my end - for now, anyway. Sometimes these custody battles can get a little nasty."

"Well, unfortunately, we've got to make it a tad bit messy earlier than expected. We need you to drop that suit."

"What? But, I can't! Only the petitioner can-" His words were cut off as I grabbed a handful of the man's hair and slammed his face into the desk. Colliding with a hard thud, the man let out a yelp of pain.

Pinning him there, I threatened, "You either drop the suit or I break your face."

"I'd choose wisely," Dante added. "If you have a busted ass face, you won't be able to put it on billboards and get out of this tiny office."

"Listen, listen, I - I - want to drop the suit. I really do, but *legally* -" Again, his sentence was cut short as I lifted his head and jammed it back against the wood of the desk. This time, I aimed to send his nose straight into the hard surface. Hearing the crack of the bone was almost music to my ears.

"I don't think you're understanding where we're coming from, Martin," Dante said. "Legalities are not our concern."

Whimpering underneath my grasp, Martin replied, "But if I drop the suit without the petitioner's permission, I could be disbarred! I could-"

I took out my gun and pressed it against the back of his neck. His breaths sped up under the cold mouth of the barrel.

"What's more important?" Dante asked. "Your career or your life? We don't give a shit about either, so that answer is completely up to you."

"Okay, okay. How - How about this? I - I'll call the petitioner and -"

"Yeah," I spoke up as I released him. "Call him."

Blood poured from Martin's nostrils as he picked his head up. Cowering in fear, he reached for the phone and dialed a number.

I made a point of watching and commit the number to memory. I might need it later.

"Hi, Mr. Bianchi," Martin struggled to upkeep his cheerful tone. "It's

Martin Geisman! I wanted to reach out and talk to you about the suit you recently filed through my office. You know, I was thinking it might not be such a good idea. You know, maybe this doesn't have to go to court if you just have a conversation with her..." His voice trailed off as another voice buzzed on the other end. Martin's eyes flicked between us and our guns. "Yes." He nodded as the voice continued to speak.

His hand trembled as he held the phone out to me. "He wants to speak to you."

I snatched the phone from his hand. "Why are you hiding behind lawsuits like a little bitch?" I asked. "Stop being a pussy and face me like a man."

"I was planning to," Leo quickly replied. "But then you went behind my back and fucked *my* girl."

"Married," I corrected. "And let me tell you, she couldn't be happier. She gets to experience a *real* orgasm every night."

"You can have the whore, but the little girl is mine. She's my flesh and blood."

"Your blood doesn't mean shit to her - and it never fucking will. Drop that fucking petition and leave Chloe out of it."

"No," Leo replied. "As her father, I have-"

"You are *not* her father," I snapped.

"Oh, but you are?" Leo chuckled. "Don't make me laugh, Ruiz."

"Chloe is a child. If you want to hurt me, then do that, but don't hurt them."

"Careful, Ruiz. Your Achilles heel is showing."

I gritted my teeth. "What will it take for you to drop it?"

"Ah, now we're getting somewhere. Hm...let's see...what do I want?" He paused for a moment, letting the tapping of his fingers fill the silence. "I think that's a conversation to be had in-person, don't you think?"

"All I need is a time and a place."

"I need assurance that this will be a peaceful conversation first."

"My men will stand down *for now*. If you send another court order to my doorstep or one of your men near any of my girls, they'll be back in full force. Are we clear?"

"Crystal." Chuckling, he said, "I'll talk to you soon, Ruiz."

Chapter 36

Brielle

"Mommy! Mommy!" Chloe's voice hummed in my ears, waking me from a deep sleep.

"Hm?" I mumbled. My brain was still hazy from the fog of unconsciousness.

I felt her small hand on my shoulder as she started shaking it. "It's time to wake up! Come on!"

I reluctantly cracked my eyes open to see my daughter standing by my bedside. She'd changed out of her pajamas and into a simple tee shirt. Her thick, curly hair, freshly washed and blow dried last night, was still pulled up into a high ponytail. A smile tugged at her lips, though her eyes were bright with anxiety. It was an expression I've learned to recognize on the mornings of a dance recital.

Chloe would always wake me up at the crack of dawn, too anxious to sleep in. But from the bright glow of the sun shining through the room, it must've been later than the six o'clock hour I was expecting.

"What time is it?" I asked as I groggily lifted myself up.

"Nine-thirty," Chloe replied. She tugged at my hand. "Come on. Get up! We need to get started on my hair, so I can be at the theater by twelve!"

Yawning, I let her tow me out of bed and down the stairs. The smell of sweet pancakes and hash browns swirled through my nose as we walked closer to the kitchen.

Javier was at the sink, washing dishes, when we walked inside. He looked

264

over his shoulder at the sound of our footsteps. *"Buenas días,"* he greeted me.

"Good morning." I continued my stride towards him, aiming for a few sleepy kisses and a hug, but Chloe shoved me towards the island.

She pulled out the chair for me and made me sit down. "Giant and I made you breakfast," she explained.

Blinking, I noticed the nice plate of fluffy pancakes, golden hash browns, and crispy bacon. A steaming cup of coffee sat beside it. "Aw, thank you, sweetpea."

"You're welcome! Giant taught me his mom's special recipe! They're cinnamon pancakes, and they are delicious!"

"Wait, you two ate without me?"

Chloe shrugged. "We were starving, and you were snoring." She wandered over to Javier's side. I didn't notice the step stool beside him until she stepped up onto it. "Do you need any more help?"

"No, I'm done here," he said. "How about you get the hair supplies? Save your mom some time."

"Okay!"

I smiled as I watched her hop off the stool and dart out of the room. "Thank you," I told Javier. "For getting up with her. You know, you don't have to do it all the-"

"I want to," he cut me off. He turned to face me as he dried his hands with a paper towel. "You're always sleeping so peacefully, and I'm up, anyway."

"Not sleeping well again?" I asked. The past few nights, I've felt him tossing and turning in his sleep. Sometimes I hear him get out of bed in the middle of the night and disappear for an hour at a time before coming back. He'll hold me close and rub my back or arms. The motion lets me know he's not asleep, but the steady rhythm of his heart tells me he's at least relaxed.

But I couldn't talk. Ever since I received the court order, my sleep schedule has been a wreck too. I spent most of my quiet time before bed overthinking and worrying about the worst-case scenarios. The only thing that drove the bad thoughts away was when Javier lay there with me. The rhythm of his steady heartbeat and warmth of his body chased away any worries I had.

But, he's busy some nights and doesn't get home until late - or not at all. On those nights, I did my own tossing and turning, struggling to fight against fear's grip on my neck.

Javier promised me nothing would happen to Chloe, but I still couldn't help but fret. Something just felt off. Out of all the motherly instincts I've gained, this was the one that I couldn't ignore.

"Yeah," he admitted.

"Come here," I told him as I held my arms open.

Obeying my command, he walked over to me and wrapped his strong arms around me.

I melted into his tight embrace, the feeling of security washing over me. "Nightmares?" I asked.

"Mhm."

"The same ones or...?"

"Different."

"About what?"

"Don't worry about it," he said as he pulled away. He nodded towards my plate. "Eat your food. I tried to save you another half hour, but I don't know shit about hair." He moved away, and I grabbed his hand.

"Hey," I said. "Talk to me."

His gaze fell to our intertwined hands. He stared at them for a moment as the walls he'd temporarily let down rose again.

I offered a squeeze to reassure him. I didn't want him to keep holding all of his emotions inside. It wasn't healthy, and I didn't want him to fall back into the mental holes he'd dug himself out of. I could help him carry whatever weight he was carrying, but he needed to let me in first.

"Later," he promised. "Today is Chloe's day. I won't put a damper on it." He brought my knuckles to his lips and gave them a soft kiss. "Eat your food. You've got maybe ten minutes before Chloe finds where I hid the hair stuff."

"Giant!" Chloe called from the other room. "I need help!"

"Ten minutes," Javier repeated as our hands fell apart.

I smiled. "You're the best."

The faintest ghost of a smile still painted his lips as he exited the room.

As promised, ten minutes went by before Chloe was marching back into the kitchen with Javier following behind her and a pile of hair products and styling supplies in his arms. She towed me out of the kitchen and pushed me onto the couch. She parked herself between my legs and fiddled with the remote to put on a movie.

Javier wandered upstairs while I started on Chloe's hair.

I ran a hot comb on low heat through her hair to straighten out the kinks of her curls. Her dark tresses fell well over her shoulders. She kept running her fingers through it, amazed at how long it's gotten. I avoided putting heat on her hair as much as possible. Recital days were one of the few instances I straightened it. Although Chloe loved her natural curls, she adored the length of them.

Once I was finished with the hot comb, I pulled her hair up into a high bun. Per her costume and ballerina standards, she had to wear the style. I tacked down her hair to lie flat on her head and used a donut hair bun to tuck the strands around.

By the time I was finished styling, loud knocks sounded at the door. Chloe raced through the hall to answer it. Cheerful greetings echoed through the hall, and I recognized the voices of my sisters-in-law.

Kiara and Lexie came strutting down the hall, dressed in vibrant sundresses and makeup bags in their hands.

Earlier this week, in a group chat Lexie created for the three of us, they offered to come over to help Chloe get ready. Both of them were eager to lend a helping hand and take some stress off of my shoulders.

Chloe curled up next to Lexie on the couch and helped her pad through the abundance of products in her bags.

"Any restrictions on her makeup look?" Lexie asked as she glanced up at me. "I was thinking of some mascara, some white eyeliner around her eyes, and some gloss. Oh, and glitter, of course!"

"That's fine," I told her. "I'm gonna go get ready. I'll be down in a bit!"

I ran into Javier on my way to the bathroom. My brow rose at his sleek black suit and freshly trimmed facial hair. "Where are you off to looking this fine?" I asked, as I looped my arms around his neck. The alluring scent of his cologne wafted through my nose and the thought of never letting him go crossed my mind.

"I have a few errands to run with Dante." He leaned down to kiss me. "We'll meet you guys at the theater later."

Content with his answer, I reluctantly released him. "Be safe," I called to him as he continued down the hall.

Upstairs, I took a quick shower and changed into a simple dress. When I returned downstairs, Chloe was glowing with confidence. Her copper brown skin sparkled underneath the artificial light pouring through the windows, and a wide smile stretched across her face. She twirled in front of the mirror, admiring her look. I could only imagine her face once she put her costume on. No one could tell her a damn thing. And I adored that for her.

The three of us dropped Chloe off at the theater hosting the recital. She barely looked back at us as she rushed towards the backstage to meet with her friends.

We still had some time before we needed to be seated for the show, so we made a quick trip to the mall. Lexie and Kiara followed me through the hallways as I made a beeline for one of the jewelry stores. I needed to pick up an order I made almost a month ago for Chloe. It was a small silver charm shaped like a swan with glittering rhinestones that resembled feathers.

When Chloe first started ballet, I had a feeling she was going to fall in love with it. She shared my love of musicals, but rather than the singing, her attention was drawn to the choreography. She loved mimicking the dance moves and adding her own flare to the songs.

The first time I picked her up from ballet class, the width of her smile as she beamed with joy proved my intuition to be true.

Before her first recital, I thought of getting her something to commemorate her efforts. One day she might make a career out of it, and I wanted her to have a physical souvenir of all the progress she makes. I bought her a charm bracelet with only one charm - a flower to represent the floral costume she wore for her first show. With every recital, I added another charm. It's become a ritual of ours for Chloe to clasp the new charm on her bracelet to seal a memory for every show.

Javier, Dante, and Adrian were waiting for us when we arrived back at the theater. All of them were decked out in suave suits and carried bouquets of flowers. My heart swelled at the sight.

We all sat together to watch the recital. While all the groups gave stellar performances, Chloe's class stole the show. At such a young age, all the kids showed such talent and discipline in their performance. They pranced and twirled and skipped around the stage with so much grace they looked like they were floating. Chloe, the center of the dance, was stunning. Her body moved as if the music had possessed her. Each twirl and kick and jump were perfectly synchronized with the chords of the songs. Even the softest notes flew through tiny jerks and waves of her joints.

As the story ended, her classmates surrounded her as she lowered to the floor and posed with her arms held high over her head and her legs in a perfect split.

A smile tugged at Chloe's face as the audience exploded into a round of applause. Breaking her pose, her eyes scanned through the crowd and fell on our small party. The bright lights caught the glimpse of the moisture forming in her eyes as we cheered louder for her.

After the show, we all shuffled through the crowded main hall to find Chloe's class. Usually, they kept them in clusters around the building to make it easier for parents to find their children and take photos against the dance academy's photo backdrops.

"Mommy!" I heard Chloe's voice before I saw her.

My eyes darted through the crowd in search of her, and I saw her jogging towards me with her arms outstretched.

Smiling, I bent down and caught her in my arms. "Hi, sweetpea!" I said as I squeezed her tight. "I'm so proud of you!"

"Did I do good?" She asked, her voice small.

"Good?" I pulled away to cup her face. "Baby, you were amazing."

She beamed at the compliment. Her smile grew as she noticed the rest of her posse walking up behind me. She left my arms to give hugs and accept flowers from the others.

Tears welled in my own eyes as I watched her be surrounded with so much love. Lexie and Kiara hyped up Chloe's grace and ability, and Dante joked about Misty Copeland having to watch her back. "You'll be the next trailblazer on the ballet scene," he told her.

Chloe giggled wildly as Adrian picked her up and twirled her around.

When she reached Javier, who was standing behind the rest of the crew, he stooped to her height and offered her the flowers. She bypassed the florals and lunged into his arms.

His face fell in shock as she wrapped his arms around his neck and squeezed him tight.

She whispered something low enough for him to hear, and his lips threatened to quirk into a small smile. His arms came around her and he returned the tight squeeze.

"We need pictures!" Lexie exclaimed when Chloe finally pulled away from Javier.

We hurried her over to the nearest backdrop and took turns taking pictures with her in front of it.

My heart pulsed with emotions I couldn't explain at the sight of the happiness radiating off of my daughter's face. Chloe has never said it aloud, but she's always wanted something like this: a tribe, a support system, a *family*. For a long time, I was afraid I'd never be able to give her one. At some point, I think we both might've accepted the fantasy would never be a reality. But, seeing these people, jagged at the edges but filled with hidden goodness, uplift and support my daughter was indescribable.

She deserved to experience love like this. And, despite the initial circumstances of my marriage to Javier, I was glad we could give it to her.

When we left the recital, we took Chloe out to her favorite restaurant. We all sat around in a U-shaped booth, chatting and celebrating Chloe's success.

Chloe, amazed by the interest the adults had in ballet after her performance, had no problem being the center of the conversation. She talked and talked about everything she knew about the dance and all the things she's learned.

"Mommy says one day we'll go to the Metropolitan Opera House and see a real ballet production," Chloe explained.

"Ooo, that will be fun," Kiara said.

"Can we come?" Lexie asked. "I need a good girl's day out in the city."

"Yeah, of course. Maybe this summer?" I glanced at Javier for confirmation, since he apparently had all the secret connections for performance tickets.

He gave me a nod.

Smiling, I squeezed his hand.

He'd been awfully quiet throughout dinner. Although he was attentive to the conversation, he rarely contributed more than a few words. After seeing him come out somewhat out of his shell in private, I missed hearing his voice.

I leaned my face into his neck and shifted my head upwards to whisper into his ear. "You alright?"

He turned his head to look down at me."Mhm." His eyes softened as he took me in. "Just enjoying the moment."

I damn near turned into jello under such a tender stare.

His dimples threatened to make an appearance as he noticed my body melting against him. Chuckling, he gave me a soft kiss on my lips.

"Isn't this a sight for sore eyes?" a familiar voice jolted us out of the short bliss.

We pulled out of the kiss, and our gazes darted towards the sound. On the other side of the table, I met a grin and a sly pair of hazel eyes. And suddenly, the peaceful high I was riding came crashing down.

Chapter 37

Javier

This motherfucker; I thought as I locked eyes with Leo. His dumb ass would have the audacity to approach me in broad daylight, surrounded by my family. He must've thought our last conversation was bulletproof. Little did he know, my words would go out the window if I thought my family was in danger.

Our temporary truce aside, the only reason Adrian wasn't putting a bullet in his head was because Chloe was sitting right next to him. My brother may condone more violence than I cared for, but he'd never commit any crimes in front of a child.

From the corner of my eye, I saw his arm dart in front of Chloe, shielding her from the sharpness of Leo's gaze as it flicked around the table.

"Aren't you all one big, happy family?" He mused.

"Adrian, Dante," I commanded my brothers. "Take the girls home. Lexie, you stay."

Chloe's brows came together as she watched her celebration dinner crumble into pieces. "What's going on?" She asked.

"Nothing, sweetpea," Brielle lied to her. She shot me a worried glance as she ushered Chloe out of the booth.

Chloe's eyes went to Leo. "Who is he?"

"No one," Brielle replied quickly.

"Don't lie to the child," Leo countered. He fixed his gaze on Chloe and offered her an off-putting smile. "I'm your daddy, baby girl."

Seeing the fear slither over Chloe's eyes was enough for me to reach for my gun. Fuck the truce. I'd be damned if I let anyone intimidate Chloe. She was too innocent, too pure - too good for the darkness of this world. Especially the hellish realm Leo crawled out of.

Lexie grabbed my wrist before I could draw it. "Don't," she hissed quietly. "Just because he's not armed doesn't mean his eye in the sky isn't."

Gritting my teeth, I released my hold on the handle of my gun. As satisfying as putting a bullet in his head would be right now, it wasn't worth putting Brielle and the rest of my family at risk.

Leo's eyes followed Brielle and Chloe as they walked out the restaurant. "A little ballerina, huh?" He muttered. "Made for the stage just like her mother."

"What the fuck do you want?" I asked.

Leo's gaze returned to me. The faux smile fell, and he shot daggers at my sister. "This conversation isn't meant for such dainty ears."

"Don't make the same mistake your brother did," Lexie warned. "This dainty body can, and will, fuck you up."

He scoffed. "And to think we almost welcomed you into our family with open arms? Now, you're off stealing mine."

"They weren't yours to begin with," I retorted. "You wanted to talk in person, so get to the point."

"How does it feel to be raising another man's family?" Leo asked, ignoring my demand. "Does it feel good, using a woman and child against their patriarch?"

"Their patriarch?" I could've laughed. "You're delusional."

"Am I? You're the one sitting here playing step-father of the year."

"What is this? You gotta get a few jabs in before you wave the white flag?" Lexie asked. "Make yourself feel like your dick is ten inches bigger than it actually is before you fuck the dirt?"

"Your sister better watch her mouth, Ruiz."

"Or what?" Lexie leaned forward on her elbows and raised a brow. "My knife will be wedged so far into your throat before you even *think* about laying a hand on me. Play with me if you want to."

"She's right," I cosigned. "It's in your best interest to stop testing us and tell us what the fuck you want."

"I want your men to stand down. For good."

"And why would I tell them that?"

"Because you don't want to see your pretty wife dragged through court. I'll go the whole nine yards - ask for full custody and make her out to be the fraud she is. Then, when my offspring is in my care, well...I guess that's a surprise you'd rather not see."

"Godless bastard," Lexie cursed under her breath.

"You really think you'll be granted custody? All it'll take is one phone call and the FBI will be up your ass with human trafficking and racketeering charges. Not only will you be denied custody, but you'll also end up rotting in prison. Do you really want to play that game?"

"I'll have both of their throats slit. How about we play *that* game?"

His words flipped one of the idle triggers in my head. Memories I tried so fucking hard to repress came rushing to the forefront. Guns in my face. Knives on my back. My siblings screams in my ear. My mother's blood on my hands.

That night, I swore to myself to never let a predicament like that happen again. I swore I wouldn't let anyone get close to me. Not enough that they could be used against me. I promised marriage, only if absolutely necessary, would only be a piece of paper, and my offspring would be my trainee and nothing more. I closed myself off so much to the idea of family outside of my siblings that I accepted I'd die alone. I'd rather that than face the same fate as my father.

But now, with Brielle and Chloe, I found myself in the same situation I was hoping to avoid. And like my father, I had two options: lose my pride or lose my family. Unlike him, I wasn't willing to take a gamble on the latter. He might've been content with losing everything that mattered to him, but I sure as hell wasn't. I could rebuild my reputation. I couldn't bring back the dead.

Leo smiled at the silence. "Ah, finally getting somewhere, aren't we?" Gaining confidence, he unbuttoned his suit jacket and took a seat on the opposite seat of the booth. "We're even, Ruiz. Have been for a while now. Both of our fathers are gone. Why fight when we don't have to?"

"Because you and your fucked up organization are a bunch of perverted scumbags," Lexie said. "And you all deserve to burn in the deepest pits of hell."

"No one was talking to you," he snapped. "I don't even know why you're here. Isn't Harris your right-hand man?"

"Sure, when she's out on vacation," I replied.

"Clearly, you haven't done your research," Lexie said. "Too busy keeping tabs on your ex that you don't even know the organization you're fucking with. Not as smart as your dad, huh? That's alright. Your brother wasn't the brightest crayon in the box either. Made him an easy target."

At the mention of his brother, Leo tensed back up. Flaring his nostrils in frustration, he turned his attention back to me. "Either you back down, or I slaughter them - *all* of them," Leo threatened, his voice laced with the darkest of intentions.

"Fine," I said. "We'll back down."

Lexie's head whipped towards me. Her brows were creased in disbelief and her eyes were wide with surprise. "What?"

I ignored her. "You're right. There's no need for any more blood to be shed. You go your way, and we'll go ours. All I ask is you keep your clubs far away from our territories - and please note there are more than you think. It'd be best if you just packed it up and went back to wherever your ancestors came from."

Leo smiled in victory. "That's alright. You all can have the States soil. Business is much easier overseas, anyway." He held out his hand to me. "Give me your word, and we'll be straight."

Without hesitation, I shook his outstretched hand. "My men will back down, and you'll get the fuck out of my face. Are we clear?"

"Crystal."

He tried to pull his hand out of my grasp, but I tightened my grip. His lips twisted in discomfort as I squeezed so tight I felt some of his bones crack under the pressure. "But, let me be clear: if you even think about coming near Chloe or Brielle, I'll dig a hole and throw you down in the devil's pit myself. *Comprendes?*"

"Yes," Leo said quickly.

I let go of his hand and watched as he yanked it back.

Rubbing his sore knuckles, he rose from his seat. "Nice doing business, and war, with you, Ruiz. Can't say it's been a pleasure."

"Fuck you," I spat.

I watched him walk out of the restaurant with his head held high and his tail hiding between his legs.

"Are you really going to let him off scot free?" Lexie asked from beside me.

"No," I murmured once I was sure he was far out of earshot. "But he'll be easier to kill if he thinks he is."

Chapter 38

Brielle

What the *hell* was that?

Where did Leo come from? How did he find us? What invisible shield was he wearing that he felt comfortable enough to walk into a den of wolves? And with what right did he think he had to speak to *my* daughter?

The look on Chloe's face when he revealed his identity was forever etched into the deepest parts of my brain. The crease of confusion between her brows. The shiver ran down her spine at the pet name he called her. The slight gaping of her lips as she looked at me for confirmation.

An honest conversation about her father was bound to happen eventually, but not right now. She was still too young and pure to understand the complexities of the situation. Here and there, she's asked questions, but I could always give her short, vague answers to keep her satisfied. My plan was to give her the whole truth when she was seventeen or eighteen. But, even then, I worried she may not be mature enough to process it. Hell, as an adult, I still struggled to cope with the events that brought my sweet girl into this world. Dancing around the topic hasn't been my favorite thing in the world, but I've only done it to protect her innocence for as long as I could. Now, with his face no longer a mystery, I don't think we could avoid such a discussion anymore.

Chloe raced up the steps when we finally arrived back at our house.

I called her name as I chased after her.

Ignoring me, she continued to sprint down the hall towards her room.

The slam of the door hit me like a hammer to the chest.

I stood paralyzed outside of the door, unsure of what to say. I wasn't prepared to have this conversation anytime soon. Let alone right now, after such a fantastic day. *Her* big day.

I fought the tears welling in my eyes as I knocked softly on the door. "Chloe?" I called. "Sweet pea, can I come in?"

Silence replied to me.

Sighing, I tried the doorknob and thanked God she didn't lock it.

Inside, Chloe was standing in front of her vanity dresser, wiping her face with a makeup cloth. Her high held head said she was fine, but the moisture in her eyes told otherwise.

"Here, sweetpea, let me help," I said as I approached her. I expected her to yank the wipe away when I reached for it. To my surprise, she handed it over without a fight.

I gently wiped away her makeup and helped her out of her costume. I didn't bother to fill the tense silence between us. Right now, Chloe just needed to process, and I will give her the time to do that. After all, there wasn't anything I could say or do until I knew the specifics of what was bothering her. Then, I'd be able to answer her questions more clearly and address the emotions wafting through her.

Once she was dressed in her pajamas, we lay down together on her bed. We stared up at the string of lights decorating the perimeter of the walls, illuminating the room like tiny stars.

"Mommy," Chloe finally spoke.

"Yes, sweetpea?"

"Was that really my daddy?"

"Yeah."

"He doesn't seem very nice."

"He's not."

She turned her head to look at me. "Is that why I've never met him? Or why you never talk about him? Because he's not a good person?"

"Yeah." I set my hand on her head and caressed her hair over her bonnet. "I've just been trying to keep you safe."

"Do you think he would hurt me?"

"I don't know."

"Did he hurt you?"

Tears pricked at my eyes from the innocence laced in her question. I didn't want to lie, but I didn't want to go into details either. A simple "yes" was all she needed to understand.

Her lips pulled into a deeper frown. "I'm sorry, mommy."

"No, no, sweetpea, you do not have to apologize - for anything. You are my saving grace. My little angel. My light that illuminates my world when it is dark. And I love you - more than words can ever explain. Nothing will ever change that. Understand?"

She nodded. "But sometimes kids can have a new daddy, right? One who won't hurt them?"

"Yeah. Some kids get lucky that way."

"Do you think I'll be lucky?" She asked, her voice now inked with hope.

"Maybe. Why? You have another daddy in mind?"

Yawning, she scooted closer to me. "I think having my giant would be nice."

More tears welled in my eyes at the sweet thought. "Yeah?"

"Mhm. He likes to play games with me, and he's been teaching me how to make breakfast on the weekends. And he makes you smile. That's my favorite thing about him." She paused as her eyes fluttered. Her body started weighing heavier with every passing moment. "Yeah," she confirmed sleepily. "I want him to be my new dad."

I couldn't help but smile. I didn't say it aloud, but I wanted that for her too. The image of all of us together was easy to picture. Javier and Chloe holding hands walking a few steps ahead. Me trailing behind with another smaller hand in mine or around a bulging belly. Life could be so simple. So blissful. So *full*.

Laying next to Chloe as she fell asleep, I closed my own eyes and let the daydreams of a better future take over. Only the alert sound of the front door opening prevented me from staying there.

I listened to the footsteps as they made their way upstairs and towards

Chloe's room.

Javier's tall figure appeared in the doorway. Lines hung around his mouth, and the frost I thought melted had returned. The muscle in his jaw bounced as he stared at me and Chloe for a moment.

I offered him a small smile and reached out my hand.

He hesitated there for a moment. His foot lifted, and I thought he was going to cross through the threshold. But he turned on his heel and continued down the hall.

An uneasy feeling stirred through my stomach as I remembered the conversation from which he'd just come from.

I wiggled my arm out from underneath Chloe's head and exited the room. Closing the door behind me, I followed Javier down to his room.

He was leaning in front of the small safe. It beeped with every number he tapped.

"What did he say?" I asked.

"You don't have to worry about those court papers," Javier replied. "You won't be hearing from him again."

I wanted to sigh in relief at the news, but I couldn't ignore the tension radiating off of my husband's back. "What else did he say?"

"It doesn't matter." He grabbed a pre-rolled blunt from out of the safe, stuck it in his mouth, and brushed past me on his way back out the door.

I almost shivered from the chill as he passed me by. "It does if it's bothering you," I said, following him. "Hey! I'm trying to talk to you!"

He ignored me and continued towards the steps. He walked to the back patio and lit the blunt. His broad shoulders rose and fell with his first puff.

The icicles of the wall protecting his soul had risen again. This time with sharper tips.

But, I didn't care. I bore the pain of their prickles as I walked up to him and wrapped my arms around him. "Javi, please," I whispered. "Don't shut me out."

"When is Chloe's last day of school?" He asked, changing the subject. It wasn't the response I was looking for, but I guessed it would do.

"Two weeks. Why?"

"Do you still want to take her to Disney World?"

"Yeah, but-"

"Tomorrow, do some research on which resort you want to stay in. Price doesn't matter. Don't tell Chloe. It'll be a surprise."

My brows stitched together in confusion. His urgent tone didn't match the words leaving his mouth. I worried his kind deed didn't hold the intentions I was hoping for. "You said you'd come with us on vacation."

"I'll be there. A day or so later, but I'll be there."

"Why? Where will you be?"

"*Dios mio*, stop asking so many questions," He snapped as he shook himself out of my grasp. His eyes burned with a blue fire as he finally turned to face me. "You wanted protection, right?"

"Yes, but-"

"Then be quiet and let me do my job."

A harsh lash accompanied his words. Only this time, I didn't flinch from the pain. I've spent too much time in the last few months learning how to be strong and stand up for myself. I couldn't let all of that go to waste because the person I cared about most was the one I needed to face. Squaring my shoulders, I matched his stern stance. "Stop being an asshole and let me do mine."

He scoffed. "What job is that?"

"Loving you," I replied firmly. I hadn't meant to say it, but there was no turning back now. If this marriage was ever going to work, if he was ever going to let me in, then he needed to know how I felt. Even if he didn't feel the same way.

The anger in his eyes instantly blew out at my words. He took a step back as if I'd hit him. His brows turned up in a mix of shock and disbelief, as if he couldn't believe what he just heard.

"Look, Javi," I softened my tone as I stepped toward him and reached for his hand. "I know this marriage was supposed to be fake, but it's real to me. It's been real...for a while now. I...I can't sleep when you're not next to me. I worry about you when you're not here. And when you are around, all I want to do is take care of you. Make sure you're fed and hydrated and nurtured and *happy*. God, I'm trying so fucking hard to make you happy. Because you have given us so much, and I love you, and you deserve all the care you so selflessly give everyone else."

"You...you love me?" His voice was so small. Like a child asking for forgiveness after sticking their hand in the cookie jar.

Hearing him sound so frail, so innocent, made me want to hug him. "Yes. And Chloe does too. She sees you like a father, Javi. *Her* father."

The ice perpetually rimming his irises melted, transforming into water that filled his lower lids but refused to fall. "No. No... She shouldn't... You shouldn't..."

"But we do." I squeezed his hand. "More than you know."

"You don't understand. People who care about me... Everyone I..." The words got caught in his throat as his voice threatened to crack. He looked away to hide the embarrassment. "It never ends well for them. And I...I can't lose..."

Oh. Stringing together the half sentences, I painted the full picture. Leo hadn't threatened Javier. He threatened *us*.

And as frightening as the thought should've been, all I felt was more sorrow for the grief-stricken man in front of me.

"Hey," I murmured. I lay my hands on his face and made him look at me. The slight movement shook his tears out of their prison. They rolled down his face like raindrops on a windowsill. "We are not going anywhere. We are right here. *I'm* right here."

His hands cupped my face, and he rolled his thumbs over my cheeks. "Yeah?"

Standing on my toes, I brushed my lips against his to solidify my point. "Yeah."

His hands slid to the back of my neck, and he pulled me in to close the short distance between our lips.

He kissed me with a passion I've never experienced before. His tongue sensually traced the line of my lips and entered my mouth, making a direct beeline for mine. Our tongues slipped and slid over each other in a tangling tango. One hand gripped the back of my head while the other slithered down to wrap around my waist. His muscular arms caged me against him in a hold so tight it almost hurt. Fire seeped through his body and burned mine, awakening the depths of desire between my legs.

As always, Javier read my silent call. He released my neck and lowered his hands to my thighs. He lifted me up off my feet, and I wrapped my legs around his waist.

Lips and limbs intertwined, he carried me upstairs into our bedroom. He lay me down on the bed, and his fingers went to the hem of my dress.

My own fumbled with the buttons on his shirt. I plucked open every one and pushed his shirt off of his shoulders. A moan of content escaped my lips as I ran my palms over his scarred skin. The way he felt was so comforting and warm - like laying underneath the covers after a long day and sinking into the mattress. He felt like home. *My* home.

He lifted my dress off my body and reluctantly broke our kiss. He pecked kisses all over my face, down my neck, across my chest, and over my stomach. I expected him to stop at my pussy, moistening with every single touch, but he didn't. He continued down to my legs in a silent mission to kiss every single inch of my body.

My neglected pussy ached as I watched his lips trail along my thighs and calves. "Javi," I whined as I tried to grab the back of his neck and pull him towards my throbbing pussy.

"Relax, angel," he murmured against my skin. He looked up at me like a desperate man who finally found his will to live. His eyes, absent of apathy and disinterest, burned with crackling blue flames. "Let me take my time to worship you."

Only this man could have his head between my legs and still give me butterflies.

He continued his journey up my thighs until he finally reached my pussy. His tongue wasted no time attending to my throbbing clit. He sucked the bud into his mouth and flicked the tip of his tongue up and down over it, soothing the ache.

I sank into the mattress with a deep sigh. My legs fell further apart to give him more access.

His tongue slithered down from my clit, further down my pussy. He traced the length of it in long, rhythmic laps.

My own hands trailed down to the back of his head, and I held his head there as I ground my hips in sync with his tongue.

He wrapped an arm around my leg and heaved it over his shoulder. Pulling me closer, he dove his tongue deep into me and devoured me whole.

I arched my back like a cat in heat from the intense wave of pleasure that washed over me. I continued to buck my hips to the movement of his tongue, riding the incoming waves like an expert surfer.

"Javier," I called his name as I felt a wave too big to surf. This one was going to fall over and consume me in an inescapable grasp.

Javier didn't slow down. He sped up his movements, determined to push me over that edge.

I dug my bare heel into his back as my body combusted underneath the intensity of my orgasm.

He still didn't stop. He licked up every single inch of my cum until there wasn't a single drop left.

I smiled at him as he came out from between my legs.

His lips glistened with my juices, and desire raged in his usually calm eyes. He climbed back up and captured my lips.

I tasted myself on his tongue, but I didn't care. Under the spell of Javier's touch, there was nothing that could tear me away from him.

I undid the buttons of his pants and slid them down his waist. I bucked my pussy against his dick in a silent, desperate request.

Our moans collided as he pushed himself into me, diving so deep that I damn near felt him in my stomach. The rhythm of our hips felt much different from before. Rather than quick, rash thrusts fueled by lust, we moved in slow, intentional grinds. Moving against each other, we pushed his dick all the way inside of me and slowly came apart to bring him back. We took our time, cherishing the sensation of being with each other.

Wrapping my arms tighter around him, I dug my nails into Javier's back. His fingers gripped my thighs in response, keeping them pinned around his waist. Our sensual kisses hid our moans, and we rarely broke besides to take quick breaths for air. Intertwined like this, it felt like more than our bodies were interlocked. Through his chest, I could feel Javier's heartbeat synchronizing with mine. Without a condom for the first time, I felt him completely. His warm skin and hot essence filled in pieces of me I thought I'd lost forever.

As we kissed and caressed and bucked into each other, it didn't feel like we were just having sex - we were making *love*.

The thought made my head dizzy, and I almost tried to refute it. For a moment, I let myself think Javier couldn't possibly feel the same way. His wall was insurmountable, and there was no way in Hell I, of all people, had broken past it.

But I couldn't deny the soft look in his eye as he lay beside me when we were through. He stared at me with such tenderness and adoration in his eyes. His thumb traced over my cheek and lips, memorizing the shape as if he were going to take a test on it. And as much as I wanted to question it - to hear him say it aloud - I knew I didn't have to. The events of the night had said more than enough.

Chapter 39

Javier

"That is the stupidest plan I've ever heard of," Adrian muttered, intentionally loud enough for me to hear.

My siblings and I were sitting around my office, discussing our last move to get rid of our enemy. I only wanted my inner circle to know about it. Most of my men may be trustworthy, but it wasn't their loyalty I was worried about. As far as everyone on the outside knew, Leo and I had come to a reluctant agreement. I didn't need word getting out that our truce wasn't sincere. If I wanted to take him out, then I needed to do it discreetly. And, like always, my brother had a problem with that.

"What's stupid about it?" I asked. My plan was to have a spiked drink delivered to him at one of his clubs in the state over. Over the past few days, he's been having special rates to rake up on money before they shut down. With all the crowds the sales bought, he'd never suspect or care where the drink came from. Especially not if it came from one of his women. One sip was all it'd take for the bastard's heart to stop beating. He'd die surrounded by his vices, and during the party, no one would blink an eye.

"It doesn't make a statement. All it says about him is that he's stupid enough to accept liquor from any pretty girl he sees."

"I'm not trying to make a statement. I'm trying to get rid of a pain in my ass."

"We should be, though," Lexie added. "Those bastards had a hit on us - *all* of us. They don't deserve fucking mercy."

"Then what do you propose? Kidnap him? Skin him alive? Dismember all of his limbs? Then, spread the parts around their clubs? What the fuck do you think that'll do?"

"Send a message not to fuck with us. When mom died, dad went down to Mexico and he-"

"I know," I cut her off. "I was there. I remember." It was one memory I couldn't forget. My father, blind with rage, executed almost an entire sector of the cartel that'd come after us - damn near single handedly. He brought Adrian and I along to reinforce the lesson he was trying to teach us. That we couldn't afford to be vulnerable. To be kids. To be fucking human.

I don't think Adrian ever had many feelings about it. After the beating we'd taken, I think he was just relieved for my father's hands to be on someone else. With the rage burning through his own veins, he took inspiration from it. If there was one thing my brother loved more than his fiancé, it was a room full of bloody corpses.

But me - I loathed that shit. The disgusting gore. The chaotic violence. The wet blood that covered my hands when we were through. All of it made my fucking skin crawl.

Making a big, bloody scene was never my style, and it only set a bigger target on our backs. My father spent a good few months ending that war. And even then, we still had to watch our backs just in case we missed one.

I always thought there was a better, smarter way to handle feuds. Not by alliances, but by giving them quiet deaths. Ones that couldn't be traced back to us.

My father liked my ideas once I was confident enough to share them. He knew if we wanted to upkeep our front as law-abiding citizens in the public, then we needed to clean up our act. Especially with the public watching us more closely after our mother's death.

And if things did ever need to get ugly, most of us needed to be as far away from that shit as possible.

As much as I wanted Leo to have an agonizing death - even the Lord knew he deserved one - I wasn't willing to risk putting my family in danger.

"Listen, I know the two of you want to avenge dad's death in a way he would've been proud of, but we can't afford to start a war - a *real* one. Leo kept the shit between us quiet because I made it personal. God knows who he's associated with or related to, nor do I plan to find out. It's best we keep this on the down low. Worse case scenario, his affiliates think his men planned a mutiny and turned on him."

"No," Adrian said. "We're letting him off too easily. He deserves to suffer."

"He will - when he gets to Hell. Not as satisfying, I know, but that's what we're working with."

"What about you?" Lexie asked. "You can't run surveillance on this alone."

"Dante will be with me on the nearby roof running command. Roman will be inside the club giving visuals and administering the poison, and Miles will be surveilling audio with wires planted inside the facility."

Lexie crossed her arms and shifted her weight onto her hip. "And where does that leave Adrian and me?"

"Back on babysitting duty," I explained. "I'm sending Brielle and Chloe out to Florida the night before. You'll go up there with them, ensure their safety until the mission is through, and then you'll be free to decide whether you want to stay or go."

"What?" Adrian exclaimed. "That's not fucking fair!"

"Life's not fair," I quickly retorted.

"No, *you're* not fair," Lexie jumped in. "You can't keep putting us on the back burner whenever something big happens. We're not little kids anymore. We are resources."

"And I'm using you."

"Yeah, as bodyguards," Adrian muttered. "Come on, Jav, you know Lexie and I have more potential than that."

"No one is saying you don't. It's just..." I trailed off as I struggled to put together the words I wanted to say. As much as I wanted to rely on Adrian's trigger happy fingers and Lexie's cunning stealth, I was reluctant to do so. But if I didn't explain myself, then my siblings were going to resent me for it. And I didn't want them to look at me the same way we all did our father.

"Nothing can happen to either of you," I murmured. "With mom and dad gone, you two...you're all the family I have."

"And *you're* all we have," Lexie said. "We almost lost you once, Javi. We don't want to risk going through that again."

I averted my eyes. I'll never forget the pain in my sibling's eyes after I woke up the day after trying to take my life. Rather than their loud ass mouths, I was met with complete silence and tear-streaked eyes. Lexie was too choked up to speak, and all Adrian could mutter was a question of how I could do that - how could I leave them?

To this day, I still don't have an answer. Not one that would make me feel less like a shitty brother who wanted to be selfish for once.

Sighing, Lexie dropped her arms and walked around my desk. Wrapping her arms around my neck, she said, "Look, I know we're pains in your ass and we don't say it often, but we love you, Javi. You're our big brother - our protector - and we need you." She squeezed me tight. "We'll *always* need you."

I put my hand on her forearm and gave it a gentle squeeze. "I know."

"So, let us help."

"I am. Watching over Brielle and Chloe may not seem like a big job to you, but it's important to me. They're our family now too, and it's our job to protect them. This isn't about your potential. This is about keeping our family safe. Can you both understand that?"

"Yeah," the twins muttered in unison.

"You really love them...don't you?" Lexie asked.

My silence spoke louder than words ever could.

Adrian chuckled. "And you swore up and down you weren't going to fall for her. Now, look at you."

I threw a pen at him. "Shut the fuck up."

The twins laughter erased the tension in the room. With Lexie's arms around me and Adrian teasing, it was almost like we were kids again. The warm sense of nostalgia sparked a yearning for home. But it wasn't my bed I was looking forward to. I wanted to see my girls.

At the late hour, I knew they were both likely asleep. But laying eyes on them, knowing they were safe, relishing knowing that they were mine, never failed to fill the gnawing emptiness in my chest.

As expected, most of the lights downstairs were out when I walked through the door. Only the stove light shone in the kitchen, putting a spotlight on the covered plate of food on the stove top.

I shrugged off my suit jacket and headed upstairs. As I passed Chloe's room door, I stopped to peek through the cracked door.

She was tucked tight in her bed with her arms around one of the stuffed animals I bought her and Bagheera sleeping at her feet. Her small eyelashes fluttered as she peacefully dreamed.

I moved away from the crack and continued down the hall to my bedroom.

To my pleasant surprise, Brielle was still awake. She sat cross-legged on the bed, her body swallowed by one of my old tees and her kinky curls pulled up into a bun. The light of the laptop in her lap illuminated her bare face, emphasizing her high cheekbones and plump lips.

At the sound of the door creaking open, she looked up at me. Stars twinkled in her eyes as she smiled at me. "Hey, Javi," she happily greeted. She moved the computer off her lap and opened her arms wide for a hug.

A smile tugged at my lips as I walked into her embrace.

Her arms wound around my neck, and she squeezed me tight. "Are you okay?" She murmured into my neck. "You're home later than usual."

"I'm fine."

She pulled away to get a better look at me. Her brows stitched together as she examined my weary expression. "You look stressed," she commented. "What's wrong?"

"Nothing," I insisted. "The twins are giving me grief - as usual."

She giggled. Her gaze, and fingers, lowered to my shirt. She undid the buttons and slid her hands beneath the fabric. Rubbing her soft palms against my chest, she said, "Well, now that you're home, you can take a load off. Relax."

I caressed her cheek and slipped my hand down to the back of her neck. Gently, I tilted her head back. My gaze lowered to her lips as I spoke. "Are you gonna help me relax?"

Her arms looped around my neck. "Maybe."

"Maybe?" I leaned in to close the distance between us. As our lips brushed against each other in a soft kiss, I flicked my tongue at the small space between hers. My dick throbbed in my pants from the tease of her sweet taste.

Her tongue met mine halfway as our kisses intensified. Eagerly, it lapped and tangled with mine.

I pushed my weight against her and lay her down on the bed. I skimmed my hands down her shirt to her bare legs. As I caressed her smooth skin, I pulled her legs up around my waist. One hand drifted over her thighs and farther up her legs.

She moaned into my mouth as I pressed my fingers against her pussy. It moistened under my touch.

I almost grinned against her lips at the sound. Applying more pressure, I started rubbing small circles into her pussy, aiming to coat my fingers in her juices.

"Wait, wait," Brielle murmured. She broke our kiss to look at me. "Did you eat the food I left out for you?"

I pecked kisses across her face towards her jaw. "I'll eat it later. I have an appetite for something else right now."

"Aht, aht," she said. She assertively pushed me away. "You'll have your dessert after dinner. Now, go."

I raised a brow. I know this girl wasn't giving me orders.

Brielle held her ground under my stare. Her own brow rose, and her lips pursed in a stern pout.

Damn, confidence looked good on her. I had half a mind to disobey just to see more of it. But it was late, and I didn't want to keep her up longer than she wanted to be.

"Fine," I gave in. "But those legs better be spread by the time I get back up here."

Leaning back against the pillows, she stretched out her legs on either side of me. In her position, I could clearly see her pussy, damp with desire. "Already done. Just don't keep me waiting too long."

"I won't," I promised. I captured her lips again, reluctant to leave her. Hell, I was hoping to distract her long enough for her to forget about her request.

All I wanted at the moment was to be inside of her. To be immersed in her divinity and all the gifts that came with it.

But Brielle wasn't having that. Again, she broke our kiss and shoved me away. "You're not slick," she said. "Go eat. Now."

"I'm trying to eat you."

She grabbed a pillow and hit me with it. "Go," she said between her giggles.

"Alright, alright." I finally climbed off of her. My eyes raked over her as I backed away from the bed. I admired the way she looked laying against the bed, her hair messy and her bare lips swollen from our kisses. It was like watching an angel lounging on clouds. A simple, yet glorious sight.

I engraved it on one wall of my mind. The image will keep me satisfied for the few minutes I'll spend away. Motivate me to shove the food down my throat as quickly as I could, so I could devour what I truly wanted.

I forced myself to look away so I could finally leave.

"Love you!" Brielle called after me.

Like a fan snagging a home-run baseball, I caught the phrase and held it close to my heart. I should've thrown it back, but just like the fan, I was so absorbed in the euphoric emotions of experiencing such a moment that I forgot about the rest of the world occurring around me. All I could do was stop, stare at the sentimental memento in my hand, and wonder how on Earth I could be graced with such an important memento.

Chapter 40

Brielle

Knock! Knock! Knock!

I rapped softly against Javier's office door with my knuckles. The tint on the glass covering the office was on again, so I couldn't see inside. Although Javier's schedule stated he was supposed to be in his office, he's stepped out a few times for meetings he didn't want held in the company building.

I almost thought he was gone again until I heard his voice on the other side of the door, granting permission to enter.

I pushed the door open and poked my head inside.

Javier was sitting at his desk with his eyes trained on the computer screen and a pen in his hands. Dark bags rimmed the bottom of his eyes, and his facial hair was getting longer than he usually kept it. As I moved closer to him, I saw how low his shoulders and eyelids hung.

He's been stressed ever since his conversation with Leo, but over the past few days, it's taken on a new level. He busied himself all day with his legitimate work tasks and went to the warehouse afterwards to take care of his duties there. By the time he gets home, I'm on the verge of falling asleep - or already there. But I always sense when he climbs into bed. Even in a state of unconsciousness, I recognized his arms around me and his breaths against my neck. I could tell from the constant circles he rubbed into my belly that he wasn't sleeping. And even when he did, it wasn't for long.

Last I spoke to him about it, he insisted he was just trying to make sure his plans to end things with Leo for good went as smoothly as possible.

"The sooner he's dead, the better," he'd told me.

I respected all the hard work he was putting in, but I was worried about him. Exhaustion hovered over him like a dark cloud, adding more rain on top of all the other things he was dealing with. He desperately needed a break before all the weight became too heavy to hold.

At least when he finally got one, it'd be on a vacation with Chloe and me. He might follow us around amusement parks throughout the days, but I thought it'd be more fun than planning his enemy's untimely death.

"Hey," I told him as I walked up to his desk. "I'm heading out to pick up Chloe. Any idea of when you'll be home?"

"Around eight o'clock maybe," he replied. "I don't have much to do tonight."

"Okay." I pecked a kiss at his lips. "Love you."

The phrase made him perk up a bit. His eyes softened, and although he didn't say it back, I could tell the reciprocating thought was crossing his mind. He grabbed my face and brought me back down for another kiss.

I left the office building and drove down to Chloe's after-school learning center. I still haven't told her about our upcoming trip. Our plan was to surprise her on the last day of school. We were going to take her out to dinner and relay the news. I couldn't wait to see the excitement on her face when we finally told her.

I tried to imagine the elation on her face as I reached the main gym area and scanned around for her head of dark curls. Something sharp raced across my stomach when I didn't see it.

I did a double-look across the room, checking every nook and cranny I might've missed. I recognized every other child who was usually here when I arrived, but I still didn't see my daughter.

Maybe she's just in the bathroom? Or took a walk with the teacher to grab something?

I prayed to God one of those options were true as I wandered over to the table where the teachers sat.

"Ms. Parker," one woman said with surprise. "Is everything okay?"

"Oh, I don't know. I was looking for Chloe, but I didn't see her anywhere."

Her brows came together. "Her father picked her up in the school yard after school."

I tilted my head, unsure if I heard her right. I added Javier and his siblings onto Chloe's emergency contact form. Maybe she meant to say aunt or uncle, instead. Or got it wrong and mistook Adrian for Javier and thought he was her father. Both of them have picked her up before. Maybe they just got the two mixed up.

"We spoke to one of the teachers at drop off and they said the office received an email and a phone call from you giving them permission to release her to him."

Their faces blurred as I tried to wrap my head around their words. There was no way in hell this was right. First of all, her father wasn't on any of her emergency contact or release forms. Hell, he wasn't even on her fucking birth certificate. Second, I didn't send any emails or make any calls to her school today. Especially not with instructions to let her go with that bastard.

Unless he hacked into my email account and had one of his girls mimic my voice over the phone. With the paternity suit he tried to file, he might've gotten access to Chloe's personal information and used it to erase any potential suspicion with the school.

"Is there something wrong?" The other teacher asked as a crease started forming between her brows.

"No," I lied. I shook the shock off of my face and feigned a smile. "I just...I just forgot. It's been a crazy day at work, and I just completely blanked on it. Sorry for the confusion." Turning on my heel, I hurried out of the building.

As I did so, I dug my phone out of my bag, prepared to dial Chloe's cell number and demand to know where and with whom she went off with.

But just before I could click on her contact information, a text notification appeared at the top of my screen from an unknown number. I clicked on it and stopped in my tracks.

At the top of the new thread was a selfie of Chloe, eyes wide with fear and her lips pulled in a distressed frown, and Leo with his arm around her shoulders and a cocky smile on his face.

My phone buzzed again as another text came through.

Unknown Number: Spending quality father-daughter time <3

I barely heard my voice as the phone fell out of my hands and a devastated scream hurled up my throat.

Chapter 41

Javier

Fuck giving that motherfucker a quiet, merciful death. I am going to rip him limb from limb and set whatever was left of him on fire while he's still breathing. That bastard deserved to die for all the shit he did to Brielle, but putting his hands on Chloe - that warranted a whole new punishment.

Brielle could barely speak when she called to tell me the news. All I could hear at first was her quick, uneven breaths and the chokes of her sobs. At first, I didn't understand what was wrong. She seemed fine when she left my office.

"He has her," she finally uttered, her voice filled with cracks. "Leo has Chloe."

And just like that, all of my previous plans went out the fucking window.

Rushing out of my office, I told Brielle to stay where she was and hung up to call Miles. He could hack into her phone remotely and track the number that sent her the photo she described to me.

As expected, it was from a burner that was no longer in service. Miles couldn't get an exact location, but he could triangulate an approximate mile range based on the nearby cell towers. The asshole wasn't far from the city.

"Send the green light message to all our associates assigned to their locations," I demanded. "I want all of them taken care of - *tonight.*"

"Yes, sir," Miles replied without hesitation.

The heart I didn't know I had crumbled into a tiny million pieces at the sight of Brielle when I finally met her in the parking lot of Chloe's after school care center.

Tears flooded over her cheeks, and her entire body shook in rhythm with her sobs. Flinging herself into me, she muttered, "This wasn't supposed to happen. I swear. I tried so hard to make sure this didn't happen."

I squeezed her tight. "I know you did. This isn't your fault." I kissed her head. "I'm gonna find her, alright? I'm gonna get her back."

She looked up at me with teary eyes. "You promise?"

I nodded. "No matter what it takes."

I drove her back to the warehouse to drop her off with Miles. On the way there, I called my siblings and commanded them to meet me there as soon as possible. Thankfully, all of them were there by the time we arrived, waiting for us in Miles's control room.

"All our men are deployed," Lexie reported when we walked inside. "The only survivors allowed are the women being held captive. And the facilities are being torched to hide all the bodies."

"Good." I handed my warehouse walkie to her. "I need you to stay here with Miles and Brielle. Run command while we're gone."

"And if he calls for negotiation?"

"Pretend to abide by his terms, trace that shit, and send the location straight to me. We'll take it from there."

"What if he has Chloe with him?" She asked. "You can't go in there guns blazing if she's still by his side."

"You're right," I said with a sigh. "Depends on the terms then. I still want the call traced and the location sent. We'll decide what to do after he tells us what he wants."

"I thought he believed y'all called a truce," Dante said.

"I guess we were both lying," I replied. After all, we'd both killed each other's kin. There was no way in hell that kind of beef was going to be squashed by a simple conversation. It was stupid of me to think he'd fall for my lie so easily. I shouldn't have let my guard down. I should've beefed up protection around the girls just in case he saw through my bluff. But, it was too late to think of what I should've done. My only focus now was getting my daughter back safely.

"I've got about four shady strip clubs within the area where the text came from," Miles explained. "Dug a little deeper, and identified two that are definitely run by Bianchi's crew."

"Alright. Dante, take Roman and some of your hard hitters from your sector down to one. Adrian, you and I will take the rest of ours and hit the other."

My brothers nodded at my command. Dante headed right out while Adrian lingered behind to wait for me.

I grabbed my wife and kissed her forehead. "Stay here," I demanded. "If Leo contacts your phone again, Miles will track it. Whatever he asks for, you tell him we'll deliver."

Her brows came together. "He's already taken what he wants. What more could he ask for?"

My head on a fucking stick.

But I couldn't tell Brielle that. She was already worried sick enough, and I wouldn't add another load to her stress. "I don't know," I lied. "Just promise me you'll pretend to comply."

She nodded. "Okay." She grabbed my face and kissed me again. "I love you."

I opened my mouth to say it back. This was the worst time to tell her, but God forbid anything happened to me tonight, she deserved to know how I truly felt about her. But before I could, I felt Adrian tugging at my arm. "Come on, Jav," he said as he pulled me away from Brielle. "We don't have time to waste."

I let him tow me down to the armory. There, we stripped off our work clothes and substituted them for all black-ensembles and bullet-proof vests. We stocked up on our rifles, Glocks, and bullets and hooked them onto our vests and belts.

"You good?" Adrian asked once we were all suited up.

"No," I admitted. "That motherfucker went too damn low. If there's even a single scratch on Chloe…" I trailed off as unfamiliar fire brewed beneath my bones.

"Even if there's not, he's still getting his fingers sliced off."

"Agreed."

The line on my brother's lips deepened. "He's looking to get even. We damn near killed his whole family. When he calls to make demands... What if he..."

"He's going to ask for one of us." I finished. "I know. And when he does, I'm going to be the one surrendering."

"What? No! You can't!"

"I am, and I will. I am the head of this family, and it's my responsibility to defend it - even if it means sacrificing my life. Besides, he's not interested in you or Lexie. I killed his father, and I took his family - he's going to want me."

"And during the potential exchange, what do you want us to do? We won't sit by and watch."

"I'd never expect you to. If it comes down to it, I'll be the bait until we can confirm Chloe is safe. Whatever he does to me until then doesn't matter. But, once she's out of harm's way, we put a bullet in that motherfucker - whether I'm still alive or not." I held out my hand to him. "Deal?"

Adrian wearily eyed my hand.

"This is *my* family he's threatening," I urged. "Let me do for them what our father didn't do for us."

A muscle jumped in Adrian's jaw as he nodded. Reluctantly, he clasped his hand around mine in a firm grasp. "Fine. Deal."

"Good." Releasing his hand, I turned towards the door. "Now, let's go finish what we started."

Chapter 42

Brielle

My leg bounced up and down as I stared at the abundance of screens on the wall of Miles's control room. The image of Chloe's face in the photo Leo sent me haunted every one of my thoughts. Her uncomfortable stance. The frown on her lips. The fear and confusion etched into her eyes.

For the first time in years, I prayed to the God I'd turned my back on. I asked Him to bring my daughter back safely to me. She was so young. So innocent. And full of potential to be something good in this horrible world. He'd saved her once all those years ago - before I even knew she existed. He needed to save her again.

"Here," Lexie's voice broke my thoughts.

I blinked out of my unseeing trance to see her holding a cold water bottle out to me. "Thanks," I murmured as I accepted it. The cool liquid eased the soreness in my throat from all the crying I've done.

Lexie took a seat beside me. "Don't worry," she assured me. "We're pulling all the stops we can to bring Chloe back safely."

"Thanks," I repeated. Truthfully, I wasn't worried about their efforts. I saw the blue fire in Javier's eyes and heard the conviction in his voice. I knew he was going to do everything in his power to find Chloe.

It was Leo I was worried about. When he wanted something, he didn't discriminate against the person standing in his way. Only God knew what he was doing to Chloe between the time they were looking for her. His comments about finding out how much she was worth lingered in the back of my mind and sent chills down my spine. Jesus, I hoped he was bluffing. After all, that was before he knew that was his daughter. He wouldn't do that to his own flesh and blood. Would he?

Before I could ponder the answer to that question, my phone started buzzing in my hand. I looked down to see an incoming call from an unknown number. Knots curled in my stomach at the sight.

"He's calling again," I told Lexie and Miles. The notification was already flashing across all the screens. Saying it aloud just made the instance seem less like a bad dream.

"Answer it," Lexie said. "Try to keep him on the phone for as long as you can."

Nodding, I hit the accept button and held the phone to my ear. "Hello?"

"Mommy," Chloe's voice replied to me. Her small voice cowered with every syllable.

Still, hearing her voice pushed some of the weight off of my shoulders. I sighed in relief as I breathed a little easier. "Sweetpea, thank God. Are you okay?"

"Yes."

"Has anyone hurt you?"

"No." She let out a shaky breath. "But, I'm scared. I want to go home."

"You will soon, sweetpea. I promise."

An eerie silence filled the air for a moment. "Mommy, my dad wants to talk to you."

"Okay. I love you, baby."

"I love you too, mommy." Static crackled through the speaker as the phone switched hands.

"Sweet girl you raised, Diamond," Leo's voice replaced my daughter's. "Respectful and obedient. She'll fit right in."

"You wouldn't dare. She's *your* daughter."

"And she'll set a great example for the other young girls. She'll reap all the benefits without having to work for them. Not until it's time for her to carry on the bloodline. I guess that's the least I could do for the girl, right?"

"You're despicable!"

"At least I'm honest," he retorted casually. "Unlike other people we know."

Sighing, I tried to contain the anger brewing in my belly. "Chloe has nothing to do with this. If it's me you want then-"

"You?" He barely contained his chuckle. "Diamond, you think this is about *you*?"

"Yeah," I murmured, confused by his response. This all started because he found out I was alive. And in sending his men after me, there's been a trail of bodies left behind. I knew Leo well enough to know how possessive and jealous he was. Knowing I was out here with another man was probably driving him crazy. What else could this whole ordeal possibly be about?

"Hm, seems like I wasn't the only one being lied to."

My brows came together. I rose from my seat and moved further down the other side of the room to get a tiny ounce of privacy. "What are you talking about?"

"Your husband didn't tell you?"

"Tell me what?"

"His family played a hand in murdering my brother and my father. *Before* I saw you in his office."

"Wait, what?"

"Mm-hmm. It's a long story for another time. But, it was quite the coincidence when I heard the two of you tied the knot after our reunion. An even bigger one when the news arrived with one of my men's dismembered hands."

"What?" My head spun from his words. He was speaking in riddles my mushy brain didn't have the energy to comprehend. I needed him to be direct. "The hell are you talking about?"

"Quite convenient Ruiz puts a ring on your finger the moment I stroll back into town, don't you think?"

"Javier married me to protect us from you."

"No, Ruiz married you as a tool to distract me. He doesn't actually give a fuck about you or Chloe. All he wanted was to piss me off. And I have to admit, it worked. Fucked me up pretty good. That and the ambushes he's been ordering on my clubs. The man has been hurting my heart and my pockets."

"What?" I repeated in disbelief rather than confusion. All the puzzle pieces started fitting together before my eyes. Leo showing up at Javier's office. Javier's generous offer to protect us, but with the specific condition of marriage. The spontaneous appearances of Leo's men.

They weren't there for me. They were there for Javier. To strike back against whatever war they were fighting. One that I accidentally stumbled in the middle of.

Leo chuckled again. "You really didn't know, huh?" He tsked his teeth. "Now, your poor daughter has to pay for her step-dad's crimes. Such a shame, isn't it?"

Pushing my hurt aside, I replied, "Leave Chloe out of it. She has *nothing* to do with this."

"And neither do you." His statement sliced through me like a knife. "So, how about I give you an offer where you both walk away and nobody gets hurt?"

I gritted my teeth. I knew I wouldn't like his offer, but I didn't have any other choice but to accept. My daughter's life was at stake. "I'm listening."

"I need you to get away from the Ruizs first. Call me back when you're alone and then I'll give you the instructions." A smile was in his voice. "I'll talk to you soon, Diamond."

I heard footsteps behind me as I lowered the phone away from my ear. "Is it true?" I asked. "You all killed Leo's family?"

"Yes," Lexie replied. "For reasons he left out."

"But, Javier was using me - as a pawn?"

"Brielle," she said as she tried to lay a hand on my shoulder.

I dodged her touch and whipped around to face her. "All of you were using us? Pretending to welcome us into the family and acting like you gave a shit?"

"No, Brielle, you don't understand."

"I understand very well!" I yelled. "All of you people in the crime underworld are the same! You don't care whose toes you step on or whose hearts you break as long as you get what you want! And to think I trusted you!"

"Brielle, you can. Listen, how about we just take a second and talk about-"

"No!" I pushed past her and started running towards the side door exit of the room. I was done listening to the Ruiz family and their lies. I couldn't rely on them to save my daughter. Like always, the only person I could rely on was myself.

"Brielle, wait!" The click of Lexie's heels followed me. "Stop!"

I ignored her and kept running through the empty basement halls. Most of their men were out looking for Chloe. There was barely anyone here to stop me - or block the exits.

Remembering the layout from when Javier brought me here before, I made a hard left through the stairwell and jogged up to the first floor. I made a beeline for the side door leading to the impromptu parking lot.

I thanked God again as I saw my car in the rows. One of Javier's men must've bought it here earlier.

I climbed inside, started the engine, and pressed my foot against the gas.

In the rear view mirror, I could see Lexie still chasing after my car. She stopped after a few moments in disbelief. The last I saw before I veered off onto the dark road was her running her hands through her hair and holding her phone to her ear.

Chapter 43

Javier

"What the fuck do you mean she's gone?" I snapped into my phone. A few moments ago, just after we finished our attack on Bianchi's shady ass club, Lexie called and told me the news.

"She just took off," Lexie said, her voice strained with frustration. "I chased after her, but the girl is faster than she looks."

"Why the hell did she leave?"

"Leo called and told her the real reason we've been at his neck. He claimed you were just using her to get back at him. She was so upset that when he gave her a bogus offer to get Chloe back, she ran out."

"Fuck!" I yelled.

My men, who were nearby, sifting through the place for any survivors we missed, stopped in their tracks and looked at me in confusion.

Ignoring them, I stepped over the dead bodies and toward the door. The metallic scent of blood sent the room into a whirlwind as I tried to wrap my head around the news. Leo's words may not have been a complete lie, but I thought Brielle knew our relationship wasn't for show anymore. She loved me, and I - dammit, I loved her too. Didn't she know that? Didn't she know how much I cared about her and Chloe? Haven't I shown it?

I should've fucking said it.

The cool breeze brushed against my face as I passed through the threshold. "Is the GPS on her phone and car still active?"

"Yeah, and I sent a rookie to tail her. We're waiting on Leo to call again, so we can know exactly where she'll go next." She paused for a moment, a sigh eluding her lips. *"Lo siento*, Javi. I should've coached her beforehand. Then, she would've been more prepared. She was just so upset, and I didn't want to-"

"This isn't your fault," I told her. "This was my plan, my wrongdoing, and I take full responsibility for it. Just monitor her location and let me know as soon as Leo gives her a location."

"What are we going to do once he does? We can't just ambush them - not with Brielle and Chloe inside."

"It doesn't look like we have a choice. We know what will happen if we wait."

"Yeah," she murmured.

"Just let me know," I repeated before hanging up. I leaned against the wall beside the door as my world took another spin. My chest was tight, each breath felt like knives stabbing into my ribcage. Each one came quicker than the last, digging into me over and over like the villain in a slasher film. Between the pain, the only thing running through my mind was: How?

How could I let this happen?

I've done everything - *everything* - in my power to make sure my family was safe. The twenty-four seven detail with my best men. The best home security system. GPS tracking on both of their phones. There wasn't a single moment I didn't know where they were or what they were doing.

Did I put too much faith in my men? Have I gotten too lax? Or was I just distracted by the one thing I thought I'd never have?

"Javier." My brother's voice pulled me out of my head.

Consumed by my thoughts, I hadn't realized I'd sunk down on my haunches and put my head down against my knees. It was a trick my mom taught me when I was younger and the pressure was too much to handle. She'd sit beside me and coach me through my breathing. At times like this, my muscle memory still resorted to the old hack. Only this time it wasn't working. The shards were still piercing my ribcage and I couldn't get my breaths under control.

This was too close - too fucking close to when I lost our mom all those years ago. I could vividly remember being in Chloe's shoes - bound and terrified and bleeding.

Fuck, did that bastard hurt her?

Raging flames rushed through my veins at the possibility. Chloe wouldn't even harm a fly. She didn't deserve any ounce of pain Leo might inflict on her. Neither did Brielle. She'd suffered enough. The thought of such scum laying a hand on either of them made my blood boil.

I needed to get to them.

Now.

Before he did the unspeakable.

"Javier," Adrian called again. His hand grabbed my shoulder and gave it a soft shake, pulling me out of the hole I'd fallen into again.

Reluctantly, I pulled my head up to look at him.

Adrian was kneeling beside me, his face scrunched in concern. "Are you good?"

"Yeah," I lied. "I'm fine."

"We're going to kill that bastard," he assured me. "*Slow.*"

I nodded. I don't think there was enough torture in the world that would equate to all the harm that asshole has done. Only the devil himself could deliver the punishment he truly deserved. Still, I had no problem working to push ours up to those standards.

My phone buzzed again. My heart skipped a beat, hoping it was Lexie calling with a location for Brielle - or my wife seeking to cuss me out. The latter would've been music to my ears. I'd rather hear her rage and know she was safe than bear her silence and wonder if I'd ever hear her beautiful voice again.

To my dismay, the notification was neither. Instead, it was a text message from an unknown number. Inside the bubble was a blue link.

What the fuck was Leo up to now?

Stitching my brows together, I clicked on the link and waited for it to load.

My heart dropped in my stomach as Chloe's face appeared on the screen. Her amber eyes were red and still streaming with tears. Her body trembled with fear as she stared helplessly at the camera. Behind her, I could see empty gray walls, steel tables, and a stairwell farther back.

Her eyes flicked up, looking behind the camera.

A small stack of large, white index cards floated towards her. It bounced lightly in assurance when Chloe was hesitant to take them.

Her fingertips shook as she accepted the cards. More tears rolled down her face as her gaze found the camera again. Shakily, she held up the cards in front of her chest. I recognized her big, bubbly handwriting on them.

Giant, please help us.

Leo appeared in the camera frame, walking around from the side to stand behind Chloe. Grinning with the most sinister of intentions, he wrapped an arm around Chloe and pressed their cheeks together.

Chloe's chest unevenly heaved up and down from his touch. Closing her eyes, she moved the card to expose another.

As she did so, Leo lifted a gun with his other hand. Tauntingly, he pressed the mouth against Chloe's head.

He's going to kill me and mommy.

Chapter 44

Brielle

My stomach rolled at the sight of the seedy club I pulled up to. It stood alone on the side of the road, cloaked by darkness. None of the bright neon letters were lit, and little light shone through the windows. Only one car loitered in the parking lot. Passing by, one would think this place was abandoned.

Once I drove far enough away from the Ruiz's headquarters, I gave Leo another call, and he instructed me to come to this address. "Alone," he emphasized. "If you bring company, all deals are off the table."

I fought the shiver crawling up my spine as I grabbed my pink gun out of the glove compartment and tucked it in my waistband. Hopefully, all my shooting lessons with Javier were worthwhile. This gun was the best shot I had at protecting myself.

I climbed out of the car and looked up at the building. It looked all too familiar to the ones I spent my time in when Leo had me under his thumb. Awful memories scratched at my brain as they tried to crawl to the forefront. Closing my eyes, I took a deep breath and reminded myself this was about Chloe - and protecting her from the same experiences I had in hell holes like this.

The scent of liquor and sex smacked me in the face as I walked inside. A single rotating white light illuminated bits of the interior. Empty platforms with silver poles. Cushioned chairs positioned in circles around them. Wrinkled dollar bills on the floor. An empty bar with a stocked liquor case.

As the light passed one platform, I glimpsed a vision of my old self, draped in shimmering silver lingerie and legs wrapped around the pole. A smile was on her lips, but pain lay in her eyes. God, I wished to hug her and assure her this wouldn't be her prison forever.

Forcing my eyes away, I caught a cloud of smoke hovering above the second floor. Slowly, I made a beeline for the stairwell and ascended them.

The upper level was covered with small U-shaped booths. Platforms similar to the ones below were placed in the middle. All of them were empty except for one.

On the other side of the room, Leo lounged against the velvet cushions. One arm was thrown across the headrest while the other held a cigar. The glow of the butt illuminated his hazel eyes, giving them a red tint.

"Diamond," he greeted me with a sly smile. "It's so good to see you."

"Where's my daughter?" I asked.

"Come here." He patted the space beside him. "Let's talk."

Gritting my teeth, I reluctantly obeyed his command. I knew how to play this game. If I wanted something, then I needed to please him first.

When I was close enough, he grabbed my arm and pulled me down onto his lap.

The smoke from his cigar wafted through my nostrils. I fought the urge to scrunch my nose from the awful smell. I needed to appear as pleasant as possible. The less defiance I portrayed, the less pleasure he received - and the faster he'd leave me alone.

"How have you been?"

"Fine."

"How's Ruiz been treating you?"

"Fine."

He chuckled. "Is that the only answer you're going to give me?"

"I'm upset," I admitted. "You kidnapped my daughter and then told me my husband is actually a conniving, manipulative piece of shit."

"I'm sorry about all that. I didn't mean to hurt your feelings. I just thought you deserved to know the truth."

"You could've told me without involving Chloe."

"Would you have believed me if I did?" Chuckling, he took another puff of the cigar. "Knowing Ruiz, he would've spun it to make it seem like *I* was lying. He's good at that, you know: making people believe things that aren't real."

I averted my eyes. "Yeah, I know."

Leo's eyes fell to the frown on my lips. "Aw, Diamond, don't tell me you really liked him?"

"He was good to me. Better than you ever were."

His hand flew to his heart. "After all I did for you, and you still hold a grudge against me. That hurts, Diamond."

"Where is my daughter, Leonardo?" I asked firmly. I wasn't interested in entertaining his games. I wanted to grab my daughter and run as far away from these people as possible.

"Downstairs," he replied.

"What do I need to do to see her?"

He smiled. "Say you'll be mine again."

"What?" I recoiled back in disgust. "Over the phone, you said we'd both be able to walk away."

"Sorry, I forgot to elaborate. I meant you'd both walk away with your *lives*. I didn't say anything about your freedom. Despite that ring on your pretty little finger, you still belong to *me*. And that little girl downstairs, she's mine too. *My* blood and flesh. And she's going to look so pretty carrying on the Bianchi legacy. She'll make a great madame someday."

I slammed the palm of my hand against his cheek. "You sick bastard!" I yelled as I rose out of his grasp. I took his moment of surprise to take my gun out of my waistband and took a blind shot at his chest. "Fuck you!"

"Ah!" He exclaimed. The cigar fell out of his hand as he clutched the fresh wound and doubled over from the pain. "You stupid whore!"

Turning on my heel, I rushed back down the hall. I jogged down the first flight of steps. Quickly, I scanned the lower level for the second flight of steps. Relying on the flashes of white light, I spotted a door near the bar. I ran over and jiggled the doorknob.

"Shit," I muttered when it wouldn't budge. I took a step back and kicked the door - *hard.* The lock didn't give on the first kick, but by the third - with some help from adrenaline and frustration - the door finally gave way.

"Chloe!" I yelled as I ran down the steps. "Baby, where are you?"

"Mommy!" her voice cried back. "Mommy, help! Please help!"

When I reached the bottom of the steps, I was met with a small array of tunnels. "Chloe!"

"In here, mommy! I'm in here!" I followed her voice down the corridor on my right. I followed the short path to a small, dimly lit room filled with steel tables.

Chloe sat at the corner of one table with her arms bound in rope. It was hooked to the leg of the table, preventing her from going anywhere. Seeing her face, red, puffy, and streaked with tears, shattered my heart into a tiny million pieces.

"Oh, sweetpea," I cooed as I sped over her to her. "It's alright. We're gonna get you out." I found the knot binding her wrists together and undid it.

Once free, Chloe flew into my arms. We squeezed each other so tight that one might've thought we'd been separated for an eternity rather than a few hours. But with all that's happened, it sure felt that way. I didn't want to let her go, afraid someone else might try to snatch her from me, but we needed to get out of here.

"Come on, baby," I told her. "We need to move."

Just as I ushered her to take a step towards the door, Leo appeared in the doorway. A red circle bloomed on his shirt from where I shot him. But, he didn't seem affected by the pain. With livid eyes and a curled snarl, he lifted his gun and shot at us.

Chloe screamed as I pushed her down onto the ground to avoid the rain of bullets.

I pulled her towards a nearby table and pushed it over to shield us. "Keep your head down!" I commanded her. Crouching down near the edge of the table, I waited for the bullets to pause. At the first sound of silence, I peeked over the side and pulled the trigger on my own gun. My aim followed Leo as he raced for cover.

"I see Ruiz taught you some new tricks," Leo yelled once he was out of sight, a smile evident in his voice. "The pink gun is a cute touch."

I ignored his comments and searched for an exit. There weren't any doors in here, but the doorway to the hallway was clear. Leo had moved a few feet away from it, and was no doubt moving closer to us. If I distracted him for long enough, Chloe would have enough time to make a run for it. I didn't care about what happened to me, so long as Chloe got out safely.

I looked over at her, crouching beside me with her hands over her ears and her eyes squeezed shut. I hated this might be our last memory together - with a gun in my hand and Chloe hunched over with fear. Children aren't supposed to see their parents die. Not like this. If the world was perfect, never. I just hoped fate would be more merciful to her than it was to me, and she wouldn't have to see the ugly that came with a death like this. Tears bit at my eyes as I grabbed her. "Baby, baby, look at me," I told her. "Look at me."

She reluctantly opened her eyes, and more water spilled over her round cheeks.

"I need you to do something for me, okay?"

She nodded.

"You see that doorway over there?"

She followed my gaze and nodded again.

"On the count of three, you run to that doorway and you don't look back. No matter what you hear. No matter what you see, you keep running. Do you understand?"

"But, mommy, I…I can't leave you!"

"Don't worry, sweetpea. I'll be right behind you. I promise."

She shook her head. Flinging herself against me, she captured me in another tight hug. "No. No, mommy, please!"

Gritting my teeth, I fought back tears and pushed my cell into her hand. "Don't stop running until you reach a gas station. Once you get there, use my phone to call Ms. Lexie or Ms. Kiara and have them come get you." I don't know how much I trusted any of their words or intentions anymore, but right now, they were the only option I had. They kept us safe for this long. They could sacrifice just a bit more of their time to make sure Chloe was taken care of.

"But, mommy-"

"I love you, sweetpea," I told her. "I love you so much."

"I love you too, mommy," she said, her voice cracking in defeat.

I kissed her forehead. "On three, okay?" We switched sides to place her closer to the door. "One...two...three!"

At the last number, we both rose from our shelter and darted to the door. While Chloe ran ahead of me, I held my arm out and let out a string of bullets around the room. The diversion worked well enough to get us out of the room.

"Go! Go! Go!" I coached Chloe as we ran down the hall and around the corner. We'd just reached the steps when a hand grabbed a fistful of my hair and threw my body against the nearest wall. With a loud thud, I collided into the concrete. My vision blurred from the impact to my head, but through it, I could see three Leo's - all with their guns aimed at my daughter's fleeing figure.

"No!" I yelled. I pushed myself off the wall and threw myself against him. I grabbed his wrists and averted the aim of the gun towards the sky. The loud bang rang through my ears. Above us, the bullet ricocheted against the ceiling and came back down. It sliced through the side of my arm. Although nothing more than a graze, the wound lit a wildfire across my skin.

Leo swung his arms and threw me onto the ground. "Oh, you are really asking for it, Diamond," he growled.

Before I could move, he mounted me and wrapped his hands around my neck. "You know, I was going to make it quick and painless." Adding more pressure around my neck, he lifted my head and slammed it back down against the concrete. More visions of him whirled around me as the pain rippled through me. He didn't stop just once. He kept banging my head over and over against the ground. "After how good you were to me, I thought you deserved a merciful death. But now..." He squeezed even tighter, cutting off my windpipe completely. "Now I'm going to make you suffer."

Chapter 45

Javier

"Is this a trap?" Adrian asked as we pulled into the damn near empty parking lot of the address Miles had pulled from Brielle's phone conversation with Leo. The building stood in the middle of nowhere with no guards, no employees, no workers - nothing. It was strange - especially for Leo. He always had men lingering around somewhere.

I scanned over the edge of the rooftop, searching for a glimpse of movement or the edge of a sniper rifle. "I don't think so," I replied when I didn't see anything.

Adrian tapped on his earpiece. "Miles, do you have anything on the surveillance cameras inside?"

"Nope," Miles's voice rang in my ear. "It looks like they're down. I did some research on the property, and records said this place closed a few years ago. Cops have driven by a few times to make sure nothing's fallen down and always reported it as vacant."

"It's probably a safe house," I mused aloud. After all, the best places to hide were the towns and areas society has forgotten about. Judging from the looks of this place, it was meant more to be a pit stop on the road than a destination. The road we'd taken was practically empty, which meant there weren't a lot of truckers stopping by for a drink and a good time. They've been hiding in plain sight for quite a while.

"Do you think he's really in there alone?" Adrian asked.

I shrugged. "His entire organization is being blown to shit right now.

Anyone who has any common sense probably jumped ship already."

Adrian cocked his gun. "Easy pickings, then."

I doubted that. A man with nothing to lose was a dangerous one. Who knew what stunts Leo was going to pull once we walked inside? We still needed to be alert and cautious.

We climbed out of the car and slowly walked towards the door. The chirping of the crickets filled the air as we tiptoed along the front wall. I led the way while Adrian stayed a few steps behind, watching for potential snipers.

Just as we reached the front door, it swung open and someone darted out.

Both of our guns raised towards the shadow. I almost pulled the trigger until I realized how tiny it was. Was that a child? Was that...?

"Chloe!" I yelled after her.

At the sound of my voice, the shadow immediately stopped. As it turned on its heel, the moonlight glimmered over the terrain, and I glimpsed my daughter's face. "Giant!" She cried as she rushed back towards us. "He's got mommy! You need to help her! They're in the basement!"

Her words were all the confirmation I needed to dart inside.

"Jav, wait!" Adrian called after me.

"Stay with Chloe!" I commanded over my shoulder. She was going to need someone to comfort her right now. I could handle Leo on my own.

I easily found the basement door behind the empty bar and jogged down the steps. At the bottom, I made out two figures. A man on top of a woman, his hands around her neck and hers clawing at his forearms.

Such a sight snapped the last bit of thread holding together my sense of control. Fuck being methodical. Fuck being strategical. Fuck being smart. I was going to kill this motherfucker - and I was going to do it with my bare hands.

Chapter 46

Brielle

The brink of death was becoming so familiar, I knew it by name. The blurring black dots around my vision. The fading of the pain as my body shut down. The relieving thoughts that maybe…just maybe, I'll see my parents again.

With every second spent with Leo's hands around my neck, the further I fell towards the dark oblivion. I scratched and kicked and writhed as much as I could, but Leo was so much stronger than me. My petty marks on his arms weren't anything but a nuisance. Fighting back only made his grip on my neck tighter. My bones quaked under his fingers, struggling not to crack beneath the pressure. Fresh air had left me a long time ago, and now I was choking on borrowed time.

I knew I was going to die. But, not this easy. Not when I had my daughter to live for.

Like a prayer, thinking Chloe's name bought me a blessing.

Leo's hands abruptly left my throat and all the air I'd been searching for flooded through my mouth. My hands flew to my neck, and I coughed from the dry sensation of suffocating.

The world around me spun in circles as oxygen rushed back to my brain. Blurry figures whirled around in front of me. Through my narrow eyes, I could make out the color of Leo's dark blue shirt. The blur was tossed around relentlessly by a dark shadow. Rage burned off of the shadow like a fiery aura. The energy, even from a few feet away, sent a shiver down my

318

spine.

Their punches and kicks blended together like a fuzzy camera resolution. I couldn't tell much of what was happening - only that Leo's blue was being slammed against the tables and walls like a goddamn ball.

It took Leo a moment to recollect himself and meet the figure with his own force. He met the shadow with his own attacks, forcing it further back towards me.

I shimmied further away, still too dizzy to stand on my own feet.

Between the ringing in my ears, I heard the cracking of bones as it made impact with the surfaces. The instinct to flinch surfaced with each one.

I turned my gaze to the nearby staircase. Remembering my daughter, out all alone in the unkind night, I rolled onto my stomach and started crawling towards it to leave.

Hands grabbed a handful of my hair before I could reach the steps. "Where the fuck do you think you're going?" Leo's voice taunted through my ears as he pulled me back up against him.

His grimy hands were only on me for a moment before my angel in black was back again. One of the steel chairs swung over my head and struck Leo in the face.

He released me, and I fell back onto the floor.

Positioned below my savior, I caught a better glimpse of his face. Brown eyes that were usually frosted over with ice were now wild, blazing with blue fire. His mouth was curled into an animalistic snarl, and he growled in frustration as he hit Leo with the chair over and over and over again. Blood splattered over his face and shirt, but he didn't seem to care. His anger possessed him, and the only thought on his face was committing cold-blooded murder.

I've never seen him so angry. Throughout all the danger we've been through over the past few months, he's always kept his composure cool and collected. I didn't know how much rage he was holding beneath the surface. Now, furious and tumultuous, I almost didn't recognize him.

"Javi?" I murmured, my voice weak and scratchy.

Despite my low tone, he heard me above the noise. He stopped mid-movement with the chair held high above his head. His livid eyes took me in, burning brighter by the second.

Leo took the moment of distraction to lunge at Javier and tackle him to the floor. Mounting my husband, he pinned him down and punched him in the face.

"No!" I screamed. This man would not harm one of my loved ones again. Gathering all the strength in my recovering body, I flung myself at Leo. I landed on his back and dug my nails into his eye sockets.

"Ah!" He yelped from the pain.

With his enemy distracted, Javier shoved Leo off of him.

As we stumbled backwards, Leo swung me off of him. The long gashes I made around his eyes outlined his irate gaze as he looked at me. "I'm getting fucking sick of you," he snarled. Glancing around the floor, he spotted a fallen gun and reached for it.

Javier caught the movement and kicked Leo so hard in his ribcage that the snap of his bones echoed through the entire room. "Not so fast, asshole," he said. He brought his foot back and kicked Leo again - this time right across his face. "You put your hands on my fucking family." With every other word, he stomped his boot on Leo's head. "My wife. My daughter." He grabbed Leo by the hair and pulled up to lean against the wall. "You caused them so much pain. So much suffering." He pulled out a knife from a hidden pocket on his dark vest and slammed the tip right through Leo's hand, pinning it against the wall.

His scream of agony sent rolls of nausea through my stomach.

Javier ignored the sound and produced another knife. Swiftly, he pierced it through Leo's other hand. He pulled out a gun from his belt and pressed the mouth against Leo's forehead. "You don't deserve any of the breaths you take."

A bloody smile bloomed on Leo's lips. "If you're expecting me to beg for mercy, you might as well pull the trigger now."

Javier lowered the gun from his head and pointed it at Leo's leg.

Bang! Bang! Bang!

I flinched from the loud gunshots as Javier sent a string of bullets into

320

Leo's limb. His howls cut through the ringing in my ears. Yet, instead of sending a dreadful feeling down my spine, I was filled with a sense of relief. Seeing the man who'd inflicted so harm on me and my life finally get the bad karma he deserved was kind of...satisfying. It was as if all the bad things I endured were coming back tenfold toward him. And as much as I didn't want to feel this way, I couldn't lie to myself. I was happy to see him squirming in a humiliating position he had eagerly subjected myself and other girls to. To hear the shrill in his voice and know he was afraid. To know his dignity and strength was being stripped away with every bullet. Hell, I almost couldn't wait to see him die.

"Is that all you got, Ruiz?" Leo challenged, his voice tight as he endured the scathing pain. "A gun is pretty boring. I expected more out of-"

Javier took something else out of pocket, a small vial, and splashed the contents over Leo's face.

Again, Leo's screams filled this room - along with the sound of sizzling flesh. The liquid Javier doused him with burned through Leo's skin. Smoke rose above the disintegrating flesh and carried the horrible stench towards me.

"Torture isn't my area of expertise," Javier admitted. "But for you, I made an exception."

Leo growled from the burns on his face. With his hands nailed to the wall, he couldn't move to wipe it off. It seeped through his eyelids and into the corner of his eyeballs. The white of his eyes turned a bright shade of red. "You son of a bitch!" He growled in frustration.

Javier's gaze returned to me as he noticed I was still sitting there, watching quietly as he punished my abuser for all of his crimes. "Come here, Brie" he demanded, his voice firm.

I carefully pushed myself up on my feet and wobbled over to Javier's side.

One of his arms looped around my waist to hold me steady while the other pushed the gun into my hand. "His death is yours," he told me. "You're the one who deserves it."

Hesitating, I cradled the gun in my hands. I've never hurt anyone before. Never planned to. But, like Javier, I was willing to grant an exception for

Leo.

After the hell he put me through, a bullet is practically nothing. It'd be quick and painless - the complete opposite of all the long nights I spent suppressing my whines and suffering in silence. I wasn't built to give him the punishment he deserved, but the little red man with horns could take care of that for me.

Leo chuckled as he watched me contemplate. "Oh, isn't this cute? You're gonna have my whore do your dirty work? She couldn't even hurt a- Ah!"

His statement was cut short as I raised the gun and shot at his groin. My bullet hit its destination, hitting him right in the dick. His screams filled my ears, and I almost smiled at the sweet feeling of revenge that accompanied it.

"Oh, you bitch! You fucking worthless, disgusting whore! I should've fucking killed you when I had the chance! You no good-"

His voice was silenced for good as I pulled the trigger again. This time, I didn't stop with just one bullet.

Multiple bullets dove into his flesh, pushing his body back and smacking it against the wall. It gyrated with the pressure of the bullets. Each movement added a new splatter of blood onto the wall behind him. Underneath him, a thick pool of red puss started to ooze on the ground.

But, I didn't stop. I pulled the trigger over and over and over - until there wasn't any ammo left inside.

His lifeless body, riddled with bullets and blood, opened the gates of a dam I built to keep all the bad memories away. All the shame, pain, humiliation, regret, and inner turmoil burst through its restraints and poured over me like a waterfall. I hadn't realized how much weight Leo and all of his evil still held over me. But now that he was dead, I could finally let it all roll off my shoulders. He couldn't hurt me, or anyone I loved, ever again.

My knees buckled underneath me from the overwhelming lot of emotions.

Javier caught me before I hit the ground. He pulled me close and squeezed with all his might. "Fuck, Brie," he murmured into my hair. "You scared the shit out of me."

322

Despite how angry I was at him, I couldn't be upset at that moment. He just saved my life. *Again.*

I sank into his embrace and buried my face in his chest. I relished in the comfort of the sanctuary within his arms for a moment. Then, the reason we were here in the first place crossed my mind. "Chloe," I murmured, shooting my head up to look at him. "Where's Chloe?"

"She's safe," he assured me. "Do you want to see her?"

"Please?"

Javier bent his knees and threw an arm underneath my knees to pick me up bridal style. He carried me up the steps and through the lobby.

The cool breeze brushed against the sweat and tears on my face like a mother wiping away her child's tears.

"Mommy!" My daughter's voice carried through the wind.

Following it, I saw Chloe jumping out of the passenger side of a nearby truck and running towards me. My heart swelled at the sight of her sweet face, stained with tears.

Javier set me down so I could rush towards her and meet her halfway.

"Mommy! Mommy!" She exclaimed as she leaped into my arms. Feeling her body collide against mine was like meshing in the last piece of a puzzle. With her in my grasp, safe and sound, my entire being felt whole and fulfilled.

"Oh, sweetpea," I said as I held her tight, determined to never let go again. "My baby. Thank God. Are you okay?"

"Yeah," she said. She pulled away enough to look at me. Her lips pulled into a frown at the sight of my bruises. "Are you?"

I nodded. "I'm a little banged up, but I'll be okay."

She threw herself back against me and nuzzled her face into my neck. "You scared me, mommy," she murmured. "I thought I'd never see you again."

"I'm sorry, sweetpea. I'm here, and I'm never going anywhere. I promise."

A sudden flash of orange light caught our eyes, and we both turned our heads towards the empty club.

Adrian and Javier stood a few feet in front of it, a few gallons of gasoline at their feet, and a pack of matches in Adrian's hand. The flash we caught was of the match between Javier's fingers. He tossed it through the front door, and the tiny flames exploded into a mass of others upon collision with the gasoline.

Within seconds, the entire first floor of the club was engulfed in flames, turning everything inside into a mass of black ashes.

Chapter 47

Javier

Life after revenge is always difficult.

There's the satisfaction of victory on one end, and disappointment on the other. The thrill of the chase, the planning and the last execution, makes you feel you're going to earn something once it's over. But you don't.

The small ounce of gratification doesn't give you what you truly want. It doesn't rewrite history and change it for the better. It doesn't erase all the pain that's already been caused. It doesn't bring your lost loved one back.

After all the sleepless nights, mind-numbing strategic planning, and bloodshed, all you're left with is wasted time.

As I reflected on this experience in particular, I guess I couldn't say my time spent was entirely without merit. Our organization gained fresh territory all over the states from the facilities taken from the Bianchis. The smaller gangs underneath our umbrella had more room to work with and could make us more money. Those neutral to us found out how much of a powerhouse our cartel really was and now knew not to fuck with us. Our role in the drug trade was stronger than ever.

And most importantly, I gained a family. One I loved and cherished more than they could possibly understand.

I wasn't able to stop by the house over the past week since I was too busy cleaning up the last bit of messes left from the war. I thought the space might've been something we all needed.

It was going to take some time for the girls to recover from such a traumatic experience. Maybe even me too. The images of a gun against

Chloe's head and Leo's hands wrapped around Brielle's throat still haunted my brain at night.

Reassuring myself they were safe through the constant check-ins with my men and Kiara's text messages when she visited them wasn't enough. I needed to see them. Hold them. Hear their breaths as proof they were still alive. And that they were still mine.

On the following Friday, once I was sure all of my leadership duties were finished, I damn near ran out of the warehouse and sped through every red light back home.

I let myself in and scanned the lower level for the girls. My stomach tightened as I didn't see or hear them anywhere.

Then Chloe's laughter echoed through the hall from the open back door, and I let out a breath of relief.

I followed the sound towards the back patio.

Through the open glass sliding back door, I saw Brielle lounging on one of the patio chairs in a pink bathing suit. A homemade charcuterie board and an array of canned drinks sat on the table they sat around. She quietly watched Chloe as the young girl swam around in the in-ground pool attached to the patio, a few inches away. The wind carried her laughter through the halls of the house.

I lingered in the doorway, admiring the sight. The girls deserved to have a nice, peaceful day after last week.

As she came back up from the water, Chloe locked eyes with me and a huge smile lit up her face. "Giant!" She exclaimed.

Her mother followed Chloe's gaze toward me. Unlike Chloe's wide smile, I was met with a tight line on her lips.

Chloe scrambled out from the pool on the ladder and darted towards me.

I stooped to her height as she approached me and caught her in my arms. Water from her bathing suit leaked through my clothes, but I didn't mind.

Her tiny arms squeezed me tight. "I missed you, giant," she murmured into my shoulder.

My chest twinged from the warmth of her words. Holding her tighter, I replied, "I missed you, too."

She pulled out of our embrace to look at me. "Do you want to come swim with me? Mommy opened the pool a few days ago, and it's awesome! I can do flips underwater!"

"In a few minutes," I told her. "I need to change my clothes."

"Yeah, I guess you can't swim around in that," she said as she glanced over my suit. "Don't take too long! I want to show you my back flip!"

I chuckled. "Okay."

Satisfied with my answer, Chloe rushed back over to the pool and hopped back into the water.

Returning my gaze to Brielle, I noticed her staring blankly at one of the soda cans on the table.

Moving towards her, I reached my arm out and wrapped it around her. I dipped my head and buried my face in her hair. Her sweet scent and ticklish curls flooded my nose, sparking a familiar warmth in my stomach. "Hey, Brie," I whispered into her hair.

"Hi," she replied, her voice small.

I sank down to sit beside her on the chair. I kept my arm locked around her waist as I planted my chin on her head. From my spot, I watched Chloe attempt different flips and tricks in the pool. Seeing her smiling and active was the best thing I could've asked for. I knew all too well how hard it could be to bounce back from traumatic nights like the one Chloe faced. I was just grateful hers didn't weigh her down the same way mine did.

"I see you finally opened the pool," I said, opening the gateway to conversation.

"Yeah, Chloe kept asking," Brielle admitted. "I was going to surprise her on the last day of school, along with Disney World, but after last week, I caved and set everything up early. I didn't see the point in withholding it any longer."

"How's she been holding up?"

"Good, all things considered. She's been climbing into my bed at night, but no nightmares or anything like that. All she wants is to be near me. I've already spoken to Dr. Quinn about seeing her next weekend. Just to check in with her."

"How about you?" I lifted my chin off of her head to get a better view of her face. "How are you?"

"I'm fine." The firmness in her voice told me she was lying.

I hooked my finger underneath her chin and made her look at me. "What's wrong, Brie?"

She avoided my eyes. "We can talk about it later."

"No. We'll do it now. Tell me what's bothering you."

Tearing her chin out of my grasp, she turned away from me and crossed her arms against her chest. "I've just been thinking a lot...about what happened with Leo."

"Yeah, me too." I scooted closer to her and tried to realign myself with her gaze. "Listen, I promise that will *never* happen again. We've been recruiting more muscle, and we'll have a team specifically for you and Chloe. None of our enemies will ever come near the two of you again."

"It's not so much that I'm worried about," she murmured. She finally looked up at me, her eyes guarded with thick shields I've never seen. "Besides, this situation was different because it was *personal...*right?"

I sighed. A part of me was hoping amid the chaos, Brielle had forgotten about what Leo told her. But how could she? Whatever he said was enough to make her flee from underneath her umbrella of safety and put herself in harm's way. No wonder she wouldn't look at me.

"Is it true?" She asked when I didn't respond. "Did you really marry me as a ploy to gain another point on your scoreboard against him?"

I stared down at her for a moment, wishing there was a lie well enough to spin this in some other direction. But none would be believable. All the incidents involving Leo fit together too seamlessly. The timeline alone would debunk any smooth words I could try to put past her. I had no choice but to tell her the truth.

"Yeah," I muttered.

Hearing the confirmation summoned some moisture to her eyes. A small tremble shook through her shoulders as she averted her eyes. She caught it halfway down her spine, straightening her composure to remain tall. "Looks like your plan was a success."

"Angel," I started. I reached out to caress her cheek, but she quickly recoiled as though my touch would scorch her.

"Don't," she said, her voice frail. "Leo's dead now. You can stop pretending you care about us."

My brows stitched together. Is that really what she thought? That I didn't care at all? Did she genuinely think so low of my feelings for her? Of me?

"Giant!" Chloe's voice echoed through the air before I could respond. She'd paused her swimming and was looking at me with a big smile. "Go change! I wanna teach you how to do a flip!"

"Alright! I'm going!" Reluctantly, I rose from my spot beside Brielle. "We'll continue this conversation later."

"Why? There isn't much else to talk about."

God, she couldn't be more wrong. We had *plenty* to discuss.

Chapter 48

Brielle

"And then what happened to the warrior princess?" Chloe asked. She was laying in her bed, tucked in tight, with Javier perched beside her. She stared up at him with wide, curious eyes as she held her plush toy tight.

We were getting her ready for bed, and she requested for him to tell her a story. For the past ten or fifteen minutes, he's been narrating a short, epic tale of a headstrong royal who raced into action to protect her kingdom under a sudden attack.

Chloe was hooked from the interesting premise and Javier's descriptive words. His words came alive as he spoke, painting pictures on the wall for Chloe to see.

I had to give him credit where credit was due: he was a damn good storyteller. And Chloe seemed to love him more for it.

I did my best to not tear up at the sight of the two of them. Chloe has become so fond of Javier. I didn't know how I was going to tell her he wouldn't be coming around anymore. I could already imagine the pout of her lip and the tears in her eyes as her heart cracked straight down the middle. She was going to resent me for a while, but I was prepared for it. One day, she'll understand all I've ever done is try to protect her. I didn't want her to experience the same hurt I was right now. The poor girl has already been through enough.

"Her armor shielded her from the force of the explosion, so she survived the blast. Her citizens deemed her a hero, and they held a huge ceremony to

330

commemorate her bravery. Her stories have been passed down throughout multiple generations."

"Stories?" Chloe exclaimed. "There's more?"

"Tons. Princess Catalina did a lot for her kingdom. This one was just the first of her many adventures."

"Can I hear another one? Please, please, please?"

"Another night," Javier assured her. "It's past your bedtime."

"But, giant, it's the weekend. Can't I stay up a little while longer?"

"You have gymnastics in the morning," I chimed in. "You need to get some rest, so you can show everyone the new moves you learned in the pool."

"Okay," Chloe caved in with a sigh.

I leaned down to peck a kiss on her forehead. "I love you."

"I love you too, mommy." She looked at Javier. "Goodnight, giant. Thank you for the story!"

"Anytime, Chloe."

We both rose from the opposite edges of her bed and walked out of the room. I kept my eyes trained ahead of me as I made a beeline for the steps. It was too hard to look at Javier right now. I was embarrassed and hurt and naïve - so fucking naïve. Javier must've been laughing behind my back at how easy it was to manipulate me for his own plans. How could a girl aspiring to be a performer struggle with playing her own part?

I took the role too seriously. Blurred the lines between reality and the script. Fed my fantasies so much that I allowed myself to live and breathe in their comfort, oblivious to the mirage.

And now I was paying the price for being such a fool. As I watched the image of the perfect, loving family crumble into a tiny million pieces, my heart did the same. I wished I could say I couldn't believe Javier would pull such a trick on me. But Javier never once disguised himself as anything other than the cold sociopath that he was. Sure, he may have feigned affections here and there, but he was always true to himself. My ass was just dumb enough to fall for him.

I heard the pinging of Javier's phone behind me as I hopped down the steps. Glancing over my shoulder, I saw him dig his cell out of his pocket and frown at the screen. "You have to go?" I asked.

"In a few minutes." We reached the bottom of the steps, and he grabbed my arm to prevent me from going any further. "We need to finish talking first."

I tore my arm out of his grasp and crossed my arms against my chest - as if it'd shield me from whatever words were about to be exchanged. "What else is there to talk about? We both upheld our ends of the deal, and we got what we wanted. This week, I'll consult a divorce lawyer and estimate a timeline for-"

"Divorce?" The word left Javier's lips in a gasp, as if I'd hit him.

"Yeah," I said with a shrug. "Unless you're worried about what news of a divorce will do to your corporate image, there's really no need for us to keep pretending we're married. I've already started looking for a new place, so Chloe and I can get out of your hair."

"You and Chloe aren't going anywhere," he replied, his voice taking a dark turn. "And we're not getting a divorce."

"Javier, please don't make this more difficult than it has to be," I said, as I turned away from him. I started walking towards the front door. "Chloe and I don't need protection anymore, and you don't need a wife to flaunt for your enemies. Let's just indulge in our victories and move on with our lives."

His footsteps stomped after me. "Is that what you expect me to do? Just move on?"

"That was the original plan, wasn't it? Once Leo was taken care of, we'd absolve the marriage and go our separate ways."

"I never said that."

I whipped around to face him. "But that was your thought process, wasn't it? You never cared about me - or Chloe! All you cared about was your stupid crusade against the Bianchis! You killed Leo's brother and father - you just needed to take out the last chess piece on the board!"

"You don't understand! The Bianchis deserved to die! All three of them!"

"Yeah, and you sure didn't mind using a defenseless woman and her child to make sure of it!"

"Brielle, I was only trying to protect you!"

"No, you weren't! Because if you were, if you truly cared about us, you never would've thought to dangle us in front of Leo's face in the first place."

Javier's face fell as my words struck a nerve. We both knew there was absolutely nothing he could say to combat that.

Turning on my heel, I continued to the door and opened it for him. "You should go," I murmured.

Javier didn't argue with me. As his familiar mask of apathy covered his face, he shoved his hands in his pockets and walked towards the door. He stopped in the middle of the threshold. He hesitated for a moment, unsure whether to leave our conversation as it was or try to mend it. Thinking better of the thin band-aid he was going to put on the immense wound I was nursing, he crossed through the doorway and disappeared down the dark pathway.

I didn't see him at our company building when I returned to work the following Monday. According to his schedule, he was out of the office at meetings all day. I guess the timing worked in my favor. I needed to start packing up my desk, anyway. My mental recovery from the horrific night of almost losing Chloe set back my start date at the theater by a few days. Thankfully, my new boss was flexible with the change, but I still needed to move my ass to make sure I was set up by the time he really needed me.

I was putting my Funk O' Pops into boxes when I heard the familiar click of heels coming into our office. I glanced up to see Lexie, stunning as usual in her pencil skirt and dark blood stained lips, approaching me. "Your brother isn't here," I told her.

"I'm not here for him," she replied. She stopped in front of my desk. "I haven't seen you since the other night, and I wanted to check on you. I was thinking we could walk over to the little cafe on Westford. They have great mocktails and grilled chicken sandwiches."

"I'm sorry, but I can't. I need to finish packing all this stuff up. But, thank you for the offer."

She frowned as she looked at my almost empty desk. "You're really leaving, huh?"

"Well, I have another job so-"

"I'm not talking about this place, Brielle." She walked around the desk and perched herself on an empty space closer to me. "I'm talking about our family."

I almost scoffed. "We were never a part of your family."

"That's not true," Lexie said sharply. "I meant what I said on the day you married Javier: we take our family values very seriously. The moment you said 'I do' you and your daughter became one of our own. We embraced you and Chloe, protected y'all, loved y'all. And I get you're upset with Javi, trust me I do, but I don't want you to make a rash decision. Not when we all really care about you."

Shaking my head, I tried to ignore her words and focus on my tasks. The Ruizs didn't care about me or my daughter. The fact Javier went through lengths of using me and my daughter as rage bait for their enemy, and his siblings letting him, told me more than enough. All they cared about was maintaining their reputation and respect in the crime world.

Lexie grabbed one of my busy hands. "Brielle, listen," she said as she whipped me around to face her. "I can't speak for my brother and your relationship with him, but I can speak for ours. Over the past few months, I've grown very fond of you. Not just as a friend, but as a sister. You know, I didn't have one of those growing up and you, and Kiara, have filled in those roles for me. And Chloe, gosh, she's the prettiest, kindest doll of a niece I could ever ask for. Seeing you with Chloe, seeing how great of a mom you are, inspires me. Makes me want to be at least half the mom you are when I finally have children of my own. You're an amazing woman, Brielle, and I don't want to lose our friendship - our sisterhood - because my brother made a mistake."

Tears welled in my eyes from her kind words. "You won't. I mean, we can still be friends, even if I'm not with your brother."

She frowned. "Do you really want to leave him?"

"No, but I just...I don't know how to forgive him. I mean, Chloe almost died."

"I know," she murmured. "And trust me, he is beating himself up about it.

But, he never meant for you or Chloe to get hurt. None of us did. Please believe that." She opened her arms for a hug.

Sighing, I willingly went into them and embraced the warmth she was offering. After the roller coaster of emotions I've rode over the past few days, it was nice to finally feel secure and safe again.

"Be upset, but give him grace," she insisted. "Knowing you both are alive is the only thing holding him together right now."

Chapter 49

Javier

"Get away from that edge!" My best friend's voice echoed through the wind.

"I'm fine," I replied, remaining in my spot on the edge of the tall building. My legs dangled over the side, but I wasn't focused on the ominous view of the ground far beneath me. Instead, my eyes were fixed on the shining city in front of me. From where I sat, I could see the lights dancing over the water. The weed I was smoking altered the view, making the reflections look like colorful eels slithering beneath the surface.

"I don't care," Dante said, his voice closer. His shoes scratched against the gravel atop the roof as he walked towards me. "Get away from there."

"Relax. I'm not going to jump," I assured him.

He stopped beside me and kneeled. Scowling, he looked over the edge at the steep drop. "How the fuck do you find this soothing?"

I shrugged. "It's quiet."

"Yeah, there's the same silence a few feet back." Carefully, he sat down and threw his legs over the edge. "You know the chaos twins have been blowing up your phone?"

"No. I turned it off."

"Why? Do you want one of them to burn this city down looking for your ass?"

Shrugging, I offered the blunt to him. "You found me, so I guess the town is safe for another day."

He took it without hesitation and took a puff. "So," he said as he blew out the smoke. "The hell are you doing up here so late?"

I took the blunt back and took a hit to avoid his question.

I came up here to think. Figure out a way to smooth things out with Brielle. Hell, the more I thought, the less likely a solution seemed to be.

Brielle had every right to be angry with me. I'd used her for my benefit - like so many other men she's come across. And I bought Chloe into it. Almost got her killed.

Her words haunted my brain over the past few days. About her getting a new place, filing for divorce, and the assumption I never cared about her to begin with. The former two I could forgive, but the latter one hit me harder than I expected.

As much as it hurt to admit, she was right: I wouldn't have flaunted our family image around if I truly cared about them. I should've kept things quiet, kept them locked away. Let the word on the street speak more than pictures ever could. After all, when we started this, we agreed our marriage wasn't real. It would've been much easier to stay on that line if I'd set firmer boundaries and didn't let them get close to me.

Looking back, the whole idea was stupid, anyway. The hell was I thinking, taking up a wife? Even a fake one? These things always end with one spouse in the grave.

I was better off letting her go now before that happened. But, for some God forsaken reason, I refused to let the thought even cross my mind.

Dante nodded to my silence. "This thing with Brielle's got you fucked up, huh?"

"Yeah," I muttered. "She wants to end things."

"And you don't?"

Again, I avoided his question and stuck the blunt in my mouth.

A chuckle rumbled in his throat. "Well, I'll be damned. I didn't suspect *she* was going to be the one breaking hearts. You know, I hate to say I told you so, but-"

"Say it and I'll push you off this goddamn roof," I threatened.

He laughed. "Alright, alright. So, what are you going to do about it? Are you going to let her walk away?"

"Hell no. But...I...I don't know what to do that'll make her want to stay. Last time we spoke, she was so upset...and it just felt like there was nothing I could do or say to fix things."

"Sometimes there's nothing you can say or do. Sometimes you've just gotta let them chew you out - give you the kick in the ass you deserve."

"Yeah, but Brielle's not the type to rip me a new one and move on. She's emotional and sensitive and vulnerable. When something hurts her, it cuts her pretty deep. And I feel like she's more disappointed in me than she is angry. She trusted me, and I let her down. I don't know how to make that up to her."

"Have you thought about sharing the same vulnerability she has with you? I know you hate talking about your feelings and shit, but maybe you need to."

"But what if I lay out my heart and she stomps on it?"

Dante shrugged. "In order to be with the one we want, sometimes that's the risk we have to take."

I kept my conversation with Dante in mind throughout the night and the next day. At work, I had a plethora of meetings scheduled, so I wasn't able to catch Brielle in the office long enough to have an actual conversation.

She's been avoiding me the best she could, anyway. Busying herself with mindless tasks whenever I came around her desk. Avoiding my gaze and offering short, one-word answers when we needed to talk. Bearing her silence was so strange after being accustomed to her spontaneous visits and long-winded babbling. The office felt so empty without her infectious, bubbly energy.

I was reminded I'd need to get used to this when I saw her packing up her desk. Seeing the little trinkets of her presence, slowly erased from my space, stung like hell. It wouldn't have hurt as badly if I knew I'd see her at home. But now, with so much distance between us, I worried she'd be moving out of there too.

Near the end of the day, Brielle surprised me by peeking her head through my office door. "Hey," her sweet voice filled the dreary silence. "Do you have a minute?"

Nodding, I motioned for her to come in.

The skirt of her dress swirled around her legs as she strutted inside. She held out a short stack of papers and set it on my desk. "I need you to sign these."

Raising my brow, I looked at the stack of papers and started flipping through the pages. "What are these for?"

"It's a separation agreement. To give you a quick review: there's no alimony and no custody or child support since Chloe is from a previous relationship. I just need your signature so I can mail it off to the courts and we can put a legal pause on our marriage. That is, until we can agree on fair terms of divorce."

Oh, so she was serious about this divorce shit, huh? She must not have heard me when I said she and Chloe weren't going anywhere.

I opened my drawer and pretended to search for a pen. Instead, I grabbed a spare lighter hidden in there. I flicked the friction wheel and placed the edge of the papers on the flame.

Brielle gasped as the fire ate up the document. "Javier, what the hell are you doing?" She reached for the burning paper, likely intending to put out the flame and salvage what she could of the document.

I yanked it out of her reach and threw it in an empty trashcan nearby. "We're not separating and we're damn sure not getting a divorce," I said firmly.

Scoffing, she crossed her arms and glared at me. "You know, I can just print out a new one. I'll make copies this time."

"And I'll burn every single one of them."

She threw her head back in frustration. "Ugh, why are you being so difficult? I am not asking you for anything besides your signature."

"That's not true. You're asking me to let you go, and that's *not* happening."

"Why? I already played my role in your stupid little revenge game. What else do you want from me?"

"I don't want anything from you. You're my wife, Brielle and -"

"Let me guess: I belong to you. Well, guess what? Just because I wear your ring doesn't mean I'm your property. Matter of fact..." she trailed off as she tugged the band off of her finger. Gently, out of respect for its origins, she set it down on my desk. "You can have it back. It's not like I need it anymore, anyway."

"Brielle," I called after her as she turned on her heel and headed to the door. I scooped up the diamond ring and darted after her. "Brielle, wait!"

Ignoring my calls, she exited through the office door and hurried down the hall.

I caught her arm before she could reach the suite lobby. "Brielle, please stop."

"Let go of me!" She yelled as she tried to rip her arm out of my grasp. "I'm done talking about this!"

"You might be, but I'm not. Shit, I haven't even spoken my peace yet."

"I already know what you're going to say, so you don't have to waste your breath. You, Leo and every other kingpin of crime are all the same: nothing but insincerity and empty promises."

I narrowed my eyes as her words cut deep. How dare she group me in with horrible, wretched men like Leo? I may not be the best person in the world, but I damn sure wasn't as evil as him.

Did I unintentionally put her and Chloe in danger? Yes. But would I ever lay my hands on her or take advantage of her body? Hell no.

I understood her feelings were hurt, but now she was trying to drag my name and morals through the mud - and that shit would not fly.

Bending my knees, I pulled her forward and threw her over my shoulder.

"Hey!" she exclaimed. She pounded her fists against my back and wriggled in my grasp. "Put me down!"

It was my turn to ignore her. I went back into my office to grab my keys, and on the way back out, I grabbed her purse out of her chair at her desk. All with Brielle kicking and screaming on my shoulder.

But, I didn't care. I would not waste my time going back and forth with her. She wouldn't let me get a word in, anyway. I needed to take her to some place where she'd be forced to listen - to *understand*.

If Brielle needed me to be vulnerable, then that's exactly what she was going to get.

Chapter 50

Brielle

"Where the hell are we going?" I asked for the millionth time. We've been driving for the past twenty-five minutes, and it seemed like we weren't stopping soon.

Like he's been doing since he scooped me up in his office, Javier ignored me. He dragged me, kicking and screaming, throughout our building as if I was a bag of potatoes. At the latter hour, most of his men were on site and didn't pay any mind to my pleas to be freed from his grasp. They've turned a blind eye to much worse.

I checked the time on my phone and sighed at the five o'clock hour. "Javier, I have to pick up Chloe. We need to turn back around."

"I texted Lexie," he finally responded. "She already got her." He finally slowed the car as we pulled into the parking lot of a local cemetery.

I raised a brow at the rows of headstones, seemingly never-ending, as they stretched across the fields. "What are we doing here?"

"I want you to meet my mom," Javier replied. He climbed out from the driver's side and jogged over to mine. He opened the door for me and held out his hand. "Come on," he said when I didn't take it. "Don't make me embarrass you in front of the dead."

Rolling my eyes, I set my hand in his and let him help me out of the truck.

We walked hand-in-hand through the empty rows. An eerie sense of déjà vu crawled up my spine as I glanced around the tombstones. I used to walk up and down the similar rows of the cemetery back home when my parents

341

passed. I'd sit for hours and hours in front of their tombstones, talking to them about school and my plays as if they were sitting across from me at the dinner table. I even told them about Leo and how flattered I was that such a handsome guy had taken an interest in me.

Years later, after I had Chloe, I returned to my hometown for an afternoon, so they could see her. As I held the tiny newborn, I imagined them holding her. I saw my father making silly faces to make her laugh and my mother gushing over her chubby little cheeks. They would've loved her if they had the chance to meet her. If she still existed, had they survived the car crash with me.

Javier's fingers tightened around mine, pulling me out of my thoughts and back into the present. He led me all the way towards the farther end of the cemetery where the larger monuments lay. We stopped at a pair in the right-hand corner of the field.

The tall tombstones looked completely different. While one was plain and empty aside from the nameplate, the other was filled with engravings of a flower garden. Vines filled with various types of flowers cascaded around the nameplate. Pale flowers of all colors were wedged between some corners of the monument. Even more lay on the ground, some of which were still full of vibrant pigmentation. A small pile of cards, still sealed tight, sat in a neat row between the flowers. Across the tops, the word "Mom" was scrawled across in three distinctly different hand-writings.

In the decorative tombstone's corner, nestled between the angles, was a faded photo. In it was a woman with rich chocolate brown skin, a waterfall of kinky black girls, and a smile that was equally fierce and kind. Her arms were stretched out over the shoulders of her three children, who stood by her side, all with baby faces and hints of innocence in their smiles.

My heart weighed a thousand times heavier at the sight.

"She would've loved you and Chloe," Javier said.

"You think so?"

"I know so."

I almost smiled as I looked up at him. "She's beautiful."

His eyes were trained on the tombstone. "Yeah." His shoulders rose and fell as he sighed. "After she died, I swore I was never getting married."

"Really?" I asked, jolting my head back in surprise. "Why?"

"Because my father's enemies used her - us - in the same fashion Leo did with you and Chloe. The only difference was my father didn't make it in time to save her." His eyes lost focus for a moment, transporting him to another phase in his life. "We were all a mess after she died. My siblings were constantly going off on their violent tangents like little firecrackers. My father was tearing everything and everyone up like a tornado, and I...I had no choice but to hold it together. Hold all of *them* together. Watching how much harm caring about someone could do turned me off of the idea of feeling that way about anyone outside of my family. So, I vowed I'd never get emotionally attached or married. I didn't think I'd be alive long enough to do it anyway, but when I survived...you know, I just...I promised myself I'd never put myself, or someone else, in a position to be taken advantage of - to be hurt at my expense."

"Why'd you go back on it?"

"Because I fucked up and got attached to you," Javier admitted. He turned his gaze away from the tombstone and looked at me. "I know you think I used you to get back at Leo, and I'm not gonna lie: I did. And I admit I was wrong. But I didn't know about you and Leo when I got that call from Chloe the night you went missing. Before then, I truly thought of you as a friend. Every day, I looked forward to seeing you in our office. Every morning, I couldn't wait for you to strut into my office like you owned the place and talk my ear off about whatever was on your mind. I savored the privilege of being graced with your presence - of your joy. So, imagine the fear I felt when I heard the one person who brightens up my day was in trouble, that I might never experience your light again. I was ready to sift through the entire city looking for you. The entire world if I needed to.

"When I found out about your situation, I could've offered a million other solutions, but I chose the one that put you closest to me - so *I* could be the one protecting you. And as much as I hated the idea of marriage, I jumped at the opportunity of being married to you. Not because of Leo, but because of my feelings for you."

Moving closer, he lifted his hand to my face. When I didn't flinch away, he lay his palm on my cheek, his touch light as a feather. "I wouldn't have done this - *any* of this - if I didn't care about you, Brie. If I didn't *love* you."

His words curled around me like a blanket, melting the ice from the cold shoulder I'd tried to give him. Tears pricked behind my eyes, and I blinked a few times to keep them back. "Javier," I started.

"No, no, let me finish," he insisted. "The other night, when I thought I was going to lose you and Chloe, I...I didn't know what the fuck I was going to do. I was prepared to trade my life for yours - or God forbid, take my own if I couldn't save you. I don't know how to live without you and Chloe. You both have given me a happiness I thought I would never experience. Every day, your smiles, your hugs, your joy, your love - fills me with more than you could imagine. And I know, I know, there aren't enough apologies in the world to make up for the danger I put you in, but I swear from the bottom of my heart, I'd lay my life down before I let anyone threaten yours or Chloe's ever again. Earlier, when I said you're my wife, I wasn't trying to claim you as property. I was trying to say you're my family, and I love you, and I want to spend the rest of my life with you."

I felt a familiar weight sliding onto my finger. Looking down, I saw his mother's diamond ring slipping onto my hand and Javier lowering down on his knee.

"I know I fucked up, and I'm willing to do whatever it takes to earn your forgiveness. But, I need you as my wife," he said. "For real, this time."

I smiled down at him as a few tears dripped down my face. "We've always been real, Javi. Don't tell me you're just now realizing that?"

A genuine smile spread across his face, and his dimples made a rare appearance. Rising to his feet, he pulled me in for a hug and squeezed me like he never wanted to let go. "I love you, Brielle," he whispered into my hair. "So much."

"I know," I murmured into his chest. "I love you, too."

Leaning into his embrace, I relished the security of being in his arms and, finally, his heart. Wrapping my arms around him, I silently forgave him for his mistakes. His heart was in the right place when he made them. Without him, Chloe and I could be dead.

He was our guardian angel in disguise, saving our lives in more ways than one. And for that I'll always be grateful to him. But, I loved him too. He was the missing puzzle piece in so many aspects of our lives, filling in the gaps I'd been ignoring since Chloe was born. Not just in our family, but in my heart as well. With him, our lives were finally whole.

"Come on," I said, giving him one last squeeze. "Our daughter is at home waiting for us."

Epilogue

Javier

Seven Years Later...

"Dad, can I go to the movies later?" Chloe asked as she leaned over the side of the chair I was sitting in. Some of the water from the pool still dripped off of her shoulders.

Summer this year bought sunny skies and high temperatures. My siblings, their spouses, and their children all came over on Saturdays like this to swim in our pool and enjoy the weather together. Chloe usually entertained her younger brother and cousins in the pool for a few hours before heading off to do her own thing. As she kept reminding us, she was a teenager now and needed a healthy social life.

"With who?" I asked, tearing my eyes away from her brother, cousins and uncle splashing around in the pool.

Chloe's shoulders curled in as she averted her eyes. "Aaron..."

I raised a brow. "Who's Aaron?"

"Yeah, Chlo," Dante chimed in from beside me. AJ, Adrian's one-year-old, was playing with a plastic shovel on his lap. "Who's that?"

"He's a friend from school."

"I've never heard of him before." I looked at Dante. "Have you?"

Dante shook his head. "Yo, Adrian!" He called my brother. "Do you know Aaron?"

My brother paused his water polo game with the younger kids to look at us in confusion. "Who?"

"Dad doesn't know about Aaron?" My son, Cristian, asked as he wiped some water out of his face.

"Isn't that her boyfriend?" Diego, one of Lexie's and Dante's twins, added.

"Boyfriend?" my brothers and I exclaimed in unison.

"Hold on, y'all," Adrian told the other kids as he climbed out of the pool. "I've gotta hear the rest of this."

"Relax, Uncle Adrian. He's *not* my boyfriend," Chloe clarified. "He's just a friend."

I tilted my head. "Have we met this 'friend'?"

"Mom has. But he offered to pick me up, so he could formally introduce himself."

"He drives?"

Chloe nodded. "He's in the grade above me. He got his license right before school ended." A smile bloomed on her lips as my brow rose higher. "Oh, don't make that face! Aaron is super nice - and smart. He's on the student council and takes AP classes.."

"How long have you been friends with this boy?"

"We just started talking this past school year. He's the one who helped me bring my grade up in Algebra II."

Oh, she was talking about her math tutor. Her school used their National Honor Society students to help with tutoring some students who struggled in their core classes. They ran a homework club program a few times a week after school so students could get some help with their work from some teachers and their peers. Chloe attended occasionally when her math work was difficult, but this year, she became a regular attendee. This Aaron kid must be the reason.

"Is it just me, or does this sound like a first date?" Dante mused. He bounced AJ on his thigh. "What do you think, AJ?"

A string of incomprehensible gibberish left AJ's mouth as he attempted to respond.

"Yeah, AJ thinks you're asking for permission on a date."

"No, he doesn't. AJ is on my side." She shifted over to where Dante sat and tickled AJ's tiny belly. "Aren't you my little stinky butt?"

AJ giggles exposed his tiny front teeth. His innocent laughter wafted through the air, ceasing whatever tension threatened to brew from Chloe's request.

Glancing over her shoulder, Chloe noticed my small smile. "So," she said. "Can I go?"

"It's just going to be the two of you?"

"Yeah."

"Hm. Let me talk to your mother first."

"I already asked her. She's fine with it, but wanted me to run it by you before I confirmed any plans."

"What time is he planning on picking you up?"

"Six-thirty, I think."

I turned to my brothers. "Are y'all trying to stay until then?"

"No! No! No!" Chloe protested. "Dad, no offense, but you are scary enough on your own."

"We weren't going to scare him," Dante said.

"Yeah," Adrian chimed in. "We were just gonna scope him out. Show him what he'll be dealing with in the case a single tear drop ever falls from your eye."

"I appreciate the gesture, but no thank you. I want him to take me out - not piss his pants."

"We'll be good," I promised.

Raising a brow, Chloe crossed her arms and shifted her arm on her hip. She stared at me with a look of disbelief.

"Alright, Uncle Dante and I will be good. I can't make any promises about your Uncle Adrian."

She turned her menacing gaze to my brother. "You scare him off and it's me and you," she swore darkly. She twirled on her heel and walked through the sliding door leading into the house.

Adrian scoffed. "Did she just threaten me?"

Dante laughed. "I believe she did. I bet she'd beat your ass, too. Have you seen her on the mats? The girl's a beast."

"Yeah, Lexie's been training her well," I agreed.

Along with ballet, Chloe has a natural talent for mixed martial arts. Ever since she's started the classes, and training privately with my sister, she's been working her way up the rankings of belts and competing in tournaments. More than a few trophies were stored in our china cabinet along with her and her brother's other accolades.

Whereas Chloe excelled in physical areas, Cristian flourished in his academics. Although he was only six, he was already showing a special interest in math and science. He loved spending time with Miles and tinkering over inventions with him. The most he's built on his own were a few Lego sets, but we had a hunch a few of his own contraptions would appear around the house soon.

I let them indulge in their hobbies for now, silently taking notes for how it'll suit them when it's time to train them to take their places in our organization. Although my siblings and I were well versed into the dark crime world before Chloe's age, we were all stalling for as long as we could to introduce our children into that side of our lives. We didn't want them to carry the same mental, and emotional, scars as we did. We just wanted them to be kids for as long as possible.

I nodded over at Adrian's daughter, who was taking command among the boys and telling them the rules of a new game they were about to play. "Before long, Melanie's gonna be giving you mouth and hanging out with boys, too."

Adrian rolled his eyes. "She isn't allowed to leave the house until she's twenty-one, let alone think about a boy."

"Ooo, I'm gonna pray for her first boyfriend," Dante said. "May God bless his poor, doomed soul."

"At that point, God isn't gonna wanna touch him either," I said.

"Man, fuck both of y'all," Adrian told us. He left us to head back to the pool with the kids.

Dante and I shared a chuckle as we watched him walk away.

We all stayed outside for a few hours longer before the younger kids grew tired and wanted to go back inside.

Kiara, Lexie, and Brielle had dinner waiting for us when we strolled into the kitchen. They'd spent the better half of the afternoon there, gossiping and cooking.

The kids sprawled across the living room and watched a movie while they ate their food. The women took over chaperoning them while we cleaned up the kitchen for them.

By the time we were finished, almost all the kids' eyelids were heavy and their tiny bodies were sinking deeper into the couch. Melanie, Diego, and Dominic, Lexie's other son, were lounging together on the couch, each of them somehow laying on the other. On the sofa chair, Cristian was curled up in a cocoon of blankets.

Smiling at their weariness, my siblings made the unanimous decision to gather their children and head out.

Chloe lucked out. They left right before her so-called date was supposed to arrive.

"Have you given her the talk yet?" I asked Brielle when we had a minute alone in the kitchen. Cristian was still in the living room, watching a movie and trying not to fall asleep, and Chloe was upstairs getting ready.

"Yes," my wife said. "When she started middle school. She's well versed in all the bases and what to do depending on whether she's ready for them. Besides, Aaron seems like a nice kid."

"Hm." I didn't want to voice it aloud, but anyone could seem nice at first. The last thing I wanted was for Chloe to get involved with some knucklehead who'd break her heart, or worse.

Brielle wrapped her arms around me and leaned her chin against my chest. "You're right to be worried. I'm worried too. But she's getting older and we've gotta let her explore what's out there. A date with a tutor boy isn't the worst place she could start."

"Yeah, I know."

She leaned up on her toes to kiss me. "Relax," she murmured against my lips. "Give the boy a chance."

"Mhm. I'll think about it."

She giggled as she kissed me again.

Her lips were still sweet after all these years. I couldn't help but take advantage of her kisses and pull her closer to me. My tongue cascaded around the perimeter of her lips, making a beeline towards the entrance. Yet, before I could even flick for the entrance, a knock sounded at the door.

We reluctantly pulled away, and Brielle laughed at the scowl on my face. "Be nice," she said.

"Yeah, yeah," I replied as I released my hold on her.

"Chloe!" Brielle called up the steps as she followed me to the front door. "Aaron's here!"

I opened the door and finally came face-to-face with the boy my daughter was smitten with.

On the porch stood an unfamiliar teenager with tawny brown skin and glasses. He was tall for his age and lanky underneath his button down. Neatly kept twists were pushed back from his face, drawing attention to his kind brown eyes and sharp jawline. Behind him, near the curb, was a lightly used Chevrolet sedan. One of his hands was wrapped around a small bouquet. Smiling nervously, he extended his free one and said, "Hello, Mr. Ruiz. I'm Aaron. It's very nice to-" His voice cut off as I accepted his hand and squeezed tight enough to relay an ounce of my strength. Yet, he still smiled underneath the pain. "Meet you," he finished.

"Pleasure's all mine."

"Aaron," Brielle sang to ease the tension from my stare. "It's so good to see you! Come in!"

Aaron shuffled inside. "Thank you, Mrs. Ruiz."

"How has your summer been so far?"

"Good. My dad works in construction, so I've spent most of my time working with him on the sites."

"Oh, that's nice." Brielle nudged me. "Having a good work ethic is a good trait at this age."

"Yeah, and the money's good. I'm using my first paycheck to take Chloe out somewhere nice."

"Where's that?" I asked.

"A steakhouse called 'Chamberlain's' near the shopping center on Westford Ave. I, personally, haven't been, but based on word-of-mouth, it's pretty good."

"And what time will you have her home?"

"Well, the movie starts at eight-fifteen, so no later than eleven. She told me she has a strict curfew, so I promise I'll abide by it."

The soft click of heels summoned our attention to the stairwell. Chloe was walking down the steps, wearing a pink cotton maxi dress, and a cropped jean jacket. Her dark, kinky curls fell around her face, emphasizing her glittering bronze eyelids and glossed lips.

"Wow," I heard Aaron murmur under his breath.

Chloe must've heard it, too. A bashful smile crept up her lips, and her shoulders threatened to curl inward. "Hey," she greeted him.

"Hi. Um, you...you look...um..."

"Flowers," Brielle whispered. "Give her the flowers."

"Right," he said, still trapped in his trance. He held out the bouquet. "These are for you."

Her cheeks darkened as she accepted them. "Oh, thank you." She turned to her mother and me. "I'll see you guys later?"

"By eleven," I reminded her.

"I know, I know."

Aaron nodded to me. "It was nice to meet you, sir."

"Hm."

He opened the door for Chloe and followed her outside.

I watched them through the window as they walked down the walkway. Aaron offered her a smile as he opened the passenger door for her.

"Isn't he a gentleman?" Brielle mused, staring at the same sight. "Chloe might have found herself a keeper."

"He better keep his hands to himself, that's all I know."

Brielle laughed. She towed me away from the door. "Come on. Let them have their night."

"Hey, Dad," Cristian called as he poked his head out the living room doorway. After his short recharge, he was beaming with newfound energy. "Do you wanna play video games with me? I've got ten bucks that says you can't beat me on Mario Smash Bros."

"First of all, that's my ten bucks in your pocket. But I have no problem taking it back."

Cristian grinned as he darted back into the living room.

"Careful now," Brielle warned. "He learned some cheat codes at school. You might be scammed out of another ten bucks."

"No, he didn't."

She pretended to zip her lips.

"That's cool. I've got some moves he doesn't know about, too. Come here: watch me teach our son a lesson."

She laughed again as I tugged her along this time. The sound mixed with my son's excited screams of competition was music to my ears.

I never thought I'd have a family like this. One filled with such love, joy, and laughter - so much fucking laughter. Every day, they lit up the darkness still lingering around my mind, giving me reasons to fight against the demons haunting my brain.

I hoped they knew how grateful I was to have them. What I'd do to protect them. How much I loved them. Surrounded by them on the couch, Brielle's head on my shoulder, my son's elbow nudging me and Bagheera at our feet, my belly was warm with sensations I was once afraid of.

Love. Comfort. Belonging.

It was the little moments like this that reminded me of all the good life had to give and all the things I had to live for. Days like this were the ones I kept filed away in the back of my mind for when the rough ones rolled through. I'll sit, watch the memories like a movie and remind myself I've finally found my peace.

I've finally found my happiness.

Acknowledgments

Firstly, I would like to thank my husband and my mom for supporting me on the journey through writing this book. This was such a personal, reflective, emotional time for me, and I appreciate how gentle and supportive you were with me as I told these characters' stories. Thank you for always being my support system.

A special thanks to my friend, Brittany, for supporting me through this journey. You were one of the first people I told about this story and your encouragement to write it was so meaningful to me. Thank you for letting me ramble about my ideas, giving me feedback and supporting me throughout this project.

Many thanks as well to my amazing beta readers. I appreciate all the feedback and funny commentary that helped develop this book into the best version of itself. encouragement. Thanks for contributing to making this novel the best it could be.

Lastly, a huge thank you to all of my readers. This series, these characters, these stories mean so much to me and I am so grateful to be able to share it with all of you. Thank you for loving on my characters and encouraging me on my writing journeys. This series may be ending, but I'm just getting started. I hope you all will stay along for the ride.

About the Author

Writing has been a hobby for Asia since she was young. During her high school and post-secondary years, she wrote an abundance of fan fictions and original stories.

Upon graduating from college with a degree in English and Education, she has continued to write romance novels and perfect the stories of the characters living in her head.

She currently lives with her husband and young son. She works as a high school special education teacher. In her free time, she enjoys reading romance novels, listening to music, making Pinterest boards for her stories, and browsing through Tik Tok.

Connect with her on Tik Tok and Instagram @author_asia_monet

Also by Asia Monet

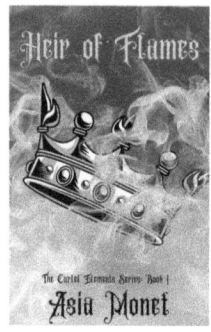 **Heir of Flames (The Cartel Elements Series: Book 1)**

 **Heiress of Roses (The Cartel Elements Series: Book 2)**

Milton Keynes UK
Ingram Content Group UK Ltd.
UKHW021427170924
1695UKWH00003B/4